NUR JAHAN'S
DAUGHTER

Tanushree Podder has written on diverse subjects ranging from travel, fiction, health and fitness and spirituality. Many of her short stories have won prizes.

For Ajoy, the light in my life

Acknowledgments

This book wouldn't have been possible without the help of the many learned and generous historians who lent and shared their books with me. Much of the information came from the public and private libraries of Bangalore, Delhi and Raipur through painstaking research of many years. I am especially thankful to Mr Imtiaz Ahmad of the Ravi Shankar University Library, Raipur, who made it possible for me to access the rare treasure of books at the library.

My deepest thanks to my editor at Rupa & Co., who shared the pangs of this book's birth with me. Her astute observations helped rectify the little details that I would have otherwise missed.

THE MUGHALS
(SELECT MEMBERS)

Ghias Baig ——— Asmat Begum

Asaf Khan | Muhamed | Ibrahim | Meherunnisa (Nur Jahan) 1576-1645

Ali Quli (Sher Afghan)

Arjumand (Mumtaz Mahal) 1595-1630

Babar 1483-1530

Mariam Makani

Humayun 1508-1556 | Kamran | Askari | Hindal

Akbar 1542-1605 | Hakim

Ruqayya Begum
Salima Begum
Bilquees Begum

Salim (Jahangir) 1569-1627 | Murad | Daniyal

Man Bai
Jagat Gosain

Laadli

Khusrau | Parwez | Khurram (Shah Jahan) 1592-1666 | Shahryar 1605-1627

Dawar Baksh

Jahanara 1614-1681 | Dara Shikoh 1615-1659 | Shah Shuja 1616-1660 | Roshanara 1617-1671 | Alamgir (Aurangzeb) 1618-1707 | Murad 1624-1660 | Gauharara 1630-1706 | Arzani

Introduction

History is replete with fascinating tales about powerful personalities. One such story—particularly interesting because it concerns a woman who controlled a powerful empire from behind the walls of the harem—is of Empress Nur Jahan, who ruled successfully for sixteen long years. While her story is often told with wonder and awe, historians and writers have largely ignored her daughter, Laadli. She was the reluctant princess on whom destiny had thrust royalty. Trapped into a life dictated by an ambitious mother, the girl travelled through tragic events of her life with stoic optimism.

The Mughals ruled Hindustan for close to 250 years. Their empire stretched across the entire subcontinent south of the Himalayas and included Afghanistan, Pakistan, Nepal, Bhutan, and Bangladesh.

In the early sixteenth century, a young prince fled across the deserts in Uzbekistan to escape treacherous nobles who had usurped his land. Babur, then a minor, eluded death and raced towards Afghanistan, where he captured sizeable chunks of land. This young prince was a military genius. Not content with the conquest of Afghanistan, he cast a covetous eye on

Hindustan and soon wrested a portion of this prosperous land after defeating Ibrahim Lodi, the ruler of Delhi. By the time he died, four years later, Babur had extended his rule over much of the northern India. He was the first of the Great Mughals.

His son, Humayun, ascended the throne after him. But it was Babur's grandson who deserves the credit for extending, strengthening and uniting the great empire. Akbar inherited the throne at the tender age of thirteen and went on to rule for half a century. He forged alliances with the proud Rajputs and garnered their support. He promoted art and music: to him goes the credit of bringing the Persian painters from whose work evolved the Mughal School of miniature paintings, which later gave rise to the Rajasthani styles.

Akbar was a connoisseur of art and architecture. His son, Jahangir, had inherited his father's interests. It was during the time of this luxury-loving emperor that art, music and architecture flourished unfettered.

Originating from the Timurid dynasty, the Mughals were Mongol by blood and bore a strong affinity to the Persian culture. They brought and nurtured Persian art, literature and architecture and beautiful gardens to Hindustan. Much of what is known as Urdu language actually originated from a lyrical amalgamation of the Persian language with Hindi.

Contrary to the common belief, the Mughal empresses were not helpless and vulnerable women. Although they remained invisible, they wielded significant power over their menfolk and advised them on various issues. Humayun's wife, Mariam Makani, had great influence over Akbar. Mughal women like Nur Jahan and Jahanara were able planners, administrators and designers.

Of all the Mughal empresses, Nur Jahan was perhaps the most influential one. As the favourite wife of the powerful Mughal emperor Jahangir, she found herself uniquely positioned to brilliantly utilise her skills in administration, politics, economics, and culture.

Nur Jahan, nee Meherunnisa, was born into an aristocratic Persian family who had immigrated to India. She grew up within the confines of the Mughal harem, amusing Emperor Akbar's wife. It wasn't surprising that the young prince, Salim, soon fell in love with her mesmerising beauty and quick wit. In a bid to free Salim from her clutches, Akbar arranged a match between seventeen-year-old Meherunnisa and Sher Afghan, a Persian soldier, a much-admired military officer.

Sher Afghan was later mysteriously murdered, leaving Nur Jahan a widow with a daughter called Laadli. In 1607, Nur Jahan was brought to court to serve as a lady-in-waiting to one of Jahangir's court women. It was here, at the spring festival of Nauroz in 1611, that Jahangir set eyes, again, upon her. Jahangir married her within a couple of months. He first gave her the title Nur Mahal, which he later changed to Nur Jahan, or 'Light of the World'.

At the time of her marriage Nur Jahan was no spring chicken. She was a widow of a man who had lost favour with the emperor, and was only one of many other wives and concubines of the emperor, with whom he had children. Yet, within nine years Nur Jahan acquired all the rights of sovereignty and government normally due to the emperor, becoming virtually in charge of the whole empire until the emperor died in 1627. The key to her success was Jahangir's addiction to drugs and alcohol, and his complete adoration of Nur Jahan above everyone else in his vast zenana, the women's quarters within the court.

Since women were not allowed to appear face-to-face with men in court, Nur Jahan ruled through trusted male envoys. But it was she who approved all orders and grants of appointment in Jahangir's name, and controlled all promotions and demotions within the royal government. She took special interest in the affairs of women; she gave land and dowries to orphan girls. She had coins struck in her name, collected duties on goods from merchants who passed through the empire, and traded with Europeans who brought luxury goods from the continent. Given her ability to obstruct or facilitate the opening up of both foreign and domestic trade, her patronage was eagerly sought, and paid for. She herself owned ships, which took pilgrims as well as cargo to Mecca. Her business connections and wealth grew. Her officers were everywhere. The cosmopolitan city of Agra, the Mughal capital, grew as a crossroad of commerce.

Nur Jahan also ruled the emperor's vast zenana, which housed hundreds of people including Jahangir's wives, ladies-in-waiting, concubines, servants, slaves, female guards, spies, entertainers, crafts people, visiting relatives, eunuchs, and all the children belonging to the women. Nur Jahan greatly influenced the zenana's tastes in cosmetics, fashions, food, and artistic expression. She spent money lavishly, experimenting with new perfumes, hair ointments, jewellery, silks, brocades, porcelain, and cuisine from other lands. Fashions at court, highly influenced by Persian culture, began to blend with local styles. Women's clothing were modified to take account of the hot weather. Nur Jahan came from a line of poets, and she wrote too, and encouraged this among the court women. Poetry contests were held, and favourite female poets from beyond the court were sometimes sponsored by the queen, such as the Persian poet, Mehri.

Both Jahangir and Nur Jahan were devotees of the elegant and sophisticated Mughal artistic style. The emperor owned an admirable collection of exquisite miniature paintings and, together with Nur Jahan, constructed beautiful gardens, notably in the court's summer retreat at Kashmir. Nur Jahan used some gardens for official functions, others were opened up for the public in general to use. Architecture, too, was an important imperial activity; some of the mosques, caravanserais and tombs Nur Jahan had built are still in existence.

Laadli Bano, Nur Jahan's daughter from her first husband Sher Afghan, was an artist, poet, and a musician. Laadli's story is that of a vulnerable and sensitive child who went through a gamut of emotions and turbulence right from her childhood. Never happy in the milieu of the zenana, Laadli was a pawn in the hands of her mother's ambitious machinations. Yet, she was the crutch that provided the empress the stability and security to plod through the rough patches in her life. Hers is a story of unflinching devotion, loyalty and steadfast support for a mother. Laadli's life traverses through the zenith of power to the nadir of deception and depravity.

I have been captivated by Nur Jahan's character ever since my childhood. Hers is an enigmatic character, both strong and vulnerable by turns. Although many books have been written about the empress, hardly anything has been penned about Nur Jahan as a mother. That facet of her personality has been totally ignored, so much so that many people are not even aware that she had a daughter.

Mughal history is full of interesting characters, some prominent and some obscure. It is the shadowy characters that are more interesting because of the veil of mystery that shrouds them. One such character is Laadli Begum. Her life has remained unveiled by historians, although it is more interesting than many. The more information I uncovered about her, the more I felt that her character needed to be brought out in the open; too long it had remained hidden amongst the dusty tomes of history. Laadli Begum has been very close to my heart and with the publishing of this book, I feel her ghost has been laid to rest. Although this is a work of fiction, I have strived to stay as close to history as possible.

Tanushree Podder

1

It was a long and arduous labour and the woman's perspiration-soaked body thrashed about agitatedly as a fresh wave of pain tore through it. Her primal groans tattooed the walls with agony, lingered for a moment near the gurgling fountain in the courtyard, drifted over the mango trees surrounding the house, and dissipated forlornly in the muggy atmosphere of Bengal. The woman's parched lips were a wounded mass of flesh as her sharp teeth sunk into them in a bid to take the edge out of the torture. Outside, the humid air teased the young leaves on the mango trees. The melodious call of the cuckoo sounded incongruous to the ears of the old nurse trying to comfort the woman.

'Just a few more moments and then it will be over. The baby is almost here.'

Another flood of pain shook the exhausted body.

'Push harder,' commanded the midwife. 'You'll have to help your baby emerge.' There was no strength left in the woman to aid the birthing process. Exhausted and teetering on the edge of a breakdown, she let out a feral cry. Her anguished scream tore through the house, its rawness stunning the chattering birds on the banyan tree outside the large mansion. The nurse heaved a sigh of relief on hearing a weak cry as the midwife pulled the baby out and subjected its red bottom to a smart smack.

The baby was washed and swathed in new muslin clothes. 'It is a girl child,' Firdaus said hesitantly, holding the wailing bundle to the mother. Screwing up her red face, the infant filled up her lungs with the humid air of Burdwan and bawled lustily. Firdaus quietly placed the baby near the semi-conscious woman and waited for a reaction.

'She is beautiful, just like you,' Firdaus said, wiping her wet brows with a scented cloth. 'Allah has been kind to us after so many years. He's sent an angel to bring joy and laughter to this house.'

A young servant girl was cleaning up the mess around the low bed. She mopped the marble floor with a rag and lit up incense sticks in the silver censers. By the side of the bed sat an Amazonian woman with a peacock feather fan, driving the flies away. From time to time she suppressed a yawn; it had been a long day. The melancholic atmosphere in the room hung over them, like the shadow of a phantom.

The gloomy air had nothing to do with the interiors of the room: it was beautifully decorated, as was the entire house. The Persian carpets, gilded candelabras and crystal chandeliers, inlaid brassware, intricately painted miniatures and bright silk cushions spread on the embroidered bedspread, all spoke of the refined taste of the mistress of the house. Lush brocade drapes curtained the spacious room of the zenana. But the heavy pall of gloom nullified all attempts to beautify it.

'You have a daughter. Thank Allah for his mercy, the girl is healthy,' repeated Firdaus, glancing at the inert body on the bed. Finding no response to her words, she bent down and checked the pulse of the young woman.

The baby let out another loud wail to remind them of her presence. The lusty cry sounded pleasant to the ears of the women in the room. 'The house has been silent for too long,' remarked the nurse.

The young woman had still not responded. Ashen faced, her thin frame quivered with each breath that emanated from the pinched nose. Long, raven locks hung limply from the edge of a tasselled pillow, spreading out like black tentacles over the pristine marble floor.

The fountain continued to gurgle like low-throated laughter. A brood of ducks paddled lazily amidst the lotus growing in the pond, unmindful of the fateful change that had taken place in the enormous mansion. The smell of human blood mingled with the scent of the frangipani flowers, creating a strange mix of odours.

Concern etched her wrinkled brows as the nurse watched Meherunnisa's motionless body.

'She has endured so much pain,' muttered Firdaus, gazing tenderly at the woman she had brought up with so much affection.

At last, the body twitched and moved closer to the baby in response to its demanding cry. Slowly a tender smile spread across the mother's face as she looked at her daughter. The long years of a discontented marriage and innumerable miscarriages melted away in a moment. The frustration of her barren existence had taken a heavy toll—the bubbling mirth in the blue eyes had gradually been replaced by frigidity; the glow of her lovely complexion had vanished, layers of disappointment replacing its radiance. *Ten long years of a fruitless marriage*, the woman sighed. But Allah had not been so heartless, after all. After ten years of waiting, He had finally answered her prayers.

Meherunnisa held the little one close to her heart.

'I will call her Laadli,' she crooned, 'the adored one.'

Disappointment had assailed her for a few moments when she was told that her baby was a girl. Her immediate thoughts had been about the barbs that would most likely fly from all quarters. After almost eleven years of marriage, she had been able to produce only a puny daughter for her swashbuckling husband. A stab of guilt tore her heart as she thought of Sher Afghan. Would he accept the little one with love or discard the baby with disappointment? He had waited for the birth of a son for over a decade.

'Shall I call a wet nurse? The baby needs milk,' Firdaus asked as she piled some cushions behind Meherunnisa.

'No!' The voice was sharp. 'I don't want any wet nurse to feed my daughter. I am going to nurse her myself.'

'As you please! But women from elite families do not feed their babies. It will make your breasts sag and you will lose your beauty.' Firdaus threw her a disapproving look. 'Our cook's daughter, Ruksana, has just delivered a baby. She is clean and healthy. She will be happy to nurse your child.'

'No,' Meherunnisa raised her voice angrily. 'You don't have to worry about the sagging of my breasts or the fading of my looks. I shall not have a wet nurse in this house.'

'Most of the royal children have wet nurses and thrive, too. Even Shahenshah Akbar had a wet nurse. Have you forgotten that I nursed you? And look at you—so beautiful and talented. Obviously my milk did not curdle in your innards,' said Firdaus emotionally.

'I'm sorry Firdaus. I did not mean to hurt you. I would not have survived if you had not nursed me. Don't misunderstand me. It is just that I want to experience every possible aspect of motherhood. It was denied to me too long.' Meherunnisa held out her hand to the old woman in a bid to mollify her.

She knew how much Firdaus cared for her. Her old nurse had left the comforts of Agra and Ghias Baig's house to be with them. Faithful Firdaus had willingly given up Agra's healthy clime to stay with her in the clammy climate of Burdwan. Meherunnisa knew how much she missed the sounds and the smells of Agra and craved for the sight of the dusty roads that led to the royal court.

Firdaus smiled understandingly and put the baby to Meherunnisa's breast. A smile lit up the wan face as the child suckled hungrily, drawing the first spurt of milk. The azure eyes gleamed with satisfaction and her womb contracted with happiness. Satiated, the newborn drifted off to sleep. Firdaus slipped away to inform Sher Afghan of his fatherhood.

Sher Afghan was entertaining his companions in the hall. She could hear their loud laughter and playful banter.

'I am sure Allah will bless you with a son. A son as strong as a tiger, as tall as a mountain and as handsome as his father,' one of the cronies was telling the strapping Persian.

Pleased with his words, Sher Afghan threw him an emerald ring. 'May your words come true!'

Firdaus hesitated at the threshold of the hall. She was the bearer of bad tidings. She knew that Sher Afghan was not going to be happy to learn that a daughter had been born in his house after so many years of waiting.

'Here comes the good news,' said one of the men, who had spotted Firdaus standing near the doorway.

'Yes, Firdaus, tell us the good news. Don't just stand there.'

Her silence distressed Sher Afghan. 'I hope everything is well,' he exclaimed.

Years of futile waiting had made him cautious. He got up and approached the nurse.

'I hope all is well with the Begum.'

His eager eyes scanned her face, trying to read the message on it. *He does care*, she thought. For many years she had disliked this man, whom she thought was far inferior to her cultured, artistic mistress. Over time, however, she had developed a grudging fondness for him because, beneath his rough behaviour, she saw the depth of his love for his wife. But no matter how much he cared for Meherunnisa, Firdaus knew that news of a baby girl would not please him.

'Huzoor, you have a beautiful daughter. The mother and the child, both are fine.' Firdaus waited for the outburst she knew would come.

'Ya Allah! So that is what held your feet woman. This is the news that made you tarry. So many years of waiting only to hear this!' he ranted. In a fit of rage, he kicked at the wine glasses.

'What are we celebrating? The birth of a girl?' he shouted. There was a wild look on his face.

There was a deafening silence as the men in the room looked abashed. Firdaus cowered in a corner, suffering the flood of curses that poured from the master's mouth. There were no words to console the heartbroken man. Ali Quli Khan Istajlu, the man who had been given the title Sher Afghan by Emperor Akbar, had been able to produce only a daughter after so many years of marriage. He ranted at fate's injustice. He had never considered bringing another wife to his zenana, the thought of divorcing Meherunnisa had never crossed his mind. He had been a faithful husband—maybe a little promiscuous at times, but a good husband nonetheless. There were others, he knew, who had taken another wife just because the first could not deliver a son.

One by one the men filed out of the room, leaving the man to his grief. They understood his feelings. A man who had no son was only half a man. They all had strapping sons. Daughters were incidental. They brought beauty and music to the house, but it was the sons who brought glory. They were the ones who looked after their parents, earned money for the household and carried the family name forward.

Sher Afghan suddenly became aware of Firdaus' presence.

'It is not your fault woman. Go away. I can't find it in my heart to reward you for the news you've brought. Leave me alone to deal with this tragedy.' He waved her away, walking slowly towards the pile of cushions on the divan. Firdaus saw him reaching for a flagon of wine as she quietly withdrew.

No one knew how long he drank or how drunk he got. All the servants in the household feared the short-tempered master and left him alone when he was in a foul mood. Even Meherunnisa kept a distance from her husband during his dark moods.

Night descended swiftly on the house, its dark shadows reaching every nook and cranny that had been earlier lit up by the sun. The cicadas began their endless chirping, unaware of the mood in the silent house. The mother and child slept peacefully, undisturbed. The mother lulled by her exhaustion, and the child sated with the first taste of her mother's milk.

The sound of the horse's hooves alerted Firdaus. Sher Afghan was riding off on his favourite horse, Mustafa, to drown his grief in some forest. The inmates were familiar with his long disappearances whenever he was disturbed or angry. He would disappear for many weeks on a shikar, only to return with trophies of tiger skins, antelope horns or elephant tusks, his mood mellower and temper restored. Or he would take off for a tour of his mansab to check on the revenues. Once again he would return with a booty of colourful silk, boxes full of condiments, heaps of jewellery or some fancy gadget. His moods were as mercurial as the weather at Burdwan.

Yet, he could be extremely kind-hearted and generous. Firdaus remembered the time when a young stable boy had injured himself critically while trying to harness a wild mare brought by Sher Afghan. Sayeed had nearly lost his life when the mare trampled him in her rage. Sher Afghan paid for the treatment of the boy and kept his job waiting till the boy recovered. He would often saunter into the huts adjoining the stables, to enquire about the boy's health.

There were many who professed that the soldier was a ruthless man, but an equal number of people swore by his generosity. Firdaus—who had been closely connected with the fortunes and the misfortunes of Meherunnisa's family—knew that her master was a simple soul who lived by his muscles rather than his wits. He was the exact opposite of his wife in every manner. She belonged to a cultured family, whereas Sher Afghan came from an impoverished background. He neither liked poetry nor understood it. He could hold his own on the breed of a horse or the advantage of using a dagger instead of a sword, but found himself out of depth when confronted with a discussion about the finer things of life.

When Sher Afghan disappeared from the house for a fortnight, Meherunnisa was relieved. She was not ready for disparaging remarks from her husband. They both needed time and space to adjust to the new event in their lives. The child had evoked in her the dormant emotions of motherhood that had been repressed for so long. She emerged from her suites, a stronger and much happier woman, cradling her infant lovingly in her arms. Motherhood was such a beautiful experience that she wanted to savour it in peace.

This was a child of many prayers. The numerous failed attempts had made both Sher Afghan and Meherunnisa despondent. While her husband had drowned his misery in wine and women, she had prayed, fasted, tied amulets on her arms, fed the poor at dargahs, just so she could hold her child in her arms.

For the first few years the couple had held on to the slender thread of hope. They clung to each other, bonded by the skeins of a common sorrow. With each miscarriage came a fresh strain on the fragile bond, threatening their relationship. The sympathy Sher Afghan had for his wife slowly turned into disdain and he kept away for long periods, seeking solace in the arms of nautch girls.

Bound by his duties at the court, Sher Afghan travelled all over the country, quelling rebellion and subjugating mutinous states. While her husband earned laurels with his valour at battlefields, Meherunnisa served as a lady-in-waiting for the Persian Sultana, Bilquees Begum, at the royal harem. It amused her to think that she had spent more time attending to the queen than with her husband in the eleven years of her marriage. She spent the long, wintry nights thinking about what could have been. She tried to cope with her barrenness. But what could she do with the anxiety that filled her heart. Would her husband take another wife because she couldn't give him the sons he wanted?

Like every woman in the harem, Meherunnisa would be delighted when the imperial army returned home after a successful campaign. The news brought joy and hope in every heart as the women rushed to decorate their homes, buy new clothes and jewellery, cook special dishes and wait impatiently for romance to return to their frigid lives. The long winter in their lives was brushed off with hopes of a romantic spring, no matter what the season. Arrival of the men brought rejuvenation and love in its wake.

Meherunnisa's eyes misted whenever she recollected the years she had spent, pining for her husband's comforting arms around her. Thousands of times she wished for a child; a child that would bring joy to her lonely life. And finally, Allah had answered her prayers. It did not matter that he had blessed her with a daughter.

She bathed the child with her own hands and dressed her in beautiful clothes. Intricately embroidered dresses in pastel colours, lace-fringed caps and pretty shoes, she made them all. Meherunnisa sang lullabies to her baby, spent sleepless nights when the child had colic, went frantic if her precious daughter as much as sneezed. The smallest indication of sickness in the baby drove her to summon the hakim.

Minutes, hours, days and weeks passed, yet Sher Afghan didn't return to his wife and daughter.

He came back after two months, only to leave immediately for another tour without meeting his wife or asking about the baby. This time Meherunnisa was distressed.

'Is it my fault that we don't have a son? Allah has granted us a daughter after so many years, should we not accept his gift gracefully?' she asked Firdaus. 'Why is he upset with me?'

'He will come around. They always do. It is just a matter of time. One glance at the innocent face and his heart is bound to melt. I wager he will love her as much as we do.'

'I hope so,' sighed Meherunnisa looking at her child who was happily kicking in the air, staring fixedly at the colourful silk ball her mother had hung above her crib. Laadli was a happy baby, smiling and gurgling through the day.

'The next time the master comes home, I will take Laadli to his chamber on some pretext. I am sure he will lose his heart to her.'

'You will do nothing of the sort,' admonished Meherunnisa. 'He will have to come here to meet his child. I want to see how long he can keep running away from her. We have a daughter and he has to learn to love her.'

Many weeks later, tired of travelling, Sher Afghan returned home. But he made no attempt to meet his wife or see his daughter. Finally, running out of patience, Meherunnisa walked into his room one evening.

She had taken hours over her bath, scenting and adorning herself with great care. Her pastel green silk bodice was intricately patterned with tiny pearls and sequins that reflected the light with each movement. The tight, green satin trousers were topped with an elegantly embroidered white kameez in diaphanous muslin. Meherunnisa had thrown a gossamer gold veil carelessly over her shoulders, enhancing the golden glow of her complexion. A heavy emerald choker adorned her slender throat, and large tear-drop pearls dropped on her bosom from a gold string wrapped around her neck. They had been a wedding gift from her father. Lodged in the parting of her lustrous hair was a string of pearls ending in a diamond-studded ornament. A string of red roses festooned in her hair let out a fragrance which mingled with the aroma of tobacco in his room.

She walked with languorous rhythm, her feet gliding over the smooth marble floor. Motherhood had caused her slender figure to fill out at the right places; her angular features had acquired a softer look. The cheeks that had carried a sunken look just a couple of months ago were glowing with pleasant plumpness; the blush on them was born out of good health and happiness. Meherunnisa had grown more beautiful with each passing day after she had become a mother.

Sher Afghan gaped at his wife. He had never seen her so lovely or happy in the eleven years of their marriage. This was a different woman, not the Meherunnisa he knew.

Meherunnisa threw him a coy smile and advanced seductively towards him. Sher Afghan felt his heart revving up with a long forgotten beat as blood surged in his loins and he experienced a rush of desire for his wife.

'Are you angry with me, my master?' she said flirtatiously, stirring up his lust.

In a voice hoarse with passion, he stammered, 'Angry...why...why should I be angry?'

'I know you have every reason to be annoyed. I do feel guilty at having produced a daughter after all these years. But, think about it—isn't it better to be a father to a daughter than to be no father at all? Haven't we waited so long to hold our child in our arms? Now that Allah has blessed us with a daughter, should we spurn his blessings and hold back our love from her?'

He could barely hear the words she spoke as he lurched towards her.

Meherunnisa knew when to use her guile; she was adept at it. There lived no man who could resist her when she exerted her charm. Neither could her husband. He grabbed her in his arms and kissed her lips, savouring the freshness of her breath. His hands strayed to her bosom and she arched her back ardently. It had been a long time since Sher Afghan had made love to his wife. His hands moved over her body impatiently, tearing away the layers of clothing while she sighed with pleasure. Her body yielded readily to his demanding hardness. The rush of passion took them by storm till at last, spent with their fervour, they lay side by side on the huge, round bed near the fountain. Smiling secretively, Meherunnisa got up and stretched sensuously. He mumbled sleepily and stretched out his arms for her but she evaded his grasping hands and walked away.

Minutes later she came back with her daughter and laid the child next to Sher Afghan.

'Don't go away, Meher,' he pleaded, turning on his back. His passions sated for the moment, he wanted to hold her in his arms and atone for his conduct. Suddenly a kick landed on his side.

'What the...' he swore. Turning on his side he found himself gazing at the cherubic face of his daughter. Fascinated, he took in the perfectly formed limbs and the bewitching smile of his child.

'Allah be praised, is the imp trying to kick some sense into me?' he laughed. Gone were his dreams of nurturing a son, teaching him the intricacies of soldiering, sword-fighting, dagger-wielding and horse riding. They were suddenly replaced by his desire to watch his daughter grow, listen to her melodious voice and to hear the tinkle of her anklets as she ran around the house.

'A daughter is better than having no child, isn't it?' he asked Meherunnisa.

'Of course, it is.'

'Yah Allah, this child is a spitting image of you,' he said, reaching out to caress the child.

Laadli gurgled happily, kicking her legs energetically.

Tenderness suffused Sher Afghan's face as he lifted his daughter.

'I have named her Laadli Banu hoping that she would be your beloved child just as she is mine.' His wife moved within the circle of his arm.

'Laadli Banu!' he mumbled, rolling the name on his tongue, trying to enjoy the feel of it. 'That's a beautiful name. Yes, she will be my beloved just as she is yours,' he promised, his words delighting his wife.

'I had never imagined that the child was so beautiful. She is perfect.' Sher Afghan opened the child's fist and spread out her fingers. Then he examined the little pink toes and the perfect pair of ears. His fingers strayed all over the child, delighting in the softness of her body. She smelt of a strange mix of milk, perfume and babyhood. He felt proud. This was his daughter, his flesh and blood, all perfect and beautiful. The powerful rush of his emotions made his eyes mist. He had waited so long for this moment.

'Tell me, does she resemble me at all?'

'Well, babies change as they grow. But I think she will be tall like you, because she seemed to fill my womb. And look at her eyes, they are grey like yours.'

'I hope she is as beautiful as her mother,' Sher Afghan's eyes were ardent as they slid over his wife's lissom body. 'I have behaved like a boor, but I shall make it up to you,' he promised, hugging Meherunnisa. 'I will try to be a good father, I promise.'

Tears of joy clouded her eyes as she clung to his strong body; he had not chided her for bearing him a daughter. *Everything is going to be all right*, sang her heart.

'We must celebrate Allah's gift to this house. It has been four months since the birth of our first child but it is not too late to rejoice. Begum, we will invite every emir in this area and throw a grand feast—a feast no one will forget. We will distribute silver and grains to the poor and the holy men.'

The next morning he donated a generous amount of money to the mosque. The elated mullah offered a special prayer for the health and well-being of the child.

The house was decorated with garlands of flowers and festoons of ribbons; the vases overflowed with fragrant flowers of all kinds. Special cooks were employed to prepare a grand banquet; Meherunnisa personally supervised the cooking, and prepared Sher Afghan's favourite kheer herself. Dozens of dishes were laid out on the dastarkhan spread in the male section, with different types of kebabs and biriyanis, roasted meats and halwas heaped on them. Inside the zenana, the women rejoiced, congratulating Meherunnisa. They sang songs and blessed Laadli.

Wine flowed liberally and there was merriment in the large mansion. A large troupe of musicians and dancers had been called from the city to perform for the guests. The large hall resonated with the sound of anklets as the nautch girls performed, their dances punctuated by the loud appreciative claps of the inebriated men while the women watched from behind screens.

Silver spoons, gilded toys, wooden rattles, yards of brocade, silk and satin, pieces of gold jewellery, pearl strings and all kinds of gifts poured in for the newborn baby, along with blessings of happiness. Matrons exclaimed over the fair complexion of the baby, and spent much time speculating on the child's resemblance to her parents.

'The next one will definitely be a male child,' they told Meherunnisa.

If ever there is one, thought Meherunnisa, smiling sweetly at the women.

'You must hurry up with the next one so that you can have many children before you are too old,' advised an old crone. 'I waited too long and then I could produce only daughters for my husband.'

There was much laughter at her statement.

'And what do you think he did?' she continued. 'He went ahead and brought home three more wives. Your husband is a good man. I guess he loves you, for he has not brought home another wife.'

The assembled women nodded their heads in agreement. Most of them had to contend with rivals.

'You are a fortunate woman,' they told Meherunnisa. She did not need them to tell her that.

Sher Afghan was true to his word. He took up the role of a father with enthusiasm. The strapping soldier spent hours in the company of his daughter. His frequent hunting trips were forgotten, and so were his visits to the nautch girls. It amused the women in the household to see the tall man crouching on all fours to play horse with his daughter. For the first time in many years, there was laughter and happiness in the house. Meherunnisa was filled with contentment. She neither had to compete with Sher Afghan's paramours nor bait him to return to her bed.

For the moment she didn't mind being at Burdwan, she cared not that it rained for months or that the musty smell was tedious. She didn't mind the isolation and the humiliation heaped on her husband by the emperor. For the first time in eleven years she was happy to be away from the royal court. She didn't miss the splendour and glitter any more.

Before Laadli's birth, Meherunnisa had waited eagerly for the letters that came from Agra, with news and gossip about the royal family. She scanned the letters carefully for mention of Prince Salim, the heir to the Mughal throne. She went repeatedly through the fine calligraphy of the missives looking for the hidden messages. Her father, aware of her love for the prince, fed her little titbits about him. Through the years of her difficult marriage, her heart remained with the handsome prince who, in his ardour, had once promised her the crown and the throne. Laadli's arrival took away some of her restlessness. She no longer pined for the exciting life of the harem—instead, she was riveted by every small step in her baby's development.

Laadli turned on her side when she was just two-and-a-half months old.

'That is pretty early. Children generally turn on their side when they are three months old,' the nurse declared with pleasure.

The proud parents delighted in narrating the exploits of their child to anyone willing to suffer their enthusiasm. Meherunnisa wrote volumes about Laadli's activities to her parents.

By the time she was a year old, the child was running around on her chubby legs, lurching all over the place, pulling out things, breaking china and creating a minor havoc. The little brat delighted in having everyone running behind her, especially her mother. The entire retinue of servants were always on the run: even a little scratch on Laadli's knees could send her father into a rage. No matter how hard they tried, the child would manage to fall or hurt herself, and there would be dire retribution for the servant who couldn't prevent her fall.

Although Meherunnisa enjoyed playing hide-and-seek with the child, she often ran out of patience. It was Sher Afghan who never tired of playing with his daughter. She loved it when he pretended that he couldn't run fast enough to catch her. The game Laadli enjoyed most was playing horse with her father.

Laadli also loved listening to Firdaus' stories. She refused to go to sleep until the old nurse had told her a story. Like a skilful weaver, the woman wove tales that mesmerised the child. Even when Laadli was just a year old, Firdaus would tell her stories of her grandfather's escape from Persia, his journey through the desert and Meherunnisa's birth. By the time Laadli was two years old, she knew all the stories by heart; there was nothing that absorbed her more than the real life stories of her grandparents.

Each night there was a tussle of wills as Firdaus insisted on telling her stories from the Persian translation of the *Panchatantra*, the *Anwar-I-Suhayli*, but the child was more fascinated by her grandfather's escapades and insisted on listening to them.

'Tell me about grandfather's escape from Persia.'

'Let me tell you a story from the Arabian Nights, the story of Scheherazade. It is about the most beautiful woman in Arabia.'

'No, I want to hear about grandpa.' Firdaus could foresee the beginning of a tantrum. The child was a consummate actress and could bring tears to her eyes in an instant if her demands were not fulfilled.

'All right, all right I will tell you the story of your grandfather's escape from Persia,' Firdaus had to concede. 'Allah knows why you want to hear the same story again and again, you must have heard it a thousand times by now.'

'Because I like it.' The child's logic was simple.

'Your great-grandfather, Khwaja Mohammad Sharif, was the Vizier of Yazd, in the far away lands of Persia.'

'Is Persia more beautiful than Burdwan?'

'Persia is the jannat on earth. It is like a fairyland.'

'Can we go there?'

'Well, you will have to ask your father. Now, the Vizier was a very influential man; even the Shah held him in great esteem and never refused anything to him. He had two sons— your grandfather, Mirza Ghias Baig, and his brother, Aka Tahir.'

The child's eyes were round with wonder as she began sucking her thumb sleepily.

'Those were the days of the glorious reign of Shah Tahmasp. He was a kind ruler—just and generous. Your great-grandfather lived in an imposing house with many rooms, scores of servants, fountains and arches, all tiled in blue and white. There were beautiful gardens filled with flowers and fruits, and birds of many kinds. Mirza Ghias Baig grew up to be a handsome young man with many accomplishments. He was not only brave and fearless, he was also knowledgeable. The Vizier arranged his son's marriage with a beautiful woman called Asmat Bano. The marriage was held with great pomp and show. All the important people in the city of Isfahan were invited to the celebrations and for many days there was feasting in the house. The poor were fed and gifted with clothes, servants were rewarded and there was great rejoicing in the house.

'The couple lived happily and soon three children were born to them,' interjected Laadli who had heard the story many times.

'Yes. Everything was going well, but the Shah was old and one day he died,' Firdaus continued, fanning the child. 'A crafty Vizier grabbed hold of the throne and a reign of terror began in the country. The Vizier was scared that Shah Ismail supporters would rise in revolt, so the wicked fellow ordered the execution of all relatives and supporters of the previous Shah.'

'What happened to my grandfather?'

'As more and more supporters of Shah Ismail were rounded up and executed, your grandfather—initially reluctant to leave his homeland—decided to flee towards Qandahar from where he intended to make his way to Hindustan.'

'Where was my mother?'

'She was not born at that time,' Firdaus said stifling a yawn. 'They packed some clothes and jewels, and along with a trusted servant, the six of them left the house at night and made their way towards the city gates. They took two of their best camels and a horse for the journey through the deserts. The city of Isfahan had massive gates which were being closely watched by soldiers so that no one could escape. Your grandfather had to bribe the soldiers to open the city gates.'

'And when the gates opened, they rode away to the desert. They had to travel through many deserts for many months to reach Hindustan,' parroted Laadli.

'If you know the entire story, why do you want to hear it again and again?' Firdaus said irritably, sleepy after the day's work. 'I will tell you the rest of the story tomorrow,' she declared.

'No, no, I want to hear it today. Just tell me a little bit more. Please Firdaus, up to the time my mother was born in the desert,' insisted the two-year-old. That was the part she loved most.

'All right, just up to the time of your mother's birth,' Firdaus warned. Thrusting a paan into her mouth, the woman continued.

'On the way to Qandahar, some robbers attacked the family and took away all the money and jewels they had hidden in their clothes. Your grandfather sent the servant back to Isfahan because there was no food, and water was also scarce. Looted of their meagre belongings, the family trudged along with their children. Your grandmother, Asmat, heavy with her pregnancy, could barely walk. The heat and the dust of the desert made it difficult for her to move. During the day, when the sun was right above their heads, they rested under any shade they could find.'

'What did the camels do?'

'The camels also rested during the day. Camels are difficult creatures to ride. They lurch and sway so violently that one needs to hold on to them for dear life!'

'But why didn't they take the horses? Horses are so nice. I can ride Sultan when Abbajaan holds him for me.'

'Sultan is a trained horse. Anyway, your grandfather had taken the camels because they are the best animals to ride in a desert. Horses are no good, they need to drink a lot of water and where do you think you will find water in the desert?'

'I would have taken Sultan even if I had to travel through the desert,' declared Laadli stubbornly.

'That's enough for tonight. I am very sleepy and so are you,' yawned Firdaus. 'We will continue the story tomorrow.' She tucked the reluctant child into bed and made her way to her room.

Laadli's questions had brought back many memories to the old nurse. As she lay on her bed, Firdaus' thoughts travelled back many years to the stormy evening when she had helped Asmat Begum deliver a baby girl in a desert tent. Images ran in a procession through Firdaus' mind. How could she forget that fateful night—the beginning of her enduring relationship with the Baig family. That night, the wind had howled frightfully, driving everyone inside whatever shelter they could find, to escape the sting of a blinding dust storm. The sun, which had been blazing just moments ago, disappeared, and a frightful darkness descended on the desert. In the makeshift tent standing under an arar tree, Asmat was groaning in pain. Lack of nourishment and the strain of a rough journey had made her feeble. Alone and untended, the woman moaned, drenched in perspiration while her distraught husband and children stood outside the tent helplessly.

From a tent pitched nearby, a trader, Malik Masood, heard the agonised cries of the woman. His caravan was travelling towards Hindustan with supplies for the great Mughal emperor, Akbar. Curious, he sent for Mirza Ghias Baig and struck up conversation with the young man. With growing dismay, he heard the story of Mirza's misfortune.

'You must allow me to help you,' offered the trader. 'Without help your wife and child will perish. There will be time and opportunities for you to repay me later.'

Masood sent his servant to fetch a local woman to help with the delivery of the baby. The first woman who crossed the servant's path was Firdaus. Despite her protestations of total ignorance about a midwife's work, she was dragged to the camp. That was how Firdaus found herself in a rickety tent with the exhausted woman.

'I know nothing about delivering a baby,' she confessed to Asmat.

'Don't worry, I'll guide you through the process,' muttered Asmat, a fresh bout of pain racking her body. 'I think the baby is already on its way. There is no time to argue.'

Together they worked in silence to deliver the baby, under the faint light of a candle which threw ominous shadows all around them. Firdaus severed the umbilical cord with trembling hands as she recited holy verses from the Quran under her breath, beseeching Allah to guide her hands. A feeling of pride suffused her as she finally held the baby in her arms. Outside, the storm abated, leaving pleasant weather. The dust had settled; the agony of the long night had passed. Mirza Ghias Baig got up from his prayer mat and faced the woman.

When she placed the child in Ghias Baig's arms, he marvelled at the perfection of the baby's limbs and thanked Firdaus in a tearful voice.

'I have nothing to give you now but, Allah willing, I may be able to repay your kindness one day.'

Like a good omen, a brilliant sun had suddenly appeared on the horizon as he held his daughter. Suffused in the glow of sunlight, the baby appeared almost divine and the father was moved to tears.

'Meherunnisa! I will call you Meherunnisa—the light of womanhood,' he murmured, kissing the little fisted hand of his daughter. Her head cradled gently in the crook of her father's elbow, the baby continued to sleep.

Disappointed at not receiving any reward, Firdaus grumbled sullenly. A servant led her to Masood's tent as she was walking away from the caravan. The trader requested her to accompany them to Hindustan.

'You must stay with the baby since the mother is too weak to look after her newborn and the family is too poor to pay you. I will pay you handsomely for your services after we reach Hindustan,' Masood told her.

Firdaus belonged to a nomadic tribe that lived in the desert. Her newborn baby had succumbed to a deadly disease and her husband, a habitual gambler and a drunkard, had run away to Kabul after running up a huge debt. With hardly any relatives to support her, her very survival was at stake. Most women in her situation opted to sell their bodies to fend off hunger. She stood hesitantly trying to make a decision between a life of hunger and possible sexual exploitation, and a journey to an unknown land with strangers. Masood's offer was tempting: the rugged desert hills had nothing to offer her and the lands afar held at least some promise. She had heard endless tales of Hindustan's riches and bounties, its reckless emperors and vast royal harems.

'You can tell me your decision after the feast,' the trader said. He had organised a feast to celebrate the birth of Ghias Baig's daughter.

The evening saw Malik Masood's tent laid out with a rich blue Persian carpet, around which sat the men of the caravan.

Heaped on platters in the centre, were delicacies like abgusht—a thick meat and bean soup; dolmeh—vegetables stuffed with meat and rice; succulent and spicy kebabs; and mounds of rice flavoured with saffron and enriched with cashew, raisins and almonds. Goblets brimmed with wine. The appetising aroma rising from the rich repast filled the tent, whipping up hunger pangs. No one went hungry that night. There was enough food to satisfy the belly as well as the palate.

In the women's tent, samovars of steaming tea and exotic sherbets sat temptingly between the food platters. Chattering and joking, the women enjoyed the rare banquet that had come their way after weeks of frugal meals in the desert. Contented smiles flashed as tiny teeth bit into the delicacies impatiently. Outside, the camel drivers, drunk and sated, began singing. The more adventurous ones began dancing around the fire, unmindful of the wood smoke smarting in their eyes.

Hunger appeased, her mind was made up. Firdaus stayed with the caravan of camels that wound its way slowly and leisurely towards promises of a brighter future and colourful dreams in another land, another empire.

2

Meherunnisa became dearer than a daughter to the tribal woman. Perhaps it was the memory of her dead infant that drew her closer to the child.

Malik Masood, the well-heeled merchant, discovered the myriad talents of his protégé as they traversed through the arid deserts and narrow mountain passes regaling each other with stories of their past. The Mirza was cultured, aristocratic and intelligent. Well versed in Persian literature, he could create couplets that evoked praises from everyone, and the trader spent many nights enjoying poems that revived memories of his romantic youth.

Ghias Baig was not only a poet and artist, but also a skilled architect and an able administrator. Such talent would be valued in the Mughal court, of that the astute trader was certain. Malik Masood knew that Emperor Akbar would be happy to appoint Baig in his court. The trader could also benefit from introducing the talented young man to the emperor. Having enjoyed the pleasures of royal living, the family was unsuited for the vagaries and hardships of a nomadic life, and the young Baig was willing to work hard to recreate the happy times for his family. Malik Masood discovered that Ghias Baig was completely in love with his wife. The shrewd trader spent generously on the young man and his family, sure of good returns on his investment.

After eight months of journeying through deserts, craggy mountains and perilous valleys, the tired and dishevelled travellers finally sighted the majestic buildings of Agra. Hopes of a brilliant future resonated in each heart as the caravan rolled into the capital of the powerful Mughal emperor. The weather-beaten and sunburnt faces lit up with expectation and loud prayers heralded their advent into the city. Masood's happy thoughts were concerned with the exchange of his bounties for imperial favours, the Mirza was hopeful of a place in the court, and Firdaus dreamt of a comfortable existence as the maid of an ambitious man.

Malik Masood housed the Mirza and his family in a modest dwelling, promising to take him to the emperor at the earliest opportune moment.

It took two weeks and substantial bribes before the trader was finally given the opportunity to attend the royal court of the emperor. Mirza was immensely indebted to Masood as the trader had paid for the very clothes that covered his body.

On reaching the Diwan-é-Aam, the trader performed a stiff kornish to the emperor and pushed forward the smartly turned out Mirza Ghias Baig towards Shahenshah Akbar. The suave Mirza, familiar with the courtesy of the Persian court, saluted the emperor in a manner that pleased the sovereign greatly.

'Welcome to Hindustan. Malik Masood has told us of your hardship and apprised us of your talents. There is always place for intelligent and able young men in the Mughal Empire.'

'The Shahenshah is most generous with his words. It is my humble request that I may be given a chance to serve the great Mughal ruler.'

The emperor, with his uncanny instinct for talent, found a position for the young man and promptly granted a generous mansab to take care of his expenses.

It did not take Ghias Baig too long to establish his credentials and prove his worth to the emperor. With diligence and loyalty the émigré soon managed to wriggle into the innermost caucus. The young Mirza was sincere, diplomatic and diligent—and it was these virtues that won him the Shahenshah's favour. Meanwhile, Asmat Begum was assigned the task of waiting on the emperor's Persian queen, Ruqayya Begum, who was always eager to surround herself with women from her land of birth.

Asmat Begum quickly became the queen's favourite. The harem was full of women who indulged in petty jealousies for the lack of anything better to do, and they took no time in joining forces against her. Since Asmat could hardly afford to antagonise the other concubines and waiting ladies, she worked hard to maintain a pleasant relationship with every member of the vast harem. Life was difficult. The ascendancy of the Mirza's family evoked jealousy in the hearts of the nobles who were struggling to win the emperor's favour. The Persians were considered outsiders and usurpers. Perhaps it was the tough circumstances that made them determined to succeed.

Unlike the other nobles, Ghias Baig spent more time with his family than in gossiping and plotting. He seemed to have no vices: neither women nor gambling interested the man. That the Baig couple doted on each other was evident from the seven children that were born to them in quick succession.

Meherunnisa, fascinated by the harem and its women, regularly accompanied her mother to the queen's chambers. Over the years, she had grown into a beautiful and intelligent child, well versed in music and arts. She could recite verses with flourish and speak many languages. It wasn't long before the child attracted the attention of the Persian Sultana, who was enchanted by her quick wit.

'Since you are always pregnant, I would like your young daughter to wait on me. You can take leave to care for your family,' the queen teased the heavily pregnant Asmat one day. From that day began Meherunnisa's meteoric rise in the royal harem. Barely twelve years old, the girl had already mastered the art of poetry, embroidery and painting. She was a skilful conversationalist and kept the Sultana amused for hours with her repertoire of anecdotes, fables and jokes.

Firdaus remembered the storm Meher had created when she learnt that she was to be married to Ali Quli. 'He is just an uncouth soldier,' she had thundered. Firdaus had seconded her, forcefully—'Begum, our Meher is born to be a queen. Have you forgotten that the astrologers predicted a glorious future for her? You must call off this wedding.'

Shaking her head, Asmat Begum said, 'The emperor wishes her to be married to Ali Quli, and we cannot defy his wishes. He may be a crass soldier but he is a favourite of the emperor.'

'It is not his fault that he is unrefined,' said Ghias Baig.

This was true: the young man had never had an opportunity to be anything else other than a soldier.

After losing both his parents at an early age, Ali Quli Baig Istajlu began earning his livelihood by working as a stable attendant at the Shah's palace in Persia. Although the work was menial, the young man gained the attention of those who mattered in the court. When things changed after the Shah's death, Ali Quli managed to escape from Persia. He made his way to Kabul, from where he journeyed to Lahore.

With no other qualification than his brawn to see him through life, the only profession he could adopt was that of a soldier. Determined to distinguish himself as a warrior, Ali Quli practised sword-fighting, hand-to-hand combat, horse riding, and many other war skills before he made his way to the camp of Abdur Rahim Khan-é-Khana, the brilliant general of the Mughal emperor, to get himself enlisted as a foot soldier. The Khan-é-Khana was on a campaign at Thatta and required as many soldiers as he could gather.

During the battle, things suddenly swung in favour of the rebels and the Mughal army began retreating. Unwilling to give up, the Khan-é-Khana charged ahead, followed by a few loyal soldiers, Ali Quli among them. Suddenly, the general found himself surrounded by the enemy. Spotting him within the enemy circle, Ali Quli snatched a horse and rode up to him. Fighting heroically, he rescued the general and reversed the tide of the battle with his intelligent strategy. The battle was won and the grateful Khan-é-Khana promoted the young foot soldier as his personal bodyguard.

As days passed, the ageing Khan-é-Khana became increasingly dependent on Ali Quli for battle plans. Ali Quli was brave, honest and loyal—three things that were uncommon during the turbulent days of war. Soldiers switched camps faster than they changed clothes, depending upon the money offered to them. Under these conditions, when the Khan-é-Khana discovered the gem he had found in his army, he nurtured and promoted the young man to become his chief aide. Loneliness, war fatigue and uncertainties are strong binding factors, and the two warriors developed a warm relationship that was based on mutual respect and trust.

When the victorious imperial army returned to the capital, it was the Khan-é-Khana who presented the young Persian soldier at Akbar's court. The tall and battle-hardened soldier performed a clumsy kornish and stood in obedience before the emperor.

'Young man, I hear that you rescued our general with absolutely no regard for your own personal safety. We are pleased to have a brave soldier like you in our army. As a gesture of our pleasure we grant you a mansab of two hundred.'

Ali Quli stood speechless with emotion. Although he had heard many tales of Shehanshah Akbar's generosity, no one had been able to describe the great ruler's charisma. As he gaped in wonder, his mentor gave him a gentle nudge to remind him about court decorum. The Persian quickly bowed to the ruler to express his gratitude and struggled to put forth a refined speech.

'I am a humble servant of Your Majesty and I only performed my duty by coming to the aid of the general. I am not worthy of your magnanimous gesture.'

The experienced eyes of the emperor immediately spotted the awkwardness of the soldier, but they were pleased with the humility of the man. In a court filled with flatterers, the emperor was happy to see a man who did not resort to sycophancy. The emperor appointed him an officer in the royal guards. News of the plots hatched by his rebel nobles reached his ears from time to time—there could never be too many loyal bodyguards around him.

With his sincerity, the young soldier soon captured the confidence of the emperor. Before long, Ali Quli was accompanying the emperor on campaigns to quell rebellions. They rode together through the empire, capturing territories and subjugating errant rulers. With each victory, the emperor rewarded the brave Persian till his mansab had risen to five hundred.

Ali Quli did not fight because he wanted mansab; he did so because he had a deep reverence for the emperor. When Akbar desired that Ali Quli should be a part of the battle at Baluchistan, the devoted Persian rode to the frontier without hesitation and proved himself to be a soldier par excellence. The tall, broad-shouldered soldier mowed through the enemy lines, his sword flashing as it reflected the sun, striking terror in the hearts of the enemy. After Baluchistan's annexation, the annexation of Makaran was a foregone conclusion. The invincible forces of the emperor conquered the cities without opposition; stories about the valorous Mughal army had already travelled from lands far and beyond.

Ali Quli returned from the battlefield triumphant and proud, a conqueror without parallel. The emperor lauded Ali Quli's invincibility and expressed a desire to reward the soldier with something more than a mansab.

'Ali Quli, we are pleased with your valour and loyalty. You have the courage of a tiger and the cunning of a fox. We can grant you a jagir, but this time we would like to gift you something that you desire. Name it and it shall be yours.'

'Jahanpanah, you have given me much more than I deserve. All I want to do is to serve you till my death,' replied the soldier earnestly.

'We are indeed pleased with your loyalty, but we insist that you name your reward.'

'In that case, I will name my reward at an appropriate time, Jahanpanah.'

'Fair enough. The day you decide on your reward, remind us of our promise and we shall grant you whatever you wish.'

It was not till many months later, when they had returned to Agra, that Ali Quli asked the emperor to fulfil his promise.

3

It had been raining incessantly for the last one week. Dark, threatening clouds covered the sky and the chirping of birds was replaced by the continuous patter of rain. Meherunnisa hated it. There was a dank and oppressive odour everywhere. Even the clothes carried a musty smell, making her feel nauseous. There was the ugly green growth of mould in every corner of the house. Insects and vermin cropped up in the store, ruining the grains. She missed the arid atmosphere of Agra and pined for the bright sunlight that was taken for granted in those parts of the country. Even the city's rains were delightful, as the first showers brought the heady smell of earth, a welcome reprieve from the heat and the dust of the long summer.

'Oh, what I would give for a patch of sunlight,' she sighed, spraying herself liberally with rose attar. She had tried everything conceivable to get rid of the mildew, without any success. Incense burned almost continuously, its cloying odour hanging over the rooms. The whining of the mosquitoes was a constant nuisance. She found the muslin nets over the beds irritating, for they blocked out whatever fresh air entered the house. Neem leaves burned continuously in the brazier, emitting a sharp odour. The suffocating atmosphere made her want to rush out and breathe the moist air.

'Yah Allah, when will it stop raining?' she exclaimed, as she snipped off an extra thread in her embroidery.

In a corner of the room Firdaus was trying to fob off the demands of the bored child.

'No, I can't play hopscotch with you. I am too old for that. Nor can I play hide-and-seek. Besides, it is raining and we can't go out.'

'Take me to the stables, then. I want to see Sultan.'

'No, you can't go to the stables either.'

'All right, if you can't take me to the stable to ride Sultan, you pretend to be my horse and I'll ride on you.'

'Allah! What else would you have an old woman do? Go and play with your doll.'

'I don't like playing with dolls.'

'Let us play chaupar, then,' suggested Firdaus.

'That is such a dull game.'

'It is the game intelligent people play. Even the emperor loves the game.'

'Does the emperor play chaupar?' The child was surprised.

'He does. He has built the squares of the chaupar board on the floor of his palace and he plays with live pieces— beautiful maidens dressed as chess pieces stand in the squares and move at the command of the players. It is a fascinating sight.'

'Anyway, I am not interested in playing that game.' Turning to her mother, the child complained—'Firdaus does not listen to me. Send her away to Bade Abba.' Bade Abba was Laadli's name for her grandfather.

'I would rather go and stay with your Bade Abba. At least no one will bother me there,' grumbled Firdaus.

Meherunnisa smiled as she listened to their banter. 'Why don't you humour her a little? She is bored.'

Grumbling, Firdaus led the child to the balcony from where they could see the pond with the lotus flowers.

'I want to hear a story,' Laadli demanded. 'I want to hear Ammijaan's story. Tell me about the time she was taken to the royal zenana.'

'When your grandfather was appointed as a courtier in Emperor Akbar's court, your mother was just a year old. She was a pretty child and a very intelligent one too: I still remember how quickly she could learn things. She was taught Persian verses, calligraphy and music by her mother. At your age, she was already reciting the Quran and painting lovely pictures.'

'I can do that too. I can do many more things,' Laadli boasted.

'All right, you are a very intelligent child and so was your mother. Your grandmother is a talented musician. She can play the Tar-é-Shiraaz, which the Persians consider the Sultan of instruments.'

'What is Tar?'

'It is a stringed instrument, much like a long-necked lute. It is carved from mulberry wood and its upper surface is shaped like two hearts of different sizes, joined at the points. The sound box is covered with lambskin. It produces a lovely melody in the hands of a talented player, and your grandmother taught this art to your mother. She can play it better than anyone I have ever heard.'

'Will she teach me to play Tar?'

'Of course, she will teach you to play it. Do you want to hear the rest of the story?'

'Yes, of course.'

'As I was saying, your mother began learning all kinds of arts at a very early age. As a girl of six, she accompanied her mother to the royal zenana. During one of her visits to the zenana, your mother played the Tar for Bilquees Begum. The empress was so captivated by the child's skilful handling of the instrument that she offered to keep your mother in the royal harem. That day onwards, your mother spent more time at the harem than at home.'

'I wish I could go to the royal harem and see what it looks like. I have heard that it is as luxurious and beautiful as jannat,' sighed Laadli. There was a dreamy look in her eyes as the child tried to visualise the grandeur of the royal palace.

'Maybe you will see it one day.'

There is more heartbreak and sorrow in those glittering palaces than I have seen anywhere, thought the nurse. She had spent enough time in the harem to know what went on behind those beautiful fretwork marble screens. Girls as young as thirteen, picked by the royal men to satisfy their lust for a night, pined away for life, separated from their beloved families, living on the emperor's charity. The concubines spent the long years of their life locked within the four walls of the harem. They amused themselves with frivolous activities to keep busy, but within their minds was an untold turmoil that sought release through vicarious pleasures and endless plotting. Many of them indulged in incessant power tussles within the harem. Lesbianism was rampant. Vices like opium and intoxicants were indulged in. Intrigue prospered behind every veil and wall of the royal harem as different factions fought for control.

'What does it looks like? Have you been inside the harem, Firdaus?'

'Countless times! I accompanied your mother to the palaces and met the queens, concubines and princesses. It is a magical world: the marble pavilions with ornate fountains set in wondrous gardens running along the Yamuna river; magnificent cupolas and exotic gardens lined by fretwork galleries; crimson and gold halls splashed with a profusion of gems, rich Persian carpets, crystal chandeliers, exotic incense in jewelled censers and the enamelled bowls with all kinds of fruits and nuts—everything takes your breath away!'

Meherunnisa smiled wistfully from the corner of the room. Her ears had caught the nanny's spiel.

Firdaus continued, 'Within the halls are elegant divans created from sandalwood, covered with intricately embroidered satin with heaps of cushions piled on them. Under the pavilions in the garden, beautiful women recline on thrones crafted out of the whitest marble, enjoying music played by the servant girls. The jewellery on their person can easily buy a few kingdoms. There is blinding resplendence all around. It would require a poet to describe the palace; I don't have the words to do so.'

It will not harm the child to conjure images of a fantastic place, thought the nurse, her mind far away. She held Laadli's hand and walked to the rain-soaked terrace. The clouds had finally floated away.

'And Ammijaan lived in the harem with the queen?' Laadli tugged at her hand.

'Yes, she literally grew up in the palace,' Firdaus said, remembering how the little girl had transformed into a beautiful maiden with long, wavy hair that fell to her hips, cascading in curls all around her lovely face. Her nubile figure had made the other girls turn green with jealousy. 'Her nimble fingers could embroider intricate patterns and she loved creating new fashions,' Firdaus continued. 'While the other women of the harem spent time in frivolous activities, your mother and Bilquees Begum discussed poetry, architecture and politics for hours, sometimes in the presence of the emperor. Emperor Akbar did not fail to notice the young girl who was always by the side of his begum.'

'Did he compliment her for her intelligence and talent?'

'Oh yes, he did. But it was his son, Salim, who was fascinated by your mother.'

'What did the prince look like?'

'Well, he was a handsome man. He was always dressed impeccably; he wore satin churidars, muslin sherwanis and velvet caftans embroidered and set with precious stones. He wore a lot of jewellery, especially set with rubies which were brought to him by traders from far away lands.'

'He must be an impressive person.'

'Oh yes, he is very impressive, both in looks and style.'

'How did they meet? Tell me about their first meeting,' the child demanded.

'It is a long story.' Firdaus stood up. 'It is late now and I am tired. Let me put you to bed. I will tell you all about the prince and your mother tomorrow.'

'You always do this to me. Just as the story gets interesting, you want to go to bed. This is not fair,' whined Laadli.

But Firdaus had made up her mind, and once Firdaus made up her mind no one could dissuade her. The little girl made her way reluctantly to her bed but sleep was far from her eyes as she tossed about, dreaming of harems and the prince.

Sleep eluded Firdaus too. Memories of Meherunnisa's romance with Salim filled her mind. How much of the story could she narrate to Laadli? The child was far too young to understand the intricacies of the royal courts. How could she explain their romance or the royal displeasure it evoked? Laadli would have to grow up before she heard the romantic escapades of the prince, Firdaus thought, remembering the first time Salim had met Meherunnisa.

The harem was abuzz with the news of the emperor's latest victory. After many months of heavy battle, the imperial forces had finally subdued the rebel king of Khandesh. Bilquees Begum decided to celebrate the event by hosting a mushaira at the harem. When Prince Salim heard of the contest, he decided to get himself invited for the occasion. He loved poetry, wine and women, and there was no way he could be kept away from a glamorous event such as this one.

Meherunnisa, now sixteen and an exceptionally attractive and witty girl, had decided to take part in the contest. She rehearsed a few verses of her favourite composer, Faiz, for the evening. Clad in a white ensemble embroidered with pearls, she looked ethereal. The diaphanous veil with its delicate silver fringe could barely conceal the excitement in her animated eyes. While the women in the zenana wore bright colours and flashy clothes, Meherunnisa favoured white. It was a calculated effort at standing out in the crowd.

As her eyes took in the conglomeration of bejewelled harem women, she felt a tremor of nervousness. This was the moment she had been waiting for. For long she had been watching the handsome prince from behind screens, but to see him face-to-face had remained a dream.

The ornate candleholder, with its solitary candle, was passed from one contestant to the other. The first in line was the princess of Mertha, the beautiful woman who was brought to the harem when her father lost his kingdom to the Mughal emperor. The proud Rajput princess, resplendent in a crimson silk lehenga and shell pink veil, wore thick gold ornaments in her hair and ears. She had beautiful doe eyes that were rumoured to have captivated the emperor's heart. Her melodious voice carried the ache of a vanquished soul as it reverberated in the extravagantly decorated harem. A loud note of appreciation echoed around the room as she ended her composition with a flourish.

The candle flickered in its crystal stand as it passed to glamorous Gulnaar, another consort of the emperor. It passed from one woman to the other and Meherunnisa's heart thumped uncontrollably as she waited for her chance. Her heart was filled with trepidation: would she succeed in attracting the attention of the prince? He already looked bored with the proceedings, his eyes scanning the faces of the women, searching for momentary diversion.

Finally, the candle was placed before Meherunnisa. Clearing her throat nervously, she began singing a romantic couplet. The prince, who was reclining on a velvet bolster, picking some grapes from the carved silver salver, immediately sat up. His glance travelled through the hall and rested on the girl seated at the far end.

The thickly lashed eyes sparkled like emeralds, confusing the prince from a distance; were they green or blue, he wondered. The delicate lips trembled with nervousness and her cheeks blushed a deep crimson as she caught his eyes. He was mesmerised.

'Allah!' the prince swore. 'Is this an angel, or am I dreaming?' he mumbled. Bilquees Begum was watching his reactions closely.

'Salim, this is neither heaven nor is she an angel. Control yourself, she is my ward,' she scolded teasingly.

'Ammijaan, I must meet this girl. What is her name?'

'Don't be impatient, prince. Come to my garden tomorrow and you shall meet her,' the queen smiled playfully at him.

Salim could barely wait for the day to break. He tossed about sleeplessly on his bed, unable to drive away Meherunnisa's image from his mind. Her impish smile and unfathomable eyes haunted him.

He sprang up from his bed as the muezzin announced the morning prayer. For the first time Salim prayed in earnest, begging for a sight of the beautiful damsel who had disturbed his mind for the past twelve hours. He petulantly rejected all the garments laid out by his valet and finally settled for his favourite white muslin fargal embellished with intricate embroidery. Golden tassels fringed with seed pearls dangled from the buttonholes. Tight satin trousers covered his legs, while the royal head was protected with a green turban from which a heron's feather jutted out jauntily. A jade hilted dagger encrusted with rubies was stuck in his crimson cummerbund.

Walking hurriedly, the prince reached the harem garden. The gurgling fountains did not attract his attention, nor did the lotus blooming in the pond. Occupied with his thoughts, the prince did not notice the flower-laden branches of the champak tree bending over the pool of water nor did he pause for a moment to admire the peacocks strutting about.

In a pavilion at the far end of the garden, Bilquees Begum reclined surrounded by her attendants.

The empress was amusing herself with the gossip provided by her coterie. They were telling her about the whims and fancies of her Rajput rival, the Amber Queen.

'...And then she demanded a goblet of the wine brought from Goa by the Portuguese Jesuits. A sip of the nectar and she got addicted to the brew. Now a regular supply has to be procured for the empress who refuses to drink any other kind of wine...'

Bilquees Begum was distracted by the announcement made by the eunuchs guarding the harem gate. 'Ba mulaiza ba hoshiyar, Shehzada Salim is on his way.'

The queen watched the prince making his way across the multi-layered garden as she nibbled on a peach. A secretive smile lurked on her face.

Meherunnisa was nearby, admiring a pair of pearly white pigeons in a gilded cage that hung from a guava tree. It was the latest acquisition of the queen, presented by a trader who had just arrived from Persia. She feigned disinterest in the prince's arrival, although her heart tattooed madly with delight. She sensed the prince's eyes on her. She let her veil slip, uncovering the striking features of her face.

Salim, who was in the act of performing a smart kornish to the queen, stood transfixed and stared at the vision till the queen coughed meaningfully.

Bowing low to her, he said, 'You commanded my presence this morning so here I am. Now, you must keep your part of the promise.'

'First, let me show you my new acquisition.' The queen was enjoying his impatience. 'I'm sure you have nothing as exotic in your menagerie.'

The prince loved pigeons and owned an impressive menagerie. But at the moment nothing interested him except the girl standing near the guava tree.

'If you must,' he sounded irritated with the queen's diversionary tactics.

'Meher, bring me the pigeons that were presented to me by Abdul Nasser.'

The girl moved with fluid rhythm across to the queen, carrying the cage in her hand.

'Allah! I have no words to express the beauty of your possession,' he declared, staring at Meherunnisa, who quickly moved away.

Too much exposure can kill interest, she had been told by her mother repeatedly. To hold a man's interest let him pursue you.

'Salim, I am talking about these pigeons. Are you listening?' scolded Bilquees Begum. 'I am willing to barter these birds for the pair of peacocks you brought from Amber.'

The prince was distracted. 'Yes, yes, definitely,' he conceded eagerly, as his eyes flitted anxiously. At any other time, he would have been delighted with the offer. Right then, he wanted to get away and pursue Meherunnisa who was walking away. She was deliberately moving towards the other end of the garden.

'Well, they are yours. Take them with you,' Bilquees Begum offered him the cage.

'Thank you so much. I will ensure that the peacocks reach your garden immediately.'

The prince bowed himself out of her presence. Carrying the cage in his hands he hurriedly walked towards the girl.

'Meherunnisa, that's your name, isn't it?' he began without any formalities.

'May...may...I take the cage from you, sire?' she stammered.

His eyes travelled from the bottom of her hennaed toes to the top of her head in a sweeping glance.

Without a word, he offered the cage to her. She took out a pigeon and stroked it absentmindedly. The prince was captivated; she knew it.

'You have not replied,' his voice was husky with desire. 'Your eyes have driven me crazy.'

'What can I say to that, my lord?' The nervousness was gone; she was in control. Meherunnisa liked to be in control, it gave her a sense of power.

He came closer and lifted her chin with his left hand while the right hand strayed towards her shoulder. Her body trembled at his touch. The pigeon fluttered in her hands and she let it escape. Glad to be released from captivity, it soared to the sky. Within minutes, it had disappeared.

The prince was aghast.

'You careless woman, what have you done? Don't you know the pigeon is priceless. How could you allow it to escape?' he raged. His passion had turned cold with anger.

Without a word Meherunnisa removed the other pigeon from the cage and released it in the air. 'Like this,' she said, laughing as the bird flew away to join its mate.

She was playing with fire—the prince's temper was legendary. It took moments for his mood to change into a dangerous one, but Meherunnisa was not afraid. The scales were tipped in her favour. The infatuated prince had a difficult choice to make—give in to his rage or to his passion.

Astounded at her audacity, the prince looked at Meherunnisa. He had never dealt with a situation like this.

'You are a fearless woman,' he seized her in his arms and whispered. 'I could have you executed for this, do you know?'

'Yes, you can get me executed,' admitted Meherunnisa demurely, lowering her head. 'But I know that you will not do so because I fascinate you.'

'What a conceited woman you are, Meherunnisa! You are right, you captivate me. I want to possess you.'

'Princes have momentary fascinations. I know of the hundreds of objects of your fascination who are languishing within the four walls of the harem, imprisoned for life. I don't want to be one of them. When I surrender myself, it will be to a man who will value me beyond the riches and the crown.' She was gambling, once again. She trembled, nervous at her own impudence, but a streak of madness goaded her on.

'Woman, you are too vain. What makes you think that I will wait for your consent? Do you know that I can possess you by force if I wish to do so?'

'I know that, Huzoor. But I also know that you will not possess me by force because I will never yield my spirit and it is my spirit that fascinates you more than my body.'

Salim walked away in a huff, angry at her words. In the solitude of his room, her words echoed in his mind and he knew she was right. She was one in a million and she knew it.

4

'Tell me the story about Abbajaan and the tigress.' The night was warm and Firdaus sat fanning Laadli with a hand fan. The child was restless. Beads of sweat glistened on her forehead and her muslin dress clung damply on her plump body.

'Hush child, try to sleep. It is late.'

'I can't sleep. Tell me the story and I'll go to sleep. Promise!'

With a deep sigh, the old nurse began narrating, 'Your father is a very brave man. Did you know that he is the tallest man in the court and everyone has to look up to speak to him? And he can wield his sword more skilfully than anyone else in the kingdom. He is the best horse rider in town and he excels in falconry and polo.'

'Even Ammijaan is very good in falconry and chaugan.'

'I will tell you about your Ammijaan's falcon. She called it Baaz Bahadur...'

'No, no, I don't want to hear about the falcon. I want to hear about the tigress,' Laadli insisted.

'Okay, then don't interrupt me. Now, Prince Salim is a very impetuous person. He rarely thinks before acting. That is the reason Shehanshah Akbar appointed your father as the prince's companion. Salim is very fond of hunting wild animals—he loves capturing them and keeping them in his palace. In fact, he owns an impressive menagerie.'

'Does he keep tigers in cages? Isn't it cruel to cage wild animals?' asked Laadli with concern. She loved animals and couldn't bear to see them locked up.

'No one can say that to a prince. Once the prince was hunting at Nagaur. It is a dense forest near Ajmer. A royal camp was set up on the fringes of the forest so that the trackers and soldiers could herd the wild animals into a specified area.'

'But why do they do that?'

'It is a classic Mughal hunting style called Qamargah,' explained Firdaus. 'One day, while the royal entourage camped in the forest, Salim rode off with a couple of soldiers. As they were going through the jungle, he noticed a few tiger cubs frolicking behind a rock. The tigress had wandered off in search of food leaving the cubs unattended. The gold-flecked eyes of the cubs attracted the tawny ones of the prince. Fascinated, Salim, dismounted from his steed and bent to caress the cubs, despite being warned not to by his attendants. He decided to take one of them back with him to the palace.'

'It is not right to separate the cubs from the mother!' said Laadli, who had a strong opinion about what was right and wrong. 'I would be very unhappy if someone were to take me away from Ammijaan.'

'That's true, but as I said, no one can tell a prince that. The prince was picking up a cub when the tigress returned. She was incensed at the sight of her cub in his hand. Before the prince could react, she bared her claws and sprang at him. Salim's attendants were too frightened to come to his aid. It was at that moment that your Abbajaan appeared. He lunged at the tigress with a dagger in his hand and thrust it deep into the animal. Everyone thought he would die but he managed to kill the tigress.'

'Was Abbajaan hurt very badly? Was he in great pain?' asked Laadli anxiously, although she knew the story by heart.

'Of course he was. You can't fight a tigress without getting hurt. He was badly mauled by the tigress, but he is a brave man. He didn't flinch or think of his own safety when he saw that the prince was in danger. Your Abbajaan stood up lurching like a drunken man. He was bleeding heavily from his wounds and then he fell unconscious. They did not expect him to live, but he is a stubborn man. He fought death like he fights his enemies. It took several weeks for the royal hakim to put him back on his feet. Upon hearing about the bravery of your father, Emperor Akbar granted him the jagir of Burdwan, raised his mansab to a thousand and presented him with a royal ring, set with precious rubies.'

'And so he is called Sher Afghan,' continued Laadli. 'We are pleased at your selfless act of bravery. You have saved the life of our beloved son. Name your reward and it shall be given to you,' the girl mimicked the emperor, much to the amusement of her nurse.

'Shahenshah Akbar was very grateful to your father. But your Abbajaan is not a greedy man. Already overwhelmed with the honour and the jagir given to him by the emperor, he did not ask for anything more.'

'But when he saw Ammijaan he liked her so much that he begged the emperor's permission to marry her.'

'Yes. He had a glimpse of your mother when she was returning from the dargah of Shaikh Salim Chisti. I was with her at that time.'

'Tell me about it. Please Firdaus,' begged Laadli.

'Shaikh Salim Chisti was a great saint. He had promised Emperor Akbar that he would have three sons who will survive till adulthood. The emperor had sought the blessings of the saint because none of his sons survived beyond a few weeks. When Prince Salim survived, the emperor constructed a dargah for the saint, as an expression of his gratitude. People believe that a wish made at his dargah is always fulfilled. Your Ammi also visited the dargah with a wish.'

'What did she wish for?'

Firdaus did not tell the child that Meherunnisa had wished to be married to Prince Salim.

'I wouldn't know that, you will have to ask your mother. Maybe she wished for a beautiful daughter like you and Allah granted her the wish. Anyway, wishes are supposed to be kept a secret.'

'Yes, I think she asked for me,' stated the child seriously. 'She keeps telling me that I am a child of many prayers.'

'We had just finished praying at the dargah and were walking out towards our palanquin when your father dismounted near the dargah. Just then a gust of breeze blew away your mother's veil. As she struggled with the veil to cover her face, the Quran she was carrying in her hand fell down. In the holy book, there was a peacock feather that your mother considered lucky. Prince Salim had gifted it to her and she never parted with it. The wind blew it away and she ran to grab it.'

'Can Ammi run as fast as me?'

'Of course not. Anyway, your father also ran behind the feather. It was a hilarious situation. All three of us were running after the feather, which kept eluding our grasp. Suddenly, the feather got entangled in a bush and both your mother and father reached out for it. At that moment, your father saw her face and fell in love with your mother. Perhaps destiny wanted the two of them to meet at the saint's shrine. He followed our palanquin to Agra and rode up to Mirza Ghias Baig's house.'

'Did he enter the house and meet grandpa?'

'No, it would not have been proper for him to enter the house or ask for your mother hand without the formalities that need to be observed. He approached the Khan-é-Khanan Abdur Rahim to take a marriage proposal for her to her father's residence. The Khan-é-Khanan was a friend of your grandfather and a very important man at the emperor's court. The old man was delighted that Sher Afghan had finally decided to marry. For a long time, the Khan-é-Khanan and his wife had been pestering him to get married. They had brought many proposals for him but he had refused all of them.'

'He couldn't have married anyone else,' Laadli's explanation was simple.

'The Khan-é-Khanan broached the topic with your grandfather but no marriage could be conducted until the emperor gave his consent.'

'Why?'

'That is the Mughal emperor's order. The marriages of all important people in the Mughal court have to be held only after they have been approved by the emperor.'

'Did grandfather seek the emperor's approval for the marriage?'

'No, it was the Khan-é-Khanan who approached the emperor for his consent. He mentioned to the emperor that Sher Afghan wished to marry Mirza Ghias Baig's daughter. The emperor was delighted because he was very fond of your Abbajaan as well as your grandfather. Besides, the two families came from Persia and there could have been no better match for the Mirza's daughter. The emperor blessed their union and the two were married.'

'Did Ammijaan see Abbajaan before the wedding?'

'She had seen him briefly at the dargah.'

'Did she like him?'

'That is a question you will have to ask your mother,' Firdaus evaded the child's queries adroitly. She remembered the heartache Meherunnisa went through when she learnt that the emperor had given his sanction for her marriage to the Persian soldier. Salim and Meherunnisa were passionately in love with each other and the prince had vowed to marry her after his return from Mewar.

Very few people knew that the emperor had sent the prince away deliberately so that Meherunnisa's marriage could be solemnised without any hindrance. The hot-tempered prince was not likely to give up his ladylove to another man easily. Emperor Akbar knew that the prince wanted to marry Meherunnisa. He also knew that the Persian faction in the harem wanted to see the prince married to her. His own queen, Bilquees Begum, had been instrumental in encouraging the romance. Salim was free to marry any woman he desired except Mirza Baig's daughter. Sher Afghan had reminded the Shahenshah about his promised reward and the emperor could not refuse his request.

When Salim learnt about the wedding, he went on a rampage. A tremor travelled through Firdaus' body as she remembered the prince's cruelty.

'You are not listening to me, Firdaus. I want you to describe the wedding. Did the emperor attend the ceremony?' Laadli was tugging at her sleeve.

'The wedding was a grand one and almost all the important people in town attended it. The emperor could not attend because he was away on a campaign, but his Persian wife, Queen Bilquees Begum, attended the wedding and gifted an expensive set of jewellery to your mother. She looked ravishing in her bridal dress of crimson brocade. The weavers at Benares had especially woven the veil and the best craftsmen of the town had spent weeks toiling over the bridal attire. It had tiny rubies and pearls embroidered into it. She was so beautiful that people could barely take their eyes off her face. No one in Agra had seen such a beautiful bride, I can vouch.'

'And Abbajaan? Did he look dashing and handsome?'

'Of course he did. There was not a man in Agra to match your Abba. He wore a white robe with fine zardosi embroidery on it, over a pair of tight satin trousers in the brightest of reds. His turban matched his robe and an ornate pin set with emeralds adorned its folds. When he rode into the house, the women exclaimed excitedly.'

'And then they lived happily ever after...' sang Laadli.

Hardly that, thought the nurse. She knew how difficult it had been for Meherunnisa to adjust to the rough ways of the soldier. Used to the elegance and refinement of the palace, she found it hard to handle the demands of a husband who was more physical than intellectual. At every stage of her married life, the prince intruded into her thoughts. For many years she continued to pine for Salim and the grandeur of the royal harem.

Her frustration showed up in constant illnesses and numerous miscarriages. With her husband away on military campaigns for long periods of time, the woman was sentenced to a life of solitude. She spent many nights tossing on her empty bed, lonely and miserable, haunted by memories of her past romance. Those were tough times. Unhappy in her marriage, Meherunnisa lost much of her youthful exuberance, beauty and wit. She was a pale shadow of her former self, with dark circles under her eyes. As the days went by, she became careless about her appearance and clothes. Firdaus felt sorry for her, but there was little she could do to alleviate the situation.

There were so many stories and memories. Firdaus' face creased with a gentle smile as she tucked Laadli into bed. Many of her fond memories were about Meherunnisa's dalliance with the prince. There were few who knew as much as she did about their romance, but those stories were not for telling. Laadli would never learn of her mother's love affair or the prince's infatuation—at least not from her. Like most people connected with the Mughal court, Sher Afghan had also heard the rumours about Prince Salim's infatuation for Meherunnisa, but he never discussed the subject with his wife. Perhaps he did not want confirmation of Meherunnisa's feelings for another man.

The spectre of suspicion, however, clouded their relationship. Sher Afghan knew that the prince wore his heart on his sleeve. Salim's love affairs were too numerous for anyone to keep count. Some of his infatuations lasted just a day, and some for a couple of weeks. Not many of his dalliances lasted long enough to cause any concern.

Of the many romantic affairs of the prince, the most tragic was the one between him and Anarkali. Everyone at Lahore knew about their romance and its disastrous end. Nadira was a servant in the royal harem. The girl was a graceful dancer and a skilled singer. One day, the empress commanded her to sing for Shehanshah Akbar. He was so captivated with her beauty and voice that he gave her the title Anarkali, meaning 'bud of a pomegranate'.

Akbar fell prey to her beauty and made her his concubine. With her beauty and wit, the girl soon became his favourite concubine. There were many in the harem who were jealous of the emperor's preference for her.

Anarkali was immensely talented and Akbar, who was a connoisseur of art, was delighted with her. She was a skilled miniaturist and often painted in the Lahore atelier.

It was the month of April, spring was in the air and Lahore was celebrating the festive occasion of Akhri Charshumba, the second month of the Islamic calendar. It was the day when the Prophet Mohammad recovered from his illness for the last time. The rituals began early in the morning with everyone bathing in perfumed water and dressing in new clothes. Sadquas, the offerings of all kinds of grains and pulses, were arranged in huge gold plates along with silver bowls full of mustard oil. The male members of the royal family touched the Sadqua and gazed at their reflection in the oil before placing gold coins in it. These were later distributed amongst the poor. After the harem women performed the rituals, everyone gathered for a sumptuous breakfast.

Surrounded by a bevy of giggling women in his grandmother's palace, Salim gazed at his reflection in the oil. The faces of some women were also reflected in the bowl as they teased the prince. All of a sudden his eyes were attracted to a beautiful image. His eyes met those of Anarkali in the golden oil, and he was mesmerised. And that was the beginning of a passionate romance.

Salim and Anarkali met clandestinely in the gardens of Lahore, professing their love for each other. It is said that fire and love cannot be hidden for long. Tales of their love affair soon began circulating around the palace and town. A jealous concubine carried the gossip to the emperor. Akbar could not believe the story, but the seeds of suspicion had taken root in his mind and he ordered a eunuch to keep a watch over Anarkali. The lovers, unaware of the emperor's spy, continued to meet each other.

When the eunuch confirmed the stories of their romance, Shahenshah Akbar was furious. The humiliation of being betrayed by his concubine was compounded by the treachery of his son. The incensed emperor resolved to award an exemplary punishment to the unfaithful woman—a penalty that would serve as a warning to all the women in his harem. He summoned Anarkali and confronted her. She admitted her guilt, convinced that the emperor would forgive her. It was not to be. Salim was sent away on another campaign and in the early hours of a quiet Lahore dawn, Anarkali was entombed alive on the orders of Emperor Akbar. Brick by brick her breath was snuffed away as the masons cemented away her life.

As expected, the jealous concubines of the harem greeted the news of her tragic death with scarcely disguised glee. Prince Salim was inconsolable when he learnt of his lover's fate. He locked himself in his apartment and spent many days mourning for his Anarkali.

Salim's history of affairs had made Mirza Ghias Baig and Asmat wary of his romance with their Meherunnisa. 'It is better to be wedded to a commoner than to be a prince's concubine,' Asmat told her husband. 'No one can predict how long the royal interest will linger. Once interest wanes, a concubine's life is no better than that of a caged animal.'

They were relieved when Sher Afghan's marriage proposal was brought before them. The marriage would serve a dual purpose. Besides winning the emperor's favour, it would give them a chance to extricate their daughter from the clutches of the prince. In any case, the idea of defying the emperor's desire never occurred to them.

The wedding did not bring happiness to Meherunnisa who had dreamt of becoming a queen. She spent her nights in Sher Afghan's arms, but her heart remained with the prince. She pined for news of her lover but, sitting far away from the court, it was not often that she learnt of the goings on in the palace. Although her father tried to give her news of Prince Salim in his letters, he was afraid of them falling in the wrong hands, so he wrote about the family and made passing references to the happenings at the court. Over a period of time, they had developed their personal codes and Mirza Ghias Baig used these to convey news of the ongoing royal conflict to his daughter.

From her father's carefully worded letters, Meherunnisa learned that her beloved Salim continuously revolted against his father. Always an unruly and obstinate man, the prince was now exhibiting streaks of ruthlessness and cruelty. Impatient to wear the crown, the prince had already made up his mind to rise in rebellion against his ageing father.

The stage for the revolt was set when the wilful prince set up his own empire at Allahabad and began holding court. He appropriated 30 lakhs of rupees from the treasury of Bihar, bestowed jagirs and titles on his supporters, gathered a force of 30,000 men and began running a parallel kingdom in defiance of the Mughal emperor.

Sher Afghan, who had taken a violent dislike for the prince, also fed Meherunnisa with news about the errant prince. It gave him sadistic pleasure to belittle Salim, because he suspected that she still had feelings for the prince.

'The history of Mughal rule has never seen a more perfidious prince. He is ready to stab the emperor in his eagerness to occupy the throne. One can well imagine the state of the empire if Salim were to wear the crown.'

Meherunnisa refused to bite the bait although she wanted to rise in defence of the prince.

'Can you imagine the extent of the prince's wickedness?' Sher Afghan commented one night, during dinner. Meherunnisa, careful not to show too much curiosity, lifted her brows quizzically. 'He has taken to skinning people alive at the barest excuse.'

Meherunnisa's heart sank with despair with each news of Salim's brutality. When had he changed into this brutal beast? Would Salim remember her when he sat on the throne? If he didn't care about his father, would he bother about her? Would their paths ever cross again?

From her father's letters, Meherunnisa learnt that the old emperor was distraught at the thought of Salim's misdeeds. His elder son, Prince Daniyal, was addicted to opium and remained sunk in a stupor most of the time. Rumours about his failing health abounded at Agra. Prince Murad, a slave of overindulgence, had also died in his prime, and now Prince Daniyal was following him to the grave. Only Salim—though not very restrained himself, when it came to liquor and drugs— remained in line for the throne. The aggrieved emperor cursed his fate and wondered if the glory of the Mughals was fated for obliteration after his death; he could not bear the thought of handing over the reins of the glorious Mughal empire to his whimsical son. Exasperated, Akbar began grooming Salim's son, Khusrau, for the throne. Khusrau was intelligent, balanced and patient.

If there was one person who had not lost faith in Salim, despite his waywardness, it was his stepmother and Akbar's favourite wife, Salima Sultan Begum. Shocked at the thought that Salim's defiance could rob him of his rightful inheritance of the throne, she intervened. The begum was determined to bring about a reconciliation between the ageing monarch and the recalcitrant prince. Undeterred by the distance, she travelled through rough terrain and brought Salim back to the royal court, after much persuasion. 'Do you want to lose the throne to your son?' she had asked, her words striking him like a blow. He decided to accompany her to Agra. The emperor had to be appeased at any cost.

The emperor forgave the repentant prince and conferred the royal diadem on him. It was an important gift, a mark of sovereignty, meant as a token of compromise between the father and son.

But Akbar was too astute to believe that his son had transformed overnight. To test the prince's change of heart, he commanded him to proceed towards Mewar to quell rebellion in the region. When Salim prevaricated, his mother rebuked him. 'Have you gone insane? After all the effort that went into bringing about the reconciliation, you are reverting to your old habits. Go to Mewar at once,' she commanded.

Reluctantly, Salim left for Allahabad on the pretext of gathering forces. Once there, however, he did nothing. The Shahenshah was convinced that nothing had changed. Salim's promises could not be trusted. The disillusioned emperor finally prepared to go to war with his rebellious son, ignoring the pleas of his queens. Sher Afghan was called to lead the troops against the prince and the loyal soldier was only too happy to ride against his foe.

Meherunnisa watched her husband riding away to the battlefield and her heart broke at the thought of him fighting against Salim. Husband or lover, she didn't know whose life to pray for. Perhaps the Almighty decided to spare her the torture, because the fateful battle never took place.

Just as the emperor and his imperial army were riding towards the battleground, Akbar's mother, Miriam Makani, died at Agra. Akbar abandoned the operation and returned to the capital. One of the major faults in Salim's character was his indecisiveness. Like a pendulum, he swung from one extreme to the other. Once again, he decided to reconcile with his father, and this time Salim decided to use his grandmother's death as an excuse to beg for royal forgiveness. His fears of losing the crown to Khusrau had gained ground. Khusrau's popularity was on the upswing amongst the royal ladies, powerful nobles and the people.

At Agra, Salim received a cold reception. After the last rites of his mother, Akbar summoned him to his private chamber. A heated altercation ensued between the father and the son till, exasperated, the emperor slapped the prince and confined him in a room under the charge of a physician and two servants. 'Wine and vice has deranged his mind. The prince needs to be kept under observation till he comes to his senses,' declared Akbar.

5

'A letter from Agra,' Firdaus said, rushing in with a sealed purse containing a missive from Meherunnisa's father. She knew how eagerly Meherunnisa waited for these letters. Meherunnisa's hands trembled as she ripped open the seal of her father's letter. She was disappointed to note that the communication was addressed to Sher Afghan.

'Dear Sher,' Mirza Ghias Baig had written, 'You must leave for Agra immediately as the empire is going through a critical period. Your absence may be misconstrued as a sign of disloyalty towards the emperor.'

Cursing the delay in receiving the despatch, Sher Afghan left for Agra immediately. He knew that Shahenshah Akbar held him in great affection, but Salim hated his guts. The soldier knew that he had to make peace with the prince unless he wanted retribution on his head. Everyone knew how ruthless and cruel the prince could be. Hundreds of servants, soldiers, spies and eunuchs who had displeased the prince had suffered horrendous punishments. From being skinned to being trampled by elephants, Salim personally watched the sentences being carried out. Flogging was a common occurrence. It seemed to give him a fiendish pleasure to see the agony on his victim's faces. His sadistic traits were a contrast to Akbar's benign nature and most nobles shuddered at the thought of Salim ascending the throne.

Even as Sher Afghan travelled to Agra, covering the distance on his fastest steed, the light of the Mughal empire was fading. Dejected with his son's behaviour, the emperor had taken seriously ill. The palace was seized with intrigues as the emperor lay on his deathbed. Prince Khusrau's uncle, Raja Maan Singh, who had been appointed governor of Bengal by Akbar, and other powerful ministers had been plotting to place Khusrau on the throne in the last few years. Much of the dissidents' activities took place in Bengal where Maan Singh was stationed. Now that the emperor was ill, the machinations were stepped up.

The clammy climate of the east gave way to the cold of the north. Icy winds tore through the forests sending shivers through the soldier who pressed forward relentlessly, urging his horse to cover the last few kilometres. He had to reach Agra before destiny played her hand. There was a sense of foreboding in Sher Afghan's heart as he tore through the countryside towards the Mughal capital. He was too late.

On 17 October 1605, Akbar succumbed to his illness. Within minutes of Akbar's death, Raja Maan Singh called a meeting of his adherents.

'It is time for the nobles to come together and make a decision. We all know that Shahenshah Akbar was disappointed with Prince Salim. He wanted Prince Khusrau to be crowned as the next emperor.'

'Yes, the last wishes of the emperor must be followed!' they cried in unison. 'Prince Khusrau must wear the crown!'

Prince Khusrau was broad-minded, learned and generous. He had endeared himself to the masses by his virtuous nature. He was the popular choice for the emperor's throne, a total contrast to his debauched father who drank excessively and lived a colourful life. Salim's violent temper, capriciousness, and cruelty made him unpopular amongst the ministers in Akbar's court. In fact, there were rumours that the emperor had not died a natural death. Muted whispers that Salim had engineered his death through poison administered by the royal hakim, travelled through the court.

But the nobles were divided. While some sided with Raja Maan Singh and Khusrau's father-in-law Aziz Koka, most of them believed that Prince Salim was the rightful heir to the throne. Swords were drawn, sides taken and war declared. Realising the futility of an open confrontation with the loyalists, Khusrau's supporters withdrew, leaving a clear path for Salim to ascend the throne.

A week after his father's death, Salim ascended the throne as emperor of Hindustan, and assumed the lofty title 'Nuruddin Muhammed Jahangir Padshah'.

Once he had been enthroned, Jahangir, much to the surprise of the nobles, decided to pardon all those who had rebelled against him. Raja Maan Singh and Aziz Koka, who had been fearful of Jahangir's reprisal, were taken aback when he declared clemency for them. The emperor ensured, however, that they were stripped of the important posts that they had held during Shahenshah Akbar's time. Although he would have liked to execute Maan Singh, the emperor could not do so as the Raja had a large following amongst the Rajputs. Jahangir was intelligent enough to realise the benefits of pardoning Maan Singh.

Mirza Ghias Baig, who had proved his loyalty, was promoted to an important post.

The responsibilities of an empire have a strange way of moulding a king's character. Jahangir, awed by the immense expectations of the people, transformed almost overnight from an indolent and whimsical prince to a magnanimous and gentle emperor. The excesses of a king, however, are not easily forgotten and Jahangir realised he would have to work hard to build a new image. He had to win the confidence of his subjects.

The first thing the emperor did was to install a 'Chain of Justice'. This was a huge chain weighing four mans, made of pure gold and with sixty golden bells on it. The chain—thirty yards long—was suspended from a battlement of the Agra Fort and the other end attached to a stone column on the bank of the Yamuna river.

Drummers went around the town announcing that the Chain of Justice had been installed to help people: all seekers of justice had the liberty to appeal to the emperor directly, by tugging at the chain.

Three times a day, the new ruler appeared at a jharoka that opened onto the courtyard of the palace. As the sun rose, Jahangir appeared at the eastern jharoka, his face aglow with the first rays of the sun. Hundreds of people began their day with his image in their minds. Again in the afternoon, the emperor appeared at the jharoka to assure his subjects that all was well with him. His last appearance was at the western jharoka at sunset. Even on days when he was not feeling well, Jahangir did not miss this routine of giving his subjects an audience from the jharoka.

Jahangir then set about establishing edicts that were to be followed throughout his dominions. With an objective of eliminating the corrupt practices of the powerful nobles in the kingdom, the emperor ordered stringent obedience of his laws. Jahangir also granted amnesty for all prisoners in his empire.

There was jubilation amongst people as the new emperor began his reign on a positive note. His ordinances found immense favour with the subjects, who had long suffered the excesses of the nobles. Tales of his largesse spread through the country.

But there was one person who he continued to treat with disdain. After weeks of travelling, when Sher Afghan finally reached Agra to pay his respects to the new emperor, Jahangir received him coldly.

Sher Afghan bowed low to perform a respectful kornish. 'May your Majesty live a thousand years,' he saluted. 'Your humble slave is at your service.'

Sher Afghan had brought expensive presents for the emperor. There were yards of expensive muslin—a speciality of Dacca, silks, strings of huge pearls and a steed of the finest Arabian breed. Meherunnisa had sent a painting of the emperor that she had done herself.

'Gift this painting to the emperor. You might succeed in deflecting some of his anger with it.'

As she had anticipated, the portrait seemed to please the emperor more than the other gifts. There was a twinkle in his eyes, lit by the memory of his past romance with the soldier's wife.

'So, you have finally decided to accept me as your emperor.' The imperial tone had softened and so had the frigid look in his eyes.

'Your Majesty, you are destined to be a great Mughal emperor. How could a lowly soldier like me think otherwise?'

'Your gifts are calculated to touch my heart. Who is the artist of this skilful portrait?' asked Jahangir, although he knew the answer. He twirled his moustache thoughtfully, his bejewelled fingers stroking the lines on the paper.

'The portrait was painted by the wife of this humble servant, Your Highness.' The Persian braved a smile.

'Sher Afghan, you once saved my life and I am indebted to you for that. That is the only reason why I have not punished you for taking a conflicting posture against me in the past. I expect your unflinching loyalty and I will not honour you with an appointment at the court till I am satisfied of your faithfulness beyond all doubt. Till such time, you may continue to enjoy the fruits of Burdwan.'

The slight was obvious. The emperor was still angry. Sher Afghan was disappointed, but he did not give Jahangir the pleasure of perceiving it. For long Sher Afghan had desired a return to Agra, but Akbar had consistently refused to heed his request. Many thought this was a conscious decision on the part of the emperor, in order to protect Sher Afghan from Salim's wrath.

'I can see that you are wearing the royal ring gifted by me,' Jahangir pointed at an expensive ring on Sher Afghan's finger. He had gifted him the ring when the soldier saved his life. 'As long as you keep it on your finger, no harm will come to you.'

With a nod of his head he dismissed the soldier.

Sher Afghan suppressed his disappointment and made his way back to his father-in-law's house. Both Mirza Ghias Baig and his son, Asaf Khan, had been granted favours by Jahangir. Over a banquet of delicacies laid out by Asmat, the three men exchanged notes.

'I was hoping Jahangir would reinstate your position at the court,' Asaf Khan remarked, reaching out for kebabs.

A shadow of anger crossed the soldier's face. 'It doesn't seem as though he wants me here.'

'You are lucky to be away from the jealousy and corruption of the nobles at Agra,' consoled Mirza Ghias Baig. He liked the unpretentious soldier and his blunt approach. There was no trace of cunning in the young man.

'I don't mind staying away at Burdwan, but Meherunnisa misses Agra and her family. Sometimes I wonder if the emperor has some ulterior motive in keeping me away from the court. It can't be possible that he doesn't know my capabilities,' Sher Afghan complained bitterly.

The Mirza sighed deeply and reached for his son-in-law's hand. 'Don't fret, it will not be long before he appoints you in the court. The emperor hasn't forgotten his tumultuous days just before the coronation.' Turning towards his son, he ordered—'Asaf, pass the delicious biriyani to Sher.' He knew Sher Afghan loved good food. 'Asmat begum has specially prepared it for you. She knows you are partial to the Persian method of preparation.'

'How are Meherunnisa and my granddaughter?' asked Asmat. 'Laadli must be keeping her busy.'

The Mirza missed Meherunnisa. He wished there was some way to bring Sher Afghan into Jahangir's good books. 'Why don't you send Meher to us for some time? Neither Asmat nor I have laid eyes on the face of our grandchild.'

'Laadli is too young to travel right now, and the journey is long and arduous. The weather is also not favourable for the long journey. They will come as soon as Laadli is a little older. To be frank, I cannot live without that little witch.'

After dinner, the men moved to the outer room where freshly made paans and hookahs lay waiting for them. The Mirza brought out an ivory chessboard and laid out the pieces with care. It had been a long time since he had played the game with his son-in-law. But Sher Afghan was distracted and he lost every game. Finally, he gave up the effort and reclined moodily on the divan.

'Tell me what is on your mind, Sher. It is obvious that you are upset about something,' the Mirza asked gently.

'I heard some rumours while I was in the court. Some jagirdars were discussing the rebellion in Bengal and my name was mentioned a couple of times. I wonder why they were clubbing me with the rebel faction.'

'That is a dangerous rumour. I would counsel you to take care. If such gossip reaches the emperor, the consequences will be dire.'

The Mirza had also heard the strange rumblings in court. Jahangir was sending his foster brother, Qutubuddin Koka, to Burdwan as the governor, ostensibly to control the rebellious faction which had renewed its activities. But there were undertones to the appointment that befuddled Ghias Baig.

The next morning, as Sher Afghan took his leave, the Mirza cautioned his son-in-law. 'Sher, I would give you a word of advice even if you don't seek it. An old man sees things that a young man cannot. It is better that you keep away from the court. You have made many enemies with your blunt tongue and undiplomatic ways. They would take great pleasure in discrediting you in the emperor's eyes. Jahangir is also unpredictable in his behaviour. It is better to avoid getting entangled with ministers who can influence the emperor.'

'I understand what you mean. I'll be careful.'

Sher Afghan knew exactly what the old man was warning him about. As emperor, Jahangir could demand and command anything he wanted. God forbid, if he still nursed an ardour for Meherunnisa, Sher Afghan's very life could be in peril.

It was a worried man who returned to Burdwan. Tired, Sher Afghan fobbed off Meherunnisa's persistent queries about her parents and the capital. But it was difficult to neglect Laadli, who clambered all over him and refused to leave him alone even for a moment.

It wasn't until after his bath and rest that a little of his old humour crept back into him and he smiled reassuringly at his wife.

'My daughter has grown while I was away. Let me see how tall you have become,' Sher Afghan said standing next to her. The little girl squealed delightedly and stood on her toes as he measured her. 'Has my Laadli grown fat, too?' he said, pretending that he could not lift her on his shoulders. 'Oh, yes, I can't carry her any longer.'

'Abba, take me riding on Sultan. Ammi has not allowed me to ride for a single day since you left for Agra,' Laadli complained from her precarious perch on her father's broad shoulders.

'Don't you begin your sessions of complaints, little girl. Go and play outside while I speak to your Abba. Your grandfather has sent some new dolls for you, have you seen them?' Meherunnisa asked, trying to distract the girl.

Eager to see the new dolls, Laadli skipped away after warning her father—'Don't go anywhere. I will be back in a minute with my dolls.'

Sher Afghan smiled indulgently at her and promised not to move till she returned.

'It is nice to be back home, begum. I missed you and my little girl. It is so quiet and peaceful here.'

'It might be good for you, but I am bored of this place, I wish we could go back to Agra. Is it just as I remember, or has it changed? Did the emperor mention anything about giving you a position in the court? Did he like the painting?'

'It was a good idea to gift the portrait to that vain man,' said Sher Afghan. 'He loved that gift more than anything else.'

They continued to discuss the trip as they moved to sit around the dastarkhan. Laadli had returned, and was sitting on her father's lap, toying with a piece of meat, refusing to eat the food Meherunnisa was pushing into her mouth. She was excited to have her father back after so many months.

'Is the emperor a good man?' she asked suddenly, taking her parents by surprise.

'Why do you ask?' Meherunnisa and Sher Afghan asked simultaneously.

'Because Hamida was saying that he had got one of her relatives flogged just because he broke the emperor's favourite china cup. I keep breaking so many cups. Will the emperor get me flogged if I go to Agra?'

'Of course not. No one can touch you as long as I am alive,' said Sher Afghan, embracing his daughter protectively. 'You must not listen to servants' gossip.'

The couple exchanged a troubled look over their daughter's head. Almost everyone at Agra knew the story of the servant who had broken Jahangir's favourite wine cup. The fellow was flogged mercilessly and put in prison till his wounds healed. After which he was given 5000 rupees and asked to travel all the way to China to procure a similar cup.

'I heard that the emperor is a changed man now. Many of the nobles I met were full of praises for the emperor's new laws,' Sher Afghan said, picking a paan from the silver salver offered by Meherunnisa, who greedily devoured all the information that her husband supplied. Her eyes widened with interest on hearing of the ordinances and the Chain of Justice. The new emperor was taking steps in the right direction by winning the hearts of his people, she thought. The hot-headed and wayward Prince Salim had matured into an able emperor.

But his position as emperor was not stable. Raja Maan Singh and Aziz Koka had not given up their hopes of crowning Khusrau. When Jahangir, who had spies scattered everywhere, learnt that the two were plotting another coup, he acted instantaneously, imprisoning Khusrau in the palace. Some nobles close to the emperor advised him to blind his son, but Jahangir was reluctant to order such a dreadful sentence.

The rumour spread, however, that the emperor was seriously contemplating blinding Khusrau. When the prince caught wind of the news, he decided to escape from the palace; he knew there were forces within the palace that would readily help him in his getaway.

Soon a plot had been contrived. Approaching his father, the prince sought permission to make a trip to Shahadara. 'I wish to pay my respects to my revered grandfather. I have wronged you, dear father, as I have wronged my grandfather. I wish to atone for my sins and beg forgiveness at his tomb,' Khusrau said, with all appearances of being deeply repentant.

Jahangir was delighted and readily allowed the journey under the escort of a few soldiers. The young prince's followers, who were lying in wait for the convoy, swooped upon the small band of the emperor's soldiers. The prince was free once again to plot a coup.

Khusrau gathered a considerable force of loyal soldiers, captured an imperial treasure convoy, and set out on the path of rebellion. When the emperor realised that Khusrau had tricked him, he was incensed. News arrived through imperial spies that Khusrau was pressing forward towards Punjab. An imperial farman (order) was immediately issued by Jahangir, ordering all jagirdars, road keepers, and ferrymen in Punjab to be vigilant. Khusrau was not to escape. They were promised a substantial reward if they captured the prince and handed him over to the emperor. The Governor of Lahore was alerted. Acting on imperial orders, the governor refused to open the gates of the city to Prince Khusrau and his band of soldiers. Jahangir, seething with anger, set out in pursuit of his son. History was repeating itself. Once again an emperor was riding against his rebel son.

After he was denied entry into the city of Lahore, Khusrau retraced his steps. To do so he had to cross the Chenab river, but no boat was available to the prince. With the emperor's army closing in, a frustrated Khusrau tried to flee in the opposite direction, but Jahangir's army had cut off his escape route. Just three weeks after his escape, the unfortunate prince was captured. Khusrau was brought manacled into the presence of the emperor who had set up camp in the garden of Mirza Kamran.

Retribution followed swiftly. Two of Khusrau's principal followers were inhumanly tortured: they were sewed up in raw hides—one in that of an ox and the other in that of an ass—and then, seated on the bare backs of asses, they were paraded through the city of Lahore. As the fury of the hot summer sun intensified, the hides dried up, tightening the enclosure and suffocating the men. One of the men died, the other barely escaped death. Surprised that he had survived, the emperor pardoned the man. The next day, about 300 of the prince's followers were either hung from trees or impaled on stakes set up along both sides of the road. Jahangir, mounted on a splendidly caparisoned elephant, rode ahead with his nobles, followed by his wretched son riding on a bare elephant. General Mahabat Khan, Jahangir's trusted minister, rode with Khusrau, calling out the names of the writhing victims. The anguished prince covered his eyes, unable to bear the sight of his suffering followers.

Not content, Jahangir decided to punish each and every man who had helped Khusrau in his rebellion. 'I have to set an example so that no one dares to oppose me any more,' he told the protesting women of the harem.

One by one the men were hounded and executed; no one was spared. Among those who were brought to trial was the Sikh Guru, Arjun Singh. While fleeing from the emperor's troops, a desperate Khusrau had begged for shelter from Arjun Singh, at Tarn-Taran. The holy man, moved by compassion, gave the prince Rs 5,000 and asylum in his camp, for a couple of days. When Jahangir learnt of this, he summoned Guru Arjun Singh and fined him Rs 200,000. The Guru refused to pay the amount, stating that he had not committed any treason but only helped a desperate man asking for mercy. The emperor, however, charged him with high treason: the Guru was tortured brutally for five days, after which he succumbed to his injuries.

That torturous summer was to see many more tragedies. The nobles of the court advised the emperor against showing any mercy to the rebels. No one should be spared, they cautioned, not even Prince Khusrau. Many of them advised Jahangir to execute his perfidious son to set an example for future generations. But Jahangir refused, citing the Timurid code of conduct, which forbade the killing of royal kin. 'I cannot execute my own son,' Jahangir told his ministers. 'Centuries back my forefather, Timur-e-leng, had proclaimed: "Do naught unto your brothers, even though they may deserve". Each and every Mughal king has observed the edicts laid down by the founder of the Timurid dynasty. I cannot go against it.'

A debate ensued over the Timurid decree, but the emperor refused to go against it.

'Perhaps Your Highness should instead consider the punishment of blinding. There is no objection to that punishment in the Timurid laws,' suggested his vizier.

The emperor considered the suggestion with a heavy heart. 'Why do I have to suffer this agony?' he wrote in his diary. 'The anguish of seeing one's own son blinded is the most painful punishment. I wish there were some way out of this muddle.'

It was an agonising night for the emperor as he tossed about sleeplessly, debating what his verdict should be. The next morning, the court was bursting with people. The deep shadow under Jahangir's eyes spoke of his tormented soul. Khusrau was brought before the court, chained and smiling, his handsome face reflecting arrogance. He was confident that the emperor, torn by paternal love, would not sentence him harshly. There was a deathly silence as the minister read out Khusrau's offence.

'The punishment for mutiny is death, in all lands,' the emperor sighed. A murmur of shock went through the court.

From behind the latticed partition came a perceptible whimper from the gathered women. 'But I am bound by the Timurid edict and I cannot sentence my son to death. With deep regret I order the blinding of my treacherous son.'

The handsome face of the prince turned ashen, all his bravado deserting him at the sight of the soldiers advancing towards him with their tools for blinding. 'Reham, reham, Shahenshah. Let not a father's name be sullied. Do not decide my fate in haste. Put me to death, for living in a world of darkness is worse than not living at all,' he cried heartbreakingly, but the emperor turned his face away sadly.

When the wire was put in his eyes, the assembled people turned their eyes away from the torture. The women in the zenana wailed loudly from the other side of the screen, unable to bear the piteous cries that resonated through the hall.

Over time, however, when Shahenshah Jahangir saw his blind son groping through the halls of the palace, helpless and forlorn, he was filled with guilt. He recollected his own rebellions: the thought of such a harsh penalty had never crossed the mind of his father, Emperor Akbar. Eventually Jahangir ordered that the most experienced physicians be put to work on the eyes of the prince so that he might see again.

Proclamations were made through the land inviting eminent physicians. The emperor promised generous rewards for the cure of his son's eyes. Many hakims and physicians arrived to try their luck. Among them was Hakim Sadra, a physician who had come all the way from Persia. The hakim undertook to cure the prince within six months and began his treatment to restore Khusrau's eyes.

Six months had passed and the emperor called for the hakim and Khusrau, impatient to see the result. Khusrau, for the first time, walked unaided into the court, much to the delight of the emperor. Khusrau had recovered partial vision in one of his eyes.

Jahangir was overjoyed. For six months he had been ridden by remorse. Now he could sleep at night, his conscience at peace once more.

'Allah is great. We were losing hope that our son would see again. We are delighted with your skills, Hakim Sadra. From today you shall be known as Masihu-uz-Zaman (physician par excellence).'

The emperor stepped down from his throne and embraced Khusrau. With great love, he helped his son to a seat next to the throne. A khilat, robe of honour, was endowed on the hakim and the emperor poured a cupful of jewels on his head. The ladies, watching the scene from behind the screen, sighed happily.

6

It was a balmy day in March. Meherunnisa woke up with a feeling of happy expectation. A tiny bird was singing near her windowsill and its chirping wrung her heart with memories of a wondrous spring she had enjoyed a long time back with her parents at Lahore. The air was laden with the sweet smell of blooming flowers and the sky was a clear, cobalt blue. Delicate wisps of straggly clouds drifted away gracefully, leaving the day bright and cheerful. The rains had ceased after a torrential week and the sun had emerged after days of hiding behind ominous clouds. After years she found herself humming a romantic song. Something in the breeze around her charged her with hope.

It was a perfect day to be spent by the riverside, to laze and loll under the trees that lined the waterfront. For long Laadli had been clamouring for an outing. Meherunnisa summoned Firdaus and instructed her to prepare for a picnic. 'We will cook in the open, under the shade of the trees by the riverside,' said Meherunnisa dreamily. 'Firdaus hurry, make arrangements for the most memorable picnic ever enjoyed by the family.'

'Can't we pack the food and take it with us?'

'No, no. It is not the same. For a perfect picnic, the food has to be cooked at the location and not carried. I know it involves more work but that is the way it has to be,' Meherunnisa said, putting an end to the argument.

Firdaus also loved picnics but hated the complex arrangements that they called for. Elaborate preparations had to be made so food could be cooked at the picnic spot; cooling drinks, snacks, games and carpets had to be carried along; tents had to be set up; and the entire area would have to be cordoned off from the prying eyes of men who were in the area, angling or bathing.

Firdaus went about instructing the servants on the arrangements to be made. Pots, pans and other paraphernalia had to be packed. Chaupar, ganjifa cards, skipping rope and durries had to be carried. Laadli would want a swing to be put up on a tree, so sturdy ropes had to be carried for the makeshift swing.

Sher Afghan was reluctant to accompany the women. 'The governor, Sahib Qutub-ud-Din, has sent for me. He has received a firman from the emperor and wants to deliver it to me personally. If I do not go immediately, he will take offence. You know what a pompous and egocentric fellow he is.'

'Can't you postpone your journey by a day? I am sure he will not take offence if you go tomorrow. Send word to him through one of the servants that you will be present at his court tomorrow morning. Please, please, let us go and enjoy the beautiful day. Burdwan rarely sees such a perfect day for an outing. Besides, Laadli will be disappointed if you don't accompany us,' insisted Meherunnisa.

'Begum, I am as keen as you to enjoy the day in your company, but I don't like the governor's attitude. The anti-Persian faction is at work in the emperor's court at Agra. They have spread rumours that I am involved with the Afghan rebels in Bengal.'

'Why should the emperor believe such rumours? You have been faithful and loyal to him at all times.'

'He has reason to believe these rumours because he has never liked me,' Sher Afghan said, casting a meaningful look at his wife.

'Despite the fact that you saved his life by slaying a tigress?' Meherunnisa said, ignoring her husband's provocative statement.

'That happened such a long time ago that the emperor would rather forget his obligations. I have always been faithful to the throne and its rulers. Jahangir knows that I am an excellent soldier and the royal army needs my services. Yet he has banished me from the court by sending me to this godforsaken place. I suspect he treats me this way because I have married you.'

At last the truth was out. The words had tumbled out before he could stop them.

'How can you say such a thing? I have never been unfaithful to you in all these years of our marriage!' Her face paled at the allegation.

'Begum, I do not suspect your fidelity, but I do have my reservations about the emperor's intentions. The fact remains that I am in his bad books and he has sent his foster brother, Qutub-Ud-Din, to act against me. I am sorry if I said the wrong thing. I am disturbed by the goings-on.' Sher Afghan was distraught.

Meherunnisa felt sorry for her husband. She suspected he was right about the emperor's intentions. Her father had told her of the rumours that Jahangir had tried to convince Sher Afghan, through intermediaries, to divorce Meherunnisa. If the rumours were to be believed—she had never discussed the matter with her husband—the emperor's treatment of Sher Afghan was obviously a reaction to the soldier's refusal to do so.

'Let us shelve all problems for tomorrow,' she said soothingly. After we return from the outing, we can think of a solution to the problem. There is no point in ruining such a beautiful day.'

At that moment Laadli ran in with her toys and tugged at her father's hands. He towered above the girl and Meherunnisa was amazed at the tenderness that suffused his face whenever he looked at his daughter. He would readily give his life to fulfil the wishes of his daughter, she thought. As he smiled tenderly at the child, Meherunnisa knew he would not refuse to accompany them for the outing.

'Abbajaan, please come with us. I will not go if you don't come,' Laadli said.

'Well, then, I cannot refuse! I guess my meeting will have to wait till tomorrow,' he said, the cloud of worry temporarily absent from his face.

His daughter skipped all around him excitedly. 'Can we take Sultan? I would love to ride him.'

'No, we will not take Sultan,' Meherunnisa said sternly. 'I don't want you riding near the river.'

'Oh, let her be, begum. I will take care of her.' Turning to his daughter, he said, 'Don't worry, we will take Sultan with us.'

As Meherunnisa had predicted, Laadli had taken after her father with regard to her height. At four, she was taller than most six-year-old girls. She was a natural when it came to horse riding and wielding the dagger. From her mother, the little girl had inherited a flair for music, poetry, and painting.

Burdwan's exotic vegetation and verdant landscape was a balm for the tired souls. The swaying palms, tall teaks, trees laden with jackfruit and papayas, banana trees with their long leaves fluttering like flags in the breeze and the wild flowers that dotted the countryside, were a poet's dream. The picturesque setting erased all the troubling thoughts from Sher Afghan's mind.

Tents were pitched and Firdaus got the makeshift kitchen fires going. Amidst the clatter of utensils, the servants began preparing lunch under the shade of a massive tree. Sher Afghan supervised the setting up of a rope swing while Laadli jumped around excitedly, adding her instructions. It was going to be a beautiful day. After a long time Meherunnisa felt a sense of total happiness, with no dark clouds smearing her horizon.

She set up her easel near the waterfront and laid out little pots of paints all around her. A boat appeared like a speck on the placid water of the river, its sails stark against the indigo sky. It had been a long time since she had painted. Busy with Laadli and household responsibilities, she had almost forgotten how to wield the brush or compose verses. 'Now that Laadli is almost four, I should begin taking some time off to do the things I love. All I have done for the past few years is embroider and stitch dresses for her,' she told her husband, as she tried to capture the magical colours around her on her canvas.

Sher Afghan, sprawled under a jackfruit tree, was amused at her complaint. His eyes swept over her svelte figure and rested on her painting. An indulgent smile played on his face as he patted her hand. 'You are good at whatever you do.' A look filled with intimacy and warmth passed between them and a delightful blush spread on his wife's face.

Suddenly Meherunnisa packed up her painting and stood up. 'It is too beautiful a day to sit at one spot. Let us walk around the waterfront.'

'I feel like playing a game of chaupar with you.'

'We will do that after we have taken a turn. I want to feel the cool breeze on my face. It reminds me of my days at Lahore when the evening breeze blew through the terraced gardens and we took endless walks discussing all sorts of things.'

As they walked around the mango grove, the smell of the tiny fruits lay thick in the air, attracting a host of insects around them. In the distance a koel cooed with ecstasy, heralding the advent of a joyous spring. Hand-in-hand they walked, with Meherunnisa humming under her breath. This is bliss, thought Sher Afghan, turning to look at Laadli trying to climb a branch of a tree. Like a monkey she clambered up the overhanging branch one minute, only to slip down the next, unmindful of her scraped knees.

They lunched under the thick foliage of the trees, seated on the ground with a sparkling white dastarkhan spread before them. Despite all the grumbling, Firdaus had managed to put together an excellent meal for the family. There were parathas stuffed with minced meat, a meat curry and a bowlful of greens with a variety of pickles and chutneys.

Even Laadli, who normally fussed over her food, stuffed herself willingly.

'There is something magical about a picnic. The most ordinary food tastes so good that one ends up overeating. I have eaten so much that all I want to do is the lie down under a tree and sleep for sometime,' Meherunnisa stated, suppressing a yawn.

On her bidding, Firdaus brought an embroidered coverlet and spread it on the ground. It wasn't until the sun decided to call it a day that they began packing up.

'We must do this more often,' Meherunnisa suggested, picking up her scattered papers.

'Yes, if the weather and the emperor permit us,' Sher Afghan agreed as he helped her pack the paints.

The setting sun sprayed the sky orange as birds made their way to their nests. The women got into their palanquins and the men rode alongside, cantering lazily. Darkness had fallen by the time they neared the house. Servants walked ahead with lit lamps to light up the path. They were a short distance away from the house when Sayeed, the stable boy, ran up to them. Panting with exertion, he cried—'Go back, go back Master! Don't go to the house. The governor and his soldiers are there. I have heard them whispering ominous things. Please go to the village and get some help!'

'Don't be a fool, Sayeed, why shouldn't I go to my own house?' Sher Afghan said brusquely. 'Move out of my way. The governor will not hurt us. We have not given him any cause for displeasure.'

He spurred his horse and rode on despite the servant's passionate appeals. Desperate, Sayeed ran towards Meherunnisa's palanquin.

'Please stop the master, I beg you. The governor's men are in a foul mood.'

Meherunnisa's heart was hammering fearfully. She cried out to Firdaus, 'Something untoward is likely to happen. My left eye is twitching. It is not a good omen. Someone please stop the master.' But Sher Afghan was too far ahead by now.

He rode into the courtyard of his mansion where the governor, Qutub-ud-din, and his deputy, Pir Khan Kashmiri, along with half a dozen soldiers lay in wait. Like ghosts, they emerged from the shadows of the trees and surrounded the lone man. This is no courtesy visit, Sher Afghan thought looking around, but it was too late to retreat.

He dismounted and walked up to Qutub-ud-din. The circle of soldiers closed in. Sher Afghan drew his sword from his cummerbund and flashed it warningly. The governor laughed at his gesture and lunged with his sword in hand. Swearing at their duplicity, Sher Afghan lunged at the governor and ran his sword through Qutub-ud-din's belly, wiping off the mocking smile.

Within a split second, Pir Khan Kashmiri struck Sher Afghan on the head with a sword, but Sher Afghan returned it so fiercely that his assailant fell dead immediately. The other soldiers now pressed forward menacingly. The Persian fought valiantly, knocking down a couple of them, but he was heavily outnumbered.

Sher Afghan's servants were stunned at the suddenness of events. They watched aghast as the governor's soldiers stabbed their master repeatedly till he fell. Sher Afghan was dead before he hit the ground. Viciously, they continued to attack him to avenge their master's death.

The palanquin and the rear party arrived at that moment and the governor's soldiers fled without suffering any resistance. Meherunnisa ran to her husband and fell on his mutilated corpse, weeping profusely. Lost in her grief she did not notice Laadli trembling in one corner of the courtyard, shock and horror written on her face. Firdaus and Meherunnisa wailed loudly, beating their chests till servants lifted up Sher Afghan's mutilated body and took it to his chamber. The courtyard was a scene of blood and gore, with the bodies of the governor, Pir Khan and two other soldiers lying in pools of blood. Confused servants ran around, debating what to do. There was mayhem in the house.

Not a tear escaped the four-year-old Laadli's eyes as she stared fixedly at the spot where her father had fallen. Meherunnisa was still lamenting loudly, cradling the body of her husband when Sayeed came running in and urged her to leave the house.

'The governor's soldiers are likely to return in greater strength. They are seeking revenge for their master's death and will take this opportunity to loot the house. I overheard one of them saying that it was not safe to leave you and the child alive. You must flee. I have arranged for your stay at the house of one of my relatives.'

'Sayeed is right. We must escape before the soldiers return. Spare a thought for your daughter. The master would never have forgiven you for failing to protect his daughter,' begged Firdaus. 'There is no time to tarry. Hurry up.' The practical woman busied herself in gathering valuables in a small bundle. They would need all the jewels they could lay their hands on.

Meherunnisa was too numb to think lucidly. She nodded mutely and allowed Firdaus to take over. Walking in a daze, Meherunnisa left the house with meagre belongings, holding the hand of her stunned daughter.

The three women left from the back door, silently walking into the night. The joyful day had turned into one of darkness and tragedy. Led by Sayeed, they rushed through the forests without halting for a moment.

'I shouldn't have allowed him to go into the house. I should have stopped him somehow,' Meherunnisa reproached herself continuously when they had reached Sayeed's relative's house. 'Perhaps the governor thought he had been offended— if only I had not forced him to accompany us for the outing, he would have been able to meet the governor. It is all my fault.'

'It was Allah's will. Why do you blame yourself? Do you think they would not have killed the master if he had gone to the court? Instead of killing him in Burdwan, they would have killed him at the governor's house. Can you not see the emperor's hand in the entire episode?'

Meherunnisa remained silent. She did not want to believe Jahangir was capable of such an act.

'Don't torture yourself with guilt,' Firdaus continued, 'you have to think about the child.' Firdaus was worried about Laadli. The little girl had not uttered a single word since the horrific scene in the courtyard. Meherunnisa turned to look at her daughter who was sitting in a corner, her vacant eyes staring into space. Gently she tried to get Laadli to talk, but the child seemed beyond her reach. Emotionally and physically exhausted, Meherunnisa held her daughter till she fell asleep.

A week passed by quickly. News from Burdwan continued to reach them through Sayeed. The loyal servant did his best to take care of them.

'I have heard that the Badshah Jahangir has sent your brother Asaf Khan to take you to Agra,' Sayeed told Meherunnisa after some days.

The very name of Jahangir sent waves of revulsion through her body. She had loved him, but now she could not think of him as anything but a murderer. Horrifying images of the brutalised body of her husband assailed her every time she tried to sleep. They kept her awake, forcing her to relive that horrible night; if she managed to fall asleep, driven by fatigue, she woke up with terrible nightmares.

Even in her mourning, she worried about the future. Sher Afghan's jagir and assets had passed on to the empire after his death. According to a law of escheat enacted by Emperor Akbar, all jagirs and properties of a mansabdar reverted to the crown on his death. It was up to the emperor to bestow any kindness or property to the kith and kin of the mansabdar. Meherunnisa did not expect any such benevolence from the emperor, since he had ordered her husband's death. She had nothing except the clothes on her back and the few jewels she had escaped with. The news that Asaf would be arriving to take her home brought some comfort to Meherunnisa. She longed to be with her parents, to surround herself with the comfort of their love.

It took four months for her brother to reach Burdwan. As he rode into the courtyard of his sister's house, a heavy feeling of despondency assailed Asaf Khan. He walked from room to room searching for a trace of human occupancy. The house was empty: thieves had ransacked it and stripped it clean of all valuables. There was nothing left of the splendour it had once seen. The looters had spared nothing, not even the expensive doors and floor tiles. Outside, the fountains had gone dry. Even the fruit-bearing trees seemed to sag with sadness and neglect. A solitary frangipani tree laden with flowers stood desolately at one side. His heart ached at the sight of the ruined mansion. He had not loved his brother-in-law, but he had respected him for his valour and openness. Sher Afghan had not deserved such a gruesome end.

Asaf rode around the village, looking for someone who could enlighten him on the fate of his sister, but no one seemed to know anything. Either they were wary of telling him or they really knew nothing about Sher Afghan's family. He pitched his camp in Sher Afghan's house and waited for his soldiers to gather some information.

Two days passed before Asaf's soldiers brought Sayeed before him.

'Sir, this boy was employed in this house. He must be aware about the fate of the women,' said the captain of the soldiers.

'Tell me where they have been taken, boy. We'll reward you for the information.'

'Are you a soldier of Emperor Jahangir?' Sayeed asked.

'Yes, I am.'

'Then I am sorry I can't tell you anything,' the boy said, his mouth set in an obstinate line. Sayeed crossed his arms across his chest in an unyielding gesture.

'Why won't you tell me?'

'Because the emperor ordered the killing of my master.'

'But I am Meherunnisa's brother. I have come to take her back safely to Agra.'

'You should have told me that in the first instance,' smiled Sayeed, flashing his strong white teeth. 'Follow me. I will show you where your sister stays.'

Meherunnisa wept when she saw her brother. The dam of grief burst uncontrollably as she clung to him. Till then, she had tried to remain composed for fear of upsetting her daughter. She cried silently in the dark, soaking her pillow at night, and maintained a calm front during the day. But now she could control herself no longer. Asaf was heartbroken at the sight of his sister. Meherunnisa was his favourite sibling and he had always been very protective about her. When Salim was romancing her, only Asaf had been supportive of the relationship. The rest of the family, including her parents, had been apprehensive about the romance and its outcome.

From behind a pillar, Laadli watched her mother crying inconsolably.

'Hush sister, everything will be all right. Pack your things and let us go. Ammijaan is waiting for you.' With open arms, he approached his niece. 'I am your uncle, Laadli. I have come to take you home. You would like that, won't you?'

Laadli's blank stare broke his heart.

Hours later, the family began their arduous journey back to Agra, where Mirza Ghias Baig and his wife waited eagerly for their daughter and grandchild.

Meherunnisa's heart grew a little lighter as the greenery of Bengal gave way to the flora of the north. The graceful palm and banana trees slowly vanished; the pungent smells of jackfruit gave way to the majestic neem, mango, jamun and kikar trees. The rice fields gradually vanished, replaced by the nodding yellow of mustard in the fields.

On their way to Agra they passed Bihar, the outskirts of which city a well-known Sufi saint resided. On his sister's insistence, Asaf agreed to halt for the night so that she could pay her respects to the saint.

Anxious about her future, Meherunnisa begged the seer to give her some indication of what her life would be like. 'My husband's death has left me bereft of all hope. I feel very insecure and helpless. Tell me, great saint, what is going to happen?'

The holy man's piercing gaze sent a shiver of fear through her body. After what seemed like ages, the old man said in a tremulous voice—'I see a crown on your head. You have a magnificent decade before you, but I see sorrow ahead if you let your ambitious nature take over.'

Heavy clouds from the incense lay between Meherunnisa and the fakir, making it difficult for her to read his features.

'Baba, tell me how I can avert the disaster,' she begged.

'Your greed will be the cause of your downfall. I can tell you nothing more; one has to face one's destiny. No one can change its course.' And the fakir closed his eyes in a dismissive gesture.

7

Unused to the heat and dust, Laadli fell ill during the journey. Meherunnisa watched over her anxiously, as she lay burning with fever and dysentery. Firdaus, worn down by her own aches and pains, could not help much in the care of the girl. Finally, after five months of hard travelling, they arrived, on a hot June day, at Agra.

Laadli had lost weight during the journey and looked wan after her illness. Through the journey, the girl had barely said anything, only responding when spoken to. Meherunnisa's heart ached at the sight of the dark rings around her daughter's face. She sat Laadli on her lap and rocked her child lovingly. 'We are at Agra, my baby. Soon, you will be at your grandparents' house. We shall have a comfortable place to stay and you will have cousins to play with. You will love the house: there are many trees there, and birds nests on the trees. Your grandmother will make many delicacies and your grandfather will bring you many new toys.' Her attempts at cheering the child barely elicited a spark of interest in the grey eyes.

But as they entered the city portals, winding their way through the crowded, cobbled streets, Meherunnisa sensed some animation in her daughter. The streets were lined with hundreds of tiny shops selling almost everything that a person could want: there were grain shops with fat men in strange turbans weighing out the requirements of the customers; perfumery shops lined with flagons of attars, their aroma wafting in the heavy breeze; sweetmeat shops arrayed with all kinds of halwas and sweets. Bales of fabric—colourful velvets, silks, brocades, printed chintz and muslin—occupied the shelves in the next shop where a group of women were haggling with a shopkeeper over a few yards of bright fabric. Beyond the street, at the head of another lane, stood an imposing jewellery shop with exotic ornaments in its showcases. An array of armlets, bangles, nose rings, anklets, hair adornments, wristbands and necklaces dazzled Laadli's eye. She had never seen such a variety at Burdwan.

'This is a beautiful city,' she said, speaking without having first been spoken to for the first time in many months. 'Will we live here forever?'

'I don't know, my child. Who can predict the future?'

A monkey performing tricks on one side of the lane caught Laadli's attention and she leaned forward, a smile creasing her face. 'Look Ammi, the monkey is doing cartwheels,' shouted Laadli, clapping her hands excitedly. Meherunnisa sighed deeply as she felt some of her own grief lift. She exchanged a smile with Firdaus.

The palanquin traversed through the maze of streets and reached the wide road leading to the fort; her parents lived in a large mansion in the same area. The avenue was lined with fruit-bearing trees, which shaded the path. The sidewalk was ablaze with the petals of fallen flowers. Meherunnisa felt a surge of nostalgia as they travelled on the well-remembered road to the haveli. *Just a few more turns before we reach home,* she thought happily.

Suddenly, their palanquin bearers halted. A posse of soldiers had ridden up to them. The emir who was leading the soldiers went up to Asaf Khan. 'Sir, I have the emperor's order to take the ladies to the royal harem. Begum Meherunnisa has been appointed as a lady-in-waiting to the emperor's stepmother, Ruqayya Begum. All arrangements have been made at the imperial harem to house the women.'

'There must be a mistake. They are on the way to the house of my father, Mirza Ghias Baig, the Itmad-ud-daulah,' Asaf Khan tried to explain. 'The emperor is aware of the arrangements.'

'I am sorry, but my orders are quite clear. I am to escort the women to the harem. They will have to request the emperor for permission to leave the harem.'

Meherunnisa was livid. Was she the emperor's prisoner? Take *his* permission to go to her father's place? The audacity of the man! She gnashed her teeth angrily. But the emir was not the man to argue with; he was just following imperial orders.

'I will seek the emperor's permission and take you home,' promised her brother before he rode off in the opposite direction.

As they entered the palace, Laadli looked curiously at the liveried soldiers, the caparisoned elephants with their golden howdahs and the sturdy steed. This seemed to be another world—so different from their house at Burdwan where the rhythm of life was languorous and leisurely. This was a bustling city, full of servants, courtiers, and women, all walking at a brisk pace, bowing and nodding constantly to the nobles who passed by in their palanquins or rode on magnificent chargers. The ahadis, the royal elite guards, clad in resplendent crimson uniforms, strutted around with naked swords. There was a purposeful air all around them.

The women, accompanied by the noble and a few of his soldiers, entered the Red Fort, which stood on the banks of the Yamuna River, through the Amar Darwaza, and progressed toward the inner gates that led to the fort. The red sandstone fort was intimidating, with its ten-feet thick walls and ramparts, which were manned by the elite imperial troops. They were stopped and their identity checked many times before being allowed to proceed on the steep ramp, flanked by high walls and turrets that led to the inner palaces. Just ahead stood the majestic Diwan-é-aam with its silver roof and ornate pillars, its walls covered with arabesque, inlaid with precious gems. The winding path from the Diwan-é-aam led to a beautiful charbagh with fountains and terraced gardens through which one could enter the palaces. At the side of the garden through which Meherunnisa's entourage passed, there was a shaded path, flanked by flowering gulmohar trees.

Climbing the steps to the palace they made their way to the royal harem, the section of the palace that was most guarded. The large and rambling zenana was buzzing with activity. Imperial guards stood outside the walls of the harem casting suspicious looks at the guests. Here, the nobleman and his soldiers handed them over to the royal harem keeper and departed hastily. The women now entered the inner parts of the zenana which were guarded by giant Uzbek and Tartar women carrying gleaming scimitars. These women were reported to be more ferocious than the royal guards; their expressionless faces appeared to be carved out of stone. Laadli clung to her mother as she looked around the cold and hostile place. They stepped into the inner courts that were guarded by eunuchs, a dazzling lot with their gaudy attires and profusion of cheap jewellery. They ceaselessly argued with the other guards, trying to establish their superiority.

Meherunnisa took in the atmosphere with disdain. She had walked the corridors of the zenana a long time back, her head held high, mingling with royal blood as she waited on Ruqayya Begum. Once again, fate had brought her back to the harem to wait on the same queen, but this time round as a married woman with a child.

There had been not much decline in Ruqayya Begum's importance, although her husband, Shahenshah Akbar, had passed away making way for his son. Emperor Jahangir's wives now held more a important place in the harem hierarchy, but kept their distance from the dowager queen. The Mughal code demanded due respect for the dowagers.

Jagat Gosain, Shah Begum after Jahangir's first wife committed suicide, was virtual ruler of the harem, and her ladies-in-waiting wielded more power than the others in the zenana. By virtue of being the senior-most wife of the emperor, the empress' word was more powerful than any other law within the four walls of the harem.

Meherunnisa had once been an important figure in the harem: her closeness to Empress Ruqayya had ensured her prominence over the other ladies-in-waiting. As she walked towards the set of rooms allotted to her in the harem, she wondered what changes she would have to face. She walked with a regal air although her heart was hammering nervously. She had to remain calm to allay Laadli's fears. They were a strange trio—the regal widow, the timorous child and the bellicose servant. The harem women watched them with a mix of ridicule and pity. News of Meherunnisa's return had already travelled through the harem. There were whispers that the emperor had ordered her to be kept in the harem so that he could reignite the love that had once throbbed between them. The concubines hated her for trespassing into their world and the queens questioned the status of the new entrant.

The rooms assigned to Meherunnisa were ordinary and stood far away from the queens' apartments, signifying her inferior position in the harem hierarchy. In the harem, as well as the emperor's court, proximity to the royals was an indication of a person's significance. Meherunnisa wrinkled her nose with disgust at the sight of her humble quarters. Within the four bare walls of this apartment lay their future. Her mind was already buzzing with a hundred ideas that could help secure her position in the harem.

As soon as they had settled, she paid a visit to Ruqayya Begum along with her daughter. Laadli was dazzled by the richness of the objects that were scattered in the luxuriously decorated apartment. It was all crimson and gold, splashed with hues of green and blue. A profusion of gems, gold embroidered hangings, Persian carpets, jewelled censors and silver filigree lamps, tinted crystal bowls, jade cups, and enamelled gold goblets covered the room. The begum sat amidst a heap of soft silk cushions embroidered with pearls. Near her stood a carved stool, on which were jade bowls containing almonds and nuts. By her side lay a golden spittoon and a gem encrusted paandaan. The queen was ecstatic on seeing her protégé after so many years.

'Meher, my child, it is so nice to see you again.' Her eyes narrowed curiously. 'And who is this lovely lady?'

Meherunnisa bowed courteously and pushed Laadli towards her. Scared, the girl stared at the corpulent matron silently.

'Come here, child,' the begum patted a cushion near her. 'Don't be afraid. Here take some of these.' She offered Laadli sweets from the silver bowl lying near her.

Laadli remained where she was. *Queens are supposed to be slender and beautiful houris, not fat and bovine. My mother would make a much better empress.* The thought had come unbidden to her mind, but she never forgot the day when she had, for an instant, imagined her mother as an empress. Laadli would wonder what had sparked that thought in her mind.

Harassed servant girls ran around serving khus and rose drinks to everyone. Realising the queen's affections for Meherunnisa, they favoured her with special attention. After a while, the attendants dispersed, leaving the two women to converse.

Unnoticed by the chatting women, Laadli sneaked out to the adjoining garden, separated from the apartments by a latticed wall. A marble courtyard—with fluted columns rising from its tiled floors—ran all around the lush garden. A host of flowers and fruit trees lined the garden's central canal, which terminated into a beautiful marble fountain. On one corner stood a pavilion with its entire roof covered in striking frieze, overlooking the river. A cool breeze blew into the chambers, laden with the smell of the frangipani trees that lined the path.

Laadli walked up to the dovecotes that lined the edge of the garden and looked at the playful white doves. She thought about all the stories Firdaus had told her about the harem and the queens. She had been fascinated, thinking the harem to be magical, glamorous. But none of Firdaus' stories had prepared her for how *intimidating* the harem was. She wasn't sure she liked the reality: she would have preferred to have them remain stories to be heard within the confines of a happy home. She felt claustrophobic: she wished she could roam around the unfettered world outside the walls of the fort. The cheery streets that had been her first glimpse of this city. The women here frightened her; their disdain of her tore into her soul, stripping it of all confidence. *If only I could live with my grandparents*, she thought wistfully. *How does Ammijaan remain so unruffled and poised?*

Things did not improve with time for Laadli. Her mother and Firdaus were busy with their official duties, and she was lonely. No one had ventured to make friends with her, and she had no one to speak to. Although there were many girls her age in the harem—the daughters of concubines as well as those of the ladies-in-waiting—Laadli kept away from all of them. It was not only because she was shy, which she was, but that the memory of her father and her home at Burdwan was still fresh in her mind. She still had difficulty sleeping sometimes; nightmares of her father's murder tormented her. She remembered what Firdaus had told her mother that fateful night, that the emperor was behind her father's murder, and she did not like to think of herself as being in the same palace as him.

Preoccupied with her own problems, Meherunnisa did not notice her daughter's unhappiness. She was concerned about their economic status. The queen was generous with her and gifted her clothes and jewels, but that was not enough.

'I have been thinking, Firdaus,' she told her faithful nurse one day, 'there must be some way we can make money so we can live more comfortably. I have to start earning money.'

'But how will you earn money inside the harem?'

'I have an idea that could work. I can sew clothes for the women.'

Meherunnisa had always been a skilful seamstress and she thought her natural talent for designing could be put to good use in the harem. 'That's a good plan—and I could help you with the work.... But...I am not sure the women will give you the opportunity. They don't know about your skill.'

'I have a plan that will get me all the orders I want,' Meherunnisa's eyes were bright. 'I will first make a dress for the begum. If she agrees to wear a dress made by me, the others would do so too, and my importance as a designer will be established within the harem.'

Firdaus was doubtful about the plan, but she didn't want to dampen Meherunnisa's eagerness.

The next morning, Meherunnisa approached Ruqayya Begum. 'The festival of Ab-é-Pashan is around the corner and everyone will get new dresses made for the celebrations. If Your Highness permits, I would like to create a beautiful dress for you.'

Ab-é-Pashan was celebrated at the court with great elegance to herald the coming of the monsoon. The princes and prominent nobles took part in the festival and delighted in sprinkling rose water over each other. It was customary for the nobles to present the emperor with bejewelled golden flasks containing rose water, jujube tree flower juice and the essence of orange flowers on the festival day.

'My dear Meherunnisa, it is so nice of you to offer to design a dress for me. You go ahead and make new clothes for yourself and Laadli, don't bother about me. Anyway, I don't wear clothes of new fashions. I am quite happy with my old seamstress because she knows my requirements and understands my body's limitations.'

'I am not talking of new fashions, but why sacrifice beauty for comfort? I can design a garment that can be both comfortable and beautiful. I am just begging for a chance to show my skills.'

'Well, why don't you design something for my niece? She is young, she can carry off beautiful garments,' the begum said dismissively.

Meherunnisa knew that the begum could not be convinced so she approached Ruqayya Begum's niece and found the young girl quite willing to try out a new seamstress. Nazneen was a beautiful, slender girl of eighteen—an ideal model for Meherunnisa's venture.

'I think apricot would be the right colour for your complexion,' Meherunnisa decided as she took the girl's measurements. The girl was delighted with the novelty of Meherunnisa's ideas and willingly cooperated with her.

Meherunnisa was excited at the thought of designing an attire for the girl. She worked feverishly: the right fabric had to be acquired, silk thread in the same shade had to be bought for the embroidery, an appropriate design had to be worked out for the dress. The final result was an exquisite creation in silk, with a liberal use of sequins, corals and pearls.

Distracted by her project, Meherunnisa barely noticed that Laadli was getting more uncommunicative. Seated in a corner of the room, the child refused to go out and make friends or play with the other children. Insecure and friendless, she spent more time with birds and flowers than with human beings. It was left to Firdaus to take care of Laadli, but the old lady had found several friends amongst the other servant women of her age and spent most of her time gossiping with them. The harem had a way of corrupting the inmates and Firdaus was no different. She succumbed to the avaricious and indolent ways of the zenana.

Ab-é-Pashan celebrations began with great pomp. Every festival was an opportunity for the harem women to show off their elaborate dresses and expensive jewellery. When Nazneen, clad in her new ensemble, made an entrance at the poetry contest in the evening, the harem women sat up and took notice. Her flame red veil, covered with tiny golden stars, was woven from the sheerest of silks. The apricot qaba that fell to her knees was a vision in fine satin. It was elaborately embroidered and fringed with seed pearls. The flame red churidar with its striking diagonal stripes in yellow was designed to reveal the slender contours of her legs and hips. A thick rope of gold and coral adorned her slender throat and the lobes of her ears were ablaze with a diamonds and coral creation, a combination that had never been tried before.

A murmur of appreciation ran through the crowd and they began enquiring about the designer of the fantastic dress. The harem women were partial to shapeless tent-like robes, fashioned from heavy materials like velvet and brocade with expensive gems and gold fringes. The dress Nazneen wore was a complete contrast: it showed off her narrow waist, slim legs and arms to an advantage. The tight-fitting bodice, the slit that travelled up to the navel and the transparency of the material, all added to a sensuousness that the garments the other women wore lacked.

The stir, however, lasted only till Meherunnisa made her entry. She took everyone's breath away with her dress, which seemed to have been spun by a diligent spider from gossamer thin strands of white silk. She was clad in a transparent white qaba, which had been embroidered with pristine pearls. Its full sleeves hugged the arms and ended in a froth of lace imported from Europe. The silver veil was deceptively simple but elaborate in texture and weave. The white satin churidar sheathed her legs in a tight embrace. The entire effect was ethereal. There was an audible gasp of admiration as Meherunnisa walked into the hall, her delicate feet shod in white satin slippers embellished with white pearls. There was barely any trace of jewellery on her person except a strand of pearls on her neck and a pair of magnificent pearl earrings. Instead of jewellery, she had made clever use of fresh flowers. White jasmines were woven in her raven tresses. She blew in like a whiff of fresh air and innocent charm into the circle of gaudily clad women laden with gold and precious gems. Crimson, gold, purple, green were the predominant colours in the hall, and Meherunnisa stood out in the crowd like an innocent dove. There was a hush as the matrons apprised her critically and took in all the details of her attire.

'You have surpassed my expectations, Meherunnisa,' complimented Ruqayya Begum, chuckling at the stir her dress had caused. 'You will be besieged with demands from the women.'

The begum's prediction proved right. The clamour for Meherunnisa's services was immediate. All of a sudden, the dark colours they had worn all their lives looked garish and dated. Hitherto, the harem women had worn cumbersome tunics of knee length, with long and straight sleeves. Over this, they wore a full-length caftan with buttons that reached the waist. Many of them wore three caftans of varying sleeve lengths—one over the other. All these were now summarily discarded. Meherunnisa had the entire harem waiting in line for her designs. Whether it was for festivals or weddings or simple feasts, it was her creations everyone wanted to wear.

Firdaus was roped in to work on the pile of fabrics as orders poured in. Even Laadli was entrusted with small errands like delivering the dresses or sewing the buttons. Unable to cope with the volume of work, Meherunnisa employed some seamstresses to work under her supervision. They worked through the day and sometimes the night, to satisfy the ever-increasing demand from the harem women. Meherunnisa's business expanded and her reputation spread all across the city, but there was a restlessness in her that didn't find solace in money or fame. The fire of ambition consumed her totally; she wanted to achieve more.

'You don't have to work so hard, now that there are so many women working on the orders,' Firdaus said, massaging Meherunnisa's tired body with hot mustard oil in which she had added eucalyptus leaves for a soothing effect. 'You have to learn to take things easy. Maybe we should turn down some of them.'

'No!' Meherunnisa sat up. 'I will employ more women to handle the orders but no one should be refused.'

The next day, four more women were employed to take up embroidery work.

It was difficult for Meherunnisa to relax. With so many women working under her, she had more time to spare, but her restlessness only increased. One morning Firdaus found her illustrating a book of poems. 'I can see that you have taken up a new business,' Firdaus scowled at her mistress.

'I have to keep myself busy. Now that the seamstresses are capable of working on their own, I need to do something else.'

Meherunnisa took her painting seriously. She gifted the first few copies of poetry books that she illustrated to Ruqayya Begum and other queens, and soon there were requests for similar books. She calligraphed the verses of famous poets like Saadi, Hafiz, and Firdausi and it didn't take much time before her work was in demand. Her fame travelled through the empire as a capable illustrator. In between illustrating books for customers, she managed to find the time to illustrate a book for Laadli. It was the Persian book of fables, *Kalila and Dimna*, comprising stories about animals. After seeing Laadli's book, every child in the harem wanted a copy of her own.

8

Within a year, Meherunnisa's business had expanded beyond her expectations and she had enough money to buy whatever luxuries she wanted for her apartment. There was more money than they required to meet their needs, and she distributed part of her earnings to the orphans who sat in the mosques, begging for money.

Laadli, meanwhile, was unable to exorcise her demons. The thought of staying amongst the people she held responsible for her father's death seemed like an act of betrayal to her father's memory. She continued to remain in a shell, and nightmares still plagued her. Seeing no signs of improvement in her daughter, a worried Meherunnisa decided to take her to the royal hakim.

The hakim's prescription was simple. 'Your daughter has suffered an immense shock. The claustrophobic environment of the harem is not good for her. She needs open and salubrious surroundings. And she needs to be around people who care for her.'

Meherunnisa confided in Ruqayya Begum about her child's problem.

·'Bring her to my apartments. Its open space and gardens will cheer her up. Besides, there are other children around. And I will also request Jahangir to send you to your parents' house for a few weeks.'

'Yes, Your Highness, I think it would be best if I could take Laadli to my parents' place. I myself would be much happier living there. I don't know why the emperor desires that I should stay at the harem.'

For many months, Meherunnisa had wondered about Jahangir's intentions. Surely he must know that she held him responsible for the murder of her husband, and that the idea of staying at the imperial harem would therefore be repugnant to her?

'I think you know the reasons, Meherunnisa.'

'I do not understand them.'

'Don't try to pretend naiveté. You can't be unaware that the emperor is in love with you. Everyone in the harem knows about his feelings for you. He wants you to remain under his protection in the harem.'

'Forgive me, Your Highness, if I disagree. I would be well protected in my father's house. Besides, I am financially independent now and I can look after Laadli and myself quite well. I do not need anybody's charity. As far as the emperor's love is concerned, it can hardly be reciprocated if I am held as a prisoner in his harem.'

'What gives you the impression that you are a prisoner?'

'If I were a free person, would I be held against my wishes in the confinement of the harem? I cannot even take my daughter to a more suitable environment.'

'I will speak to Jahangir about your problem. I am sure, he will not refuse you permission to visit your parents,' the queen promised.

Meherunnisa began bringing her daughter to the queen's apartments every day. The girl would sit in a corner, watching the women giggling, playing tricks on each other, and nibbling at the delicacies laid before them. They spent hours discussing jewellery and the emperor's moods, playing chaupar and ganjifa, or composing inane verses. She hated their foolish chatter, and when she could no longer stand the noise, she escaped to the garden to stare at the sedately flowing river winding its way along the palace walls.

Her closest companions were a parrot called Mithoo, and a white dove named Minna. Laadli had taught the parrot to speak a few words and the dove to carry little notes. She spent hours training the two birds. *At least they can fly. They don't have to live in the harem*, she thought.

One day when she was sitting in the pavilion watching the peacocks preening with delight at the sight of black, rain-bearing clouds, her thoughts were intruded upon by a voice. She turned around and saw the teenaged Prince Khurram standing close to her. She got up and, after a self-conscious bow, began walking away from him.

'Please stay,' he commanded, his voice stern. Laadli stood transfixed, her eyes downcast. 'Do you like this place?'

Laadli nodded obediently, resentful at the loss of her privacy.

'So do I. It is beautiful, isn't it? I could spend many hours staring at the river,' he said, taking a seat next to her on the marble bench. The six-year-old girl cringed at his touch as he put out a hand to point out the flurry of pigeons near the steps.

'That white pigeon is called Shirin. And that one with the spotted tail is known as Farhad. They have been named after the famous lovers.'

His interest in the doves calmed her. *He's not as bad as I expected him to be*, thought the girl. Firdaus had repeatedly warned her against talking to the princes. 'They are a spoilt lot. It is best not be get close to them,' she had cautioned Laadli.

'And that dove near the cote is a short-tempered one,' said Laadli hesitantly, pointing to a grey dove hovering near the lovers. 'It keeps pecking angrily at the others all the time so I have named it Naraaz.'

They both burst out laughing as Naraaz suddenly pirouetted and pecked violently at another bird that had dared to pick a grain from its food bowl. All of a sudden Minna, the white dove, appeared from nowhere and settled on Laadli's shoulder.

'Minna is the most intelligent bird I have seen. She can carry letters and understand most of what I tell her. I have a parrot called Mithoo that can speak a few words. Do you want to see her?' Laadli called out to Mithoo and the parrot dutifully landed near her. It began pecking at the grains the girl held out in her hand.

Khurram burst out laughing. 'You seem to have trained them very well. I wish I had the patience to train a few birds.'

'It takes a lot of time, and yes, patience is essential if you want to train them.' Laadli's serious face brought a smile to the prince's face. He wanted to make her smile. She looked so pretty when she smiled. He felt sorry for the girl. He had heard all about her father's murder and how her mother had been incarcerated in the harem. It was common knowledge that his father, the emperor, loved the woman and would not let her out of his harem.

'Do you like riddles?' asked Khurram suddenly.

'Yes, I know many of them. My mother knows more riddles than anyone in the harem. She can keep Ruqayya Begum amused for hours with her riddles.'

'Well, tell me one and let me judge whether they are any good.'

'All right, try this one. Two partridges ahead of one, two partridges behind one; tell me how many partridges in all?'

Laadli waited with an amused look on her face while the prince mused over the riddle.

'Five?' he asked.

'No. Guess again.'

'I think it is five.'

'Silly, it is three.'

'How?'

'See, there are two partridges before the one at the end of the line and two partridges behind the one in the front, that makes it a total of three,' Laadli was animated as she explained the riddle by drawing three birds on the wet earth.

'You draw quite well for a girl your age,' remarked Khurram pointing to the partridges she had casually drawn on the ground.

'I can draw all kinds of birds. When I was very young my Abba presented me an album with paintings of birds. I began drawing the birds that roamed around Burdwan. I have a good collection of those drawings. I'll show them to you one day.'

'I would like that very much. Do you come here every day?'

'Yes, my mother insists that I accompany her to Ruqayya Begum's palace although I find it very boring to listen to those stupid women chattering away about silly matters. So I escape to this garden to watch the birds and the river.'

'Will you bring your album tomorrow? I will also bring a few paintings that I have done.'

'That will be nice. We can exchange the paintings, if you like.'

Laadli liked the prince. He was friendly and kind, unlike the picture painted by Firdaus. Perhaps it was because they had common interests. For the first time since she had arrived at Agra, Laadli felt that she had a friend. Meherunnisa noticed the change in her daughter and so did Firdaus.

'I think Laadli has found a friend, finally,' said Meherunnisa. Laadli was busy painting.

'Yes, she has stopped chattering with the parrot and seems to be in a very happy mood. She has been sketching birds since this afternoon.'

When the prince and the girl met again, they sat together near the fountain and exchanged notes on the paintings.

Over the next few days, they spoke about verses, riddles and paintings. They mimicked the women at the harem; they laughed over the silly eunuchs and tested each other's cleverness with their riddles. Laadli felt happy in his company. She shared her dreams and aspirations with him. No one, not even her mother had been privy to the girl's innermost thoughts. Gradually she felt herself warming to the prince. On his part, he found her innocence appealing. Most of the girls he met fawned over him, flirting and batting their eyelashes. They had just one thought in their minds—marrying royalty. Laadli was different. She was like a fresh whiff of breeze that delighted him.

'I want to be a painter when I grow up,' she told him one day.

'You must do that. My father has a huge atelier and there are many painters there. You must have heard of Mansur and Abul Hasan. But there are only male painters in the court. Maybe you should speak to my father some day. He can ask one of the artists to teach you the art.'

'I don't want to speak to the emperor,' Laadli said, shaking her head resolutely.

'Why not? Are you afraid of him? You don't have to be afraid of him. The emperor is very fond of children and he is partial towards girls.'

'Should I tell you something?' Laadli glanced around cautiously. 'But first you must promise not to tell anyone.'

'I promise. I won't part with your secret.'

'I hate the emperor. He killed my father.'

The prince was taken aback by the hatred in her voice. Khurram had heard whispers about his father's role in Sher Afghan's murder, but had believed them to be mere rumours.

'That's not true,' he said.

'I saw my father butchered by the emperor's foster brother and his men,' Laadli said, agitated. 'The coward came with so many soldiers to fight a lone man. He tricked my father because he did not have the courage to face him in the battlefield. My father was a hero who fought so many battles for the Mughals. He saved your father's life, yet the emperor got him murdered.'

'Why would he do that?'

'I don't know,' Laadli said, uncertainty creeping into her voice. 'I have only heard some women saying that he likes my mother.'

'Laadli, I wish you wouldn't listen to those silly women. You have been laughing about their stupid chatter, how can you believe anything they say?'

Khurram wanted to help the girl. She was a sensitive person, an artist who should be focusing her energies on creative things, instead of nursing this rage against a powerful emperor. Her anger would only be destructive. Even if there was any substance in the allegation that the emperor had engineered Sher Afghan's murder, there was little she could do. In fact, there was little anyone could do.

One day, he told her that he was leaving for a campaign; he had to go to Mewar and would be away many months. Once again Laadli was thrown into the deep abyss of loneliness. Only this time, she didn't retreat into the dark, gloomy cave of depression. Instead, she began painting with renewed fervour. That she had found someone who shared her interests was solace enough for Laadli. Her involvement with art gave her a sense of peace and purpose. She would have a new album of paintings to show the prince when he returned, she told herself.

While Khurram was away, Laadli discovered a new passion. The whole city was agog with news of the arrival of Ustad Hussein Ali Khan—reputed to be the best sitar player in the country. His first recital was arranged in the Diwan-e-Khas, and all the harem ladies had been invited to hear the maestro. As the Ustad's fingers weaved its magic with the instrument's strings, Laadli sat enthralled. She had never heard the instrument played before. It was a music that stirred hearts and brought peace to the soul. *I have to learn to play this instrument*, she decided. *It calms my restless soul.* Long after the recital was over and everyone had left the hall, she sat there alone, the music reverberating in her mind.

Laadli was a strange girl. Neither interested in clothes nor jewellery, she had never asked her mother for anything. So

Meherunnisa was taken aback when her daughter approached her the next day and said, 'Ammijaan, can I ask you for something?'

'Of course, Laadli, tell me what you want. Is it a necklace or a new dress?' Meherunnisa was delighted.

'I want a sitar.'

'You won't just need the instrument, Laadli, you would also need a teacher. Where will I find you a teacher?'

'Buy me the instrument and I'll find a teacher,' the girl declared resolutely.

The instrument arrived from the city of Benares after a few weeks. It was a beautifully crafted piece, with a shining exterior and a melodious tone. But a teacher was impossible to find. Although there were many women who could sing and dance, none could play the sitar. After spending a few hours with the instrument, Laadli gave up in frustration. 'It is so difficult to play without a teacher,' she complained.

'Didn't I warn you about that?'

'I *will* find a teacher to teach me the instrument.'

Meherunnisa detected a streak of obstinacy in her daughter and it surprised her. She had always assumed Laadli to be a pliant person. *The child is growing up*, she thought, looking at her daughter critically. Her daughter was now six years old; two years had passed since the day they had entered the portals of the zenana. *I should spend more time with her*, she decided. *My work has made me neglect her for too long.*

With her mother's decision to spend more time with her, Laadli's education began on a serious note. She plodded painstakingly through tomes of painting, music, history, poetry and the Quran. Not satisfied with these, Meherunnisa also taught her daughter the art of embroidery, designing, architecture, and gardening.

'I want her to rise above the others,' declared the mother. 'She is special.'

Slowly, with her days and nights now spent trying to absorb some new information, Laadli felt the fearful shadows of the past receding. For Meherunnisa too, this time had a beneficial effect: the restlessness she had been suffering receded as she formed a special connection with her daughter.

The festival of Eid-ul-Fitr was around the corner, and Meherunnisa finally obtained the emperor's permission to visit her parents, through Ruqayya Begum's recommendation. Laadli was ecstatic. She had heard so much about her grandparents' house from her mother.

Her heart beat a fierce tattoo as their palanquin crossed the threshold of the huge harem. It was so good to step out of the harem. Her eyes feasted hungrily on the sights. The bustling streets, colourfully attired townsfolk, business houses, gaily-decorated shops, and the street performers—everything attracted the artist in her. She tried to memorise each detail, to be painted on her canvas later. Her spirit soared. Even Meherunnisa was elated, her face glowing with the prospect of spending a full week with her family.

The palanquin wound its way through the narrow bazaar streets towards the elegant mansion of Mirza Ghias Baig. How well she remembered the courtyard with its huge mango tree in the centre, the rows of plants, tended by her mother, fringing the large open space. Bright sunlight filtered into the rooms through the branches of the neem tree in the backyard. Her mother was an avid gardener. No one knew more about herbs and their potent qualities than Asmat, but roses were her weakness. She excelled in inventing different uses of her favourite flower: as an edible sweet paste to be smeared on paan; an attar extracted from fragrant rose petals; or a sherbet made from bright red petals of the flower.

As Laadli entered the house, the brilliant Bukhara rugs brought a warm and joyous feeling to her heart. The lovely brocade curtains, silver-legged divans covered with skilfully embroidered coverlets, the comfortable pile of cushions and the hordes of pigeons feeding on the scattered grains in the courtyard, all looked so homely and comfortable. Her nostrils flared as she breathed in the familiar smells of a home. Laadli always associated smells with important events in her life, and the scent of roses always brought back happy times to her mind. Laadli felt a sense of peace after a long time.

Her grandmother hugged her in a tight embrace as her cousins rushed out to greet them with enthusiasm. They led Laadli to the inner chambers with Arjumand, soon to become her favourite cousin, teasing her mercilessly: 'You are so tall, you look like my aunt!' Although Arjumand was a full eight years older to her, they two cousins quickly developed a strong bond of friendship. The other cousins were too immature for the serious and sedate Laadli.

The atmosphere in the house was ebullient. After the ritualistic fasting through the month of Ramzan, it was time to rejoice and spend time with loved ones. Asmat had bought new clothes and jewellery for everyone in the house. A bangle-seller was invited into the courtyard and the women enjoyed themselves choosing from an array of colourful glass bangles.

Laadli and Arjumand decided to wear green. Clad in pastel green qaba and mustard-golden veils, they looked delightfully fresh and youthful. Arjumand wore her mother's emeralds on her neck and ears, with pearls strung in her hair, but Laadli decided to wear bright ochre marigolds as adornment. It was a novel experiment that caught the fancy of the other girls. Soon, everyone was clamouring for flowers to match their outfits. Meherunnisa smiled happily: Laadli was showing a distinctive flair for dressing. She had inherited her mother's panache and creativity.

The arrangements for the Eid feast began with the preparation of sweets and savouries, which kept the women busy for hours. Laadli, who had observed the rigorous month-long fast without drinking a drop of water from sunrise till sunset, looked forward to the feast eagerly. The cousins gorged themselves on the delicious food laid out by their grandmother on the traditional dastarkhan, and laughed till their sides ached. The warmth in the house made Laadli glow with happiness. She wished she could live with her cousins and grandparents forever. The very thought of going back to the harem was unbearable to her. The riches, jewels and gold were a poor compensation for love, laughter and happiness. Laadli wondered if her mother felt the same.

It was a quiet and depressing journey back to the palace. Meherunnisa was in an unusually contemplative mood. It was two-and-a-half years since they had arrived at Agra, but she had not once met the emperor nor had she heard from him. Why did he want her in the harem if he was not going to communicate with her?

The emperor was, in fact, impatient to meet her, but was shrewdly biding his time. Much as he wanted to meet Meherunnisa, he knew that the memory of Sher Afghan's death still haunted her. As long as the memories were fresh, the proud woman would ruthlessly toss out his proposal, of that he was sure. Ruqayya Begum, who was privy to Meherunnisa's feelings, had warned her stepson to tread carefully unless he was prepared for a rejection from the lady.

Soon after Meherunnisa and Laadli returned to the harem, they were taken up with preparations for the Nauroz festival. Laadli hoped that she would see Khurram at the festivities: she had not seen the prince for a long time and missed his company. She knew the prince would definitely attend the Meena Bazaar that was held during the Nauroz period.

At last the day arrived. Hectic preparations had been going on in the harem for weeks as the women amassed their precious ware to be sold to royalty and noble men at the Meena Bazaar. Some were preparing sweets and savouries, while others were busy creating various types of artefacts and embroidered items for their stalls. This was a much-awaited occasion, and every woman wanted to use it either to make money or attract the attention of the nobles. Laadli was too young to run a stall on her own, so she was assigned the job of helping Arjumand in her kiosk.

Gaily striped canopies were put up all around the harem gardens. Between the tall cypress trees stood colourful stalls with their wealth of wares. The women vied with one another to occupy vantage positions and laid out their wares on beautiful Bukhara rugs and Persian carpets. There were caged birds, bolts of velvets, muslins and silks, embroidered cushions, garments and brocade dresses. Fragrances, unguents, henna, lotions and potions rubbed shoulders with illustrated copies of the Quran and poetry. Goblets, cups, bowls and chinaware stood along with crystals, porcelains, vases, enamelled metals and decorations. There were sweetmeats, savouries, and dry fruits, herbs, spices and medicinal concoctions. Each stall had something unique to sell.

Eunuchs, servant girls, concubines, queens, princesses and attendants bustled about trying to attract customers to their stalls. The concubines were flirting outrageously with the nobles. There was loud laughter and banter as they tried to peddle their wares and bargained furiously with the men. The Meena Bazaar was a pleasant excuse for varied activities, trading of goods being just a façade for them. Catching the eye of an eligible nobleman or a prince remained the paramount reason for those young women who did not belong to the emperor's harem. They lisped and fluttered their eyelashes, pouted and tried every trick to entice the men.

Meherunnisa had been planning for the event for many days. In her stall she exhibited beautifully embroidered veils and turbans for the nobles; gorgeous albums of paintings and verses; especially designed aigrettes, daggers, anklets, necklaces, and earrings. Also displayed were ivory chess pieces sculpted in attractive shapes, jewellery boxes with gold latches, and ornate night stands and cabinets carved from the most expensive teakwood with ivory inlays.

But the most treasured items on sale were her stunning collection of jade articles, which she had amassed over several months just for the Meena Bazaar. Jade was in fashion; everyone wanted to own some article fashioned out of the precious stone. The delicacy of the stone and its cost made it a status symbol. Jade in its many hues—white, pink and shades of green—carved into dagger handles, wine cups, bowls, tiny plates, mirror frames and bookstands, were in great demand by the nobility. The beauty of the jade wine glass, reflected in its thin, almost translucent, quality, had been eulogised by poets in the court.

Meherunnisa's jade bowls were fashioned to fit perfectly in the palm of the hand, as that was how the emperor held it when drinking. It was believed that jade changed colour if the liquid in it was poisoned, so the emperor favoured jade bowls to the enamelled gold ones. Meherunnisa had designed the wine cups to match the organic form of leaves and flowers. She sought to capture the fullness of a flower, the twist of a stem, the web of veins and the gentle curve of the edge of the leaf.

Compared to Meherunnisa's precious ware, Arjumand's stall was insignificant. A heap of silver trinkets, some gold jewellery, a few embroidered cushion covers and coverlets were lined along with the albums of paintings done by Laadli. The two girls were not hopeful of catching the eyes of royalty, they were more excited by the idea of running a stall. Too inhibited to call out to the men, the girls huddled together, hoping that someone would wander to their stall and make purchases.

The emperor made a grand entry with his princes and emirs. He was resplendent in a scarlet brocade robe. On his head rested an embroidered dark green turban with a long plume dangling playfully. Stuck on one side of his broad green cummerbund was the famous sword, Alamgir, inherited by each Mughal emperor from the time of Humayun. On the other side was a dagger with its jade handle shaped like a tiger. Strands of large sized luminescent pearls adorned his neck; his wrists and arms glittered with heavy gold bracelets inlaid with diamonds and rubies. His fingers were covered with several rings of varying designs, sparkling with neatly inset precious stones. Everyone knew that Jahangir loved expensive jewellery—the ornament on his turban, with its walnut-sized ruby, diamond and emerald, was rumoured to have cost several lakhs of rupees.

The men swaggered to the stall closest to the entrance. It belonged to Jamila Begum, the wife of a high-ranking noble. In a generous mood, the emperor picked up a few pieces of expensive jewellery and then the bargaining began. The lady asked for an astronomical price, and the emperor teased her mercilessly. At last they settled on a price, and the emperor walked on while his attendant paid and collected the item.

From her corner Meherunnisa watched the emperor. As if sensing her eyes on him the emperor turned and their eyes met across the teeming stalls and held for what seemed to be an eternity. She felt herself redden as she held his gaze in a steady manner, not blinking for a moment till another woman claimed his attention. Meherunnisa waited for Jahangir to walk up to her, but he studiously avoided looking in her direction again. Talking in low tones with his queen, Jagat Gosain, who was walking by his side, the emperor turned towards another stall at the end of the garden.

Prince Khurram was loitering around aimlessly, surrounded by his friends, when his eyes alighted on the green-eyed Arjumand, dressed in a golden yellow qaba and ochre churidar. Arjumand exuded an inner beauty that dazzled everyone, and the young prince was no exception. He got rid of his companions and made his way towards her.

Laadli had gone to fetch some refreshments for Arjumand. When she returned, she was surprised to see Prince Khurram dawdling at their stall. He seemed to be hesitating between a gold trinket and a painting made by Laadli. Arjumand stood tongue-tied before him, unable to quote the cost of the articles.

'Salaam Alekum Shehzada Khurram. Does that painting interest you?' Laadli asked, diverting his attention from Arjumand's face.

'Alekum Salaam Laadli. How much are you asking for it?'

'It will cost you fifty gold mohurs.'

'You are a heartless shopkeeper. Such a high price for so little a thing!' laughed Khurram. 'I daresay no one will pay you more than ten mohurs for that.'

'This price is only for Prince Khurram. Others will not be able to afford my paintings,' quipped Laadli.

'I'll take it,' he said, placing a purse full of gold coins on the counter. Then he turned to address Arjumand. 'What have you to offer, beautiful damsel?' Stammering with embarrassment, she appealed to Laadli for help. But Laadli refused to come to her aid. She was enjoying her cousin's discomfiture.

Blushing furiously, Arjumand pointed to an enamelled wine goblet. 'That will suit your highness. And it costs just twenty gold mohurs.'

'Is that all? I will pay fifty mohurs for it. If Laadli can command fifty for her painting, you deserve nothing less.'

Watching the two, and sensing the strong attraction flowing between them, a sudden stab of jealousy struck Laadli's heart. She quickly packed the purchases to hurry him away from the stall, but the prince hung around, looking for more objects to buy. His eyes constantly sought Arjumand's, but she refused to meet his gaze. With growing alarm, Laadli realised that the prince was truly enamoured by her cousin. Her only true friend had succumbed to another's charms.

After that day, the prince sought Laadli only as a messenger to convey his love notes to her cousin. He also borrowed her pigeon, Minna, to carry his missives of love to Arjumand. Laadli complied with his wishes because he was dear to her. She painstakingly gathered the crumbs of his affection, aware that she would never get more than that. His heart would belong to just one woman, and that was Arjumand.

9

Meherunnisa waited patiently for the communiqué from Jahangir. Although he had avoided meeting her at the Meena Bazaar, she was sure that he would send word to her through someone. She was right. A couple of weeks later, Ruqayya Begum broached the subject.

'How long can a widow mourn her departed husband? Meherunnisa, I feel pained at your lonely existence. Can you imagine living your entire life in this manner? You have a daughter to support, too.'

'With all due deference to your views, Begum Sahiba, I think I can support myself. As for Laadli, I will do my best to provide a decent life and a worthwhile dowry for her when she grows up.'

'It is not just the matter of financial security. What about your life?'

'I am fortunate to have your concern and affection. But there must be hundreds and thousands of unfortunate widows like me in the Mughal Empire, who do not have either a decent shelter nor the comforts that I enjoy, yet they continue to live their life.'

'But they do not have the emperor at their feet. Meherunnisa, my son adores you. He would like to make you the queen of his heart.'

'Your Majesty, I am flattered to hear that. A poor widow with a child can hardly be worthy of his attention. I still mourn for my slain husband and cannot dream of giving myself to another man.'

Meherunnisa was raising the ante. Succumbing to the emperor without any assurances from his side would put her in the same position as that of an ordinary harem woman. At most, she would be regarded as a concubine. But Meherunnisa dreamed of being the Empress of the Mughal Empire. Nothing less would do. She had waited for many years for her dreams to materialise, and she was in no hurry to ruin them by walking into the emperor's bedchamber. She would bide her time till his desire for her overcame him enough, to make her his empress. Queen Jagat Gossain was the Shah Begum, and nothing could change that, but Meherunnisa could still become an empress.

In his chambers, Jahangir paced the floor, irritated with Meherunnisa's obstinacy. *I will not be spurned; she has to yield,* he decided. He was emperor, and could command any number of women to subjugation; he was not going to beg Meherunnisa. Yet, he faltered. She was special. She held his heart. The emperor sought solace in the arms of other women, but Meherunnisa's face refused to leave his mind.

'What can a man do if a woman denies him her heart?' he asked Mohammad Sharief, his trusted minister and stepbrother.

'If it is an ordinary man and an ordinary woman, he can force the Qazi to perform a nikah, but the emperor is no ordinary man and she is not an ordinary woman. I have no solution to your dilemma, Your Majesty.'

'That woman has the nerve to snub me! What a paradox: I am revered by entire Hindustan, hundreds and thousands of beauteous women want to share my bed, but I am obsessed with one woman who won't respond to my love. If I just wanted to possess her physically, I could have brought her to my bed, but I desire more. I feel tongue-tied in her presence! Isn't that ridiculous?'

'You could offer to make her your concubine,' suggested Sharief, after a short pause.

'You think I haven't done that already? I have sent several missives proposing a place for her in the harem, but she has rejected them all. Her spirit amazes me.' The emperor's looked balefully at his stepbrother. 'Sharief, I want that woman at any cost.'

'At the cost of offering her marriage?' asked Sharief.

'Yes, if that is what she wants.'

'Mughal emperors have always married for political or economic gains. Right from Shahenshah Akbar's times, the policy has been very clear. In Meherunnisa's case, it is neither a politically beneficial union, nor is she from a royal family.'

'She may not be royalty, but she belongs to a reasonably good family. Her father belongs to a noble family from Persia. And he is one of the most intelligent and able ministers of the empire. Her brother, Asaf, is an important emir. Do you know that he has studied Sanskrit and Hindu scriptures in great detail? As for her younger brother, Ibrahim Khan "fatehjung", he is one of the ablest generals in the empire.'

'That may be so. But do not forget the fact that Mirza Ghias Baig was under a cloud of suspicion during Shahenshah

Akbar's time when he was caught accepting bribes. Have you forgotten that he had fallen from royal grace? Your Majesty also seems to have forgotten about the unfortunate eldest son of Mirza Ghias Baig. Was Mahmud not executed by your order because he had conspired with Khusrau to have you assassinated?'

'There could be one black sheep in every family. Just because one of his sons tried to assassinate me, I can't paint the entire family with a black brush. The Mirza was accused of taking bribes, but he has been warned and he is not likely to jeopardise his position by resorting to such folly in future.'

'What about Sher Afghan's unfortunate murder? I am sure that the lady fends you off because of that incident.'

'That was most unfortunate. I wish the fellow had agreed to divorce Meherunnisa as I had suggested. Let us not discuss what has been. It depresses me to think of all those unpleasant things. Tell me what should I do to make her accept my love?'

'Speak to her. Tell her how much you love her. How can any woman spurn the genuine feelings of an emperor?'

Jahangir shook his head, 'I wouldn't be able to bear her rejection.'

'There is another solution. Why don't you speak to her father, Mirza Ghias Baig, or even her brother, Asaf Khan? Put in a word through her family. It could have a better impact.'

'That is a very good idea. I shall summon Asaf Khan and speak to him.'

Not wanting to lose any time, the emperor immediately summoned Meherunnisa's brother. Asaf Khan was an important member of his court and an intelligent man.

'Asaf, I wish to speak about a private matter for which I need your counsel,' the emperor began hesitantly. Asaf

Khan instantly understood that the emperor was referring to Meherunnisa. Every member of Meherunnisa's family knew about the emperor's love for her. Both Mirza Ghias Baig and Asaf Khan were aware that the family could benefit greatly if Meherunnisa accepted the emperor's proposition. They tried to coax her, but she remained adamant. Only her father understood that his clever daughter was angling for the crown.

'Your Majesty's desire is my command. I shall do anything in my power to satisfy the desire of my emperor.'

'This is a delicate matter concerning your sister, Meherunnisa. I wish to marry her but she refuses to agree to my proposal.'

'My sister still mourns for her husband. A mere widow, she can hardly refuse you, sire. She must be delighted by your proposal; it is just that her grieving heart deters her from accepting it. I can assure you of that, Your Majesty.'

'How long must she mourn? It is well over three years now! My patience has its limits. You must convey my impatience to your sister.' The emperor paced the floor agitatedly.

The very next day the emperor presented a Khilat to Mirza Ghias Baig, in the Diwan-é-aam. In the presence of all the nobles he announced, 'Mirza Ghias Baig, we are very pleased with your selfless services to the empire and now we wish to reward you. From today, you shall be known by the title Itmad-ud-daulah, the pillar of the empire.'

The Mirza bowed low before the emperor and accepted the honour humbly. He had guessed the reason for his promotion. In fact, most of the nobles knew the reason for the emperor's generosity towards the Mirza.

As the days passed, the emperor continued to pine for his beloved Meherunnisa, but she kept him away with the excuse that she was still mourning for her dead husband.

On the other hand, the affair between Prince Khurram and Arjumand Bano progressed at a fast pace. The young couple met clandestinely and exchanged vows of love.

'I can no longer live without Arjumand,' Khurram confided to Laadli. 'She has become the orbit of my world. Sometimes I wonder if it is possible to love someone as much as I love her.'

His deep sighs and lovelorn looks moved Laadli, but she could do little to help him beyond carry their missives. It was the emperor who held the fate of the young lovers in his hands. Without the imperial permission, Prince Khurram could not marry Arjumand.

'Why don't you ask the emperor for his blessings?'

'He wants me to marry the daughter of the Shah of Persia because he wants our relationship with them consolidated. Has he forgotten his own romantic escapades, I wonder.'

'Marry the Persian princess and then ask for Arjumand's hand,' Laadli suggested pragmatically. 'You have to please the emperor to obtain his blessings. As long as he does not refuse the match, there is hope for the two of you.'

'You're right. I will broach the topic tonight when the emperor retires to his private chamber,' Khurram said determinedly.

That evening the prince approached his father and begged him to grant permission for his marriage with Arjumand. Jahangir was relaxing in his quarters, a wine glass and hookah by his side, and an open book of verses before him.

'Princes cannot decide their marriage. It is for the emperor to decide who they should marry.'

'But I love Arjumand. I cannot live without her.'

'You must learn to be patient. We have decided that you will marry the daughter of Mirza Muzaffar Husain Safavi of the house of Shah Ismail of Persia so that our relationships with the Shah can improve.'

'If I agree to marry the Persian princess, will you allow me to take Arjumand as my wife?'

'Don't place conditions on us. We will think about the matter after your marriage with the princess.' And the emperor dismissed his angry son. The fact was that Jahangir was annoyed with the Baig family. Every time Meherunnisa turned him down, he found it difficult to control his rage or the urge to punish her family. *Khurram will not marry Arjumand till Meherunnisa agrees to my proposal*, decided the emperor.

Four years had now passed since Meherunnisa had come to the imperial palace at Agra. The emperor's impatience grew, as did his temper tantrums. He was no longer content to pass his time at the court or harem. Neither hunts nor animal fights amused him. He found no solace in alcohol or dancing girls.

His stepbrother Sharief noticed the pinched look on the emperor's face. *He has been drinking too much*, he thought, *he has to be distracted*.

'I have found some nice hunting spots just a few kilometres away from Amber. The dense forests there are full of rare wild beasts and birds. Would the Shahenshah like to indulge in the sport?'

'Hunting no longer interests me, Sharief. My soul is shattered with grief. I can neither sleep nor eat. There is so much restlessness in my heart that I can't find peace. My mind knows no joy. It is all because of that woman who refuses to understand my feelings. Could she really have transformed into such an unfeeling person? Has she forgotten the vows of love we exchanged?'

Jahangir's face, lined and weary, invoked pity in his companion.

'Jahanpanah, sometimes it is better to wait than to push a matter. Do not fret over her obstinacy. Leave it to the Almighty to take care of the affair.'

The emperor halted his agitated pacing. His tawny eyes emitted liquid fire. 'Sharief, if you were suffering the way I do, you wouldn't be talking in this manner,' he admonished. 'I wish to travel to Lahore. Maybe the beauty of that city will awaken romance in the heart of my beloved. Agra is too much of a practical city, it is Lahore where love and romance flourish.'

It was useless to argue with the emperor. Sharief bowed himself out of Jahangir's presence muttering—'I shall personally supervise the arrangements for the travel, Your Majesty.'

Outside, away from the emperor's hearing, he cursed Meherunnisa and the problems she had brought to the court. *Why can't the woman surrender to the inevitable? What a mess! Allah, I pray that the emperor snaps out of his infatuation or the woman realises the futility of her inflexible stance.*

The emperor's decision translated into frantic activity as the court began packing up for the long journey. When the court moved from one city to the other, it meant that almost everyone moved. From nobles and soldiers to petty traders and even beggars, everyone joined the caravan: no one wanted to be left behind. There would be no business when the royal camp moved and the enormous capital city would become like a ghost town. Life existed where the emperor lived. No less than fifteen hundred elephants, ten thousand horses, hundreds of palanquins and thousands of foot soldiers formed the entourage.

Meherunnisa also travelled along with the emperor's harem. With more than three hundred concubines and eighteen wives, the harem was a magnificent procession. Laadli travelled with her mother in a palanquin that tailed the procession. The important queens and concubines travelled at the head, and women lower down in the hierarchy, at the rear of the convoy.

It was the first time Laadli was travelling with the royal retinue and she was delighted with everything. On her insistence, her friend, Benazir, was sharing their palanquin. In the past year, ever since Khurram was lost to her, Laadli had made two friends—Ratnavali, the niece of a concubine, and Benazir, the daughter of a concubine. The three girls were of the same age and shared the same interests. They also shared a common hatred for the emperor.

Benazir had grown up with the image of her frail mother endlessly waiting for a visit from the emperor. Benazir's mother was the daughter of a Hindu noble, low down in the hierarchy. She had caught Jahangir's eye when she attended a royal function and was brought to the harem by force and converted to Islam. For six months Jahangir had been enchanted with his new paramour, then he tired of her and discarded her forever. Benazir's mother had been in love with a young Hindu soldier when the emperor had her brought to the harem. Jahangir had ordered his execution when he learned of their romance. Benazir had often heard the story from her mother.

Ratnavali was the daughter of a proud Rajput chieftain. She had been left orphaned after the emperor's army attacked her town and killed her family members. The imperial soldiers had gone on a rampage, plundering and raping the women, killing children and causing mayhem. Roop Kunwar, a childless concubine and a distant aunt of hers, took care of her now.

The girls giggled as they noted the strapping Uzbek women guards who galloped alongside their palanquin. The one on the right of their palanquin had a discernible moustache and her demeanour added to her masculine appearance.

About two kilometres ahead of the main column, a few soldiers rode with several yards of white linen. This was used to hide from view any animal carcasses or corpses that might lie on the way, so that the sight of a dead body did not offend the royal sensibilities.

Right in front of the procession walked the elephants, with bearers carrying the Mughal standards. The Timurid standard of a crouching lion set against the rising sun was followed by white Arab stallions adorned with gold saddles, reins and stirrups carrying the personal banner of the emperor Jahangir, calligraphed in Persian. A dozen men sprinkled rose water and fanned the air free of flies so that dust or pests did not bother the emperor.

The emperor travelled on a golden howdah under a gem-encrusted umbrella. He was flanked by four artists and calligraphers who noted events and the emperor's thoughts, to be recorded later for his memoirs. Jahangir never travelled anywhere without his memoirs. Alongside the emperor's elephant rode a vizier with many documents about the places the procession was passing through. His vast store of documents contained each and every detail about the area. Next to the vizier rode the imperial treasurer with bags full of gold and silver coins to be distributed by the emperor to the people on the wayside, who gathered to pay their respects to him. A posse of elite guards, who were the emperor's privileged soldiers, followed these riders, decked in crimson uniform, their faces solemn and determined.

A regal palanquin crafted out of silver and decorated with pearls and rubies, and covered with brocade curtains, carried the empress. A thoroughbred stallion walked alongside in case the empress wished to ride when she got bored of sitting in the palanquin. A number of imperial palanquins carrying other queens, according to their ranks, followed the empress's palanquin. Ferocious looking Uzbek women guards with drawn scimitars surrounded the palanquins, ready to attack any man who dared cross the path.

Behind them rode another troop of riders with naked swords. After them came the palanquins carrying noblewomen and emirs followed by the procession of lesser courtiers, musicians, servants, slaves and traders. Hundreds of horses, camels and elephants carrying provisions, water, and tents followed in the rear. There were makeshift baths, the emperor's menagerie and other stores loaded on the animals. A ragged group of beggars and mendicants formed the tail end of the procession.

Finally, the entourage reached Lahore Fort. Covering a vast area, the fort had been constructed with red sandstone by Shehanshah Akbar, but Jahangir insisted that marble pavilions be added to the palaces. The emperor was partial to glazed Kashi tile work and frescoes, and his architect Mamoor Khan was instructed to use these elements extensively in his renovation efforts.

'Mamoor, we wish you to make generous use of glass mosaic for the embellishment of the Sheesh Mahal so that it will reflect the grandeur and beauty of a Mughal emperor's court. The Sheesh Mahal would require extra thick walls and ceilings to provide adequate depth for different layers of the plaster background, and the openings will have to be minimised to necessitate the use of artificial light. This will bring out the effect of the glass mosaic work. And, of course, it will also ensure coolness.'

The emperor's understanding of architectural details impressed Mamoor Khan.

Pointing to the fort, the emperor continued. 'I want this to look more like a palace than a fort. I want you to design the Khwabgah with paintings on the ceilings and the walls. You can also use stuccowork on the walls, like we did in my mother, Queen Jodha Bai's palace at Fatehpur Sikri. I want similar work in the Diwan-é-khas. And the gardens—they should be as beautiful and ornate as the ones in Kashmir.'

While reconstruction work was going on at the fort, the emperor camped in the Dilkhusha gardens, on the banks of the river Ravi. Double-storied royal tents in bright crimson were pitched in the lawns of the garden amidst the fruit trees. The emperor's tent, containing several rooms, was covered with exotic paintings and its floors were furnished with bright carpets. Carved screens of Kashmiri walnut wood provided privacy from prying eyes. Ivory caskets and jade wine cups with couplets inscribed on them, gold spittoons, enamelled flower vases filled with perfect blooms, porcelain plates with fruits, carved sandalwood side tables, almost everything that brought comfort and luxury to the emperor in his palace, was replicated within the tent.

The mammoth tent also accommodated the Diwan-é-khas and council rooms, just as they formed a part of the emperor's quarters in the fort. Tents for the other nobles occupied the rest of the garden, their distance from the emperor's marquee indicating their status. In the evening, the emperor sat in the marble pavilions shaped like stone thrones, standing in the centre of an enormous pool, as he listened to the ethereal music played by his musicians. Sheets of cool, quiet water contrasted with shawls of fast running water cascading over chadars—deep-throated marble chutes inlaid with coloured marble. The play of water in countless fountains covered the surface with ripples. Tiny oil lamps set in marble niches sparkled from behind cascades. Rows of trees lit with Chinese lanterns lighted up the path around the garden.

The breathtaking scene didn't alleviate Jahangir's pining heart, however. 'If only Meherunnisa were by my side,' he sighed, 'this would be paradise.'

'Meherunnisa is housed on the other side of the river Ravi. Your Majesty can travel by the royal barge on a moonlit night and capture her heart. I am sure the lady will respond, for who can ignore the magic cast by the moon on a night like this. A direct appeal is always favourable to the ones made through mediators,' Sharief suggested.

Jahangir felt convinced of the truth of his stepbrother's statement. That night, the royal barge, lit like a chandelier, floated on the waters of the Ravi, as it made its way towards the mansion that housed Meherunnisa and Laadli. His heart beating hopefully, Jahangir advanced towards his destination. He went as a lover, not an emperor, to woo the woman of his dreams.

From her balcony Meherunnisa watched the illuminated barge approaching the shore. She walked to the outer hall where her maid was lying in deep sleep.

'Wake up, you fool, the emperor approaches this mansion,' she kicked the girl.

The girl got up, sleepy and disoriented.

'Run to the door and bring in the emperor while I dress,' instructed Meherunnisa calmly, as she entered her room to complete her toilette.

Soon they were standing alone in the hall, she heavily veiled and he, hesitant. His escorts waited outside in the garden.

'What brings you here, Your Majesty, at this hour of the night? I do have a reputation to defend. Words of your night adventure will soon leave the four walls of this mansion and people will smirk.'

'I have come to you Meherunnisa, because you have not heeded to the appeals sent through emissaries.'

'Your Majesty should have patience. I am a grieving widow who has no reply for the emperor's missives.'

Her cool manner enraged the emperor.

'Enough, Meherunnisa. Enough time has been granted for your mourning. For how long does a woman mourn a husband she didn't love?'

Her green eyes spewed fire as she directed her gaze at him. They seemed to burn a hole in the veil that covered them.

'You are insulting me, Your Majesty. Is love to be worn over one's sleeve, to be declared in public, for everyone to see? I mourn a man who was my husband for thirteen years.' The rebuke took him by surprise.

Anger flickered in his eyes. 'It is a deadly game you are playing with me. You continue to dangle me on a slender thread. I have no more time to give you for your grief. Four years I have waited for you. I can wait no longer.'

'How can a mere women play deadly games with an emperor? That is the sole prerogative of the royals. I play no games with you, sire. I just want you to leave me to my fate. I am too small a person with no rank and status to challenge the grand Mughal emperor. Do I detect a veiled threat in the emperor's statement?'

Her words were sharp and the tone uncompromising. The volcano of rage simmering inside his bosom turned into cold lava in an instant. Its ashes seemed to choke him as the mighty emperor grovelled helplessly before her. 'Meherunnisa, my darling, how could I threaten you? I love you more than anything else in my life.'

'More than your throne? More than the hundreds of beautiful women in the harem?' she asked archly, delighting in his discomfiture. She felt powerful and potent before her helpless lover.

'Yes, yes, more than the throne and the crown, more than the women in my harem, more than everything!'

'Is that why you got my poor husband killed? A valiant soldier, who fought bravely for the empire, saved you from death once, and rode with you many times, protecting you from the hail of arrows and bullets. Did he deserve to die so miserably, killed so brutally, his body hacked to pieces by your henchmen? All because he happened to be married to a woman who caught your fancy?'

'Don't you dare make such allegations, Meherunnisa. Don't test my patience just because I love you.'

'I am sorry, Your Majesty, for a moment I forgot that you are the emperor. For an instant I saw my husband's murderer standing before me. You may punish me in any way you want. Behead me, have me trampled by elephants or bury me alive within the walls like Shahenshah Akbar buried Anarkali. I shall not complain.'

'Why are you intent on torturing me? Believe me, I had no role to play in your husband's death.'

'For four long years I have lived with the gory image of my husband's brutalised body. How can I forget his murder, sire? The entire empire knows that your foster brother, Qutubuddin, was instructed by you to kill my husband. And you are telling me that you had no role to play in his murder?'

Jahangir was pacing the floor agitatedly.

'What do you want from me? Tell me, how can I atone for the murder of Sher Afghan? Since you believe that I was instrumental in causing his death, tell me what I must do to erase that idea from your mind?'

'I am no one to pass judgement, Your Majesty. I can't dictate terms to the powerful emperor of Hindustan. Please leave me to live the rest of my life in peace.'

Rejected again, the emperor left to drown his misery in endless cups of wine.

'Sharief, I am trying to be tolerant, but she tries my patience. I must be the only Mughal emperor to be spurned by a woman. I feel ashamed of my weakness.'

'Your Majesty must not lose heart. I have no doubt that a persistent approach can make her heart melt. No woman can reject a penitent man.'

Every night, for eleven nights, the emperor travelled on his barge to Meherunnisa's mansion, trying to mollify her. Hidden behind a pillar, the eight-year-old Laadli watched as the emperor wooed her mother with expensive gifts, laid the imperial treasures at her feet, bared his heart and tried every ploy he could think of. The innocent child applauded what she thought was her mother's courage in rebuffing the emperor. Laadli gloated in the emperor's discomfiture. She was convinced that her mother's love for Sher Afghan would not allow her to submit to Jahangir's wishes.

Seated in the garden of the mansion, Laadli told Benazir, 'My mother will never acquiesce to the emperor's desires. How can a woman marry a man who murdered her husband? Is the emperor so naïve that he doesn't understand that, or is he so vain as to think that he can win any woman's heart with his throne and crown?'

But Laadli's delight did not last long. Appalled, she watched as her mother's frozen heart slowly thawed and warmed to the ardent lover's pleas. On the twelfth night, Jahangir could control himself no longer. He fell on his knees and pleaded— 'Don't send me back, I beg you.'

Taking her in his arms forcibly, he murmured against her black fragrant tresses—'Meherunnisa, I can't live without you.'

'I do not give my heart to form until the course of action is known; I am a slave to love, and the seventy-two sects are known,' she recited, closing her eyes in ecstasy.

Her pliant body receptive to his caresses, she whispered back—'Your Majesty, you will have to pay a high price for me.'

Intoxicated by her soft voice and aroused by the sensual scent of roses on her warm body, he promised, 'I am willing to lay my crown at your feet, just say yes to my proposal, my Meherunnisa. From today you shall be known as Nur Mahal, the light of the palace, if you agree to my proposal.'

With bated breath, Laadli listened from behind a pillar. She clapped her hand on her mouth to stop herself from gasping as she heard her mother respond—'I shall not acquiesce to being a concubine, even if you bestow that title on me, that is my first condition.'

'You will never be a concubine, that is a promise. I shall make you a queen.'

'The second condition is that my daughter, Laadli, will wed your son and your heir.'

Laadli could barely control her revulsion. Why was her mother succumbing, and why was she including her in her list of conditions? In that moment she knew all was lost. She realised that her mother had only been playing a game with the emperor: all she had wanted was a good bargain. It had nothing to do with emotions or mourning or love. Laadli's heart broke. A sob escaped her throat. She watched helplessly as her fate was sealed.

'I agree to that condition too,' the emperor said, ready to acquiesce to all her demands.

'If you make me a queen, it may cause a stir in the harem. Queen Jagat Gosain, the Shah Begum, will not take kindly to your decision.'

'You are a hard bargainer, Meherunnisa. Don't forget that she is much senior to all the women in the harem and I cannot displace her. It is against the rules of the Timurid dynasty.'

Meherunnisa knew she had reached the limit of her bargaining strength and pushing harder could jeopardise all that she had managed to inveigle out of Jahangir, so she gave up graciously.

'I respect the Timurid laws and will not insist on breaking any of them. I am yours, Badshah, from today, both in flesh and spirit.'

The emperor's eyes lit up with her words. He embraced her with happiness. 'My Nur Mahal, we shall get married at the earliest and you shall be my chief consort. Allah is great! He has blessed me with happiness. We will have the grandest wedding ever seen in Lahore. There will be rejoicing and celebrations throughout the land,' he said, holding her tight, his grip hurting her.

'Not at Lahore, Jahanpanah, let us get married in Kashmir. It is the most beautiful place on earth and I want our relationship to start from there.'

'That is a fantastic idea. Why did I not think of it? We will set out for Kashmir immediately. Sharief,' he called out to his foster brother who was waiting in the garden. 'Congratulate us, brother. She has agreed, at last.'

Mohammad Sharief bowed low to both of them and expressed his delight at the momentous decision. He was relieved at the development. *At last I will be able to rest in peace*, he sighed, as he accompanied the ecstatic emperor to the barge.

Laadli's world shattered as she watched the emperor returning to his barge, elated at his victory. Soon she would be the daughter of a queen. At that moment, she hated her mother more than the emperor. For Laadli, her mother was a traitor who had let her husband down.

'But why does she have to marry that murderer?' she wailed in her room. Neither Benazir not Firdaus, sitting by her side and trying to console her, had an answer to that.

News of Meherunnisa's reconciliation with the emperor spread like wildfire. There was consternation in the harem. Would the wily Meherunnisa demand a higher status than she was eligible for? There was much anxiety in the Rajput faction, but the Persian bloc was jubilant.

Jahangir met Mirza Ghias Baig and expressed his wish to get married immediately. There was little time to prepare for an elaborate ceremony, but the elated Mirza Ghias Baig and Asmat got busy with their daughter's wedding arrangements with enthusiasm. The household bustled with the constant arrival of jewellers, seamstresses and traders who brought the finest of silks from China, the best of muslins from Dacca and embroidered velvets from Gujarat. Cooks were brought in from different parts of the country. The most famous nautch girls, musicians and singers were called to accompany the royal entourage to Kashmir to perform for the festivities.

The wedding was a grand affair. Meherunnisa was resplendent in a royal blue silk qaba embroidered with pearls, her slim legs encased in a matching churidar, and her radiant face covered in a gossamer veil of pure woven gold. Her feet were shod in velvet slippers embroidered with seed pearls and gold thread. She wore the most exquisite jewellery, which had been gifted to her by the emperor: a delicate ornament, crafted out of gold filigree and set with huge blue diamonds and rubies, sat on her head; an emerald and gold choker adorned her neck, along with five strings of pearls which hung to her waist; dangling earrings fell to her shoulders; her arms bore pearl and gold bracelets and armlets; each finger had a ring; and a crescent shaped ornament covered the back of her palm. The bride shimmered with each step she took to walk up to the flower bedecked dais, followed by her maids.

Musicians heralded the arrival of the emperor as he walked to the hall with his sons and Mirza Ghias Baig. Only Khurram seemed to be brooding about something—his handsome face dark with anger. Jahangir wore a pure white silk qaba with gold embroidery and a pearl encrusted, richly embroidered crimson cummerbund, in which was stuck his dagger with its jade handle. A flank of nobles followed the emperor, resplendent in their finery. Dozens of slaves sprinkled rose essence and strewed the path with petals of roses and jasmine, as the bridegroom approached the stage that had been covered with a canopy of gold. Strings of jasmine, roses and pearls hung from the ceiling to divide the men and the women. Sombre-faced mullahs and qazis began the nuptial rituals.

The emperor was impatient for the formalities to be over. He could not wait to hold Nur Mahal in his arms. His heart leapt with pleasure as Nur Mahal whispered her acceptance and the qazi announced that the ceremony was complete. A volley of greetings rose from the spectators. Each noble wanted to be the first to congratulate the couple and offer precious gifts.

With a voice shaking with emotion, Jahangir read out a long ode he had composed for his queen, eulogising her beauty and intelligence, her grace and goodness, her generosity and benevolence.

'From this day, Begum Meherunnisa will be known as Nur Jahan, the Light of the World. With this wedding I adopt her little daughter, Laadli, who will, henceforth, be known as Shehzadi Laadli Bano,' he announced to the assembled nobles.

Earlier that day, wedding gifts from the emperor to Meherunnisa had filled the chambers of the harem. Jahangir had been extremely generous. There were caskets full of gold coins, totalling eighty lakh gold asharfis. Eunuchs carried in over five hundred sets of exquisitely tailored and embroidered dresses in muslin, silk, velvet and satin, in various colours, for the empress. There were heaps of priceless pearl necklaces, each pearl the size of a nugget, chokers set with diamonds, rubies and emeralds, gold bracelets and armlets, hundreds of gold rings set with precious stones, countless casks of perfumes, musk and ambergris, satin and velvet slippers embroidered with seed pearls. He had also given her dozens of caparisoned elephants, pure-bred Arabian stallions and palanquins ornamented with gold plating and inlays. Finally came the royal Farman, which endowed Nur Jahan with jagirs of Rampur, Kanauj and Qandahar, along with a command of thirty thousand troops. It was the largest jagir ever given to an empress.

After Jahangir's announcement, poets read out their compositions in praise of the emperor, nautch girls danced with abandon and the musicians played divine music as the couple was led to their bridal chamber. There were fireworks and joyous celebrations, clothes and food were distributed generously to the needy.

While the entire valley resounded with laughter and merriment, a tearful Laadli sat in a dark corner of her room, weeping inconsolably. She had refused to attend the marriage ceremony despite the pleas of her friends. The sounds of laughter, music and revelry seemed to scorch her soul as she tried to block out the sounds of her mother's wedding. Firdaus found her lying in a heap on the floor the next morning.

As the days passed, Laadli felt increasingly miserable. Preoccupied with her new husband, Nur Jahan had no time for her lonely daughter. The couple spent endless hours in the beautiful gardens by the Dal Lake and Jhelum river, where distant shikaras bobbed in the placid waves. Jahangir, gazing at the snow-clad peaks of the distant mountain ranges, sighed with happiness.

'Kashmir has never been more beautiful to my eyes,' he declared ardently.

Kashmir was the emperor's favourite resort, and its saffron fields, undulating grasses specked with nodding blooms of daffodils, irises and roses had never appeared more enchanting to the emperor. The flock of exotic birds hovered around them, their colourful plumes brightening the surroundings. The tall chinar trees stood like sentinels at a distance. Fruit trees laden with cherry and apple blossoms sparkled from a distance. A cup of wine by his side and his Nur Jahan near him, the emperor wanted nothing more from the Almighty. He felt blissful and sated.

'The placid Jhelum, beautiful lakes, willow-shaded canals, deep green rice fields, wooden bridges across rivers, water lilies and lotus—these are the things that make this place so wonderful. This is a place I never want to leave. When I am in Kashmir, Agra and Lahore seem so miserable that the mere idea of going back to them depresses me.'

Nur Jahan sighed contentedly and snuggled closer to the emperor under the black marble pavilion. 'The heart is one held prisoner by beauty and perfection, a cry of "blessed" arises from the nightingale's soul.'

'Wah, wah, Nur, is that your couplet?'

The empress nodded modestly.

'I am thankful to Allah for giving me the most beautiful, intelligent woman on earth. What more could a man want? Nur, wine, and Kashmir, I have it all,' Jahangir sighed contentedly, burying his face in her bosom.

When he looked up, he saw Nur Jahan's brows knitted in concentration. 'What is it that troubles my queen?'

'I do not want to mar the perfection of your day with my problems,' she demurred.

'Don't I have the right to share your worries? Tell me what troubles your mind, begum.'

'It is Laadli, Your Majesty. She has taken this marriage badly. The child does not understand. She has locked herself in her room and refuses to speak to me.'

'I noticed her absence at our wedding. The child has lost her father and it is difficult for her to accept me. Don't worry, she will come around.' He soothed her brows and kissed her lovingly.

'She is a sensitive child, not given to expressing her feelings. Sometimes I feel I have failed her as a mother.'

'Begum, you are a wonderful mother. Laadli is only a child, I'm sure she will soon be happy about our marriage.'

Nur Jahan clung to him ardently and whispered: 'You are so wonderful. How will I ever repay you for all that you have done for me?'

His voice thick with passion, the emperor murmured in her ears, 'Just love me with your body and soul.'

While the royal couple wallowed in love, the nobles and courtiers immersed themselves in merriment. Wine, music, romance and beauty, these were the only things on everyone's mind. News about unrest in the south came as a shock to the emperor and his ministers. He quickly despatched Khurram to quell the rebellion and ordered the grand vizier to make arrangements to return to the capital. The honeymoon was over.

Reluctantly, the royal entourage made its way back to Agra, travelling through the dusty plains, its enormous size slowing it down.

10

Her sharp scream rang through the silent corridors of the harem, shaking up the slumbering occupants of the adjoining palaces. Her perspiring body felt cold and numb in the clammy July morning. Images of the nightmare she had had lingered in her mind. She wanted her mother to hold her tight, and comfort her. She didn't like sleeping alone in the large room, isolated from the rest of the harem by the walls that seemed to haunt her nights with ghostly visions.

Nightmares had haunted Laadli's regularly in the first year after her father's murder. Meherunnisa's constant closeness had helped her. She slept with her daughter, hugging her in the warmth of her breast. Slowly, Laadli had stopped having bad dreams. But now her mother was no longer by her side, the nightmares had returned to disturb her once again.

Firdaus slept on the floor near her but it was small consolation. The old woman, after a few pellets of opium, snored loudly through the night. Wistfully, Laadli recalled Burdwan, when both her parents were always with her. The past four years had been full of changes—a new environment, new friends and new lifestyle. Many adjustments had had to be made, but the constant company of her mother had made it easier for Laadli. Things had altered drastically in the past six months however; ever since her mother had got married to the emperor, she had become a stranger.

Everyday, Nur Jahan's influence increased as the besotted emperor became increasingly dependent on his wife, leaving important state decisions to her. For the first time in Mughal history, a queen was endowed with so much power. No grants of land was conferred upon any one except under her seal. The emperor granted Nur Jahan the rights of sovereignty and the imperial seal was handed over to her. On all firmans receiving the imperial signature, the name 'Nur Jahan, the Queen Begum', was jointly inscribed. She even sat by the emperor during his daily public appearances at the jharoka.

The emperor was happy to remain in the background and let the empress take over the running of the empire. When his advisors asked for decisions, he said, 'Let Nur Jahan rule, I require nothing beyond a seer of wine and half a seer of meat.'

Nur Jahan was aware that her daughter was not happy that she had married Jahangir, although Laadli had never dared to actually voice that opinion to her mother. But with an empire to take care of, she had no time to spend with her daughter, to try and make her understand, or even to adjust to the new situation.

Dazed after the alarming dream, the child ran out of her room, looking for her nurse. Firdaus was standing near the courtyard, wiping her face. *Why is Firdaus crying?* Laadli felt a stab of fear strike her heart. Something was wrong. She had never seen Firdaus cry, apart from when Sher Afghan had been killed.

'What happened? Why are you crying?'

'Nothing my child. I am not crying. A speck of dust fell into my eyes. Don't worry. Come, let me give you a wash, and then you can breakfast on the delicious keema parathas the bawarchi has made especially for you. You love them, don't you?'

'You are trying to hide something from me, Firdaus,' probed the girl. 'Tell me what happened, I insist.'

It has always been difficult to fool the girl, thought Firdaus. She was too intelligent and sensitive.

'Your mother has been imprisoned by royal order. The emperor will hold a public trial today,' she finally disclosed.

'But why? What has Ammi done?'

'It is all due to that stupid Chain of Justice the emperor installed. That terrible thing has not stopped ringing ever since it was set up,' Firdaus cursed bitterly. 'I knew something terrible was likely to happen, my left eye has been fluttering since yesterday morning.'

'But what has Ammi got to do with the Chain of Justice?' exclaimed the bewildered girl.

'Last night your Ammi and some concubines were walking on the terrace. As you know, the river Yamuna flows along the fort and during the night many wild animals come to drink water from the river. Everyone knows that your mother is a superb archer and most of the concubines are jealous of her skills. They wagered that she would not be able to shoot a target without seeing it. Nur Jahan declared that she was skilful at shabda bhedi—shooting an animal by the sound it makes while drinking water. Only the most capable archer can boast of this skill. Your mother should not have accepted the challenge.'

'She had to, they questioned her skills,' the girl said seriously.

'Your mother waited with her bow and arrow, listening for the lapping sound made by an animal. After a while there was a lapping sound and your mother shot an arrow.'

'Did it hit the animal?'

'Meherunnisa's arrow never misses its mark, but it was no animal; your mother had shot a poor washerman who had come to fill water in his pitcher. As he dipped the ewer in the water, it made a lapping sound and your mother shot in that direction. The poor man died on the spot. When the imperial servants were sent to bring back the target, they found the washerman with the arrow in his heart. His wife was called and she began wailing loudly, cursing the person who had killed her husband. When she learnt that it was none other than the empress, she tugged at the Chain of Justice to seek the emperor's judgement.'

'Ammi would never kill an innocent man consciously.'

'But the emperor is bound by his duties. He has promised impartial justice to anyone who calls for it, and now he has to prove that he can do so even when the accused is his favourite wife.'

'Where is my mother? I want to meet her.'

'You cannot meet her now. She is nazarband, under house arrest, in her palace. No one is allowed to meet her till the trial is over,' Firdaus sniffled pitifully.

'I will appeal to the emperor for mercy. He has to grant clemency to my mother! She is an empress.'

'Even empresses cannot kill people without reason. To pardon her will destroy the emperor's image. Only the Almighty can save the empress,' cried the woman.

Tears clouded Laadli's eyes. First her father and now the mother, was she destined to be an orphan?

'Can we attend the trial?' she asked.

'I think so. The trial will be held in the Diwan-é-Aam. Most of the royal ladies will be there to witness the trial.'

With heavy hearts the two made their way to the Hall of Commons, where the trial was scheduled to take place. The hall was bursting with people, all eager to watch the trial. Wagers were being laid on the final verdict: some said the emperor would not order the execution of his beloved wife, while others vouched for his determination to be fair. The hall had never witnessed such interest in a trial nor such crowds to hear a verdict.

Firdaus and Laadli tried to find a place in the balconies that lined the hall. The entire harem seemed to be there. The concubines, who numbered no less than 300, and the emperor's eighteen wives, were there to watch the trial. The Shah Begum, Jagat Gosain, occupied a vantage position. With her sat two other wives. The rest sat in different balconies with their attendants who fanned the ladies with peacock-feathered fans. Eunuchs guarded the entrances. Cool khus sherbet and lemonade were served in enamelled tumblers along with almonds, walnuts, fruits and sweets.

To the distraught child, it seemed as if the harem women saw the trial as entertainment. It seemed so cruel to be enjoying oneself while someone's life was at stake. Laadli looked at the women with hatred. Then she remembered what her mother had told her—'Laadli, my child, there are many women in the harem who hate me. They want to hurt me in any way possible because I have succeeded in rising to a position they can only dream about. In trying to hurt me they might hurt you in some way. You have to understand why they are so insecure and why they hate us so much.'

She recalled those words now. She didn't want any part of this. She despised the deviousness of the harem ladies. Laadli ached for a normal life in a normal home. Her gaze travelled across to the balcony where her mother sat, guarded by eunuchs. Nur Jahan knew she had more enemies than friends, and they would use every opportunity to seek her downfall. The only loyalty she could count on was from Firdaus and her own daughter. Laadli felt her heart lurch uncontrollably as she watched her mother's impassive face.

Down below in the hall, the attendant announced: 'Bashaksh, ba mulaija, hoshiar, shahenshahe alam badshah Jahangir padhar rahe hain.' The emperor walked in, followed by his nobles, ministers and advisors.

Laadli craned forward to have a better look. The emperor had dark circles under his eyes, evidence that he had spent a sleepless night grappling with his decision. He was in an unenviable position. But Laadli felt no sympathy. *Oh, how I hate him,* Laadli thought, clenching her fingers in a tight fist.

The trial began and a hushed silence fell over the crowded hall and the balconies. The washerman's wife was ordered to narrate her charges. The poor woman seemed too nervous to speak and cried inconsolably. The emperor waited patiently till she could talk.

'You have charged the Malika-e-Alam, Nur Jahan, with the murder of your husband. Is that true?' he asked gently.

The old hag continued to whimper pathetically. She had pulled the chain instinctively, without thinking of the consequences. Once she had entered the opulent hall and witnessed the crowd, the widow had lost all her courage.

'Speak woman. You have charged the empress with the murder of your husband and now you refuse to speak,' said one of the ministers. 'If you do not repeat your charge, you will be punished severely for falsely accusing the empress.'

There were many in the Mughal court who hated Nur Jahan. This was their chance to get rid of the powerful woman who ruled the empire by proxy.

Scared that she would be punished, the woman rattled out her statement. 'Jahanpanah, I am a poor woman. My husband washed clothes for a livelihood. We stay in a hovel near the river. The empress shot my husband—and now I have no one. I want justice.' She prostrated herself before the emperor.

'You shall have justice,' declared the emperor. 'What do you want? The law favours death penalty for murder. Blood for blood and death for death,' he announced gravely.

There was commotion in the hall as women began to wail and the men sighed. Laadli screamed and rushed forward but Firdaus grasped her and pulled her back.

'Reham, Shahenshah, reham,' cried the crowd begging the emperor for clemency on behalf of the empress.

The concubines, who had been stunned into silence, now looked fearfully at each other. The devious ones among them gloated at the prospect of getting rid of Nur Jahan, while the more compassionate ones had tears in their eyes. Many of them had her to thank for several acts of kindness. Queen Jagat Gosain's eyes misted with grief. She did not wish such a dire punishment for her rival, who had always been respectful to her.

The crowd appealed to the washerman's widow to retract her statement.

'Stupid woman, do you want the empress to be executed?' scolded the Khan-é-Khanan. 'What will you gain with her death? Ask for money in return so that your life can be comfortable and secure.'

The poor woman was so perplexed that she stood tongue-tied before the emperor, sobbing loudly. The crowd began chanting—'reham, reham, reham.'

Overwhelmed, she cried—'Jahanpanah, what will I do with the empress's life? It is of no use to me. My husband is dead and cannot be brought back to life with the life of the empress. I do not wish any harm to come to her.'

'Do not allow yourself to be swayed by the crowd. You have every right to ask for justice and I will do my best to grant it you. The empress has brought you grief by killing your mate; you have the right to bring her grief by taking my life. It is not the empress's life, but mine that I offer,' the emperor said at last.

There was a stunned silence in the hall. Behind the fretworked windows, a lament went up amidst the harem women.

'Jahanpanah, this is not possible. You must not offer your life in lieu of a washerman's life,' the Khan-é-Khana said. He turned towards the old woman and whispered—'Ask for money and be done with it, woman. This is the moment of judgement. If you ask for the Badshah's life, your life will not be spared by the loyal subjects of this country. But if you accept money, your name will be written in history as a merciful woman who pardoned a powerful empress.'

The woman looked nonplussed. She had not expected that the emperor would offer his life. This was the emperor's shrewd move to dissuade the woman from asking for Nur Jahan's life.

'Shahenshah-é-Alam, all merciful emperor, it is a colossal sin for me to ask for your life in lieu of my husband's. I want nothing but two square meals a day and some clothes to cover my body. I do not require any riches. I will take anything you offer me, but please release the empress. I take back my charges against her.'

A loud cheer went up in the hall as the crowd expressed its satisfaction.

'Are you sure?' the emperor asked once more. Life had crept back on his face and his eyes were dancing merrily now that he knew that Nur Jahan was absolved and he was free from any reproach that posterity may lay at his door.

'Release Malika-e-Alam and give this poor woman gold coins equivalent to the empress' weight,' ordered the emperor, giving his final verdict.

A loud cry of joy went up in the hall and Laadli began dancing with happiness. All around her women were chattering excitedly and congratulating each other. Queen Jagat Gosain discreetly wiped a tear from her eyes. There were loud murmurs of the emperor's greatness as the crowd in the hall melted away, their curiosity satisfied. Jahangir had emerged as an impartial emperor.

'I want to meet Ammijaan,' declared Laadli rushing towards the balcony where her mother stood receiving the congratulations of the harem women. Firdaus and Laadli pushed their way through the thronging crowds and reached Nur Jahan. Without waiting for any formalities Laadli threw herself into her mother's arms, her tears staining the pristine white dress of her mother. 'Don't ever allow anyone to see your tears, Laadli,' she patted the tearful child. 'They will presume you are a weak person and take advantage. You have to remain strong. There will be many incidents of this kind in the palace. Don't let them break you,' Nur Jahan told her daughter.

It was advice Laadli was not likely to forget in a hurry.

For days after the incident, the girl followed her mother like a shadow. Laadli was determined not to let the empress out of her sight. Early in the morning, when the empress stepped into her hamamgah, the girl would sit patiently in a corner watching her mother being massaged by her attendants. She would take in the details of the unguents and lotions that were used to keep her mother's skin glowing. Her keen eyes noted the different kinds of cosmetics used. There were specially prepared herbal oils, in which basil and hibiscus flowers had been boiled to bring sheen and prevent greying of hair. A special concoction of soap nuts, shikakai and gooseberries was used to shampoo the tresses.

The elaborate bath rituals seemed an inordinate bother to the girl who spent no time on her own toilette and resented the fuss created by her nurse. Wide-eyed, she watched her mother step into the marble tank filled with rose petals and overflowing with sparkling water heated to just the right temperature, while a slave rubbed and washed her body with scented soap.

When she stepped out of her bath, the servants flocked to cover her body from the gaze of the girl as they wiped it dry with fragrant towels. The empress lay down on a marble bench while a brazier filled with sandalwood incense, covered with a cane basket, was laid under her head to dry her hair.

After her bath Nur Jahan made her way to the prayer room. An onyx bookstand with her Quran stood in the centre of the room, with incense censers around it. Lighting up the agar and sandalwood joss sticks, Nur Jahan settled down to pray. This was one ritual that the empress never took lightly, for she was a devout woman whose faith had given her the throne of a magnificent empire.

From the prayer room they walked to the empress' chamber, where the attendants waited with petitions from destitute women and orphans. The empress had a soft corner for widowed women and their children—perhaps because of her earlier plight—and she spared no effort to help them. Nur Jahan had arranged the marriage of many orphan girls. Laadli was amazed at the efficient manner in which her mother handled all kinds of problems. Whoever asked for her protection was given refuge.

To the nine-year-old Laadli, her mother's virtues knew no bounds. She worshipped the ground her mother walked on: she followed her around like a tame dog, waiting for the crumbs of affection thrown at her by the empress. When Nur Jahan was busy with state affairs—which was most of the time—the girl wandered around the harem corridors, uncertain and unsure of herself. Laadli had neither the self-assurance nor the bravado to handle her new status as a princess. Although the emperor had stated that Laadli would be known as Shahzadi, and conferred upon her a tiny jagir after his marriage to Nur Jahan, she knew that the other princesses of the harem sniggered and called her the usurper's daughter. They called her mother the Persian usurper and a Persian whore.

'Can a Persian vagabond's daughter be a princess, even if the emperor grants her the title? Princesses are not made; they inherit the title when they are born in royal families,' Laadli once heard Princess Zohra Banu remarking to a friend.

With so many real princesses floating around in the harem, no one bothered about a surrogate one.

The frightened girl—who still cowered each time she was brought in the presence of the emperor—struggled to keep up a brave front, her mother's words ringing in her ears: 'Don't let them break your spirit.'

She tried hard to emulate the royal ladies, aping the ways and manners of the princesses. She watched her mother closely, although she realised that no one could ever imitate her mother's powerful presence. Whether it was the nobles who came with their representations regarding some problem, the artists who came to her for guidance, or the harem women who wanted her counsel, everyone went back satisfied with her judgement. The emperor seemed to require her guidance on every matter, from English and Portuguese trading contracts to the layout of a new garden. Her vibrant energy, diplomatic excellence, perception, shrewdness, calculative intelligence, artistic skills—everything seemed to have an overpowering effect on Jahangir. Those who dealt with her either hated or loved her, but no one could ignore her.

'I can't help feeling sorry for the girl. It is no fault of hers that she is born to an ambitious woman like Nur Jahan,' Queen Jagat Gosain had been heard remarking. For, now that Meherunnisa was empress, she had transferred her attentions to ensuring that her daughter would inherit the title one day.

The idea seemed to obsess the empress. 'You *will* be an empress one day. No one can stop you from becoming one. I will ensure your ascendancy to the throne, if that is the last thing that I do.'

It frightened Laadli to hear her mother's words. Wasn't it for Allah to decide who would be a queen? How could a mere mortal control destiny or create royalty? Whatever be her powers, wasn't the empress just another puppet in the hands of the Almighty? Besides, Laadli had no desire to be an empress; she didn't even want to be a princess. But there was no way she could tell her mother that. How could she describe to her mother the joy she felt sitting in the marble pavilion overlooking the river, enjoying the gentle breeze and the flitting butterflies? Or tell her that she only wanted to play the sitar. Fine dresses, jewellery and cosmetics didn't interest her. The crown held no lure for her.

She pined for the open spaces and the luxuriant banana trees, mango groves, waving palm fronds, and the jackfruit trees with their cloying smell that had dotted the countryside of their Burdwan residence. She missed the soulful songs of the cuckoo, flamboyant parakeets, lark's warble and the spirited chirping of the birds that nested in the trees. In her mind, she could see the black darters that combed the rice fields for food.

At Burdwan, she had had the freedom to wander around the large farm at the back of their house, searching for the different kinds of nests built by the birds on the trees. She remembered how she had marvelled at the lovely nest made by a weaverbird in a mango tree. A servant had offered to bring it down for her, but she had told him not to. She hated seeing any bird or animal hurt. Sher Afghan had once presented her a pair of canaries in a golden cage when he realised how much she loved birds. But Laadli had set them free. 'I am sure they don't like being caged,' she told her father.

'You are right, no one likes being imprisoned,' he responded. 'I think I know what will please you,' he added mysteriously. A few days later he had given her an album filled with pictures of birds, drawn by a local artist. It became one of her prized possessions, and she carried it with her wherever she went. Over the years, Laadli had added pictures of different birds to it.

Laadli spent hours day-dreaming. Not for her were the many amusements that occupied the inmates of the harem. 'The girl has a romantic nature,' exclaimed her mother when she caught Laadli reading the Persian poetry of Sa'adi. To keep her daughter occupied, Nur Jahan arranged for tutors to teach her Persian, Arabic, Turkish and Urdu. Besides, there were lessons in painting, literature and music.

With the passing years, as Nur Jahan's responsibilities increased, so did the time between her meetings with her daughter. Sometimes it was weeks before they saw each other. Firdaus could see that Nur Jahan's preoccupation with state matters was affecting the girl, and it upset her. One day, during one of her visits to Laadli's apartments, Nur Jahan sauntered over to the balcony from where she could see her daughter sitting in the garden.

'How quickly the years have flown by, Firdaus. Laadli seems so grown up,' she said, a tinge of regret in her voice. 'I have not been around for her.'

'You have no time for your daughter. I can't understand what the point is in involving yourself in all kinds of matters. Can't the gardens be left to the architects and designers? Aren't there enough ministers to think about the empire?' Firdaus complained.

There was a sudden flash of anger in Nur Jahan's eyes. The empress did not tolerate advice. 'Mind your own business Firdaus, and let me mind mine.'

Realising that she had overstepped her limits, Firdaus bowed herself out of the empress's presence, muttering under her breath as she walked down the corridor. 'What is the point in designing palaces and running an empire if one doesn't have any time to spend with one's only child? My suggestions rankle because they are blunt.'

At another of their rare meetings, the ten-year-old Laadli asked her mother, 'Is there anything you can't do?'

Nur Jahan was sitting propped against some cushions in her bed. The empress was unwell. For Laadli, it was a special occasion—just the two of them sitting together, without any distractions.

'Of course, there are so many things I wish I could do but don't have the time. For instance, I love music and would have loved to take lessons in singing from an Ustaad.'

'People say that it is your ready wit and fantastic sense of humour that has the emperor enthralled. I wonder how you can remember the vast number of jokes, anecdotes and riddles.'

'You can do whatever you want, provided you want it enough. Just remember those words, Laadli. I expect that someday you will be able to do the things I can do and your child will wonder at your inexhaustible capacities,' laughed the empress, pinching her daughter's cheek lovingly.

She drew her daughter close and hugged her tight. Guilt and remorse ran through her as she kissed the girl's forehead with affection. 'Laadli, you must remember that I love you very much. I may not spend much time with you, but you're always on my mind and I am doing everything I can for your future and happiness.'

'Of course, Ammijaan, I know you love me. It is just...it is just that I get a little lonely sometimes.'

'You must make more friends and devote more time to the arts. No one is lonely when they read or create. It is only the uncreative who indulge in gossip.'

The warmth of her mother's tone pleased Laadli. She sighed loudly, wishing the moment would never pass. It was as though Nur Jahan had read her thoughts, for she continued to hold her daughter in a tight embrace.

Although it was now six years since she had come to stay in the palace, Laadli continued to feel intimidated by the palace and its inhabitants. The harem was divided into many groups—the Rajput clique, the Persian faction, the Hindustani Muslim bloc—and she belonged to none of them. No one spoke to her—she was an outsider, the daughter of the empress, to be avoided and kept at a distance. Since no one could afford to offend the empress, the women who disliked Nur Jahan vented their resentment on the daughter. Unkind remarks came her way almost every day.

Laadli waited for festivals because then she could escape to her grandparents' home and rejoice in the warmth of the large family. She was particularly close to her grandmother and her cousin, Arjumand. They mimicked the queens and concubines, laughed, bantered and poured their hearts out to each other.

11

Marriage had changed Jahangir. With Nur Jahan by his side, he became a different person—generous, tolerant, and good-humoured. Gone was the tyrannical, sadistic man who had derived pleasure witnessing cruel torture sessions. He now spent more time in pursuit of the finer things of life—music, arts and architecture became his passion.

On Eid, Jahangir granted freedom of movement to the captive prince Khusrau. The semi-blind prince was allowed to ramble around the palace with an escort. But it was Prince Khurram who benefited the most from his father's change of heart. One evening, the emperor invited the prince to his chamber and shared a drink with him. This was a rare honour. In fact, it implied the emperor's permission for the request of a gift. Not willing to let the chance slip away, Prince Khurram asked for the gift of Arjumand's hand in marriage.

'Your Majesty, I have been waiting for your consent to marry the daughter of your trusted vizier, Asaf Khan, for a long time now. I beseech you to consider the match favourably.'

Inebriated with wine and happiness, the emperor smiled benignly at his son. 'I can understand the agony of waiting. I waited for many years to marry the woman I love.'

'I don't want to spend the prime years of my life pining for Arjumand. I married the Persian princess on your command, what else can I do to please you, father?'

'No, you don't have to spend any more time pining for her. We are pleased to sanction your wedding with the lady of your choice.'

The news spread like wildfire in the palace. The emperor had conceded to the match. Khurram and Arjumand would be wedded at last. Nur Jahan decided she would personally make her favourite niece's bridal attire and jewellery. Nur Jahan was fond of Prince Khurram and the two had formed an alliance of sorts, despite the tension that occurred when Prince Khurram had stonewalled her attempts to get him married to Laadli. Nur Jahan had now begun considering marrying Laadli to Prince Khusrau.

From the jharoka, pushed and jostled by excited harem women, Laadli watched Prince Khurram, resplendent in his bridal finery, riding a bejewelled white stallion. Slaves strew his path with rose petals, and sprayed perfumed water from silver sprinklers. A band of musicians dressed in brilliant clothes, followed the royal groom. The crowd cheered lustily and scattered petals in the path of the long wedding procession comprising hundreds of horses, elephants, soldiers and nobles.

The pageant wound its way through the streets of Agra towards the bride's mansion leaving clouds of dust and dazzle in its wake. Gold and silver coins were thrown to the eager spectators who lined up the streets to catch a glimpse of the emperor's son, who was finally marrying the woman he loved.

The story of Khurram and Arjumand's romance was as popular as the one of Laila and Majnu.

With a heavy heart Laadli retired to her chamber. She was about to lose the affections of Khurram, the only male friend she had ever had. Would he ever find time for her, wondered the girl.

'Don't you want to attend the wedding?' asked her excited friends, 'We are all going with the procession.'

'I don't think I will go. I am not feeling well.'

'Don't be stupid. It is not every day that a prince gets married. Besides, it is your cousin Arjumand's wedding. She will be an empress one day and then she will recollect that you did not share her joy on the most important day of her life.'

'To be truthful, I would have felt offended if I were her. Besides, the empress wouldn't like your not attending the wedding,' said Benazir.

Fearing her mother's wrath, Laadli finally agreed to attend the wedding. There was a bustle of excitement as the harem women dressed up for the occasion. Nur Jahan had already left for the wedding venue early in the morning, laden with costly gifts for the bride. Hers was a dual role, for she was both the groom's stepmother and the bride's aunt. Arjumand had to be bathed and the ritualistic toilette of a bride had to be completed with the assistance of her aunt, before the ceremonies began.

'Laadli, don't loiter and day dream. We should have reached your grandfather's house by now,' Benazir goaded.

Laadli stood undecided between a green ensemble and a shell pink one. Her mother had designed the gorgeous dresses for the occasion—one for the morning rituals and the other for the evening feast. Alongside the dress, Firdaus had laid out the matching jewellery and accessories.

'Let me help you dress,' offered her friend picking up the green costume.

'No, not that one. I will wear the pink one,' said Laadli, snatching the dress away from Benazir. She remembered the occasion when both Arjumand and she had worn a green dress at their grandfather's house to celebrate Eid.

Hurriedly, she dressed in the shell pink silk qaba embroidered with pink pearls. A pink churidar, and a crimson veil embroidered with silver thread work completed the attire. For jewellery, she wore diamond and amethyst encrusted earrings that reached to her shoulders, their pearl extensions pinned into her hair. A string of pink pearls rested on her hair, its crescent shaped diamond pendant falling gently on her temple. Her slender neck was adorned with a collar of gold ablaze with rubies and diamonds. Her arms were clasped with broad bands of gold inlaid with precious gems. Dozens of gold bangles tinkled on her wrists and her anklets jangled musically when she walked.

Benazir braided Laadli's hair and stuck rose buds in each twist of the hair. Her eyes were darkened with kohl and her lips coloured with a red salve.

'You look beautiful,' Benazir declared, standing back to admire the result of her labour. 'But why do your eyes have sadness in them? A smile would certainly suit you better.'

'Does it matter how I look, Benazir? We both know that these looks are not good enough to attract the attention of the princes. If I were beautiful, wouldn't I be getting married to Prince Khurram today, instead of my cousin, Arjumand?'

'Hush, don't say such things. Destiny plans things for us; nothing can happen unless Allah wants it to happen. Not even a leaf can stir without His wish. There are better things lying in wait for you,' the faithful Benazir consoled her friend. 'Now, let us hurry before people miss us. We will enter from the back gate and mingle with the ladies. The empress will be very angry if she learns that you did not arrive on time.'

The girls climbed into a festooned palanquin and rushed towards the bride's house. They were just in time to see the prince entering the house with his entourage.

The groom was led to the nuptial podium decorated with strands of jasmine and rose buds. Mullahs seated on the side recited from the holy Quran, their eyes not wavering for a moment from the text. The emperor showered a handful of diamonds, rubies, emeralds, gold and silver coins and many other precious stones on his son's head. A large platter, full of gold and silver coins, was thrown to the beggars who lined the streets outside the house, after it had been touched by the groom.

Laadli rushed inside and joined the giggling women who were leading Arjumand towards the wedding dais. The mammoth hall had been divided into two—one for men and the other for women—separated by a screen made with strings of flowers.

The bride was glowing with happiness. Her bright eyes were lowered modestly as she walked across to the bedecked podium, surrounded by the harem women. As she passed Laadli, she looked up and gave her a mischievous wink. Laadli smiled and returned the wink. Her cousin looked stunning in a midnight-blue attire, embedded with tiny diamonds and pearls, winking like a million stars on a dark night. A silver veil obscured her radiant face.

'Are you nervous?' whispered Laadli. Arjumand's hands were chillingly cold.

'Oh, Laadli, at last you are here! I am so nervous—my hands just won't stop trembling. Is this how brides feel on their wedding day? My heart is beating so hard I can barely breathe.'

'I guess all brides go through this experience. Don't worry, this feeling will last for a couple of hours and then you will be flushed with happiness.'

'I wonder if he's feeling the same way,' mumbled the bride stealing a glance towards the other end of the hall where the prince was sitting.

'I don't think men feel the same way,' announced her practical cousin. 'They are much too engrossed in ribald talk. I do hope you are happy.'

'I don't have the words to express my happiness. It has been a long wait. Laadli, wish me luck and pray that I am never parted from him,' Arjumand's hennaed hands clasped hers tightly.

'Of course. I want you to be happy.'

The two girls walked side-by-side, Laadli much younger but taller than her cousin, her serene loveliness a foil to the dazzling Arjumand. Their steps were sure as they walked—Arjumand towards her destiny and Laadli towards the beginning of a new chapter in her life. For the first time she realised that nothing was permanent in life—friends, circumstances, riches or parental love. Her heart ached with this insight. Even her mother's affections could not be taken for granted anymore. The umbilical cord had snapped long ago.

12

It was early summer and the emperor was at Ajmer, the city of the great Sufi saint, Khwaja Muin-ud-din Chisti. It was said that, while returning from a hunt in the forests near Ajmer, Emperor Akbar—resting near a tree—heard songs of wandering minstrels praising the saint. The mendicants lauded the greatness of the saint and spoke about his mystical powers. Hearing them, the emperor decided to seek the saint's blessings. Akbar was so impressed by the great saint, that he refused to take any major decisions without consulting Chisti.

After the birth of Jahangir, Akbar—in gratitude for the saint's blessings—walked for seventeen days from Agra to Ajmer. Jahangir himself made an annual pilgrimage to the city.

But Jahangir had another reason for being in Ajmer this year. Prince Khurram had returned to the family fold after conquering Mewar, which had been a thorn in the emperor's flesh for a long time. The link between the fertile Gangetic plains and the emporiums of trade on the Western coast passed through Mewar. So long as Mewar was independent, the merchants of the Delhi Empire could not expect adequate security of person and property on the highways.

The proud Rana of Mewar laid down a few conditions before he submitted to the Mughal emperor. He wanted the withdrawal of the Mughal garrison from Mewar, a pledge that the Mughals would honour the sanctity of the shrine of Eklingji, and lastly, that the Rana would be recognised as a sovereign prince within the borders of Mewar. The vanquished Rana also asked that no girl from the Rana's family would ever be demanded in marriage by any Mughal, and that their heirlooms would be returned.

Jahangir acceded to all the conditions, but insisted that Prince Karan Singh, along with his son Jagat Singh, should attend the Mughal court in lieu of the Rana. It was Karan Singh who arrived to render homage to the Mughal ruler, along with his nobles. Emperor Jahangir sent Prince Khurram, with his most important ministers, to receive the scion of Mewar. The grand entourages met outside the city gates and then traversed the dusty lanes of Ajmer to arrive at the emperor's residence. The spectators were being treated to one of the greatest events to have ever taken place in that town.

Kettledrums boomed and joyous shouts followed the young prince of Mewar as he rode through the streets. People showered his path with rose petals. In a rare gesture, Jahangir stepped down from his throne and crossed the hall to meet Prince Karan. Nur Jahan, seated behind the marble screen watched incredulously, as the emperor escorted Karan Singh to a seat of honour to the right of the throne. This was an unprecedented honour given to a defeated prince. From her vantage point, Laadli watched the proud Rajputs taking their seats in the durbar hall.

'Who is the victor and who are the vanquished? The Rajputs seem to be honouring us with their presence,' she whispered to her friend.

Grand celebrations followed the signing of a historic treaty. The empress had outdone herself in arranging the festivities. The best of food, wine and entertainment were laid out, surpassing any other festivity witnessed by the town of Ajmer.

Two days after the grand celebrations, there was another event to celebrate. The entire harem was buzzing—Laadli had come of age. From a child to an adolescent, the princess had blossomed unnoticed by the inmates of the royal zenana. 'Late bloomer,' some of the harem women sniggered behind her back. Laadli was almost twelve, a little too late to mature by their calculations.

To celebrate the occasion, Nur Jahan decided to hold a feast for ladies of the harem. The most exquisite tapestries were brought out and hung on the walls. Bright Kashmiri carpets covered the marble floors and fresh flowers were placed in the jade and porcelain vases that lined the courtyard. Silver incense containers were placed in the empress' chamber, along with bright silk cushions embellished with pearls and sequins. Festoons and decorations were put up on all the pillars that surrounded the chamber. Musicians were called and nautch girls invited to perform for the evening.

Laadli, meanwhile, was bathed with saffron and milk after her body was massaged with unguents made out of almonds and cream. Her hair was washed and dried over the fragrant smoke of sandalwood sticks. Her hands and feet were embellished with intricate designs of henna, and her eyes were carefully lined with fresh kohl. Strands of jasmine and roses were wrapped around her plaited hair and rose attar, especially made by her grandmother, was liberally sprinkled over her body. She was now ready to wear the beautiful dress designed by her mother.

The purple and pink striped trousers were topped with a diaphanous knee-length qaba in lavender, embroidered with small roses in dark purple and set with tiny amethyst stones. Nur Jahan seemed to favour the colour purple for her daughter. Left to herself, Laadli would have preferred to wear soft colours like ivory, shell pink or white. The lilac silk veil was held in place with a gold tiara set with diamonds. Her tiny waist was clasped with an ornamental belt—a gift from the empress. On her slender throat Laadli wore a necklace made of pink Basra pearls. A hair ornament made of diamonds dangled on her right temple. Gold bangles jingled on her slender wrists, and a solitaire glittered on her nose.

The queens and concubines strolled in to take their place on the assigned carpets, carrying gifts for the princess. Nur Jahan's sharp eyes evaluated each gift to ascertain the level of allegiance to her. There were gold coins, pearl strings, diamond brooches and gold necklaces studded with precious stones. Yards of silk and velvet lay scattered along with embellished hand mirrors and perfume bottles.

Laadli felt suffocated with the attention. Her jewellery and clothes felt heavy on her body. If she were not the centre of attention, the circus around her would have amused her. But now, the music, chatter and the vulgar jokes irritated her. She wished she could escape from it all. It was all so tedious, to be smiling at women she knew disliked her. The harem women just needed an excuse to celebrate. Laadli would have given anything to escape to her grandfather's house for the day. But that was not to be.

'Tonight I have invited the emperor and his sons for the feast. I want you to dress up in your best clothes. Amreen will help you dress. I want you to pay special attention to Prince Khusrau, Laadli. I don't want any trouble, is that clear? No running away to the garden or ignoring the prince. He is going to be the next emperor and I want you to impress him.' Her mother's instructions were loud and clear—Laadli was to flirt with the prince. She knew that her mother was trying to make a match between the two of them. She intended making an empress out of her daughter.

'Did you hear me, Laadli?' Her mother's voice took on the ice-cold tone she was so familiar with.

The morning entertainment ended with a grand feast that sated the women. Stuffing their mouths with fragrant *paans* they complimented the empress for the arrangements as they sauntered back heavily to their chambers.

There would be a short reprieve for Laadli, before the evening function began. Nur Jahan had made meticulous arrangements for the evening, with music, dance, amusements, ending with a feast. Only the emperor, his Shah Begum, the princes and their wives, were invited. It was to be a close-knit family function. The empress did not want any distractions while she thrust her reticent daughter onto the unwilling blind prince. Khusrau, happily married to Rukhsana, was most reluctant to have anything to do with Laadli. He had always behaved like an indulgent elder brother and treated her like a child.

The empress, however, had not given up. She intended him to marry Laadli only because she knew that he was the most likely successor to the emperor. Nur Jahan tried to seduce the prince with promises of freedom and hinted at the possibility of her support in the matter of inheritance, if he married her daughter.

The idea had come suddenly to Nur Jahan just a couple of days earlier when she visited her father. 'I have been toying with an idea for a long time now,' she declared, seating herself amidst the soft silk cushions on the comfortable divan in his study. Illustrated copies of all kinds of books lay scattered around the room. She picked up a copy of the Quran, beautifully bound, and read through the first page, waiting for her father's reaction.

Ghias Baig shot her a quizzical look. He was familiar with his daughter's quirks and impulsive decisions. *What now*, he thought, taking in Nur Jahan's opulent attire and bejewelled appearance. *She has changed so much. I can't find my Meherunnisa among the jewels and royal trappings. Malika Nur Jahan is a stranger.* He sighed wistfully.

Patiently, he waited for the empress to speak.

'Don't you think it would be a good idea if Laadli were to be wedded to Khusrau?' she asked, toying with the quill that lay on his writing desk.

The old man was stunned. 'Marry Laadli to that blind, unfortunate man who is living on borrowed breaths? Even Allah has abandoned the wretched fellow. Mehru, his days are numbered. Don't you know that your brother, Asaf, and Khurram are waiting to murder the man? He is the only obstacle in the path of Khurram's accession to the throne.'

'I know everything. There is not a thing in this empire that I don't get to know. I am aware that Asaf and Khurram will try to murder Khusrau. But don't forget he is still the eldest son of the emperor.'

'If only that old fool, Aziz Koka, Khusrau's father-in-law and his uncle, Raja Maan Singh, had not been so impatient to make him an emperor, Khusrau would have ascended the throne after the emperor's demise,' the minister sighed deeply. Like most people, he was fond of the prince. His tragic plight saddened the Mirza.

'He can still be an emperor,' stated his daughter enigmatically. 'If he marries Laadli, I will champion his cause. He is young, intelligent and popular. He can be the next emperor if he collaborates with me. But the young fool does not want to listen to good advice.'

'Mehru, my child, you must not involve yourself in the royal squabbles. You must remain steadfast in helping the emperor deliver justice to those who deserve it, without any ulterior motives. Advise the emperor to do the right thing,' begged the Itmad-ud-daulah. But his words fell on deaf ears.

When did this change take place? he wondered. *When did his daughter transform into the ambitious and ruthless queen who stood before him. Was this the child Asmat had borne in the harsh desert of Qandahar?* Ghias Baig shook his head dejectedly. She wouldn't listen! She never did. His heart turned cold with premonition as he watched Nur Jahan stride out imperiously from his chamber, without a backward glance.

Amidst the rejoicing and the dancing of the audacious nautch girls, Nur Jahan watched the blind prince groping his way through the hall to reach his brother's side.

Moments later she beckoned Laadli and said—'Offer some wine to the princes. See that they are comfortable.'

Reluctantly, Laadli made her way to the princes.

'Come Laadli, join us,' invited Rukhsana, seated by Khusrau's side. She liked the girl. There was no guile in her.

'Did your mother ask you to come here?' asked Khusrau, laughing loudly. 'The scheming bitch.' His mouth drooped with bitterness and he shook his head and repeated, 'The most venomous adder sits on the royal treasury. Does that satisfy her? Of course not; she needs to control each and every breath inhaled in the palace.'

Laadli was shocked. She threw a terrified look at her mother, but Nur Jahan was busy feeding grapes to the inebriated emperor who was lying prone on her lap. If she had heard the comments, she displayed no signs of having done so.

'Well spoken brother, just don't let her hear you or you will not go back to your prison. She holds the slender reins of your life. It is up to her to snap the thread at any moment she desires,' warned Prince Khurram.

'You won't miss me, brother. I am sure that would delight you more than anything else in the world,' retorted Khusrau.

'Enough, enough, please don't quarrel,' Rukhsana intervened. 'Let us talk of pleasant things. Prince Khurram, when are we to hear the good news?'

Arjumand was in labour.

'Any moment now. In fact, I should check on her.' Khurram left the party in haste, glad to find an excuse to leave the depressing company of his brother.

Khusrau turned to Laadli—'So, your mother wants me to marry you? To save my life, I must succumb to her majesty's desire?'

He was in a foul mood.

'I don't mind marrying you if it will save your life,' confided Laadli. 'It must be terrible to remain imprisoned for so long.'

She liked Khusrau and pitied him. Like Khurram, Khusrau had been kind to the friendless girl when she had entered the harem. Laadli remembered the day he had rescued her from the clutches of heartless harem girls who were teasing her mercilessly. He had warned them of dire reprisal if they dared to tease his sister. The girls kept away after his threat.

'Poor child! I wish your mother were half as kind as you. How could a nice child like you have emerged from her wicked womb?' Laadli flinched at his words.

Khusrau patted her hand affectionately. 'No dear Laadli, I couldn't marry you to save my life. My days on this planet are numbered, thanks to your mother's plotting. You deserve someone who will take good care of you.'

'But I really don't mind marrying you,' insisted Laadli.

'I do. Brave princes do not hide behind petticoats of women; they face their punishment with courage. If I have to die, I will die honourably, but I shall not succumb to the tricks of that vile woman who has reduced my father to a mumbling idiot.'

'I do not want you to die.'

'Pray for me, Laadli, the odds are stacked too high against me. Not just your mother, but my brother and his father-in-law also wish me dead. If it is written in my destiny that I should die young, I will,' he ended philosophically.

His dark mood overwhelmed Laadli. 'How can you bear to listen to all this and remain cheerful?' she asked Rukhsana. 'Does it not depress you?'

'Is there any point in being depressed about it? Should I spoil the few moments that I have with him? No, Laadli, I am trying to enjoy the time that remains for us and then I shall leave the world with him,' Rukhsana smiled gently at the wretched girl. 'Tell me what happened to your desire to learn sitar?' she asked, changing the subject. Everyone in the harem knew about Laadli's fascination for the instrument. 'Did you find a tutor?'

'Not yet, I am still trying to persuade my mother to find me a good teacher. I did find one but lost her soon enough.'

'And how did that happen?' asked Khusrau.

'Jabeen, the daughter of our Meer Samaan, can play the instrument reasonably well. She agreed to teach me the basic lessons. Just after we began the lessons, she fell prey to Prince Shahryar's attentions. I lost a teacher and he gained a lover. So ended my lessons.' A wry smile flashed on Laadli's face as she recollected the incident.

Khusrau guffawed at her words. No one knew his indolent, half-witted younger brother better than he. Prince Shahryar was always surrounded by his cronies, drinking, or spending time with the harem women and slave girls. He had no time for intellectual efforts.

'Next time, try to find a male tutor. That way, you will not lose your teacher to Shahryar.'

'Who can be sure?' commented Rukhsana, meaningfully. Rumours of Shahryar's sexual preferences abounded in the harem.

The three of them broke into laughter and the clouds of depression seemed to lift momentarily.

'I want an honest reply to my question,' Laadli suddenly turned serious. 'Would you have married me if I were beautiful?'

Her question took them by surprise, and the couple exchanged troubled glances. They knew that Laadli suffered from low self-esteem.

'Who said you are not beautiful, Laadli? You are very pretty and only a fool will refuse to marry you,' Rukhsana consoled her.

'That is not true...' the girl said tearfully.

Laadli was not conventionally beautiful. With her lanky, long limbs, she stood out among the other women and that made her so self-conscious that she had begun to stoop. Her lack of self-assurance and over-sensitive nature made things worse for her. Besides, she never bothered about her appearance, nor made any attempts to look pretty.

Rukhsana looked the girl over critically and wished Laadli would submit herself to the harem women. They could make anyone look glamorous. A little shaping would have helped the straight brows over her sensitive, deep eyes. She had beautiful grey eyes that could make any man swoon if she learned to use them to advantage. The gentle-hearted woman wished she could take the girl under her wings, but she dreaded the empress.

'Do you know what is wrong with you, Laadli?' Khusrau held out his hand to her. 'You are too critical of yourself. Give yourself a chance. Both Khurram and I are in love with other women. It is not because you are not beautiful. Besides, I am blind and too old for you! Why do you torment yourself with such ideas? Let me assure you that you are a very pretty girl and any man would love to marry you. Anyway, you are too young to be worrying about all this.'

'I am not too young. Khurram was in love with Arjumand from the time she was my age,' Laadli was petulant. 'And how do I convince my mother who believes that I repel men.'

'Does your mother really believe that?' Rukhsana was appalled.

From her end, the empress watched them and wondered what they were talking about. She could see the forlorn face of her daughter and thought that Khusrau was not being kind to her. Seething inwardly, she gently pushed her sleeping husband to a side and made her way towards them.

Laadli noticed and quickly escaped before her mother could reach them. Outside in the garden, she sat on a bench amidst the rose bushes and gave vent to her tears, her slender body shaking uncontrollably with sobs. In her misery she remembered her adoring father, Sher Afghan. There were very few moments when Laadli did not miss him, and still fewer moments when she did not hate her stepfather. As for her mother, it was difficult for the lonely and miserable girl to decide whether she loved or hated her.

It was a glorious morning when Arjumand Bano gave birth to a beautiful daughter. They called her Jahanara, Jewel of the World. The delighted prince walked all the way to Salim Chisti's dargah in thanks and distributed gold and silver coins to beggars.

Ajmer was witness to so many happy events occurring simultaneously, that the palace reverberated with constant celebrations and activity. The victory of the Mughal troops over the Maharana of Mewar, and the birth of Prince Khurram's first child—it was a glorious period, to be celebrated and enjoyed. Convinced that the town of Ajmer, with the holy dargah situated in it, was lucky for him, the emperor decided to stay there for a longer period.

The emperor loathed Agra for many reasons, one of them was his belief that the city was unhealthy. Jahangir had been having breathing problems and he believed that the climate at Agra aggravated this ailment. 'Sometimes I feel that I should shift my capital from Agra to Ajmer or Lahore. Agra is definitely not lucky for me.'

'What about Kashmir? I thought that was the place closest to your heart,' teased Nur Jahan.

'Ah! Kashmir! That is a heavenly place. But begum, one can't rule the country from Kashmir.'

Those were happy times and even the empress took time off to relax from her vigil. There were no rebellions to control, no wars to wage, peace prevailed in the empire.

The emperor spent more time writing his memoirs, noting each event with painstaking zeal. A pair of Sarus cranes that had been captured when they were just a month old, travelled with the emperor wherever he went. He had named them Laila and Majnu. The emperor watched their growth and habits with great interest. Royal artists had been instructed to draw images of the two cranes at every stage and the chronologists had been commanded to record each move of the pair.

The emperor fretted continuously about the cranes because they showed no inclination to mate. When the cranes were about five years old, they finally decided to oblige the emperor. A soldier, who had been commanded to monitor their movements, carried the happy news to the emperor.

Rushing to the birds, the emperor and his artist watched the pair with eager eyes as they performed an elaborate mating dance. Pirouetting gracefully around each other Laila and Majnu romanced, blissfully unaware of the watchful eyes. The birds alternately circled around each other with opened wings, bowed their heads and leapt into the air. Then they mated. The emperor was delighted. He described the mating ritual in great detail in his diary.

When Laila laid her first egg, Jahangir recorded the date, size and the description of the egg. The emperor was passing more and more time in such activities, leaving the task of ruling the empire in the hands of his empress.

One evening, as the emperor sat with Nur Jahan in the garden, under a canopy of stars, he asked her—'Malika, what is the item that is circulated the most in our empire?'

The empress thought for a moment and then replied—'The Imperial coins, of course! They travel from hand to hand, from trader to the common man and know no boundaries or religion.'

Jahangir was delighted. 'As usual, you are right. Indeed, it is the coins that represent the ruler's power. I have been toying with the idea of redesigning the coins. Right from my grandfather to this day, there has been little change in their appearance. Don't you think it is time we made some changes?'

'What does the emperor have in mind?' asked Nur Jahan, enthused about the idea.

'I thought that in place of the month, the coins could carry a figure of the constellation which belongs to the month. For instance, the figure of a ram could be engraved in the coins released in the month of Farwardin, and the coins released in the month of Urdbihist could carry the figure of a bull on them.'

'What a wonderful idea! Let me design the series of coins. They will be so beautiful that people will want to possess and retain them instead of just trading with them.'

The coins were designed and struck in the royal mints. The special coins were released on the emperor's birthday and found immediate approval amongst people. They were exchanged for twenty times higher than their face value and, as Nur Jahan had predicted, people began hoarding them.

The nobles were not surprised. The emperor's fixation with coins was well known throughout the court. No one had forgotten the four gigantic gold asharfis weighing 400 tolas,

300 tolas, 200 tolas and 100 tolas presented to the Persian ambassador on Jahangir's birthday. These were the world's biggest gold coins and the most expensive ones. The largest coin contained almost twelve kilograms of pure gold!

Inscribed on the huge coin, in Persian, was a couplet eulogising the grace of Nur Jahan.

Ba Hukm Shah Jahangir yaft sad zewer,
Banam Nur Jahan Badshah Begum zar.

(By the order of Jahangir, gold had a hundred splendours added to it by receiving the impression of the name of Nur Jahan, the Queen Begum.)

13

Many people wondered what it was about Nur Jahan that made the emperor so besotted with her. Nur Jahan was thirty-four years old when she married Jahangir, middle-aged by all accounts, besides being encumbered with a daughter. She was beautiful, no doubt, but there were more beautiful women in the harem. Nur Jahan's magic lay in her intelligence, artistic temperament and quick wit. She could compose poetry with the fluency of a bard, design a garden with the skill of an accomplished architect, and hunt with the expertise of a huntsman. She could entertain the emperor with her verses and vast treasure of riddles, while impressing him with her dazzling beauty and political proficiency. She could pit her brains against the best politician and emerge a winner.

'You have to work hard at being an empress,' she told Laadli. 'It is not easy. The harem women are jealous of my position because they only see the glitter and the power. They cannot see the toil and stress that lies behind the sceptre and the crown.'

The royal entourage was back at Agra to celebrate the ninth anniversary of the emperor's accession to the throne.

The public jubilation lasted a full week. The bazaars and public places were decorated with colourful velvet, silk and flowers. Firework displays and various kinds of amusements occupied people throughout the empire. At the royal court, celebrations began with a display of elephants and horses in their finery, and with the emperor inspecting his cavalry and infantry.

In the Diwan-é-aam, nobles, emirs and princes gathered to pay homage to the emperor, who was seated on his magnificent throne that stood within the boundaries of a golden railing. On the right of the throne stood a pedestal with a golden scale, promising justice to every citizen. No one, not even his own sons, were allowed to step inside the golden boundary. A step lower, inside a silver railing, the princes stood, along with the highest-ranking viziers. With them stood an attendant with a gold sceptre. Another step lower, enclosed inside a circle of crimson wooden railing, stood the rest of the nobles and emirs, and with them stood an attendant with a silver sceptre. The commoners were allowed to stand beyond the crimson railing.

Gifts and valuable offerings arrived in abundance as the nobles rushed to seek the emperor's blessings. The offerings ranged from priceless gems and jewels, precious gold and silver articles, ivory, and jade artefacts, to expensive Arabian horses, mammoth elephants procured from the jungles of the northeast frontiers, and slaves brought from far-off lands. Silk from China, muslin from Dacca, velvet, porcelain, crystals, pearls, rubies, emeralds, diamonds, and rare paintings were given as gifts.

The emperor, in turn, handed out grants in the form of jagirs, horses and promotions. The cost of the gifts was translated as the degree of loyalty towards the emperor and the grants were in keeping with the presents that the nobles offered. Whether it was the coronation anniversary, Nauroz or the emperor's birthday, all the emirs were expected to make lavish offerings. If the emperor decided to visit any of the nobles, it was the officer's duty to make offerings worth the emperor's visit. Many nobles were known to have gone bankrupt trying to make a suitable offering.

The dowry that each marriage brought in for the emperor also helped fill up the royal coffers. When emperor Jahangir married Man Bai, her father, Raja Bhagwan Das, presented him with several strings of Persian, Arab, Turkish and Kutch horses with gold saddles, together with a hundred elephants with gem-encrusted gold howdahs, Abyssinian, Circassian and Indian male and female slaves, and vessels full of gold and jewels. Each emir who attended the wedding was given pure-bred Arabian horses with gold saddles.

Once the gifting ritual was over, the emperor moved to the palace to enjoy himself. The list of entertainments ran long. First, there were tournaments of all kinds, with generous rewards being given to the winners, and then a procession of amusements in the harem. Dance and music accompanied with wine and an elaborate feast lasted till every muscle was exhausted and the mind dulled with opium. Only when the emperor was incapable of rising to his feet were the celebrations brought to an end.

Soon the emperor and his royal entourage were on their way to Ajmer again, to pay homage to Chisti's dargah. The emperor was in high spirits. The forests near Ajmer were his favourite hunting grounds and he enjoyed the thought of spending leisurely time near the banks of Ana Sagar Lake, which were being beautified jointly by the empress and Prince Khurram. Sitting in one of the curtained palanquins, Laadli found herself amused at the wasteful luxury of the journey that could have fed thousands of poor people for many years. At one time, as a child, she had been impressed by the procession, but now it seemed such a foolish effort at impressing people who barely managed a couple of meals every day.

Barely had the royal caravan reached Ajmer when news came that Arjumand had given birth to a son. Prince Dara Shikhoh's birth brought great jubilation in the royal quarters. The child was Jahangir's first grandson and would one day inherit the empire. Trumpets belted out happy notes along with cymbals and drums. Jahangir and Nur Jahan visited the young couple and gifted a gold cradle studded with precious jewels along with seven gold cups filled with pearls.

While outwardly all seemed well between Nur Jahan and her stepson, a rift was slowly sundering their alliance. With each passing day, the emperor's dependence on alcohol grew: he was consuming twenty cups of wine along with several pellets of opium each day. This addiction did not help his already failing health. It was enough to send the royal physician into a frenzy, but Jahangir was unperturbed. In the backdrop of his father's ill health, Khurram's many victories had made him a contending power in his own right. Nur Jahan intended to scuttle Khurram's plans to inveigle himself with his father. She kept Khurram on the move, not allowing him to remain by his father's side. He was sent from one campaign to another, travelling constantly with his wife and children through different lands.

This time, his days of luxurious leisure at Ajmer were cut short by the imperial command instructing him to travel to

Deccan to subjugate the Abyssinian slave, Malik Amber, who possessed tremendous military and administrative talents. The Deccan rulers had never been completely subservient to Mughal emperors, often rising to revolt. Jahangir desired to punish the lot and sent Khurram to vanquish them. Autumn was on its last leg and winter chill was itching to spread its tentacles when Khurram started from Ajmer for the Deccan. In his excitement, the emperor loaded the prince with presents as he set out on the grand campaign. The prince was honoured with the title of Shah, which no Timurid prince had ever received. The stylishly crafted and bejewelled swords presented by the emperor were valued at over a million rupees and a dagger with a jade sculpted, gem-encrusted handle was worth rupees forty thousand.

'Khurram is the only one I can depend on,' the emperor lamented. 'Khusrau is a traitor, Pervez is busy drinking himself to death and Shahryar is a nashudani, good for nothing.' Nur Jahan said nothing.

After Khurram left for the south, Jahangir expressed a desire to travel to Mandu. A lavish reception awaited him and his seraglio at the palace of Baz Bahadur and Roopmati. Perched along the Vindhya ranges, Mandu, with its natural defences, was originally the fort capital of the Parmar rulers of Malwa. Towards the end of the thirteenth century, it was ruled by the Sultans of Malwa, the first of whom named it Shadiabad—'City of Joy'. And indeed the pervading spirit of Mandu was of gaiety. Its rulers built exquisite palaces like the Jahaz Mahal and Hindola Mahal, ornamental canals, baths and pavilions which were graceful and refined, reflecting those times of peace and plenty.

Towards the end of the thirteenth century, Mandu became the pleasure resort of the Sultans of Malwa. Sultan Baz Bahadur, the romantic ruler of Mandu, decided to give up battling after he suffered a disgraceful defeat at the hands of Queen Durgavati. Instead, he decided to give himself up to the pleasure of music.

'Benazir, do you know the legend about the lovers Roopmati and Baz Bahadur?' asked Laadli. Below them the clear waters of the river Narmada flowed calmly, its silvery stream meandering through the forest. They were standing on the spot known as the Roopmati's Pavilion. The pavilion— which stood on one side of a steep cliff—had once been a retreat for Roopmati. Here, the queen had stood near the windows, gazing at the river flowing through the Nimar plains. The passing of a gentle wind through the gorge sounded like sighs of an anguished lover. Far away, a balladeer was singing. The notes were unfamiliar and the lyrics unclear. All that Laadli could decipher was that he was singing about the immortal lovers, Roopmati and Baz Bahadur.

'I know you are dying to hear of the love story, aren't you?' Benazir said, her eyes twinkling with mischief.

'Of course I am. Is it possible to stay in the palace and remain untouched by the legend?'

'It is said that Roopmati was the daughter of a Hindu noble. Her name means "one endowed with beauty". She was gifted with a melodious voice—it is said that wild beasts from the jungle would come to her door to hear her singing. One day, she was singing in the garden and the Sultan of Malwa, Baz Bahadur, happened to pass by. He was enchanted with her voice and kept returning to the garden so he could catch a glimpse of the singer's face. And one day he saw her. People say that it was love at first glance. Roopmati became his favourite wife and he constructed this beautiful palace for her.'

'Their love story has a tragic end, doesn't it?

Benazir nodded. 'Adham Khan was Akbar's foster brother and a very powerful general in the Mughal army. The emperor sent him to conquer the lands of Malwa. After defeating the ruler, he unleashed a reign of terror, killing innocent people and molesting the women. His unruly soldiers went on a rampage. Adham Khan had heard of Roopmati's beauty. He sent her a proposal, which she refused. The queen waited for Baz Bahadur to rescue her from the lecherous general but Baz Bahadur had fled from Mandu to escape the Mughal army.'

'How terrible!' Laadli was appalled, her mind conjuring images of the desperate woman caught between a ruthless victor and a cowardly lover.

'Roopmati waited in vain. Finally, unable to fend off Adham Khan's advances, she swallowed poison. People say that her ghost still wanders around Mandu, calling out to Baz Bahadur.'

Laadli gazed at the tiny lake nearby, abloom with pink lotuses, as she thought about the heartbroken Roopmati's soul still searching for her lover.

'But who knows what is the truth?' Benazir was saying. 'These are stories people tell. I would like to see the ghost myself before I lend any credence to the stuff.' Noting Laadli's far-off look, she added, 'Now stop dreaming of the queen's ghost and get ready for the hunt! The empress will not take it kindly if you are late. And don't you try to wriggle out of the arrangements.'

'You know how much I hate to go for these blood-thirsty expeditions,' Laadli said, shaking her head slowly.

'Since there is no escape for us, shouldn't we accept the inevitable and get ready to join the others? The hunting party has already begun gathering on the grounds.'

With a deep sigh, Laadli began dressing for the hunt, her mind still captivated by the stories of love.

The salubrious climes of Mandu delighted the empress and she had planned endless excursions in the forests around the palace. The news that thousands of people were dying across Punjab and Lahore due to a dreadful scourge did not disturb the mood. The dense Malwa forest offered plenty of sport and the emperor, addicted to hunting, looked forward to slaying some tigers and leopards. Camps had already been set up at vantage points and the rounding of the beasts had begun.

The hunt party set out. The emperor, astride a mammoth tusker, a falcon perched on his gloved hand, took the lead. Nur Jahan was seated on an equally impressive elephant. Behind the royal couple rode the English ambassador, Sir Thomas Roe, and other ministers.

Far behind, maintaining a comfortable distance from her mother, Laadli rode with her friend Benazir, reluctantly kicking her mount. She hated hunting, but the empress would brook no objection.

'A princess must hunt. She must be skilled at everything— administration, politics, hunting or hawking, she is expected to accompany the emperor at all times.'

'But I don't want to hunt, I would rather remain at the palace.'

But as usual Nur Jahan's word had been final. No one could argue with the empress, her wishes were expected to be followed, unquestioningly.

From far off came the sound of drums being beaten by the hundreds of foot soldiers that were herding the wild beasts. Behind them came thousands of horsemen who gathered together to form a circle around the forest, trapping within it countless animals like tigers, leopards, wild boars, and deer. The circle grew smaller as the soldiers advanced. And then the hunting party stepped in.

The smell of fear hung heavy over the atmosphere as frightened animals darted for safety. Birds screeched and fluttered their wings fearfully, reaching for the highest branches in the trees. As the hunters closed in, the frenzy amplified in momentum and the beasts emerged from their hideouts. Laadli wished the morbid exercise would end soon.

Four tigers sprang out of the bushes and approached the empress' elephant menacingly, but she was unperturbed. The emperor looked at Nur Jahan and said, 'All yours!'

She asked, 'Arrow or bullet?'

The emperor raised two fingers, put them down, and raised them again without saying a word. He was careful not to make any sound that would disturb the animals. The couple, with their complete understanding of each other, didn't need words to convey their thoughts. Nur Jahan understood that he wanted her to shoot two of the tigers with arrows and the remaining two with bullets. She loaded two guns and kept them ready. Then she took up her bow and selected two arrows. In the twinkling of an eye she raised the bow and let fly two arrows at the tigers. Her aim was unerring and two large beasts fell with arrows stuck in their hearts. She then picked up the guns and dropped the other two tigers in quick succession.

Not a shot was wasted and not a beast escaped. There was loud appreciation of her marksmanship. Jahangir smiled proudly and glanced at the English ambassador.

'Fantastic! Unbelievable! I have never seen anything like this. You are a great hunter, Empress,' cried Thomas Roe, realising that he was expected to shower compliments on the empress for her prowess. Much of his compliment was, indeed, heartfelt. He had never witnessed such marksmanship.

The emperor chuckled delightedly—'Would any one your English women be able to duplicate the empress' accomplishment?'

'Frankly, Your Royal Highness, I don't think any woman in England, or even Hindustan for that matter, would be able to imitate it.' The ambassador was sincere in his praise.

Laadli, however, felt nothing but revulsion at the sight of the creatures lying in a pool of blood. What were human beings trying to prove by killing helpless creatures? she wondered sadly.

There was to be no respite from the empress' pursuit of pleasure. She was either playing chaugan with her ladies or engaging in falconry. The emperor, ever willing to match his hawking skills with hers, bantered over the rewards.

'I bet your falcon can't beat Jaanbaaz.' Jaanbaaz was the emperor's favourite falcon, trained by the master hawker, Mirza Arshad Khan. It could swoop on its prey and bring it back to its master within a matter of minutes.

Not one to accept defeat, Nur Jahan brought out her hawk that she lovingly called Altaf. Almost immediately the nobles and ladies began betting excitedly. Laadli watched sadly as the two falcons were let off to lunge on their preys. Minutes later, the falcons laid two bloody pigeons at the feet of their masters.

That evening, she sat in the pavilion of Rani Roopmati, gazing at the rippling waves of the river down below.

'I will never hunt, no matter if people take me to be weak and incompetent. I don't have to prove my ability by shedding the blood of innocent creatures,' she muttered under her breath.

14

The day was just about to break as the three girls crept away to the stables. The camp was quiet, with most people sleeping off the previous night's excesses. Even the guards were lax, lulled by the knowledge that the royals slept peacefully. The girls walked their horses to the deep end of the forest, praying that the animals would remain silent. After walking for ten minutes they rode away, thrilled by their escape. The cool air stung their faces as the horses galloped into the forest. All around them, birds twittered loudly, preparing to leave their nests for the day.

It was Ratnavali's idea to escape for an unescorted ride, before sunrise.

'There is no charm in being surrounded by the eunuchs who demand that you stick to the rules. I want to experience the magic of the forest without anyone watching over me.'

The idea appealed to Laadli and Benazir, who loved to slip away from their escorts whenever possible. They rode through the dense foliage, enjoying the multitude of smells. A small waterfall with sparkling water tempted them to halt. They dismounted, tethered the horses on one side and stepped into the cold water of the small pool under the waterfall. Laadli shivered as she dangled her feet in the icy pool.

'It is so nice here, away from the stifling atmosphere of the court. I wish I could stay here forever,' she said dreamily.

Ratnavali sighed loudly and said, 'Yes, wouldn't it be lovely? But it is all very well for you to speak like that—my days of freedom are coming to an end.'

She was already betrothed to a Rajput prince and the marriage was to take place shortly.

'If the empress' plans are successful, it won't be long before the Shehzadi is also tied in knots with some prince,' joked Benazir.

'I hope none of them live to wed me. The feud between the sons is growing each day and I won't be surprised if they finish each other off before the emperor dies, leaving no heir to the throne,' laughed Laadli.

All of a sudden Laadli spotted a cave at one end of the water pool. The dark, cavernous interiors loomed mysteriously, provoking their interest.

'What do you think occupies that cave?'

'Some wild bears, most probably,' replied Ratnavali, splashing her feet in the water.

'Or some lioness with her cubs,' hazarded Benazir.

'Or a hermit with immense knowledge of the past and future,' said Laadli. 'Let us go and find out. Shall we wager on our guesses?'

'I think it is dangerous to go into the cave. None of us is a good shot, and if there are wild beasts inside, we will be dead geese. No one will know where to find us.'

'You have always been a coward Benazir. Come on, let me lead you into that cave. My Rajput blood is challenged at the thought of proving its valour,' laughed Ratnavali.

The girls picked their way gingerly through the brambles and the puddles to reach the mouth of the cave. Laadli peered inside and gasped. A hermit sat cross-legged on a tiger skin with a lamp before him. His eyes were closed in meditation and a glow surrounded his face like a halo.

'You have won,' whispered Benazir.

'Sshhhhh! Let us go away before we disturb his meditation. It is said that breaking a hermit's meditation is not a good omen,' Ratnavali hissed.

Laadli continued to gaze at the hermit, unwilling to move.

Benazir tugged at her arm but she brushed it away impatiently. At that moment the hermit opened his eyes and beckoned them. The girls were transfixed. They slowly made their way to his side without a word. It was as though he were pulling them to his side with an invisible string. 'So you have finally arrived,' the deep voice rumbled like a thousand waves splashing against a rock. A tremor passed through the girls. 'You have kept me waiting for long. There is no reason to be afraid. Your arrival here was ordained at birth. None of us can do anything against our destiny. We are mere puppets in the hands of the Almighty who pulls the strings whichever way He deems right.'

The girls prostrated themselves before the hermit.

'Baba, can you predict our future?' asked Ratnavali, who was a great believer in the Hindu philosophy of rebirth and destiny.

The sage smiled. The girls were surprised at the gentleness of that smile. 'Do you really want to know what fate has written in your palms? Sometimes it is better to leave the future unknown.'

'I am curious.'

'Ah, curiosity! That disagreeable characteristic which makes us so impatient and vulnerable at the same time.'

'Will it harm me if I tried to find out a little bit about my future?' Ratnavali probed, her heart beating fiercely.

'No, it will not harm you to know a little bit, but too much curiosity could definitely harm you. I will allow you a brief glimpse into your future.'

The sage commanded her to look into the bowl lying before him. 'Look into the water and you'll see a shadowy picture of your destiny.'

Cold and clammy fingers climbed slowly down her spine as Ratnavali gazed into the bowl. Her mind felt numb as a strange compulsion propelled her body into a vortex. 'Gaze into those ripples and when they are steady you will see the man you are to wed,' the prophet commanded.

The frightened girl peeped closer into the bowl and discerned several disturbing figures of violence. Amidst them she found a handsome warrior riding on a white steed. He was the prince she was to marry. Involuntarily she shivered.

'Don't be afraid. He is a brave man who will overcome many enemies and wars. Can you see those figures?' he asked, pointing at the indistinct silhouettes. 'They augur many wars. You are betrothed to a great Rajput prince.'

The figures were hazy and Ratnavali leaned closer to see them clearly. The voice went on: 'Your life will see many hurdles as your husband wages numerous wars. But there will be compensations—he will bring glory to your kingdom and you will find great love with your husband. You will be a mother to many children. Is there anything else you wish to know?'

Ratnavali shook her head silently. Laadli was eager to ask him about her future, but she hesitated. Her religion did not allow any room for prophetic visions.

'Do not hesitate to ask whatever is in your mind. It is not wrong to be curious about the events in your life, but it is wrong to try to alter the course of those events. As the empress' daughter you are destined to face many challenges in your life.'

Taken aback, Laadli glanced at her friends. How had he known that she was the empress' daughter? Hesitantly she asked, 'Tell me Baba, if my mother will be able to get me married to one of the emperor's sons.'

Laadli's question seemed to amuse the hermit and he burst into loud laughter, his mirth echoing within the womb of the cave. The girls shivered. 'The mysteries of destiny don't unravel themselves so easily, child.'

'Baba, I want to know what the future holds for me,' Laadli insisted as she crept closer to the bowl by his side. The ripples were violent and the figures reflected on them, unsteady. 'Why can't I see anything?' she cried.

'Look closer. Close your eyes tight and then open them slowly,' the voice commanded. 'You will eventually be wed to one of the sons of the emperor, but before that I see love arriving in your life. You will be surrounded by music, art and beauty. There will be many happy moments when the handsome man comes into your life, but beware. He does not belong to a royal family. I see a horrendous end to your romance. There will be much bloodshed and tragedy. I can't tell you more than that.'

Laadli watched fascinated as the ripples turned steady and the haze lifted. The figures were clearer and she glimpsed herself mirrored in the water, dressed in bridal finery, beside her stood a handsome man. Suddenly, the man disappeared and a pool of redness occupied the place next to her. She was petrified as she stared at the bloodstains that were reflected clearly in the bowl. Horrified, she covered her eyes with her hands.

Benazir, horrified with the tragic predictions about Laadli's life, had no desire to know her future. It was much better to remain ignorant than to suffer the horrific visions of a violent destiny. As if he sensed her feelings, the hermit closed his eyes in a dismissive gesture. The girls bowed to him and walked out of the cave. A coldness crept through them as they turned back towards the royal camp. Laadli was greatly disturbed. The vision in the bowl tormented her.

'Don't bother about the predictions, Laadli. How will you fall in love with a commoner when you never get to meet any? Just ignore the prophecy and live your life the best you can,' said Benazir, trying to console her distraught friend.

Laadli shook her head and said, 'No, the hermit was very learned. How did he know all those things about me?'

The light-heartedness of the morning had evaporated. The dark predictions of the hermit loomed ominously before them, his warnings echoing through their minds. They rode back to the camp in silence.

15

The year rolled by and the royal couple continued to enjoy their leisurely life at Mandu. They amused themselves with long rides in the forest, chess and chaugan, falconry hunting, and boat rides on the river. Neither were overly concerned about Prince Khurram, who was still carrying out his seige of the fort at Ahmadnagar, his heavily pregnant wife by his side. Arjumand accompanied her husband for every campaign—no matter how difficult the terrain or how uncomfortable the living. The doting couple had made a pact not to separate, ever.

Eager to keep the emperor entertained, Nur Jahan arranged for a fishing trip. The emperor loved angling and no one knew it better than her. She discovered that the river Narmada, flowing at the footsteps of Mandu, was full of rohu, Jahangir's favourite fish. Several large barges were equipped with fishing gear and the entourage set out for the day. Camps were set up on the other side of the riverbank for the fish to be cooked and an open-air picnic was arranged. Jahangir was delighted when he drew no less than twelve large rohus in his net.

An impromptu poetry contest was organised by the empress and the nobles vied with each other to win the huge ruby ring promised to the winner by the emperor.

'*If the rosebud can be opened by the breeze in the meadow, the key to our heart's lock is the beloved's smile,*' recited Nur Jahan opening the contest, and the emperor immediately declared her the winner. Modestly she declined the prize and gently rebuked him for his favouritism.

'Laadli, why don't you recite the couplet you composed yesterday?' the empress said suddenly, turning to her daughter.

The very thought of reciting her couplet before the assembly sent a shiver up Laadli's spine. 'The verse is not ready,' she demurred politely. 'I am still working on it.' Murmuring her apologies, she quickly made an exit before her mother insisted.

Campfires were lit and musicians entertained the emperor while the cooks roasted the fish. Kebabs were made, curries tempered and pulao garnished. A delicious aroma wafted from the makeshift kitchen. Lanterns, swinging from the branches of trees, lit up the riverbank, their bright flames of light setting the ripples aglow. Colourful carpets covered the grass, soft bolsters lined the edges and dozens of silk cushions were heaped to support the corpulent bodies of the nobles.

'What a delightful way to spend an evening,' remarked the emperor. 'It is these ideas of yours which bind me to you so faithfully,' he told the empress, sipping his favourite wine.

A fresh bout of celebrations began to herald the emperor's birthday and the entire harem turned into a beehive of activity. Great rejoicing for an entire week took over the entire Mughal Empire. Mandu was besieged by visiting nobles and emirs who had travelled all the way from various parts of the empire to pay their homage. Special dancers and musicians were brought in from Agra. Mellifluous music and the sound of the heavy metal anklets of the dancers rang through the halls. The night sky was made resplendent with fireworks displays.

It was the lunar birthday of the emperor and the day began with the traditional weighing ceremony. Seated in the courtyard of the palace, Jahangir was weighed twelve times on a giant golden scale. The first weighing was done with gold on one side and the emperor on the other; this was followed by silver, copper, iron, spices, silk, perfumes, ghee, rice, milk and two types of grains. Jahangir's weight was carefully noted and there was much commendation by the gathering, for the emperor had gained weight.

Standing at the end of the hall, Laadli and her friends giggled; after all the feasting, it was not a surprise that the emperor had put on more weight and that his girth was flabby.

All the things that the emperor was weighed against were distributed amongst priests, fakirs, poor and destitute. Prayers were chanted continuously to augur good fortune and health for the emperor. In the temples and mosques people prayed for the emperor, while another knot was tied on the silken thread that kept an account of the emperor's age.

Cauldrons full of food were distributed amongst the poor and sacks full of special feed for birds were given to servants, to be scattered on the streets. The emperor personally gifted purses to the dancers, musicians, artists, poets, craftsmen, architects, and royal servants.

In the royal kitchen, Nur Jahan cooked Jahangir's favourite dishes with her own hands. Wines of all kinds had been procured from different parts of the country. Bards composed special poems, and miniaturists painted pictures of the emperor's profile to adorn the palace halls.

After much deliberation, Laadli decided that she would present a beautiful muslin turban to the emperor. She knew of his partiality to Dacca muslin, which was the lightest imaginable fabric, almost magical in its texture. She had picked up exquisite material from a trader during Eid and saved it for a special occasion. Royal purple in colour, it was a full thirty yards in length, but so exquisitely fine that it hardly weighed anything. The old man had called it Shabnam.

'It is a rare muslin,' he had said. 'Do you know that this muslin, when laid wet on the grass, becomes almost invisible, and because it becomes indistinguishable from the dew, it is named Shabnam.'

When she presented the turban to the emperor, he was ecstatic. 'This is the best gift I have received on my birthday. Tell me, child, what would you want in return?'

The empress delighted in his appreciation of her daughter. And for the first time Laadli had not flinched at the emperor's touch as he patted her head. It was a good sign.

'Your Majesty, I want nothing in return. Your pleasure is more valuable than any material thing that I can ask for.'

'Nur, your daughter is blessed with a sweet tongue. We are charmed by her speech,' the emperor said. 'Laadli, you may ask us for anything and we shall be glad to grant it to you.'

'Right now I don't need anything, Your Majesty. When the need arises, I will ask you for it,' promised Laadli.

'Laadli, don't you covet anything? You have never asked us for anything.'

'Your Majesty, my desires are not conventional. I would like to ask you to feed all the poor in the kingdom, or set all the animals in your menagerie free. You wouldn't like that, would you?'

A frown of annoyance crossed the emperor's brow as he looked at the young girl. Realising the intensity of the moment Nur Jahan intervened. 'Laadli, you forget that you are speaking to the emperor. Besides, your wishes are too lofty and unrealistic. Keep them to yourself.'

Her reply was impertinent—'That is why I did not ask for anything.'

The empress blushed at the unnatural insolence of her daughter. Laadli had never spoken so rudely before. *What made her so angry*, she wondered, as she distracted Jahangir so he would forget his anger at the girl. *She needs to be married*, thought Nur Jahan. *She is getting unmanageable.*

Twice a year the emperor celebrated his birthday—once according to the lunar calendar, and then according to the solar calendar. Amidst the revelry celebrating his solar birthday, Prince Khurram returned to Mandu, having signed a treaty with the Abyssinian ruler, Malik Amber. The victors were welcomed with great pomp by the emperor. So pleased was Jahangir with the accomplishments of his son, that he bestowed on him the title of Shah Jahan, Sovereign of the World. Besides the lofty title, he was made a commander of 20,000 cavalry and 30,000 zat.

Shah Jahan was presented with the important jagirs of Hissar and Punjab, along with jewels and precious stones, which alone amounted to rupees 22,60,000. There were fireworks and grand feasts; prisoners were released to celebrate the occasion.

The empress was now convinced that he would inherit the kingdom. In the privacy of her boudoir she began to plan ways by which Laadli could seduce the prince. 'Shah

Jahan must marry Laadli. We have to make it happen,' she told Firdaus.

'But he is not interested in marrying her,' Firdaus, who sympathised with the girl, said. 'We can't force him to wed her.'

'Leave it to me. I will think of something,' Nur Jahan said, with a determined look.

The empress organised a magnificent feast for the royal family to celebrate the reunion. Her mind began ticking off the tasks at hand as she prepared for her bath. The marble pool of sparkling water was ablaze with crimson rose petals and jasmines. The empress sat on a marble bench while her personal attendant, Azra, rubbed a special cream made from sandalwood, almonds, saffron, and camphor on her body. The gentle hands of the maids untangled and soothed her taut muscles as they ran over her neck and shoulders, sensuously massaging the back of her body with strong movements. The expert hands kneaded her muscles till they relaxed, traversing from her back to her thighs, legs and feet.

'A good massage is more satisfying than sex,' the empress believed and she abandoned all inhibitions for the ritual, as she lay prone on the bench while Azra did the four finger spinal walk down her vertebral column. The technique never failed to put her in a tranquil mood. The cool, shadowy interiors of the hamamgah were designed for repose. It was her own private haven, an escape from the ceaseless demands on her time.

An hour later she sank into the refreshing bath gratefully. The cool and refreshing rose scented water washed her troubles away and she felt rejuvenated, ready to take on the demands of her role once again.

As the maids helped her dress, Nur Jahan's mind was already on the task at hand—Laadli's marriage. Her daughter was already fourteen years old and the empress was worried. As Azra helped her into a sheer ivory muslin qaba with delicate gold embroidery, Nur Jahan's mind was in a whirl. The knee-length jacket with embroidered rosettes and dark crimson churidar set off her translucent skin to an advantage. The emerald choker on her neck highlighted the flashing green of her eyes making them appear deeper. She decided to don a turban style headgear for the day. A heron feather and diamond stones adorned her turban.

'Azra, I want you to help Laadli with her toilette today. Ensure that she looks her best.' commanded the empress walking out of the bath.

Accompanied by Benazir, who was her inseparable companion, Laadli submitted herself to the elaborate ritual of massage, bath and dressing up. She emerged from the hamamgah perfumed and bejewelled, and made her way towards her mother's chambers. Nur Jahan had left instructions that she wanted to see her daughter after the bath.

The empress critically took in the pale-pink costume her daughter wore and nodded her head appreciatively. The colour suited Laadli. Nur Jahan had especially designed the dress. The bright red arabesque pattern on the dress gave it a dramatic effect and the grey pearl necklace she wore set off her daughter's calm grey eyes.

The evening feast was an elaborate affair. Hira Bai, the famous dancer from Agra, had been invited to entertain the gathering. Leaning against the softness of silk cushions and bolsters, the emperor looked relaxed. By his side sat the empress, her witty remarks amusing her indolent husband.

Shah Jahan reclined at one end with Arjumand, who was pregnant again. Prince Shahryar sat in another corner with his cronies, his mood swinging from petulant to boisterous. Laadli had been ordered by her mother to sit with Shah Jahan, so she dutifully took her place near the prince, trying to make conversation. Arjumand was fond of her cousin and accepted her company with pleasure.

'Tell me, Laadli, did your mother instruct you to sit with us?' asked Shah Jahan.

Blushing with embarrassment, Laadli confirmed his suspicions.

'So, now it is my turn to be wooed by the princess. I am flattered,' he raised his wine glass with a flourish and saluted the empress. She returned his mocking glance with a sweet smile.

'Don't be offensive,' scolded his wife. 'She means no harm.'

'Oh, my innocent Arjumand. If only you could read your aunt's thoughts the way I can, you wouldn't be so charitable to her.'

'Please...I am not here to cause any problems. I know that my mother intends to push me into your company but, honestly, I have no option,' stammered Laadli. 'I would rather be with you than be with Prince Khusrau or Prince Shahryar. Being with Prince Khusrau is depressing, while Shahryar is downright nasty.'

'My poor sister,' clucked Shah Jahan. 'I really pity you. With a mother like the empress, you don't need an enemy. Khusrau is likely to be relieved now that she has taken him off her list of eligible husbands for you. He is besieged with problems of his own. As for Shahryar, he is a total disgrace to the Timurid dynasty. I just hope that your mother does not entertain even the remotest idea of including him in her list.'

'He scares me. There is something quite abominable about him,' admitted Laadli. 'I do hope the empress will never ask me to entertain him.'

Their eyes travelled to Shahryar who was making lewd gestures at the dancing girl. He was totally inebriated and behaving in his usual offensive manner.

'I sincerely hope that my aunt doesn't take it upon her to thrust poor Laadli on him,' agreed Arjumand, who felt genuinely sorry for her cousin.

The freezing winds of November burst through the forests of Malwa. Laadli walked through the vast gardens that were denuded of their blooms; browning leaves lay on the ground. A severe water shortage affected the royal camp, forcing people to buy water from the villagers who carried it from long distances. The emirs complained about the high cost of water and began putting discreet pressure on the emperor to move camp. By now Jahangir had tired of Mandu and was equally eager to move to a new place.

Winter faded away into spring, bringing back beauty to the hills. It was summer by the time the emperor began his journey towards the sandy shores of Gujarat. It was the empress' wish to spend a couple of months near the port of Surat. Neither Jahangir nor Nur Jahan had ever seen the sea and were looking forward to the trip. But the long journey to Ahmedabad was neither pleasant nor enjoyable as the weather began to deteriorate, much to the unhappiness of the royal family. The sand and dust displeased the emperor who was more at home with the greenery of the hills.

The arid landscape and the heat turned the emperor into a cantankerous person and he constantly complained about the journey. Disgusted, he recorded in his memoirs—I do not know whether to call the place Samumistan [the place of hot winds], Bimaristan [the abode of sickness], Zaqqum zar [the thorn or cactus bed] or Jahannumabad [the house of hell].

To make matters worse, a strange sickness afflicted the royal party at Ahmedabad. It began with a high fever and the appearance of large, dark blisters on the body that multiplied at a fast rate. Death ensued in a matter of hours. The emperor as well as Shah Jahan fell prey to the pestilence and it was only after intensive treatment by the royal physician and a prolonged period of recuperation that they recovered. This illness prompted the emperor to order an early departure from Gujarat.

The jagir of Surat belonged to Nur Jahan. It was a prosperous port and a constant bone of contention between the Portuguese, English and the Dutch who were fighting for sole trading contracts. The English were currently not allowed to purchase or construct forts in the area, restrictions which the English were now trying to have removed. Sir Thomas Roe, the English ambassador, had accompanied the royal caravan all through the journey from Mandu to Ahmedabad, looking for an opportunity to present his case. Throughout the journey, Roe endeavoured to negotiate with Asaf Khan, but was perpetually thwarted by Shah Jahan and Nur Jahan, who were both wary of the English. 'Why do they need to build forts when we have allowed them trading rights?' she raged. 'Traders don't need forts. All they need is permission to trade.'

The Portuguese, meanwhile, had been encouraged by Jahangir's response to the overtures of the Jesuit priests. He had already agreed to the conversion of three princes to Christianity. Three nephews of Jahangir, his brother Prince Daniyal's sons, had been baptised and the priests had taken them under their wings. The Jesuits hoped that the emperor would eventually consent to being converted to Roman Catholism. Jahangir had adorned his courts with Biblical paintings and the Jesuits—mistaking his curiosity in an art form for religious fervour—took it as a sign that he was keen to be converted.

But there was also a lot of ill-will against the Portuguese as well. They had plundered a few trading vessels belonging to the empress, taking many slaves and robbing the ships of expensive carpets, gold, precious stones, dry fruits and other expensive commodities. The owners of the trading vessels appealed to the emperor to control the activities of the pirates. As the Mughals had no naval strength, they could hardly take it upon themselves to do the task. The only way out was to grant privileges to the British. Supporters of the English traders in the court argued that privileges given to them would help in controlling the Portuguese.

The emperor vacillated on the decision, finally leaving it to his empress. He was raring to return to the comforts of Agra after his stay in the inhospitable climes of Gujarat. The march to the capital began in the midst of the rains that washed the landscape with a muddy brush. Wading through the deep slush, the royal caravan, with its innumerable elephants and horses, soldiers and slaves, wound its way slowly through the vast stretches of forests, crossed several rivers in spate and climbed the frightening ravines, passing through insignificant villages, impressive towns, poor and impoverished hamlets as well as prosperous cities.

Exhausted, the royal court finally returned to Agra. There was not a soul who didn't feel elated at the sight of the lofty gates of the city.

Back at Agra, it was business as usual for the empress. Seated behind a screen, Nur Jahan listened to every petition presented to Jahangir. On the empress's insistence, Laadli accompanied her occasionally.

'The only way to learn the intricacies of politics and administration is to be present when the court is in session. You have to learn these things, Laadli. I expect you to know them since you will be an empress one day,' Nur Jahan rebuked her when she expressed her reservations about attending court.

It wasn't always boring to attend court. Some of the incidents that took place were rather amusing. One morning the ambassador of an African country presented his credentials to the emperor. Among the expensive gifts presented by him was an animal with black and white stripes.

'What kind of animal is that? It is neither a horse nor a mare, although it looks like an ass. I think the ambassador has got black and white stripes painted on it to make it look different. It is a ruse to please the emperor,' whispered the ministers.

The emperor was perplexed. If this were a painted horse, would the colour not fade after a few months? Finally, the ambassador, amused at the reactions, explained that the animal had not been painted—its stripes were natural.

'Your Majesty, this animal, found in our jungles is known as a zebra. The Almighty God has painted it with his own brush.'

Still not convinced, the emperor commanded that the animal be washed and scrubbed. It was only when he saw that stripes remained despite being scrubbed, was the emperor convinced that they were natural.

Jahangir immediately ordered the court artiste to paint a picture of the exotic animal and preserve it for posterity. He also commanded that the animal be weighed and measured. Then he made notes in his diary about the peculiarity of the animal.

'We would like you to bring us a mate for this strange animal so that they may produce more of their breed and Hindustan may possess many of these funny beasts,' Jahangir told the African ambassador. For many days he watched the zebra with great interest, noting its habits and manners in great details.

While the emperor occupied himself thus, a deadly disease was spreading like wildfire in the countryside, leaving a trail of death behind. The stench of rotting corpses permeated the air. Hundreds of people were dying every day. Food was scarce and so was drinking water; there were no farmers left to till the lands and no doctors to tend to the sick. Jahangir, finally realising the intensity of the disaster, granted several thousand rupees to the villages, but it was too meagre an amount to contain the disastrous effects of the plague.

16

Amidst the tragedy, the emperor was struck by wanderlust once again. This time he was pining for his favourite city of Lahore. 'Nur, what is it about the magical city of Lahore that lures me time and again. Is it the dense clumps of the tall eucalyptus and cypress trees lining the Grand Trunk Road, or is it the lofty minarets of the mosques? My heart rejoices in anticipation of a visit to Lahore.'

Nur Jahan knew it was futile to argue with the emperor once he had made up his mind. 'It is the most beautiful city in the entire empire,' she agreed. 'The buildings, the roads, the trees and the gardens, in fact the very air of Lahore is wonderful. When the wind whistles through the tall trees, and twilight floods the beautiful face of the fort, the Ravi flows in gentle rhapsody, mist fills the ancient streets and the havelis come alive with strains of classical music; the sublime spirit of Lahore suffuses even the hardiest of souls with tender emotions.'

'That was beautifully said, Nur. I have also composed a couplet on the city. A *glance tugs at the heart's skirt, saying–this is the place!*' recited the emperor.

'I only wish we didn't have to travel so much in the heat. Besides, the scourge is creating unlimited fear in every heart. Most of the nobles are unwilling to stir out of their houses for fear of the disease.'

'Don't they realise that they may be safer at Lahore than they are here?'

'Your Majesty, the plague has taken over the entire country without exception. The royal historians are claiming that only once have they heard of such a widespread scourge. Entire states of the northern and western parts of the country are suffering from the tremendous onslaught of the disease. We will not escape it in Lahore.'

'Begum, I loathe Agra during the hot months. Even Yamuna seems to boil and the sands blow in from the deserts of Rajput lands. The weather brings unhealthy effects on my constitution and that is why I prefer to reside at Lahore.'

The emperor was suffering from breathlessness and his asthma attacks had resurfaced. So, once again the royal caravan took to the road, winding its way through the deserted and dusty streets, in a slow and tired march across the plains. They rested during the afternoon and covered small distances by the cooler hours of the morning and evening.

Even the usually imperturbable Uzbeg and Tartar women, who rode alongside the harem palanquins, wore an expression of irritation on their countenance. The Meer Samaan, who was in charge of making suitable arrangements for a comfortable stay enroute, looked harassed. Each evening, he would leave ahead of the rest of the entourage with an advance party of workers to find a restful site where the tents could be pitched for the emperor's party. The preferred site would ideally be next to a body of water with good green coverage for shade. The tents had to be pitched in strict hierarchical order. Bathing tents and a kitchen had to be set up, arrangements for drinking water for the men as well as the beasts had to be made in advance. The next morning the caravan would arrive at the chosen spot to find everything waiting in readiness for them. Even the slightest discomfort could lead to the most severe punishment by the emperor.

It was weeks before the emperor reached the city of Lahore. It was a warm May month and Lahore was sweltering with the northwestern heat waves blowing into the city from the deserts. It was Nur Jahan's second visit to the city. Like Jahangir, she had grown to love Lahore.

The sun was yet to rise when a eunuch announced the approach of the emperor to her chamber. She was surprised. It was unusual for her husband to wake up so early. 'I want to take you to a lovely place and we must go there early in the morning before the sun gets intense,' Jahangir told her.

As the empress dressed in a hurry, she wondered what the unexpected visit would entail. She couldn't stop laughing when she saw that they were to travel by a bullock cart. Drawn by a pair of strong bulls, the sturdy cart was decorated with tassels. 'Why, Your Majesty. It is a delightful idea to travel by this cart instead of the elephants or horses.'

'I thought we should do something different this time. Besides, I did not want to be accompanied by our retinue. A ride in a bullock cart is much more comfortable than riding a camel or an elephant. I am sure you'll find it quite enchanting.'

'I am sure I will. It was a good idea.'

They rode forty kilometres away from the fort. The green spread all along the jungle path was delightful. The thought that they had eluded their escorts was thrilling enough to amuse the two of them.

'Agra will always remain Shahenshah Akbar's city. I prefer Lahore. We have purchased Lahore with our soul; we have given our life and bought another paradise,' the empress recited with feeling while relaxing under the mango grove near Hiran Minar on their way to Jahangirabad, which was the emperor's favourite hunting spot.

'Do you know why I built this memorial? My pet antelope Hansraj was more intelligent than many human beings. He could understand everything I said and could follow all commands. Only dogs are known to do that. I came across Hansraj during my first hunt in the forest. The beauty of those limpid eyes struck a blow to my heart.'

It had broken the emperor's heart when the antelope died. He ordered an imposing monument to be raised over its remains, on which a life-size stone statue of the deer was placed. Nur Jahan walked over to the memorial and read the Persian inscription engraved on a slab of stone affixed to the grave:

'At this beautiful spot an antelope was caught by the pious king, Nur-ud-din Jahangir, which, in the course of a month, abandoning its savage and wild habits, became the head of the royal antelopes.'

The lofty, carved octagonal memorial tower stood boldly in the forest challenging the tall trees in the vicinity. Nur Jahan let out a sigh of contentment. It was nice to be away from the royal court. She had the emperor to herself and the world was hers for the moment.

'Why don't you build a hunting lodge at this place? It would be delightful to stay here for a couple of days while you hunt in the nearby forest. In fact, I think it would be a good idea to have tunnels that connect the Hiran Minar and the Lahore fort. We could escape undetected from the fort to this lovely place whenever we wish to be on our own.'

'It is uncanny how you think of the same things that go through my mind, Nur. I have been toying with the idea of constructing a tunnel for quite some time. Your idea is a brilliant one. In fact, why don't you make a plan for the project and it shall be executed without any delay. I am not as talented at designing buildings. '

Nur Jahan gave him a sly look—'What about the mausoleum you constructed for your lady love? You aren't too bad a designer, either.'

'Which mausoleum are you referring to? And which is this lady love?'

'I have heard many stories about the pomegranate bud that stole your heart and caused you to rebel against the Shahenshah. Entire Lahore talks about the edifice you built in her memory.'

A cloud of sadness misted the emperor's eyes as he remembered Anarkali. 'It was such a long time back. The luckless woman became the target of the Shahenshah's wrath. She paid for the folly with her life.'

'Do you think love is a folly?'

'When a commoner falls in love with a prince, it is a folly.'

'I was a commoner, Badshah, and I had the temerity to fall in love with you. So, will I have to pay for the folly with my life?' jested the queen.

'You are my queen, my world. I have given my empire to you. But Anarkali was different. She was very innocent and her love for me was selfless. She desired nothing more than my love.'

Was the emperor being sarcastic? Was he referring to her political machinations? Nur Jahan felt a stab of jealousy.

'You still love her, my darling.'

It was not a query and the emperor's eyebrows shot up protestingly.

'Begum, why do you fret over a story long forgotten? How can I love a dead woman when the light of my life is with me?'

'I will visit the mausoleum you built for Anarkali. I want to pay respect to the woman who sacrificed her life for your love,' the empress stated haughtily, her stiff bearing and unsmiling face speaking volumes about her feelings.

'As you wish.'

Nur Jahan fought back the angry retort that came to her lips. *Why grieve about a woman who is no more? Why hadn't he forgotten Anarkali, after all these years?* The magic of the morning was lost in the gloom that suddenly seemed to have descended at the mention of Anarkali's name. Saddened, the emperor got up from her side and began pacing agitatedly. Nur Jahan regretted having brought up the topic; the morning had been ruined.

'Shall we return to the palace?' asked the emperor after a while. 'It is getting very warm and soon there will be hot winds blowing across the city.'

They travelled back in silence. This time the empress did not notice the beauty of the wild blossoms, nor did she delight in the vivid plumes of the peacocks. She did not heed the musical call of the mynahs nor quote a couplet at the sight of the fluttering wings of a parakeet. The shadow of a tragic memory blotted out the beauty around them.

The empress was determined to visit Anarkali's tomb and she went there at the first available opportunity, without the emperor's company this time. Instead, she took Laadli and a few ladies with her. Flowers of all colours danced against the background of gushing fountains. There was a strange melancholic air around the tomb, which was set in an octagonal building covered with a dome. At each corner of the building stood a turret, on top of which was a cupola.

A hushed silence fell over the giggling women as they stepped on the marble floor. The tomb reminded everyone of the courtesan's tragic love affair with the emperor. What a heavy price to pay for love, thought Laadli, as she studied the sarcophagus on which was inscribed the ninety-nine names of Allah and a Persian couplet:

Ta qayamat shukr goyam kard gar khwish ra
Ah! Gar man baz beenam rui yar khwish ra
I would give thanks unto my God till the day of Resurrection.
Ah, if I could behold the face of my beloved again
— The Bereaved Salim, Son of Akbar

The couplet expressed Jahangir's feelings more than anything he could have said. The sadness reflected in the words brought a lump to her throat. This was true love! Laadli sighed.

For Nur Jahan, the trip helped her make peace with the past. The jealousy she had felt a few days ago left her in an instant and she felt sympathy for the dead woman as she sat down beside the tomb to pray for a while. She hated the woman no more; Anarkali was just another unfortunate woman to have fallen prey to the whimsical ways of the royal Mughals. After a while, she placed a wreath of fragrant flowers she had brought with her and quietly walked away from the mausoleum.

17

Everyone was talking about the talents of a new young painter at Agra. Within months of his arrival in the city, he had eclipsed most of the artists in the royal atelier. Imraan Khan was extraordinarily talented and soon there was a clamour for portraits made by him as word about his expertise spread around the town. He could paint the finest miniatures with a single-hair brush fashioned out of squirrel's hair. When word reached Jahangir, who prided himself as a connoisseur of art, the artist was summoned to the court.

Just a few days back, Sir Thomas Roe had presented a miniature painting of Madonna and her Child to Jahangir. It was beautiful and intricate. After inspecting it closely, a scheme had unfolded in the emperor's mind. 'We have heard that your talents surpass those of our royal painters. The entire town is talking about your matchless skills as an artist. We want to see if these claims are true,' Jahangir told Imraan.

The young man bowed to the emperor and replied— 'Jahanpanah, I am just a humble artist who earns his living by painting portraits of rich nobles and their families.'

'You are a modest man and we like your humility. The English ambassador has given us a miniature made by a firanghee artist and he claims that it is one of the best in the world. We want you to replicate the miniature in such a way that the ambassador has to eat his words. Will you be able to do that?'

'I will certainly try my best to carry out your command.'

The emperor ordered the miniature to be given to Imraan and gave him two days to produce a copy of the painting. After two days, when the artist brought his reproduction to the court, Jahangir was ecstatic. 'This is fantastic! We can't decide which one is better. They are exactly identical in form and quality.'

He passed the copy to his ministers and asked them to identify the original. None of them could differentiate between the two miniatures.

'We had not expected you to do such a good job. From today we appoint you as assistant to the Nadir-ul-Zaman, Abul Hasan. Since you are so good in copying Angrezi paintings, we wish you to start a special section in which you will create miniatures of their work.'

Then Jahangir summoned Sir Thomas Roe and handed him the miniatures. 'Well English Khan, can you tell the difference between the miniatures?' he asked, smiling mysteriously.

The ambassador turned them over and over in his hands, trying to find a flaw in the reproduction, but after studying them for a while, he failed to find any difference that would tell the original from the reproduction.

The courtiers smiled at the discomposure of the ambassador.

'You will not be able to find it even if you spent the entire night studying them. The Mughal artists are as good as any in the world. In fact, we would say that they are superior in their artistry and mastery than the others in the field!' The emperor then ordered Imraan Khan to point out the original miniature to the English ambassador. Imraan bowed respectfully to the emperor and approached the envoy.

'Sir, if you inspect the details carefully, you will notice that the difference is very minor and not easily noticeable. The original portrait has been done with a brush that is slightly cruder than the one used in the copy. If you look very closely, you may notice the difference. While the Angrezi artist has used a sable-haired brush, I used a squirrel hair brush to get a finer finish.'

'By God, that's true. I could never have told the difference. Please accept my compliments for your fine artistry,' stated the envoy.

Jahangir was so pleased with the work of his new artist that he immediately conferred a mansab of two hundred on him.

'Young man, I would like you to do my portrait. Although Mansur has been appointed as the official portrait artist, I would like you to do my portrait in the rose garden,' ordered the emperor.

One morning, Jahangir summoned Imraan to the royal garden at Lahore. 'Come young man, we would like you to begin the portrait that you promised to make for us. This is the most pleasant season of the year and Lahore is at its beauteous best.'

Since no one but high-ranking nobles were ever allowed inside the empress' private rose garden, Imraan knew that

Jahangir was endowing special privilege on him. As he entered the royal garden, the artist understood why the Persians referred to gardens as paradise. To them, paradise was interpreted as the ideal garden, and water was considered its soul. The royal garden was divided into four quarters and enclosed by a high wall with massive wooden doors studded with heavy iron nails and pikes. From a distance he could make out three terraces that formed a pattern. Water drawn from the adjoining river descended from one terrace to another after flowing through a network of canals, tanks and water chutes. As water streamed from one level to the other, it gathered momentum and descended with force, spraying a hundred droplets that appeared like tiny marbles let loose by a mischievous child. Marble steps ran along the sides of the water chutes, ending in a marble pond in which bloomed dozens of lotuses. Ornate niches, made of agate, marble and onyx, occupied the walls behind the waterfalls. At night, oil lamps—sheltered behind ornate glass shades of different geometrical shapes—were placed in the niches, making the waterfall appear like a curtain of flowing light.

Pathways along the central canal were lined with tall cypress trees, alternated with orange and lemon trees abloom with fragrant flowers. Imraan knew that the Persians believed that trees like orange, pomegranate, plum and white kachnar symbolised youth, life and hope, while the cypress was the symbol of death and eternity. The Mughals also believed in the efficacy of gardens to cure them of all ailments, mental and emotional. Water, trees, flowers and fruits: they surrounded themselves with these elements to bring a sense of peace and tranquillity to their war and strife-torn existence.

Hosts of carnations, hollyhock, peonies, lotus, marigold, violets, tuberose and zinnia shrubs dotted the landscape. The garden contained more than a hundred species of plants, including evergreens and screw pines. There was a profusion of roses standing against the lush background. Parrots and pigeons moved around freely among the flowers. Several peacocks strutted around fearlessly. Ornate pavilions with adorned cupolas and marble benches lined the garden. A wooden bridge covered with creepers ran over the water canal at one end.

For a few moments, Imraan stood mesmerised by the view before him, and then a few lines from the verses of Faizi came unbidden to his mind—

'If there is paradise on earth, it is here, it is here, it is here.'

His creative energy was at its peak as Imraan rushed about selecting the right space and light for the emperor to pose in. Cool breeze from the river Ravi blew into the garden.

'There is music in the air,' said Jahangir. 'It makes me wonder if this is what heaven looks like. The bliss in this garden makes one forget all worries.'

With a smile Imraan replied—'Jahanpanah, it takes a poet to recognise the beauty of nature and express it in words and an artist to reproduce the beauty on canvas. You, Sire, are the poet, and I am the humble artist.'

The emperor chuckled at Imraan's compliments—'Young man, I believe that your skills extend beyond the limitations of a brush. You also have a way with words. Maybe you should try composing poems.'

Imraan adjusted the emperor's robe so that it fell in graceful folds around his lap, and he began sketching the royal profile. The emperor was clad in perfect white muslin with a heron feathered turban adorned with emeralds and rubies; his feet, shod in green embroidered slippers, rested on a velvet upholstered footstool. It was a perfect setting. Imraan plucked a bright red rose from the garden and handed it to Jahangir. The flower softened the emperor's appearance.

Jahangir watched as the artist's charcoal flew in swift motions across the paper, his brows knitted in concentraton. There was no doubt about his proficiency. All of a sudden, his hands seemed to freeze. Muttering an oath, Imraan threw away the charcoal and wiped his hands with a disgusted look.

'What holds you up, Imraan?' The emperor was irritated at the artist's tardiness. Jahangir was not known to be a patient person, and the delay annoyed him.

'I am sorry Jahanpanah. Someone is attempting to play Raag Bahar, but the notes are absolutely wrong.'

'How can you tell? You are an artist not a musician,' said the emperor.

'With all due respect, Jahanpanah, I am first a musician and then an artist. My uncle, Mian Tansen, was employed in Emperor Akbar's court and I learnt some music from him during my childhood. I will not call myself an accomplished musician, but I can distinguish the right notes from the wrong ones,' replied Imraan modestly.

'Yah Allah! We have none less than Mian Tansen's nephew in our court and no one has informed us. This is unpardonable. Why didn't you let us know before?'

'Pardon me Sir, I did not want to boast about my lineage. My talents are in no way comparable to those of my uncle.'

'Besides being a talented person, you are an unassuming person. In any case, you have solved our problem. We have been looking for an Ustaad to teach our stepdaughter the sitar. Laadli has been trying to pick up the raag for a few days, quite unsuccessfully, as you must have realised. Our royal musician has stayed behind at Agra so she is unable to get his help. Will you teach her the correct notes?'

'Your wish is my command, Jahanpanah. I shall strive to do my best to impart to the princess whatever knowledge I possess.'

'Our daughter will be delighted to know that we have found her an Ustaad. We will also ask her to stop assaulting our senses with the wrong notes. Then there will be peace and you can paint my portrait without any disturbance,' smiled the emperor. There was a twinkle of humour in his eyes.

Imraan knew that Laadli was the daughter of empress Nur Jahan. She was rumoured to be a recluse—a gentle and shy girl. He spent the rest of the morning trying to sketch the emperor, but his mind was restless. The thought that he would be imparting music lessons to a princess was a disturbing one. In all his twenty-three years, the young artist had not dealt with a woman. To be seated in the presence of a shehzadi seemed an incredible idea to him. His hands trembled; they had always been very steady. Was it nervousness or apprehension? he wondered, trying to steady his fingers.

Suddenly the emperor rose and began walking away— 'Your art will have to wait, young man,' Jahangir told Imraan. 'It is time for us to present ourself at the jharoka. We shall continue with the portrait tomorrow. You will be told when you have to begin music lessons with the princess.'

The young artist was relieved to be dismissed by the emperor. His mind in a whirl, Imraan tried to remember the words of caution uttered by Peer Shah Buland, the Sufi saint whom he visited regularly. Just after he was commissioned by the emperor for a portrait, Imraan had visited the holy man for his blessings. The Sufi fakir had been very precise in his advice: 'Follow three edicts and you will never be sorry. Firstly, no matter how pleased the emperor is with you, keep your distance from him. The moods of an emperor are like the rain clouds that can be harmless one moment and spark lightning the very next moment. Secondly, no matter how many opportunities fate provides, do not get intimate with any woman from the royal zenana. They will bring you nothing but sorrow. Lastly, to be a good artist, do not let the lure of gold overpower your creativity.'

Imraan recalled the Sufi's words as a eunuch approached him with the instructions that he was to present himself at the royal garden in the evening for the music lesson.

Later that evening, Imraan, dressed in a spotless white muslin dress, headgear in place, walked towards the royal garden. Dangling from his cummerbund was a brocade pouch with paan in it. He wasn't rich enough to wear rubies or diamonds in his turban, but a string of small pearls adorned his neck. He had taken care to dab himself with the attar he kept aside for special occasions, and this was as special an occasion as any. Not everyone gets an opportunity to enter the royal garden or tutor a princess, he thought.

The evening was a pleasant one as Imraan arrived at the royal palace. The empress' chief eunuch, Hoshiyar, met him as soon as he entered the rose garden. The eunuch led him through an aisle to a pavilion overlooking the gently flowing river. An elaborate arrangement had been made for the music lesson. Hundreds of red roses alternated with white jasmine buds were strung together and suspended from a golden bar to form a floral curtain. They fell from the roof to the floor, effectively dividing the pavilion. The air was heavy with the fragrance of flowers. The setting sun in the horizon completed the idyllic picture. Imraan experienced a sense of peace as he entered the pavilion. It was the perfect setting for a music session.

Piles of silk cushions lay on a spotless white sheet, which was spread over a thick Persian carpet. Jade and china bowls heaped with fresh and dry fruits were placed on one side while an ornate silver spittoon stood at the other end of the carpet. A sitar completed the picture.

A few eunuchs stood around the pavilion, whispering in low tones. Minutes later, one of the eunuchs announced the arrival of the princess. Imraan stood up and bowed his head so that the princess could arrive unseen. The melodious tinkle of anklets heralded the entrance of his pupil. The whiff of her perfume reached him. It was almost impossible for the young man to keep himself from stealing a look at the princess, but the words of the Sufi saint echoed in his head and he willed himself to keep his eyes down.

Imraan bowed in her direction and said—'Salaam Alekum, Shahzadi, I am here on the Badshah's command.'

'Alekum Salaam,' from within the veil emerged a soft voice; it had depth and melody. She settled down on her side of the pavilion with her ladies. With a resolute shake of his head, Imraan brought himself to the task at hand. He picked up the instrument and began tuning its strings.

From her vantage position, the princess stole a glance at her Ustaad. She took in the tall and graceful figure of the young man. He was more handsome than anyone she had ever seen. Something about him reminded her of her Abba. Maybe it was his stature. Her heart began to beat faster as she picked up the sitar in her hands.

The moment Imraan's hands touched the sitar he became oblivious to the intoxicating ambience and the shehzadi. He performed a thanks giving prayer to his own Ustaad and, closing his eyes, he began strumming the strings with precision, remembering each note of the raag he was about to play. Laadli listened with growing fascination. This was the kind of music she wanted to play. It was magical. Even the eunuchs who were hovering around protectively stood enraptured. The ladies accompanying the princess cried out 'Wah, wah, Subhan Allah,' without any restrain. They were spellbound by his skilful rendition of the raag.

'Subhan Allah,' the princess exclaimed as he ended his rendition. 'That was a superb piece. Will I be able to play the instrument as expertly, ever?'

Imraan blushed happily at the praises heaped by the small audience.

'Why not? With devotion and dedication, you can learn to play even better than me. But before I begin teaching you, I would like to tell you something about raags themselves. You must be aware that Hindustani music is replete with raags which have been created very scientifically. Each raag is played at a specific time of the day. For instance, Raag Malkauns is a late night raag that is played between nine in the evening and midnight, in the third quarter of the night, while Raag Bhairavi is an early morning raag to be played between six and nine in the morning. You should not attempt to play a raag at the wrong time. The magic is lost when you do that. I heard you playing Raag Bahar at eleven in the morning, which was not correct. It is supposed to be played only between midnight and three a.m. This is the first rule you must obey. Since it is almost six in the evening, we will play Raag Bhoopali.'

Laadli sat captivated as Imraan taught her the basic rules. She picked at the strings in all earnestness, willing herself to learn the intricate notes of Raag Bhoopali. The magic of the setting sun and the melody of the notes mingled with the cool breeze laden with the scent of the roses. It was another world, another time. For the inexperienced girl, the atmosphere was intoxicating; it seemed nothing short of bliss.

Immersed in the music, neither the Ustaad nor his pupil realised the time gliding away silently. Slave girls placed crystal candelabras with dozens of candles flickering in them. A couple of silver incense burners were placed on either side of the pavilion to ward off mosquitoes. A bright new moon had made its silvery appearance before Imraan realised it was late.

'I think that is enough for a day. I would like you to practice the notes I have taught you today. Tomorrow we shall take up another aspect of the same raag. Khuda Hafiz,' he said tersely, and performed a respectful kornish to the princess. Then he stood with his head bowed to allow the princess to pass unseen. Once again he was fiercely tempted to steal a look at her, but the Sufi's words echoed in his mind, warningly.

The princess reciprocated his salutation and made her way towards the royal harem, surrounded by her slave girls and eunuchs. Only after she had left the garden did the artist make his way back to his quarters outside the royal palace. As he walked through the narrow streets to his humble quarters, Imraan was overcome with the feeling that, in some way, his life had changed and would never be the same again.

In the royal harem, Laadli thought of her music lesson and smiled to herself.

'I know what occupies the royal mind,' teased Benazir, who had been present at the rose garden during the music lesson. 'I don't blame you. He is very handsome. It would be impossible for a woman not to fall in love with such a good-looking man!'

'Don't you dare tease me! I was not thinking about him. I was just wondering if I will ever learn to play sitar the way he does. He was quite marvellous, wasn't he?' she asked.

'Yes, and he is said to wield the brush as expertly as he handles the sitar. The entire city is talking about his painting skills and the emperor has already commissioned him for a portrait.'

'I wish he could teach me to paint,' the princess sighed, as she playfully pulled at the zari tassels of the brocade cushion on her bed. There was a wistful look in her eyes.

'Now, don't be greedy,' rebuked her friend. 'Isn't it enough that he has is teaching you music? Or, is it the desire of spending more time with him that makes our princess so restless?'

'Don't be silly, Benazir,' the princess said, turning away. She could feel herself blushing. *What has happened to me? Why do I feel so strange?* she wondered. The truth was, her friend was right. For whatever reason, she could not wait till the next evening came.

As they sat in the pavilion the next evening, separated from each other by a freshly erected floral curtain, she wondered if he could hear the thumping of her heart. It beat loudly as he explained the birth of Indian music in his rich voice. 'Your uncle, Mian Tansen, was a great singer. It must have been an wonderful experience for you to learn music from him,' Laadli said, wanting to prolong the conversation. She liked his voice.

'He was one of the world's greatest singers—unparalleled in talent. He was also a great composer. In fact, Raag Darbari Kanada was created by him.'

'It is said that when he sang Raag Deepak, the lamps would light up on their own. And when he sang Raag Megh Malhar, rain clouds appeared in the sky. Is it true?'

'I never had a chance to hear him sing these two raags, but people have told me it is true. There is a tamarind tree next to his tomb and it is believed that those who eat a leaf from the tree will be bestowed with musical talents.'

'If you happen to go there, will you get me a few leaves from the tree?' Laadli asked.

'I am afraid that the tree will soon lose all its leaves since every person wanting to learn music has been tearing them down in great profusion!' Imraan said.

Laadli's laughter rang through the garden. It wasn't just what he had that had made her laugh. She experienced an inexplicable cheerful feeling in his company. She had not laughed in such a blithe manner for a very long time.

The eunuchs threw them a disapproving look, but neither of them noticed. 'Do you known any of Emir Khusro's compositions? I am very fond of his khayals.'

'You like Khusro? I am a devotee of his music. His verses are simple and yet so eloquent:

You've taken away my looks, my identity, by just a glance.
By making me drink the wine of love-potion,
You've intoxicated me by just a glance.

The entire assembly sat spellbound as they listened to Imraan reciting Emir Khusro's compositions. Even the eunuchs crept closer to hear the words. The moon waned, its silver beams reflected in the pool of water. The princess sat enthralled in the company of the musician, as his rich voice recited the lovely verses. She wished the night would never end. There was magic all around her.

The music lessons continued. Resolved not to get into trouble, Imraan forced himself to remain detached. The Sufi's warning rang constantly in his mind, and he made no attempt to see the face of his important pupil. Four months passed. Laadli had finally admitted to herself that she was in love with her tutor. She was not sure when it had happened—perhaps it was the instant she had first heard him play—but she knew that her feelings for Imraan were real. She realised there was not much she could do about this; in her usual self-effacing way, she did not think that he would ever return her love. It did rankle, however, that he did not seem in the least curious about her. Finally, she spoke to her her friend. 'Benazir, why is he not even interested in looking at me? Would a man not be curious about his pupil? How can he remain so indifferent?'

'Please Laadli. You must not think about him. It can lead to nothing but sorrow and will endanger Imraan's life. It is my advice that you let the affair die before it begins. And you must be careful what you say. There will be trouble if the empress hears you.'

'All my life I have done my mother's bidding! When she thrust me on Prince Khusrau, I didn't object despite the fact that I considered him like a brother. Then her next target was Khurram and she pushed me on him. Tell me, am I a puppet in her hands, to fulfil her ambitions? Do I have no say in the matter of my matrimony?' Laadli cried.

'Hush! The walls have ears. You must be careful about what you say. Your mother wishes you to be the Malika of Hindustan one day.'

'She wishes nothing but to continue her rule over the empire!'

Benazir's heart broke to see the unhappiness in Laadli's eyes. Silently she snuffed out the lamps and left the chamber. Sleep eluded Laadli. She tossed on her bed restlessly. She knew it was impossible, but she wanted Imraan to fall in love with her, to woo her with lovely verses and music. Her body craved for his touch.

Over the months, the eunuchs became lax and the number of ladies accompanying Laadli also dwindled as the novelty of the experience died. They found other sources of amusement, leaving the princess to her lessons, undisturbed. Only Benazir continued to accompany her friend every day.

It was a winter evening. The nip in the air was pleasantly chill. Laadli was intent upon winning her tutor's appreciation as she struck a chord on the sitar. For many days she had been practicing intently, just so she could impress Imraan. The rendition was near perfect.

For the first time, Imraan complimented his pupil. 'That was wonderful, Shehzadi. You have picked up the nuances of playing the sitar quite well in the short time that I have been tutoring you.'

Laadli blushed at the compliment. Gathering her courage she replied—'Thank you. It is four months since you began teaching me and it is due to your guidance that I have been able to handle the instrument. Soon the royal entourage will be moving to Kashmir. I wonder whether I will be able to continue with the music lessons.'

'I will request the emperor to allow your music lessons to continue,' assured the Ustaad. He was confident about the talent of his protégé and wanted her to move beyond the boundaries of amateur playing.

'I do not know whether the emperor will agree,' Laadli shook her head sadly. 'We will have to appeal to my mother. She is the one who decides everything.'

'You will have to do that, Shehzadi, since I don't have access to the empress.'

'Something has been bothering me for a few days,' her voice quivered nervously. 'Will you give an honest reply to my query?'

Imraan heard the edgy note in her voice. 'What is it that you want to know, Shehzadi? I am a truthful person by nature and I will try to give you an honest reply.'

'Don't you...don't you feel curious about me?'

Laadli's question took him by surprise.

'I beg your pardon. I don't understand your question,' Imraan said, his instincts alert.

'Don't you want to know more about me?' persisted the princess.

Benazir shot a warning look at her friend, but Laadli was determined to carry the matter to a head.

'She means, you've never displayed any interest in seeing the princess in all these months,' Benazir finally explained.

'Shehzadi, I am here to teach you music, not to gaze at your face. I have heard that the empress is beautiful enough to distract the emperor. So I assume her daughter must be beautiful, too. Beyond that I have never hazarded a thought. It is my duty to impart music lessons to the princess and I intend carrying out my duty without any hindrance,' Imraan spoke resolutely.

'But I am not beautiful. My mother is, that is true, but I take after my father,' Laadli's voice seemed to float around him. 'My eyes are too close together and my brow stands straight over them. The nose is all crooked and the lips too bulbous. The teeth, well—the less said the better. They protrude over the lower lips in a most ungainly manner. Tell me, great artist, can you imagine my plight. No man ever wants to look at me.' There was bubbling mirth in the dulcet voice that came across the floral divide.

Imraan was horrified. He had heard tales about her rejection by the princes Khusrau and Khurram; the rumours abounded in the city. Now he knew the reason. He felt sorry for his pupil and consoled her. 'Well, princess, beauty is not everything. There is something more important than physical beauty, and that is, the beauty of the mind and spirit. You have the talent to rise above physical attributes.'

'Your words are meant to console me. The fact remains that no man will marry an ugly girl, no matter how talented. For that matter, will you paint the portrait of an ugly princess?' Benazir and Laadli suppressed their giggles.

'Why not?' Imraan did his best to comfort the unhappy princess.

'How can you do so without seeing me?'

'If you described your features well, I could paint your portrait without seeing you.'

'Let's wager on that. The Nauroz celebrations are a week away, let us present each other with portraits. You will paint mine and I will paint yours, without seeing each other.' The challenge seemed to excite the princess. The artist humbly agreed to her wager.

That evening, Imraan was in a thoughtful mood as he walked down the Lahori Bazaar lane towards his house. He barely noticed Abrar, the aphrodisiac seller, who was trying to entice his customers with glib talk. Abrar stood by his tattered rug, which was laid out on the street with a heap of dried herbs and potions in minuscule containers. His little son was beating a small drum on one side. Soon a little crowd of curious people had gathered around the vendor.

'Janab, you must be wondering what are those little straw-like dried things. Well, they are the most potent herbs that were ever found on this side of the Himalayas. They can turn an impotent man into a potent bull; a man who is unable to satisfy a single woman, into a stud capable of siring a hundred sons. If you have only daughters, I have a potion that will give you only sons. It is a guaranteed, sure-fire, fail-safe, herbal concoction. For double efficacy, there is the Shabnam herb for your spouse and the Mardangee potion for the men.'

The crowd grew larger by the minute as the vendor continued in his singsong voice, lauding the powers of his herbal treasure.

'You don't believe me? You don't believe Abrar, who has sired a dozen sons? Well, it is my misfortune that no one has realised my worth as yet, but ask those who have bought the potions. They will tell you about the power trapped in these little bottles. The cost of the potion, you asked dear sir, it is nothing. Just a few dams. For the cost of one kebab you can be a potent man. Buy a surkh of Mardangee for a dam and I shall give you a surkh of Shabnam for free. How is that for a bargain?'

A few people had picked up the dried herbs and were debating over the merits of the vendor's offer. Soon the demands began pouring in.

'I'll take a surkh of both.'

'Give me a packet of the best.'

Abrar got busy packing his stuff into small pieces of white muslin.

'How do I consume this dried twig?' asked a customer.

'Yes sir, you've asked the most important question. You have to soak the herb in a bowl of milk and place the bowl in moonlight for a single night. The best time for the treatment is during the full moon nights. Combine the concoction with a little sugar in the morning and drink it up and by night you will be charging like a bull.'

There was a titter of laughter as the men tried to overcome their embarrassment. Imraan smiled despite himself. He had once asked Abrar if the ware he peddled was of any use. The vendor had been candid. 'Janab, I will not lie to you because you are a neighbour. My forefathers peddled the same ware and they swore by the efficacy of their products. I have just inherited the trade. Whether it works or not is a different matter.'

The artist recalled those words as he watched the crowd. Men will do anything to prove their manhood! he thought. Ahead, a lame beggar blocked his way and Imraan parted with a dam before he made his way to the next street. His mind was abuzz with several plans. The princess had challenged him to a tough wager and he had to find a way to accomplish it.

For long, Laadli had wanted to see the portraits and other paintings done by Imraan and he had been postponing it. The next evening, he carried a few of them with him as he made his way to the garden. Once there, he bribed one of the eunuchs to put the paintings up on Laadli's side of the pavilion before she arrived.

Laadli was ecstatic when she found the paintings hung on the wall. She inspected them closely and raved about their superiority over anything she had ever seen before.

'I think your talent is far greater than people credit you for. Not for a moment did I imagine that you could paint so well despite hearing stories about your skills with the brush. If only I could paint half as well as you!' she sighed.

Imraan was modest. 'I don't think I am such a great artist. A lucky one perhaps.'

'I have also brought something for you,' said the princess. Quickly she passed a sketch from under the jasmine curtain. The artist caught a glimpse of the artistic fingers of his pupil before they were quickly withdrawn. He looked at the sketch and asked, 'Who is this supposed to be?'

'Well, I thought that you would find it very difficult to draw my portrait without some help so I have done this self-sketch.' The mirth in the princess' voice belied any seriousness she might have tried to convey.

The sketch showed the face of a rather ordinary looking girl. It was just as she had described herself—rather unattractive eyes huddled close together under severe, straight brows, and a broad mouth with sunken cheeks. Imraan smiled to himself as he looked at the sketch and then began sketching furiously on the canvas that he was carrying with him that evening. Occasionally he glanced to his right, towards the pillar of the pavilion where his paintings were hanging. Hidden amongst the paintings was a tiny mirror, which at that moment reflected the face of the princess as she stood near the paintings. He had a good view of her profile as well as the front of her face.

Imraan had spent an entire night thinking of some way to see the princess without her knowledge. It was towards the early hours of the morning that the idea had occurred to him. He hit his forehead for not having thought of it before; it was so simple. All he had done was to hang a small mirror at a height on one of the pillars, at a forty-five degree angle from where he could catch the reflection. The mirror was well camouflaged by the flower vase that was placed in the niche of the wall. Unseen by anyone, the mirror did its job of providing the first glimpse of the princess to her tutor.

If this face is ugly, I'm a monkey, the artist thought, smiling at the countenance reflected in the mirror. Perhaps she was not as beautiful as her mother was said to be, but there was a certain character in her face, a tenderness in her features that arrested attention. Unlike her mother's blue-green eyes, the princess had calm, grey eyes that reflected her innocence. Her hair, unlike her mother's curly tresses, was a raven silk—straight and fine. The chin was tapered and weak unlike her mother's strong jawline; she had her mother's rosebud mouth, however.

Her complexion was a pale marble with brows that were neatly arched. Taller and broad shouldered than most women, the princess was a bundle of contradictions. Her tall stature belied her delicate appearance. She was like a drooping flower that could, with a little effort, become a tall and beautiful bloom. It required an artist's sensitive eyes to appreciate the girl's inner beauty. To Imraan, the princess was far more beautiful than any woman he had seen.

Despite the Sufi saint's words of warning, Imraan found himself attracted to the young girl as he sketched furiously, capturing the childlike beauty of the damsel. He would give the final touches in the privacy of his room when he could draw unhindered and unhurried by curious eyes.

'Shall I continue practicing the notes you taught yesterday or will you start a new one?' Laadli's voice drew his attention. He quickly packed away his sketch and pulled the sitar towards him.

18

The Nauroz festivities were inaugurated with much fanfare by the emperor. The women vied with each other in adorning themselves with henna and all kinds of ornaments. Tresses were oiled, perfumed and washed with soap nuts and other herbs; novel hairstyles were devised and tried out on each other. Professional masseurs were much in demand for their services. For weeks, excited women had exchanged notes about the latest fashion in clothes: most of them originated within the walls of the harem as Nur Jahan's clothes tended to set the fashion for each season. No one was allowed to wear the fabric favoured by the royal couple, nor were they permitted to use the same colours or copy their styles, but most women stuck close to the original, with little deviation.

Bazaars and public halls were decorated with costly materials and fresh flowers. Across Lahore, people whitewashed and decorated their houses with green branches to herald the first day of spring. A large number of people flocked from neighbouring villages, to amuse themselves. For a full eighteen days there would be merry-making, when people visited gardens, played various games and attended parties. Even restrictions on gambling were relaxed for the festival: Nauroz was the eighteen-day period when one could do what one wanted.

The public was allowed free access to the emperor once a week during this period. The Mughal emperor distributed special kinds of coins called nissars that were specially struck for distribution among the people. Verses were composed by poets eulogising the emperor. Singers and musicians flocked to the court from all quarters—during the Nauroz festivities, the nobles indulged in all-night song competitions. Contests abounded in the royal courts. Nautch girls made a fortune as their skills were in great demand in the city.

There was a lavish display of wealth and magnificence on the occasion. The first day of Nauroz saw the front courtyard of the palace occupied by a large body of glittering cavalry, all dressed in coloured embroidered silk, while the horsemen wore brilliant silken robes. Royal elephants with golden howdahs followed the cavalry.

Processions of the nobles occupied the streets all through the morning. They competed with each other in displaying their riches. There were jewels and expensive artefacts on all sides. Seated in the balcony of the great hall, Laadli and her friend watched the pompous emirs as they arrived in the court.

They giggled at the sight of Meer Muzaffar, the governor of Allahabad, arriving in his beautifully decorated palanquin. The corpulent governor was seated cross-legged against a thick cushion of brocade, his lips stained red with paan. There was an opium-strengthened, tobacco-filled hookah to keep him in good humour. On one side of the palanquin rested a silver spittoon, on the other walked two servants to flap away flies with a peacock fan. A couple of slaves spread rose petals and sprinkled perfumed water on the ground to flatten the dust. A few footmen marched in front to clear the way and a soldier on a stately steed followed in the rear.

'Isn't he a sight?' giggled Laadli as Benazir mimicked the governor's posture.

The governor's wife, Salma Begum, had an equally impressive carriage. A minor princess from one of the princely states, she was entitled to more privileges than the other nobles' wives. The begum sat in a beautiful golden howdah on a majestic elephant. Five other elephants, carrying other wives of the officers, followed the leading elephant. Surrounding the women were the beautifully dressed and finely mounted chief eunuchs, each with a wand of his office in his hand. The female bodyguards, Tartars and Uzbeks, rode their handsome steeds. There were, besides, a large number of eunuchs on horsebacks and foot soldiers with canes in their hands to clear the way. The minor nobles' wives, whose retinue were in keeping with their husband's rank and pay, followed the royal princess.

There were many arrangements to be made for the stabling of the horses, and the boarding of servants and slaves. The Lord High Stewart's office worked around the clock making elaborate arrangements. They could not afford to leave anything to chance.

The noblemen's processions were easier to handle than those of the princes and their consorts. Princess Bahar, notorious for her short temper, drove the administrators to desperation when she arrived with her huge entourage. She was travelling in a palanquin which was covered with a rich net of gold. The eunuchs around it had peacock feathers with handles of enamelled gold adorned with precious stones. The palanquin moved very slowly through the streets. A number of water bearers ran ahead sprinkling rose water to settle the dust. Soldiers with sticks of gold in their hands warned people to keep out of the way as the procession passed through the streets.

No one could dare to cross till the royal procession had passed, otherwise he was sure to be beaten back ruthlessly. It was proverbial that three things were to be carefully avoided: being caught among horses where kicking abounds; intruding in the hunting ground; and approaching ladies of the harem.

The right to way followed a strict hierarchical order. It was customary for a person of junior rank to show respect to his superiors. Emirs had to stand aside to let the royal palanquins pass. At times, the emperor would send a gift of several pieces of betel in a gold brocade bag ornamented with precious stone as a mark of honour to a waiting noble. No breaking of protocol was allowed and severe punishment followed any breach of the rules.

On the first and the last day of the festival, the king took his seat on the throne in the midst of great rejoicing. The nobles stood in rows in order of their rank and offered presents. Jahangir then bestowed jagirs, robes of honour, titles and promotions. Money was distributed generously to the faithful and loyal subjects, artists and artisans.

As usual, the Meena Bazaar was to be held in the harem gardens. This year, however, Nur Jahan had planned an al-fresco luncheon after the bazaar and entertainment programme that followed had ended. When the emperor entered the zenana, an astonishing sight encountered his eyes. As he entered the empress' quarters, he found all the women clad in a striped, colourful ensemble. He was still recovering from the sight when Nur Jahan walked up to him. The empress was decked in a green and white striped churidar embellished with silver stars, over which she wore a bright tunic embroidered with tiny emeralds and pearls. Her striped veil was edged with zari and on her neck she wore an expensive emerald set within a double row of diamonds and pearls. A profusion of pearls hung from her ears, spilling down to her shoulders. Her eyes shone with a mischievous glint reflecting the emeralds. She looked bewitching.

'Begum, I have never seen such an enchanting sight!'

Smiling, the empress led him to the rose garden where the rest of the harem ladies were gathered. The path to the marble pavilion by the riverbank was festooned with garlands of fragrant flowers; millions of rose petals were strewn along the path. Royal musicians sat in a special enclosure. Doves floated around freely, feasting on the grains scattered for them. Elaborately dressed eunuchs sprinkled rose attar all around the place.

The stalls for the bazaar were set up on the fringes of the garden, canopied with gaily-striped material to compliment the leheriya dresses of the royal ladies. As usual, the women had outdone themselves: the items for sale ranged from Chinese printed silk yarns to specially-designed hookahs, from ivory chess sets, to exotic love birds in golden cages. The theme of striped decor found echo all over the garden, in the stalls, layout of the food and the dresses. Impressed by Queen Jagat Gossain's diagonally striped, bright, silk odhni, Nur Jahan had asked about the origin of the material. Her spies had told her that the material was called, leheriya, after sea waves. 'The name comes from the effect of the diagonal stripes. The dyers of Amber are very skilled in preparing this special kind of design on silk as well as muslin.'

Immediately, she had commanded the royal tailors and clothiers to create special dresses from this material for all the Persian women in the harem. Hordes of tailors and royal clothiers travelled all the way to Amber to get the fabric created in the desired patterns and colour combination.

Queen Jagat Gossain was amused—'She will do anything to gain the emperor's attention. So much expense for her whims and theatrics! What next?'

Jewellers travelling from the far coasts of Gujarat and Bengal had been stationed in the city for the past few months, struggling to cope with the orders for new jewellery that poured in from the royal harem. This year's speciality was the studded necklaces crafted out of gold medallions with a dazzling diamond set in the heart of the flower that made the pendant.

The jingle of colourful glass bangles resounded through the corridors of the harem along with the giggles of excited women. This was a special day for most of them; some of them had not had the good fortune of meeting the emperor for more than six months. The tinkle of anklets as the women ran around playfully arrested the attention of the nobles.

After the emperor and his entourage finished bargaining and purchasing from the stalls, they settled down in the elaborately arranged marble marquee for the entertainment to begin. Cool sherbets and wines were served to the guests along with silver salvers loaded with all kinds of nuts, almonds, sweets and savoury snacks. Several slaves and eunuchs went around serving paans and dry fruits. Hookahs and silver spittoons were strategically placed for the ease of the nobles.

The entertainment programme began with the singing of ghazals. The harem women sang verses composed by famous poets and the emperor presented generous gifts to the singers.

'My lord, there is a surprise in store for you,' Nur Jahan smiled secretively, enjoying the emperor's curiousity.

She clapped her hands and a slave girl carried forth an instrument covered in silk and laid it down on the carpet. Minutes later, Laadli entered the hall and performed a graceful kornish to the emperor.

She looked stunning in a purple and white striped leheriya. A purple veil covering her silky hair; several strings of pearls layered her neck and her ears were adorned with a matching set of dangling earrings. Her long fingers teased the strings and the hall filled up with music. The lilting notes of the sitar held the audience spellbound.

Loud compliments followed her recital. 'Wah, wah, Subhan Allah,' the words came from all around.

Clapping joyously, Jahangir beckoned his stepdaughter. Laadli walked towards the dais where he sat with Nur Jahan, and bowed charmingly.

'What a lovely composition! Begum, I was unaware that she had learnt to play sitar so well! You certainly deserve a gift today.'

Saying this, the emperor removed the precious necklace of diamonds and rubies he wore around his neck and handed it over to her.

'I think her tutor deserves a reward, too. He has excelled in his job,' remarked the emperor, summoning a minister. 'See that Imraan Baksh is present at the court tomorrow morning. I want to reward him for making a musician out of the princess.'

An enormous dastarkhan had been laid out in the central baradari for the royal family, while the nobles were led to their designated areas. Slave girls carried silver platters heaped with aromatic pulao, various kinds of meat dishes, kebabs, and lotus stems cooked in the Kashmiri style. Exotic fruits like pomegranate had arrived all the way from Persia, cherries had come from Kabul, pineapples were procured from Europe, melons from Badakshan, dry fruits like makhana, dates, walnuts, pistachio and almonds, from Kabul.

Nur Jahan delighted in the sight of the nobles satiated with the fare, while she tasted a few kebabs and biryanis. She was a light eater and loved feeding people more than she liked eating. Laadli, lost in her thoughts, picked at the food. She was eagerly waiting for the hours to pass. Excited about her rendezvous with Imraan in the evening, she barely noticed the delicacies lying before her.

In the end, the guests were served specially prepared paans with cardamoms. The princesses could not help giggling at the sight of the nobles and emirs who, stuffed with food, found it difficult to get to their feet. Eunuchs and slaves helped them up, and then, tottering, they made their way out of the garden, singing praises about the food and entertainment. It was a satisfying start to the Nauroz.

Amidst all the revelry, no one noticed Laadli and Benazir slipping away to the public park where Imraan waited. They had decided to meet away from the palace, to escape the spies and the vigilant eunuchs. The moon played hide-and-seek behind the woolly clouds as the princess walked stealthily towards the palace gate. The girls had no difficulty in passing the guards who assumed them to be maidservants from the royal harem as they were dressed up in a cotton lehengas and thick veils like the Rajput women. Since the royal palace gates were kept open for visitors during the Nauroz festivities, passing through the portals was an easy task.

Laadli did not know where she was getting the courage to do this. Getting caught by the guards would mean severe punishment for her and for Imraan—he could even lose his life. But, at that moment, all she wanted was to meet him. Clutching Benazir's hand, she walked swiftly till she reached the massive gates of the park.

An acrobat was walking on a rope near the gate. The crowd cheered him on as he balanced himself with the help of a long bamboo pole. For a moment, Laadli halted, her feet arrested by the entertainers. Across the park, a fire-eater was swallowing flames from a torch. His tongue licked the trembling flames drawing appreciation from the crowd. As a child, she had read stories from the *Arabian Nights* and the scene seemed no different from the ones described in the classic. A flock of peasants stood around a snake charmer who was making a cobra sway, dazedly, drawn to the movement of his been. Nearby, a monkey performed tricks, much to the delight of the observers who provoked it with loud cries.

This was such a different world from the cloistered one in the harem. She breathed in the air greedily, exulting in her new-found freedom. For the first time in her life, she had stepped out of the harem without the protection of the eunuchs. It was an exhilarating experience.

'Laadli, don't loiter around. It could be dangerous if we are recognised,' Benazir gave her a push.

They entered the far end of the garden and made their way towards the fountain in the centre. Imraan was lounging on a marble bench at one corner of the garden. As soon as he saw them, he hurried forward and greeted them with a bow. The three of them moved into the shadows of the trees to escape notice.

An uncomfortable silence hung like a thick curtain between them.

'I hope you did not have much trouble arriving here,' Imraan finally said.

It had been Laadli's idea to meet him in the park. He had been appalled at the idea. 'It is dangerous for you to move out of the harem.'

'We all have to die some day. If the fear of death binds our feet, we will never live anyway,' Laadli had commented philosophically.

Living a life of seclusion could not be a very happy thing for a young girl, thought Imraan.

'Shehzadi, as promised, I have brought your portrait.' He handed her the painting and stood back to watch her reaction.

Benazir moved closer and peered over Laadli's shoulders as she unwrapped the portrait.

'Yah Allah, it is an exact copy of you,' she exclaimed.

'Do I really look so beautiful?' Laadli whispered. The artist had captured the startled look in her grey eyes and given them a mysterious depth. The rosebud mouth seemed to quiver with some secret passion. She seemed like a hunted gazelle poised for flight. There was näiveté and purity in the eyes.

'You must have seen her face!' Benazir exclaimed. 'It is not possible to create such likeness without having seen someone. But where and how did you catch a glimpse of the princess?'

'I have a confession to make: I have seen the princess.'

'How? When?' There was incredulity in the girls' voices.

'It is not possible to make a portrait without seeing someone, so I made arrangements to catch sight of the shehzadi.'

Imraan went on to relate how he had placed the mirror near the paintings and observed her, surreptitiously.

'You would have been executed if any of the eunuchs had seen you looking at the princess.'

'That was a risk I was prepared to take for the sake of a glimpse of her beautiful face.'

He risked his life to see me, she thought, trembling with excitement. It was just as she had dreamt. He was the lover she had craved for, seated at Roopmati's pavilion at Mandu. After a moment's hesitation, she threw back her veil and gazed into Imraan's eyes.

'You can look at me without any fear now,' she announced bravely.

They looked into each other's eyes, drinking deeply. The artist could not help falling in love with the nubile girl. She was so eager and so undemanding. The saint's words of caution were thrown to the winds as he gazed into those fathomless and yielding grey eyes. Fired by passion, they were more beautiful than he remembered.

'We must go now,' Benazir's voice seemed to come from a distance.

'You haven't kept your part of the wager, princess. Where is my portrait?' Imraan asked huskily.

She withdrew a canvas from under her bodice and gave it to him.

'Not bad,' commented the artist.

The portrait bore a close likeness to the artist although it was far from perfect. 'Some day, I will teach you to draw better,' he murmured, kissing her hands.

Laadli withdrew her hands as though live charcoals had singed them. His lips were hot with passion. Without a backward glance, she ran out of the garden followed by Benazir, her heart thumping dangerously.

'Oh Benazir, I had never imagined I could be so happy!' Laadli said when they were within the safety of her chamber. The journey back to the palace had been uneventful: the inebriated guards had taken no notice of them.

'You are treading on dangerous grounds, princess,' she warned.

'I cannot live my life wondering what could have been, Benazir,' Laadli told her friend earnestly. 'I am truly happy for the first time in so many years. How can I let it go?'

Days turned into weeks and weeks into months as the two lovers stole moments in the niches and corners of the garden. Laadli's faithful eunuch, Nissar Khan, arranged the meetings. The eunuch had been the emperor's personal valet till he entered into Laadli services after she rescued him from the emperor's wrath. The incident had taken place a year ago when, one evening, the emperor was seated in the royal harem near his beloved Nur Jahan. Inebriated with wine, Jahangir ordered for a bowl of dry fruits. The eunuch ran to obey his bidding and in his haste tripped on the edge of a carpet. The emperor was beside himself with rage—his favourite crystal bowl had slipped out of Nissar's fingers as he fell down. The incensed emperor swore at the eunuch and ordered that he be imprisoned. Jahangir was known to declare severe punishments like lashing and even death sentences to his attendants for such petty mistakes. The eunuch stood trembling with fear and there was silence as the entire assembly waited for the emperor's pronouncement. No one dared intervene. Even Nur Jahan remained silent.

Laadli suddenly rushed to the emperor and fell at his feet to beg for clemency. 'Jahanpanah, I beg you for forgiveness. Please pardon the hapless fellow,' she cried. Her heart tore at the sight of the trembling eunuch. 'You had asked me to name a reward on your birthday. I remind you of that promise, Sir. Grant me this eunuch as the reward and I shall remain ever grateful.'

The emperor was trembling with rage. His intoxicated brain, clouded with opium, could hardly comprehend much of her garble. Grunting with anger, he brushed her away. Laadli clung to the emperor's feet without flinching as he tried to kick her away.

'Stupid child, why do you want to waste away a precious reward for the sake of a eunuch? Have you gone crazy?' he shouted.

Nur Jahan tried to intervene. 'Laadli, what foolishness is this? Get up and go to your chamber immediately,' she ordered.

But the princess was determined to have her way. 'Don't let your ideals of justice be tarnished, merciful emperor. I am asking for this eunuch's life in exchange of a reward you granted me a few months ago. Surely, His Majesty has not forgotten his promise.'

The Mughals were proud of their reputation as people who kept their promises. Jahangir vacillated, unable to deny her the custody of Nissar Khan's life. 'All right, he is yours from this moment. Let his cursed face never appear before me, for then I shall not be responsible for his life.'

Everyone sighed with relief and the eunuch collapsed in a heap at Laadli's feet. He was dragged away by the other attendants. From that day, Nissar became a constant shadow of the young princess. He proved to be a valuable attendant as he provided her with all the gossip and spied for her. It was the grateful eunuch who became the main channel of communication between Laadli and Imraan. Nissar ensured that they could meet clandestinely. He carried missives between the two lovers and warned them of any imminent dangers that may arrive in the form of spies or guards.

It was dangerous for the lovers to meet in the palace gardens so they met outside the fort, in the commoner's gardens. Laadli and Benazir, clad in coarse cotton lehengas to pass off as Hindu maids who worked in the harem, travelled on foot to meet the artist. Sometimes, Ratnavali would go in a palanquin on the pretext of visiting some temple and Laadli would accompany her as a maid, her face hidden behind a veil. Although they met almost every day, the lovers were not content with the stolen hours. They craved for the togetherness of a lifetime.

'Let us run away somewhere,' Laadli proposed one day. 'We will travel far away to Persia where no one will know our identity. There we will live like ordinary people, far away from the Mughal court and the empress.'

'Do you think she will let us go? Your mother will hound and follow us till she finds us and then she will execute both of us. She will never allow us to escape. You know that better than me, Laadli.'

'How long can we live in this manner—hiding and snatching moments together? The tension of being discovered is becoming unbearable. The emperor has decided to move to Kashmir for the summer. Does that mean that we will be separated for the season? I will die without you. You must convince him to allow you to accompany the royal retinue,' insisted Laadli.

But even before Imraan could ask Jahangir's permission to accompany the royal party to Kashmir, the emperor summoned him for an interview.

'Imraan Baksh, we want you to accompany us to Kashmir and paint for us all the beauty and glory of that place so that we can surround ourselves with those beautiful paintings when we return to Agra.'

Laadli was overjoyed when she heard the news.

19

On his way to Kashmir, Jahangir received news that the Deccan was besieged with problems once again. Malik Ambar, the Abyssinian slave who had been subjugated by Shah Jahan, was creating trouble again. The emperor despatched Shah Jahan to take charge of the campaign.

Once more, the harried prince found himself travelling to Burhanpur with his family. Arjumand Bano was pregnant and the journey was difficult, but no amount of coaxing by her husband could convince her to stay back in the palace.

Shah Jahan, frustrated at being made to travel constantly, seethed within. He knew that the crown should rightfully come to him, but the emperor was vacillating and bestowing too much power on Nur Jahan. Realising the uncertainty of his position at court, Shah Jahan decided to get rid of his rivals at opportune moments. As his first move, he insisted on having charge of his elder brother Khusrau, who still languished as a prisoner in the palace. Although the emperor did not trust Shah Jahan with the custody of Khusrau, he had to accede to the prince's wish because he was the only one who could subdue Malik Ambar.

The two brothers left their father at Lahore for Ahmadnagar where Shah Jahan managed to chalk out a hasty reconciliation with Malik Ambar. The prince was keen on returning to the capital: the Mughal troops were a harassed lot as there was a scarcity of food and material in the camp.

The journey to Kashmir was doomed from the start. Jahangir's intemperance had now begun to tell seriously on his health and his asthma was getting worse. The royal physicians appealed to him to reduce his dependence on wine and opium. The hazardous journey took several weeks, but the emperor was ecstatic as he sighted the lofty mountains in the distance.

'At last, I sight peace and happiness for my tormented soul,' he declared tiredly.

Once they arrived in the vale of Kashmir, Jahangir worked furiously on his journal. He penned descriptions of the meadows, the stately trees, the springs, cascades, and the brooks running down the valley and swelling into majestic rivers. He wrote of the clear rivulets springing from the mountains and escalating into picturesque lakes. At Kashmir, he indulged in his favourite hobby of planning the layouts of new gardens.

And then news of Khusrau's death arrived from Burhanpur. The blind prince had died, the messenger said, of colic while in Shah Jahan's custody. No one in the court believed that the death was natural. The body had been hastily interred on the orders of Shah Jahan, denying the emperor the last glimpse of his eldest son's body. Jahangir was devastated. Although Khusrau had rebelled and caused him a lot of grief, Jahangir had always nursed a soft corner for him. He had hoped that the prince would eventually succeed him to the throne.

'Nur, how could he have died so suddenly, he left us just the other day with his brother. I can't believe that this could have happened,' the emperor wailed.

Nur Jahan knew that the death had been manipulated to clear Shah Jahan's way to the throne, but she held her tongue.

In the meanwhile, Laadli and Imraan continued to meet secretly in the maze of the innumerable gardens of Kashmir, exchanging vows of love and promises to spend their lives in each other's arms. It was far easier to romance in secret in the lovely valley than it was in the plains. The strict vigil of the eunuchs and guards had relaxed, lulled by the serene beauty of the surroundings.

Their idyll came to an end when the camp received news that the empress' mother was seriously ill. Nur Jahan was agitated and insisted that they travel back to Agra in time to see her mother.

'We always assume that those whom we love will live forever,' Laadli cried, leaning her head on her lover's shoulder as they sat on a cold stone bench near a stream. Imraan was staring moodily at the water that gushed happily on its journey over the smooth rocks. The news that the royal entourage was to make its way back to the capital disturbed him. He was aware that meeting Laadli would be extremely difficult once they left Kashmir.

'I have always been close to my grandmother. I have so many happy memories of the days spent in my grandparents' house,' she continued, her heart heavy with despair. 'I can't imagine her gone.'

'We are just puppets in the hands of the Almighty, Laadli,' Imraan tried to console her. 'Who knows when he will call us back to be with him?'

'I am thankful to Allah for bringing you in my life. I can bear anything as long as you are with me.'

20

Before the emperor's camp could reach Agra, Asmat died in the arms of her husband. Ghias Baig was inconsolable; he had loved his wife deeply. The tragic blow seemed to sap him of his will to live: overnight he seemed to show his age, transforming from an upright, proud noble, into an old, bent man. Asmat had been the trunk that supported the sprawling family tree, with its many branches, binding them in a mesh of togetherness with her love. Under her benign shade, the tender branches had grown and flourished, unaffected by the storms of events that shook up the others around them.

The empress' palanquin arrived at her father's mansion on the fifth day after her mother's demise. Laadli and Nur Jahan stepped out of it and stood helplessly at the threshold of the quiet house. Silence hung over the huge mansion like a heavy shroud. Tears clouded her eyes as Laadli recalled the joy she had experienced there. She could almost smell the rich flavours of her grandmother's cuisine as she stepped into the house. The gentle and loving touch was still there, hanging around them like a protective cocoon.

Quietly she walked into the large, sunny room that had once been Asmat's chamber. She had spent so many happy hours in that room listening to stories, feasting on the delicacies prepared by her grandmother. Laadli sat down on the floor and, closing her eyes, she attempted to recall each smell, taste, touch and emotion that she had experienced in the room. The cool floor embraced her in its fold, stoking memories of her grandmother's comforting touch.

Her heart overflowing with grief, Nur Jahan crossed the open courtyard with its trees and fountains and walked into her father's darkened study. She could see the old man framed against the light filtering in from the window, seated cross-legged near his desk, lost in his thoughts. His vulnerability touched her. Sitting close to him, she held his hand and pressed it gently. They remained sitting that way for many moments. At last she spoke—'Come father, you are much too important a man to waste your life in the darkness of this room. You are much too strong and capable.'

But he shook his head and pleaded—'Meher, the light has gone out of my life. Let me dwell in the darkness, steeped in my grief.'

There was no point arguing with him. Resolving to return another day to try and convince him, she went back to her palace. The empress returned six months later, this time to talk about a subject she had not discussed with anyone. Her father still rarely stepped out of his study. After the initial greetings and small talk, Nur Jahan broached the subject of Laadli's marriage.

'There is something I need to discuss with you. I need your advice in the matter. Abba, you know that the emperor's health has been failing. If only I could get Laadli married, my responsibility would be over.'

Ghias Baig was absentminded as he responded, 'And whom do you have in mind for your daughter this time?' He felt much too tired to continue any discussion with his strong-willed daughter and wished she would leave.

'I know that mother's death has struck a devastating blow to you, but Abba, you can advise me on this subject without being caustic about it.'

'You don't need my advice any longer, you are the all-powerful empress. You can do whatever you want.'

'Please don't speak to me like that, Abba. You know I love you and respect your judgement. I am pleading with you to help me decide about Laadli's marriage. She is as dear to you as she is to me, and I know that you will never give wrong counsel about her life.'

'If you really want my advice, forget about getting her married to any of the princes. Khusrau is no more. Khurram is already married to Arjumand and he will not marry Laadli. Who else is there to consider?'

Nur Jahan hesitated. 'I was thinking of Shahryar.'

The Itmad-ud-daulah could hardly believe his ears. Outrage roused him from his grief. 'Have you gone crazy? Your greed for power has gone to your head! Are you seriously contemplating getting your daughter married to that good-for-nothing? Do you want to ruin her life? Meherunnisa, think for a while, that girl has suffered enough. Let her be. Don't involve her in your foolish plotting.' He rose from his seat and began pacing agitatedly in the room, shaking his head with disbelief.

Nur Jahan parried his remarks with a counter offensive. 'How can you accuse me of trying to ruin my daughter's life? I want the best for her. I want her to be an empress.'

'Don't try to convince me that you are thinking of your daughter, you are only concerned about yourself! You don't want to lose the reins of power after Jahangir's death. You want to control the empire by proxy. Getting Laadli married is just one of your foolish attempts at clinging to power. Let me make it clear to you—after Jahangir's death, no one can stop Shah Jahan from ascending the throne. With Khusrau out of the way, there is nothing you can do to deter him. He is able and ambitious. As for Shahryar, he is an imbecile with all the wrong habits. He will never become the emperor. All you will succeed in doing is ruin your daughter's life.'

The empress was shocked by her father's anger. She had not anticipated such a vehement objection to her idea. 'Meherunnisa,' her father said, now trying to cajole her, 'I know that you are a very adamant girl, you have always been so, but I beg you to reconsider. If you have any concern for Laadli, please don't pursue this plan of yours. We will find her someone with whom she can find happiness. I love her too much to be able to bear her unhappiness. Forget Shahryar. Have you not heard all the rumours about him?'

'They do not affect me. Whether he visits nautch girls or sleeps with teenaged boys: all that can be brought to an end. Once Laadli is married to him, I will take the responsibility of changing Shahryar's behaviour.'

'You are silly if you think that you can change the ways of a delinquent when the emperor could not do so,' Ghias Baig shook his head sadly. He knew now that his daughter's mind was made up and nothing he said could alter it.

'Poor Laadli,' whispered the old man as he watched Nur Jahan walking away angrily.

Unaware of what was brewing in her mother's mind, Laadli decided to keep the rendezvous she and her lover had planned later that day. The two girls, Benazir and Laadli, crept out of the palace and made their way towards the garden where Imraan was waiting at the usual corner seat by the fountain.

The artist was lost in contemplation when he heard a few voices behind him. Turning, he spotted a few familiar faces. The young men were staggering drunkenly.

'Mian Imraan, what are you doing here, all alone?' one of them said. Altaf was always high on opium.

'He is thinking of his next painting, I presume,' said Amjad, who resented the young artist's meteoric rise. A failed artist, he was perpetually searching for someone to pay for his wine.

The third man, less drunk than his friends, tried to drag the other two away. 'Come on, we have a rendezvous with Zeenat Bano, the nautch girl,' he reminded them.

As the inebriated men were walking away, they ran into the two girls. Not realising what lay in wait for them, Benazir and Laadli were hurrying towards Imraan.

Amjad lurched towards them. 'So this is the reason for our great artist's presence in the garden. What a lovely reason for waiting.'

'Hold your tongue, Amjad,' threatened Imraan. With his hands he gestured to the women to turn back to the palace, but he was too late.

Altaf caught hold of Laadli's arm and pulled her towards him, while Amjad had caught hold of Benazir and was dragging her towards the bench. As Imraan rushed towards them, the third man struck him on the nose. Spotting the blood spurting from his nostrils, Laadli screamed and began struggling against her captor—'Imraan!' she cried.

'Well, well! The heart cries for the lover! Lift your veil and let me see your beautiful face,' Altaf slurred.

As she thrashed about to escape his embrace, her veil dropped.

'You fool, do you think you will go unpunished for this dastardly act of yours?' her eyes blazed. With her free hand she slapped him on his surprised face. The man tightened his hand around her in a fearful grip that hurt. 'You slapped me,' he shouted. 'I will show you what it means to slap Altaf!' His voice was cruel.

'Let them go,' shouted Imraan, trying to grapple with the men. 'You do not know who they are.'

He pleaded with the drunken fellows to release the girls but they jeered at him. 'Yes, yes, tell us who they are. Are they from the royal harem?'

'Of course they belong to the harem. Look at the jewellery and the fair faces,' chuckled Altaf.

Attracted by the shouts, a crowd soon collected and began taking sides. The girls, realising their opportunity, quickly made their escape in the resulting melee. Harassed and scared they ran back to the palace but trouble awaited them when they reached the gates of the harem. An overzealous guard decided to establish their identity before letting them in. Despite Benazir's pleas that they worked for the empress, the guard was not satisfied. He was a new recruit and wanted to prove his sincerity to the bosses.

As the girls were cajoling the guard to let them in, Hoshiyar, the chief eunuch of the harem, strolled by. 'What goes on there?' he shouted, walking towards them.

'Sir, these women wanted to enter the harem and when I asked them to prove their identity, they told me that they work for the empress. They say that they were out on an errand.'

'Is that so? I know all the women who reside within the walls of the harem. I can tell you whether they belong here or not.'

Laadli knew all was lost. Hoshiyar smirked sadistically when he lifted their veils. 'Well, well, it is none other than the empress' daughter. But what might the princess be doing in those coarse garments. Was it a rendezvous outside the palace walls?'

'It is none of your business,' snapped Laadli, moving past the gaping guard. Even as the girls made their way to their apartments, they knew that Hoshiyar would report the matter to Nur Jahan.

'With all her spies around, she was bound to find out about Imraan one day. I will just have to seek my mother's forgiveness, ' Laadli said.

'I doubt if the empress will be merciful in this matter.'

Benazir was right. The empress was incensed. She had suspected that something was going on behind her back, and now she was convinced that Laadli was meeting someone secretly. She decided to find out. Her network of spies was efficient and it was just a matter of a few hours before Nur Jahan learnt that Laadli had regularly been meeting her tutor, Imraan. She called Hoshiyar and issued explicit instructions to the eunuch.

That night, Benazir rushed into Laadli's apartment. 'Nissar has brought news that the empress has got wind of your affair.'

'Hoshiyar must have reported yesterday night's incident to her,' said the princess. 'Don't worry, I've decided to meet my mother and tell her everything.'

'It is too late, Laadli! I think Imraan's life is in danger. The empress has decided to punish the artist,' Benazir cried.

Laadli was full of trepidation—'What should I do? If she has decided to end the affair, she will do so at any cost!'

'Send Nissar with a message. Instruct him to leave Agra immediately.'

'I will die without him, Benazir!'

'Would you rather lead that unfortunate fellow to his grave? Don't you understand the peril he is facing by staying in this city? Control yourself, Laadli. Let him go away for the time being. We will find a way out later. The empress must not find him.'

That night Laadli had a horrifying nightmare. In her dream, she saw the emperor seated on his throne and Imraan standing in chains before the court. He was being tried for the temerity of falling in love with the empress' daughter. The nobles and soldiers were jeering at him. Then, Laadli saw herself, her veil askew, clothes dishevelled and tears streaking her cheeks. 'Jahanpanah, I beg you to spare Imraan's life. Take my life instead,' she begged. The courtiers sniggered at her as she clung to the emperor's feet. Her mother glared at her from behind the jaali. The harem women laughed at her but she wouldn't let go of Jahangir's feet. Tears streamed down her face as she sobbed loudly, 'Your Majesty, I beg you to let him go.' The guards dragged her away, even as Imraan struggled futilely against his shackles. Then she dreamt that a mammoth elephant stood with its enormous foot poised to stamp out the life of her lover. Imraan was entrenched in a hole, only his head visible above the ground. As the foot came down on her lover's head, she screamed.

Her scream brought Firdaus running to her. Laadli was soaked in perspiration and her heart was hammering wildly. Tears were flowing down her cheeks. As a child, nightmares of her father's murder would wake her up, and now it was the nightmare of Imraan's death that had terrified her. Would she be haunted by nightmares of death forever?

Laadli passed the rest of the night pacing her chamber agitatedly, as she waited for the first light of dawn to light up the east. At last, her mind was made up. She quickly penned a note for her lover and despatched Nissar to Imraan's house.

'Nissar, you must hurry. Run to Imraan's house and warn him of the danger. Ask him to leave immediately for Marwar. Ratnavali is married to the prince there. I'll write her a note to grant asylum to Imraan for some time. Carry this note to him immediately. His life is in grave danger.'

Without a word, the eunuch hurried off with the message. Laadli's note never reached the artist. It was intercepted by Hoshiyar Khan. The cunning eunuch, anticipating Laadli's move, had waited near the harem gate. As soon as Nissar emerged from the gate, he was seized along with the missive by the guards.

Within moments, Laadli's letter was with the empress, who ordered that the eunuch be thrown into the dungeon. With despair, Laadli learnt of Nissar's fate. All her attempts to contact Imraan failed; he seemed to have disappeared into thin air. No one knew where he had gone. She could only hope that he had been able to escape before the royal guards had reached him. Nur Jahan noticed her daughter's wan face but refrained from discussing the matter with her. She determined to have her married to Shahryar at the earliest.

A few days later, Laadli entered the empress' chambers. 'I want to speak to you, Ammijaan.' She had used the term Ammijaan to address the empress after a long time. The chasm between the two women had grown increasingly wide. 'Why did you have to do this?'

'Do what, Laadli?' the empress feigned innocence.

'You have punished Imraan and sent Nissar to the dungeon. Neither of them has done you any harm to deserve such a terrible end. You should have punished me for the misdemeanour.'

'I have no idea what you are talking about.'

'You know very well what I am talking about. Imraan has disappeared, no one knows his whereabouts.'

'How am I to blame for that? May be he got tired of romancing you, or may be he did not have the guts to face the repercussions. Anything is possible.'

'You know that is not true. He would never desert me. As for guts, he has much more of it than many so-called brave men. In my entire life, I have met just two valiant men—my father, Sher Afghan, and Imraan. Unfortunately, both of them were victims of your machinations.'

'Hold your tongue, Laadli! You are crossing your limit. I had nothing to do with Imraan. As for Nissar, this is what he deserves for having encouraged you to indulge in indecent escapades. He is paid by the emperor to restrain you, not to assist you in your dalliances. You may go now.'

Laadli fumed at her mother's words and stomped out in a rush. She almost collided with Shahryar who was strolling towards the empress' chamber. He was the last person she wanted to meet at the moment, she despised the effeminate prince.

'Well, well, why are you rushing Laadli?' he drawled.

She ignored him and kept walking towards her apartment, her vision blurred by tears.

21

Laadli flung herself down on the bed. The sharp shards of her dreams seemed to litter the floor of her apartments. She lay in her bed wondering if her lover was alive. The cool breeze coming from the river fanned her hot, feverish body. As if in trance, she watched a huge spider waiting patiently in the silken web it had spun in a corner to ensnare its prey. She watched as a tiny insect walked into the web. It struggled to free itself from the silken skein unsuccessfully, while the wily spider watched calmly from a corner. Suddenly, the spider pounced on the unsuspecting creature. Within minutes, the insect was dead.

Laadli woke up with a fever that the hakim's prescriptions seemed unable to cure. By the third day, even Nur Jahan was perturbed at the strange illness. 'What is wrong with the girl?' she asked the royal physician. 'Why doesn't the fever go?'

The old man shook his head. 'I don't think it is a physical problem. It is in her mind.'

Guilty, Nur Jahan shouted angrily: 'What is the use of your knowledge if you can't heal the princess?'

The physician shrank back in fear. Nur Jahan's temper was legendary. 'I will prepare a special potion for the princess tonight,' he whispered, bowing himself out of her presence.

A week passed, but the fever persisted. The shadows under Laadli's eyes deepened even further, as the pallor on her face became more pronounced. Laadli refused to speak a word to her mother. The worried empress expressed her anxiety to Jahangir.

'I don't know how to deal with her sickness. It is all because of that artist. I wish we had never set eyes on that man.'

'Begum, I am to blame for all the problems. If I had not suggested that he tutor her to play the sitar, things would not have gotten out of control.'

'No, no, Jahanpanah, don't blame yourself. It is destiny.' Nur Jahan was contrite.

The days passed and Laadli's fever receded of its own accord. She realised the futility of her position. There was nothing she could do either to trace Imraan or be with him. With Benazir and Firdaus by her side, she slowly began to recover. Sitting in the garden one evening, she held Benazir's hand and said, 'It does not matter if he is no longer with me. I had some time with him, and for that I will always be grateful. No one can snatch his memory from me nor wipe his image from my heart.'

Laadli's run of misfortune had not ended however: news reached her that Mirza Ghias Baig, who had been ailing ever since his wife died, was on his deathbed. Laadli's heart skipped a beat at the information. First her beloved grandmother had passed away, then she had lost Imraan, and now the only other person she loved in the world was also leaving her.

'Why am I so unfortunate? Everyone I love is deserting me,' Laadli lamented to her friend. Without waiting for her mother's permission, she summoned a palanquin and rushed to see her grandfather.

The old man lay helplessly in his bed; his breath coming in shallow rasping bursts. His once imposing body seemed to have shrunk in size. 'Abba,' she cried, tears pricking her eyes. Sitting on the floor by his bed Laadli stroked the old man's feet lovingly.

The tired eyes flickered in response and the Mirza tried to speak. With his hands, he weakly gestured at the girl as if in benediction and closed his eyes.

Half an hour later, Nur Jahan arrived with the emperor. They rushed to the old man's side. Laadli moved away towards a window and stared out at the gigantic mango tree in the courtyard. Her mind was numb with grief.

As if in acknowledgment of his daughter's presence, Mirza opened his eyes and a rueful smile lit them up for a moment. He clasped her hands in his shrivelled ones and tried to say something. The lips moved but no words emerged from them. The exhausted soul finally soared and left the body with a shudder. Loud wails filled the room and Laadli knew her grandfather was no more. She felt abandoned and desolate.

Jahangir was grief-stricken. The wise old man had been his advisor for many long years. There were very few dependable ministers in his court, and Mirza Ghias Baig had been one of them. He had been unbiased in his counsel and sincere in his efforts. With the death of her father, Nur Jahan lost her friend, philosopher and mentor. For many years she had depended on her father for guidance.

A few months after her father's demise, she approached the emperor for permission to construct a mausoleum in Agra for her parents. Realising that the work would serve to divert her, the emperor quickly granted her all the monies required for the grand monument she intended to build.

'It will be all marble and silver, standing tall near the banks of the Yamuna, a memorial that will take people's breath away with its grandeur,' she declared one evening.

Jahangir had a great respect for his wife's architectural abilities. The beautiful monuments she had designed spoke of her talent. There was one last thing that needed to be done before she put her energies into constructing the mausoleum.

'Jahanpanah, you have given me everything I have asked for, but my mind is besieged with worries about Laadli's future. I will know no peace till the girl is settled.'

'You are right, begum, it is time Laadli got married. After her unfortunate romance with that artist, it is necessary that she gets married.'

'Shahenshah, I want to remind you of the promise you made during our wedding. You had promised that Laadli would be married to one of the princes and that he would ascend the throne.'

'Who do you have in mind? Prince Khurram has already declined to marry Laadli. We can't force him to do so.'

'I was thinking of Shahryar.'

'Shahryar? Have you taken leave of your senses, Nur? He is inept and stupid. Laadli is an intelligent and sensitive girl. I do not think it is right for us to tie her down with that fool. Have you heard the rumours about his preference for boys?'

'I have heard them but I think it wiser to discount the rumours. They could just be the products of malicious minds.

I have no doubt that Laadli will be able to change his habits. Besides, I will personally take it upon myself to reform his wayward nature.'

The emperor could sense the rising anger in her. Lately, he had been feeling fatigued and the very thought of arguing with her tired him. All he wanted was to rest in the gardens of Kashmir, writing his memoirs.

'As you wish, begum. It was just a thought I expressed. If you feel that he is right for your daughter, I have no objection to the marriage. Now stop fretting and sit by my side. Will you read aloud the latest set of verses composed by Sa'adi for me, in your dulcet voice? It calms my disturbed nerves.'

Now that she had got her way, Nur Jahan happily indulged his whims and read out the verses aloud in tune. Jahangir loved nothing better than listening to her sing verses of famous composers. He sipped his wine and closed his eyes. This was far better than indulging in futile arguments, where the empress would have the final say in any case. In all the years of their married life, the emperor had never revoked her decisions. They were final and brooked no opposition. His consent was incidental.

Laadli was not surprised when her mother announced her marriage with Shahryar. She had sensed it coming. Like the emperor, she submitted to her mother's desire rather than get into a fruitless argument with her. Grief-stricken, she did not have the spirit to fight Nur Jahan. The hermit's prophecy haunted her. But Laadli decided to make at least one attempt at dissuading her mother.

The empress was seated in the pavilion enjoying the evening breeze that wafted in from the river across the fort. The musicians were playing a soft evening raag and the servants were lighting up the candles in embellished candelabras.

'I want to speak to you,' Laadli performed a hasty kornish as she approached the empress.

'If it is about the marriage, there is no use. My mind is made up. And I do not want to hear anything about Shahryar, either.'

'I don't want to marry, not now, not ever. Emperor Akbar had proclaimed a law against the marriage of Mughal princesses. According to his diktat princesses were destined to maidenhood. I want to exercise that right to remain unwedded.'

Nur Jahan's laughter sounded harsh in the serene surroundings. 'You are not a princess. You forget that your father was a common soldier and you are a princess by name, not by birth. The edict of Shahenshah Akbar was meant for Mughal princesses, not for pretenders. I am an empress because I married an emperor, but you are a princess because the emperor was generous enough to grant you the title.'

At that moment, Laadli hated her mother more than she had thought possible. She was a ruthless woman and nothing touched her insensitive heart.

'Take my advice, Laadli. Try to accept whatever Allah has destined for you. Stop lamenting about the lover and prepare for the wedding. You shall be an empress one day and empresses don't cry. Shahryar may be a fool but he is also a prince and one day he could ascend the throne. A small sacrifice has to be made for the comforts of the throne.'

'I do not want to be an empress. I want to be happy. Do you hear that? I want to be happy. I want to escape from the disgusting environment of the harem. I want to live a life of freedom. Please set me free,' she begged, clutching her mother's feet.

'Freedom to marry a man off the streets?' Nur Jahan's brows arched with disdain as she took a drag from her hookah. 'That can never be allowed. You have to marry a prince.'

Laadli stared at her mother with pity. 'Why am I grovelling before you?' she said. 'You can give me nothing. Your very ambitions make you powerless.'

The bejewelled woman sitting before her was the most powerful woman in the country, but no one knew better than her that Nur Jahan was just an insecure woman who lived in constant fear of losing everything. Nur Jahan dreaded the thought of her besotted husband dying, leaving her bereft of imperial powers. She knew that Jahangir's days were numbered—he was a sick man. His overindulgence with alcohol and opium was slowly disintegrating his innards and leading him to death. Laadli knew that she was her mother's only insurance.

Drawing herself to full height, she stood up tall before her mother. 'I will agree to marry the prince if you set Imraan free from the dungeons or wherever you have sent him. I will trade my life for his.'

'You are living under an illusion, Laadli. I do not know your lover's whereabouts.'

The truth finally dawned on the young woman. Imraan was no longer alive. Nur Jahan could not agree to the trade off because he was already dead. With a sinking heart, she walked slowly out of the room.

Shahryar was elated with the match. Although no love was lost between Laadli and him, his dreams of power suddenly seemed within reach. Being on the empress' side would bring handsome rewards. Already the emperor, prodded by Nur Jahan, had bestowed several important jagirs on him. These brought him substantial wealth and had far-reaching consequences in the struggle for power between him and Khurram. He hated his elder brother's guts and nursed secret ambitions of ascending the throne. All his life, the delicate and feminine prince had been taunted and belittled not only by his father but within the harem also. He would never forgive Khurram for the vile name he had given him. The moniker Nashudani had been Khurram's gift to Shahryar.

Right from his childhood, the dull-headed prince had avoided the company of men. He hated the combat training and studies that he was forced to take up. The merest hint of violence could send his heart aflutter. There was nothing that attracted him more than spending time in the dance halls and the bars. Addicted to opium, he spent most of his time with dubious companions who took advantage of his position. Sunk in wine and debauchery, Shahryar spent time away from the court and shunned the harem because of the mocking women. He feared the wrath of his father and hated the derisive remarks of his brother, Khurram. No one gave him any importance nor asked him for his opinion.

But now, with the support of the empress herself, he could step up the royal ladder. Much as he disliked Laadli for her supercilious airs, he had no objection to marrying her, if that was what it would take to get the throne.

The occasion of the betrothal of Shahryar, the fourth son of the Emperor of Hindustan, with the daughter of Nur Jahan by Ali Quli Beg, took place at Lahore and was marked by great rejoicings through the city. The emperor gave gifts and valuables valued at a lakh of rupees as a betrothal present. The bride's uncle, Asaf Khan, the new Itmad-ud-daula, threw a grand feast for the royal guests in his new palace at Lahore.

On the day of the wedding, Laadli was woken up in the early hours of the morning by giggling attendants and led for the ritualistic bath. Laadli sleepwalked to the hamamgah where Benazir was waiting with a specially prepared unguent of turmeric, sandalwood powder, fresh cream and hundreds of other herbs, all designed to make her skin glow. The attendants smeared her body with the concoction amidst much jesting about the size of her breasts and the proud upward slant of her nipples.

Warm, scented water was poured over her body to wash away the remnants of the sandalwood paste. Her hair was washed and shampooed with herbal potions and then dried over aromatic fumes. It was braided with a profusion of rose buds and pearl pins were stuck at regular intervals. An old woman applied henna on her feet and palms, tracing delicate patterns over them.

Laadli sat with the drying henna on her limbs, lost in thought about her future. Imraan still haunted her mind. She didn't love Shahryar, and she was sure that he did not love her. A maid brought her lemonade fortified with a dash of opium, intended to alleviate her nervousness. All around her, the harem women sang songs of love and ardour, the lyrics loaded with erotic connotations. The rhythm and the music grew faster and Laadli's mind began reverberating with the music and opium. Her body had grown numb and a languorous feeling overtook her as she was dressed in bridal finery.

Nur Jahan had taken pains to design the wedding costume of her only daughter. It was a vision in the softest of muslins, a transparent peach qaba with sequinned embroidery, which highlighted her peaches and cream complexion to perfection. The flaming orange veil set with emeralds and pearls, and the orange churidar were ideal bridal wear. The empress had presented her personal hair ornaments to the bride. A heavy gold tiara was pinned on her head to hold the veil in place. The edges of the veil ended in tiny pearls and her ears were covered with gold and rubies. Layers of pearl strings reached up to her chest and her diamond nose-pin dazzled in the light. Her arms were covered with dozens of gold bangles studded with rubies and emeralds. The armlets were intricately designed ropes woven out of gold with strings of pearls and rubies dangling from them.

Her eyes were rimmed with kohl, the lips were made redder with a special unguent made from ripe pomegranate, the pale cheeks were rubbed with the extracts of rose petals to give them colour, and a splash of gold dust was sprayed on her eyelids. Her clothes smelled of exotic essence and her entire body was glowing with the effort of the women. She looked beautiful. Benazir stared at her friend and whispered— 'You look angelic. I hope you are happy.'

'I was not destined for happiness, Benazir,' the princess replied, a sardonic twist on her lips.

As Ratnavali and Benazir led Laadli to the flower-festooned canopy under which the marriage was to take place, Nur Jahan hugged her daughter. 'I am doing what I think is best for you. I hope you are happy,' she said emotionally, choking over the words.

Laadli threw a disdainful look at her mother and walked haughtily to the beautifully decorated podium. She was not going to assuage her mother's guilt. Viciously, she delighted in punishing the empress with her silence. The emperor was seated near Shahryar, across the hall, in a flower-decorated enclosure. The prince was clad in crimson brocade with zari work and a golden cummerbund. Always a rakish dresser, Shahryar had outdone his costume this time. Jewellery covered every inch of his body. Jahangir was feeling morose and unwell. From time to time he drifted into a stupor. Nur Jahan, radiant and happy, was too preoccupied to notice his condition.

Once the marriage was solemnised, the assembled nobles began their congratulatory rounds. Gifts flooded the couple: eager to please the empress, most of the nobles and emirs had gone overboard. Nur Jahan, in return, gave away precious pearls and gold mohurs to the guests. Jahangir declared that the important jagir of Dholpur would be given to the young prince. He gifted Laadli with a jagir in Gujarat and several caskets of pearls and diamonds. This was the last wedding that he was likely to attend for many years.

A grand feast followed the wedding. Special chefs of the royal kitchen had worked around the clock to create the mouth-watering fare. The chef for the preparation of the array of meat dishes came from Kashmir, a Shirazi cook was in charge of the succulent kebabs, for the spicy pickles a cook had been brought in from Amber, and so was the cook who made the papads. For the fish delicacies, a cook came in from the Konkan coast and a Persian chef was responsible for the delectable pulao. For the delicious variety of halwas, a Choubey chef was brought from Mathura, while a chef from Bengal prepared the sweetmeats. After the feast, a platter of paan was passed to the guests. Tied in silk thread, the betel leaves were packed with fragrant zarda, ambergris and dates. For weeks, Lahore would talk of nothing but the marriage feast of the emperor's youngest son.

As the feasting continued, the women led Laadli to an inner chamber in the harem to prepare her for the bridal chamber. They undressed her and began massaging her with perfumed oils. Dozens of expert hands moved in tandem all over her body, tantalising and teasing, their touch sensuous and intimate. Hundreds of sparks burst in her nerves, firing them with passion. Her opium-ridden mind tingled her senses with delightful warmth. A slow flush rose in her cheeks as she felt herself aflame with desire. Benazir looked slyly at her as a woman gently parted her legs and rubbed the insides of her thighs sensuously. A moan escaped her lips and she closed her eyes in ecstasy. They teased and excited her, laughed at her reactions, as her groin grew moist with molten desire. Her entire body ached for the touch of a man.

Laughing and teasing, they led her to the bedchamber. Seated on the flower-bedecked bed, she awaited her husband. The overpowering scent of the flowers made her senses swoon and she felt light-headed. It all seemed like a dream. Only Benazir remained by her side till, at last, Shahryar lurched drunkenly into the chamber. He approached his wife with a silly smile that vanished the moment Laadli directed her blazing eyes at him. Desire drained out of her body within moments at the sight of the drunken prince, and her nerves turned taut with loathing. She resisted his clammy hands, which wandered all over her body like serpents. She pushed him away and stood up. Shahryar looking surprised but relieved, sank into the cushions in a drunken stupor. Moments later he was snoring while Laadli stood forlornly staring at the garden beyond, the image of Imraan flooding her mind. Tears of frustration ran down her painted cheeks, leaving ugly lines in their wake.

Next morning, the women inspected the virgin white sheets on the nuptial bed and shook their heads knowingly. The marriage had not been consummated. Rumours about Nashudani's impotence began rearing their head and the harem women gossiped about Laadli's misfortune. The gossip soon reached Nur Jahan. Determined to make a man out of the foolish fellow, the empress began thinking of ways and means of making Laadli seduce him. Nur Jahan knew that she would never be able to stop the tongues wagging until Laadli produced a child. Throughout the empire, people were talking about how she had ruined her daughter's life.

She wrung her hands tiredly, so many matters were awaiting her nod. Ever since Jahangir's health had deteriorated, he had stopped taking even the minutest interest in state affairs. Nur Jahan had no one to guide and advice her. She wished her father were alive. He was the only one who could have helped. There was also the unfinished construction of the mausoleum she was building for her parents. So many responsibilities, sighed the empress, but the most important one was to put Laadli's life in order.

Shahryar had suffered rejection for many years, which had driven him to find solace in the company of nautch girls. They did not condemn nor judge him the way his royal relations did. In their company, Shahryar found comfort and camaraderie. Laadli's haughty and aloof personality doused his passion. Her frosty looks condemned him to impotence. The moment she directed her glacial grey eyes at her husband, he shrank in his clothes. Frustrated, he would seek the company of his friends and drink with them till he lost consciousness. After a few months, Shahryar stopped going to his wife's chamber. It suited Laadli. She hated the cowardly man she had married; his very touch repelled and nauseated her. No matter how much the empress compelled her, Laadli could not bring herself to seduce her husband. She knew that her mother was distraught at the turn of events. Truth be told, even she had not expected things to turn out so disastrously.

It was during one of her visits to the mausoleum site that the empress thought of a solution to Laadli's problem. She would seek the help of Hira Bai, Shahryar's favourite courtesan, to solve the matter, Nur Jahan decided. The marriage had to be consummated. It was already several months since Shahryar had married Laadli and the tongues had not ceased wagging. In fact, the rumours had gained momentum with each passing day as the prince openly flaunted his relationships with courtesans and young boys. He did it more to spite Laadli than for any other reason. It was his way of seeking revenge.

As soon as she returned to the palace, Nur Jahan summoned Hira Bai to her chamber and explained the plan to her. In return for her services, the courtesan was offered a vast amount of gold and gifts. According to the plan, Hira Bai would seduce the opium-dulled prince in her chamber and then Laadli would replace the courtesan in the darkness. At first Laadli baulked at the idea proposed by her mother. It was beneath her dignity to seek consummation of her marriage by deceitful methods. She acquiesced only when the empress explained that the pretence was necessary if she wanted to bear a child. Laadli desperately wanted a child of her own, to nurture and love. She agreed to her mother's plot with great reluctance.

Shahryar, impassioned by the vulgar gyrations of the courtesan and her crude seduction, tottered to the bed, half conscious and flung himself on the woman who lay in the dark, barely realising that it was his wife he was making love to. Laadli bore the violent and brutal coupling with disgust, suppressing her screams as he mauled her body ruthlessly.

For several days the switch of bodies continued till, at last, Laadli could endure it no more. Her body was covered with bruises and her soul felt lacerated with the deception.

It was a humid morning and the court was in session. Jahangir was listening to the presentation of a bribery case against one of the nobles. Laadli watched the proceedings from behind the screen, seated near her mother. She felt bored and listless. At first, she discarded the sudden wave of nausea as the outcome of foul weather, but she couldn't ignore the dizziness for long. She swooned and fell in a heap on the floor. The empress immediately had her daughter carried to the harem and the royal physician was summoned. He confirmed what Nur Jahan had already suspected. Laadli was pregnant.

Relieved and exultant, the empress whispered the news into the emperor's ears. There was rejoicing and celebration in the harem. The overactive tongues that had been spreading rumours fell silent at the news. Laadli was ecstatic.

'Congratulations, Shehzada,' the eunuch sniggered as he carried the news to Shahryar.

The prince was livid when he heard the news. *Laadli has been unfaithful*, he thought to himself. *But how could she have had a lover? She has been under the constant vigil of the eunuchs ever since the Imraan affair.* He knew he had not slept with her, then how had she gotten pregnant?

The thought that he had been cuckolded haunted his mind till the empress sent for him. 'I had to resort to trickery,

Shehzada, since you were not willing to consummate your marriage with Laadli and the rumours were getting more colourful with each passing day,' she rebuked gently. 'When your manliness is challenged it is best to set rumours at rest, isn't it? It would be prudent not to discuss the matter any more,' she warned, offering him a bowl of kheer.

'But Hira Bai will talk. They like to brag about such things,' he mumbled sheepishly.

'She will be taken care of. You don't have to worry about her,' assured the empress.

With his suspicions laid to rest, Shahryar strutted proudly around the court accepting the congratulations of the nobles. His manhood had been redeemed. That evening, while playing chaupar, the empress told Jahangir about how she had brought about the consummation of Laadli's marriage. The emperor guffawed loudly when he heard the story.

'Begum, you always come up with the most brilliant ideas. It is amazing how your pretty head thinks up such devious plans. I could never have thought of such a solution,' he complimented. 'Do you have any solutions for us? We have been married for so many years, fruitlessly.'

'Your Majesty, we should look forward to our grandchild's birth. I am too old to bear children.' There was a sorrowful look in her eyes. There would have been no problems of inheritance if she had borne the emperor's child.

'You will never be old,' the emperor remarked loyally. Nur Jahan looked as beautiful as the day they had first met. The slight rounding of her figure and the maturity in her lovely eyes suited her better. If anything, she looked lovelier than he remembered. Pride lit up his eyes as he stared at her admiringly.

'Check and mate,' declared Nur Jahan triumphantly, demolishing the potent piece on the ornate chessboard. The emperor always lost, but he didn't mind losing to his brilliant wife; she was par excellence where strategy was concerned.

22

As the baby grew in her womb, Laadli found herself surrounded by advisors. Suggestions poured in from all sides. She had taken to drinking milk by the gallon although she detested the stuff. Her arms were covered with half a dozen amulets procured from soothsayers.

'You are going crazy with anxiety. Everything will be all right, don't worry so much. And stop following each and every tip given by those stupid harem women,' Benazir said, massaging Laadli's swollen feet. Benazir herself had recently gotten married and lived in Agra.

'You will not understand, Benazir. This baby is my only reason for living. I will do anything to have a healthy baby.'

'Tell me honestly, do you want a son or a daughter?'

'I know that my mother is pining for a grandson so that her reign can continue for another generation. Her craze for power never ceases to amaze me. I want a daughter so that I can bring her up the way I want. Moreover, if I have a son, I will soon have to part with him, whereas a daughter can live with me in the harem, forever.'

'You don't envisage getting her married?' Benazir joked.

'Of course. She'll be free to marry whoever she wants,' Laadli replied seriously. 'I will not impose any restrictions on her.' Laadli's eyes clouded over as she remembered Imraan and her ill-fated love affair. So many nights she had lain wondering if he was alive, so many hours she had spent re-living the happy moments she had passed with him.

'Benazir, do you think Imraan is alive?' she asked her friend.

It was the hundredth time that Laadli had asked her that question. Benazir knew where the conversation would lead and tactfully changed the subject—'Laadli, I saw the baby move. Did it kick just now?'

Laadli, sensing the baby turning inside, nodded happily.

The empress keenly monitored the progress of her grandchild's growth inside Laadli's womb. Astrologers and soothsayers made a fortune as her anxiety grew with each passing day. Despite her busy schedule, she found the time for a journey to Ajmer to pray for a grandson. For a while she forgot all about the throne and Jahangir's successor. She tore herself away from state affairs to spend time with her daughter.

'Laadli, you should not be running around in this manner. It is not good for the baby,' the empress scolded her daughter. 'And did you take the potion sent by Hakim Abdul Khan?'

It amused Jahangir to see his wife so excited about Laadli's pregnancy. 'One would think that this is the first time anyone has borne a baby in the harem,' he joked.

'Well, this is the first time my daughter has borne a child. And it could be the last,' there was a tinge of regret in her voice. 'Unlike Arjumand who is forever pregnant.'

Arjumand had been pregnant at least ten times in the last eleven years of her marriage, although only five of her children had survived. Nur Jahan realised that Shah Jahan and his sons could rule the empire for the next two generations if she did not stop him from ascending the throne. The only option was to install Shahryar as the emperor. If Laadli produced a son, he would be anointed as the crown prince and she could rule over another generation.

Meanwhile, reports of Shahryar's ambitions reached Shah Jahan at Burhanpur. His father-in-law Asaf Khan warned him that the empress intended backing Shahryar's claim to the throne. Annoyed at the developments, Shah Jahan began to plan out his next move. He wanted to return to the capital and be near his father to thwart the empress' designs. Just then, news arrived from the western frontier. Qandahar had fallen to the soldiers of Persia. The emperor could hardly believe the tidings since Shah Abbas, the King of Persia, had from time to time sent ambassadors and expensive gifts to him professing friendship. Qandahar was an important city, strategically located, as the bulk of trade that took place between Hindustan and Persia on the land route, passed through it.

Jahangir commanded Shah Jahan to proceed on a campaign to Qandahar. However, not wanting to remain away from the politics of the capital, Shah Jahan remained entrenched at Mandu refusing to proceed for the battle. In the meanwhile, Jahangir's health was failing rapidly. Repeated visits to Kashmir and the treatment of royal physicians did him little good. Though outwardly the empress retained a calm demeanour, she realised that she would have to convince the emperor about Shahryar's suitability for the throne quickly if things were to work out to plan.

The pain struck Laadli as she was strolling around the garden. She clasped her belly and sat down heavily on a bench, her breath coming in short gasps. Benazir took one look at her ashen face and quickly rushed to her side.

'Can you make it to your chamber or should I summon the women? Shall I fetch the hakim?'

'No, no, the pain is still not so intense. I like it here, it is so cool and pleasant.'

'Let me help you inside,' insisted her friend.

A fresh wave of pain hit her even as she tried to get up. With a whimper, she sat down on the marble bench once again. Drops of perspiration ran down her temples as she fought the excruciating pain. Benazir ran back to the harem and came back with a few servants. Between them, they helped Laadli to her feet and carried her back to her rooms.

When Nur Jahan heard the news, she hurried to her daughter's side. Meanwhile, the hakim had also arrived. It was almost noon when the puny baby finally emerged from the comfortable darkness of the womb and announced its appearance with feeble wailing. To Laadli's delight and Nur Jahan's disappointment, it was a girl.

Once the baby was bathed and dressed, the empress carried her to Jahangir. He peered at the screwed up, red-faced baby cradled in his wife's arms and smiled gently.

'It is too early to be sure but I think she looks like you, Nur,' he declared. The emperor said it to placate his disgruntled wife because he knew how disappointed the empress must have been on learning that it was a girl. The empress was not amused. It had taken a lot of planning and plotting to get Laadli impregnated. It might not be very easy to cajole Laadli into sleeping with Shahryar once more. There was not much chance that she would have another baby.

'What are you going to call her?' asked Jahangir.

'I think Laadli has already decided on a name. I can't imagine how Laadli was so sure that she would give birth to a daughter.'

'That daughter of yours has a mind of her own. She may seem to be a meek person, but the girl has inherited your stubbornness.'

Suggestions for the child's name came from all quarters but Laadli stuck to her decision. She would call her daughter Arzani. 'Isn't it a beautiful name? I have always liked that name. When I was a child I would often pretend my name was Arzani. All my life I have hated my name. Laadli is so unimaginative and commonplace. My mother wants me to be an empress—imagine an empress called Laadli Begum!'

As the days flew by, Arzani grew up into a chubby and happy child. Laadli took her role as a mother seriously. She missed Firdaus tremendously—her old nurse had died after a prolonged sickness a few months back. Shahryar often dropped into her chamber to meet his daughter. He adored the little child because she had restored his pride. Thoroughly pampered and spoilt by her doting parents, Arzani won hearts easily with her childish prattle and lovely looks. Even Nur Jahan, despite the initial reserve, soon warmed up to the child. Jahangir, who loved children, spent much of his spare time playing with his foster daughter's child. At two, she was already picking up the nuances of playing chaupar and sat with her grandparents when they played the game.

Increasingly, however, Nur Jahan had no time for other activities. With growing alarm, she realised that Jahangir was losing all interest in governing the empire; he spent all his time writing his memoirs or studying the paintings produced by his artists in the ateliers that were running at great costs to the treasury. Whenever she insisted on his attending the court or spending time on state matters, the emperor would find some excuse to keep away. 'In any case, I rarely take a decision without consulting you, Nur. All I need is some peace to do the things I love.'

The loss of his son seemed to play on his mind. 'I am to blame. If I had not agreed to send Khusrau with Khurram, he would be alive today. Khurram is ruthless; he will remove any obstacle to his attaining the throne.'

'You can't blame yourself for the turn of events. It was destined to happen,' Nur Jahan soothed, trying her best to console her guilt-ridden spouse.

As the emperor spent more time away from the court, Nur Jahan involved herself completely in the affairs of the empire. Ever since her father passed away, there had been a void in her life. She missed his wise counsel and sincere advice. Now she turned to Laadli for suggestions, using her as a sounding board much of the time. Her daughter was the only person she could trust.

'The Afghans are on the path of revolt in Bengal once again. I wonder what can be done to check their growing unrest?' the empress contemplated aloud one evening.

They were seated in the garden watching Arzani play. The child was running after the peacocks, trying to grab their colourful feathers.

'I think it is because we have been following a wrong policy for many years. Whenever the emperor decides to punish an emir, he banishes the fellow to Bengal. As a result they don't try to solve the local problems. Instead, they while away their time collecting enough revenue to bribe the emperor to get back in his good books.'

'So, what is the solution?'

'Well, it is simple. Send the most trusted and able minister to Bengal with a promotion. Let it not seem as though it is a demotion. Promise him a higher rank and riches if he can quell the Afghan unrest.'

Nur Jahan was impressed by Laadli's suggestion. Her meek, self-deprecating daughter had grown into an astute politician. Motherhood had brought a lot of confidence and poise to Laadli's personality. The empress felt proud. Years of sitting behind the fretwork screen of the Diwan-é-aam, watching the emperor take decisions, had taught the girl many things.

'She will make a better empress than me,' thought Nur Jahan, 'because she is not as rash or ruthless as I am.' To her credit, the empress was objective about her own faults.

She watched appreciatively as Laadli rushed to pick up her daughter who had taken a tumble on the grass. Picking up the girl, Laadli smothered her with kisses and wiped away the tears that were threatening to run down the plump cheeks. Reassured by her mother's voice, the child resumed chasing the birds across the garden.

'I have always underestimated her,' thought Nur Jahan. 'I can easily handle state matters with a little help from my daughter.'

The empress began consulting Laadli for most matters, taking her opinion seriously. It was Laadli who restrained her mother from making rash decisions, and advised moderation when Nur Jahan lost control of her temper. Gradually, the daughter became her mother's most trusted advisor. They sat together for long hours, discussing the merits and demerits of petitions, debating matters of promotions and transfers of the nobles, granting of jagirs and juggling resources. In Laadli, Nur Jahan found the perfect foil—intelligent, mature, calm and even-tempered.

Soon the two had a new problem to cope with. Shah Jahan had decided to make his move towards seizing power; if he did not do it now, he thought, he could be left out in the cold. His first step was to seize the jagirs of the empress and Shahryar. The emperor was livid when he learnt of the revolt. In anger, he transferred Shah Jahan's jagirs in Punjab to Shahryar.

'It is time Shahryar was given a chance to prove his worth,' suggested the empress one evening as they sat in the jharoka watching an elephant fight. Two massive bull elephants decorated with colourful tassels, ribbons and jewellery, were brought to the courtyard, their mahouts sitting atop. Nobles, commoners and royals surrounded the courtyard to watch the event. The harem ladies were seated behind the fine marble jaali, bejewelled and excited as they wagered on their favourite elephant. Jahangir gestured for the fight to begin and nodded absently at Nur Jahan, riveted by the elephants.

With a tinge of impatience in her voice, the empress repeated her statement—'Shahryar must be sent on the battlefield to keep him away from the bad influences that surround him. He has to learn the lessons of war just as everyone else.'

'Let him enjoy life. There is time enough for him to go to battles.'

Trumpets blew and cymbals sounded as the mahouts urged their animals forward for the attack. The creatures, majestic in their bearing, charged at each other. A roar of excitement went up around the courtyard as the bigger beast engaged his trunk with the opponent. Jahangir clapped excitedly. 'I will place my bet on the bigger brute. He has the advantage of height as well as girth.'

'I will back the smaller one. Size doesn't necessarily offer an advantage. It is one's tactics that matter,' Nur Jahan said, throwing a disdainful look at the emperor who was bending forward in excitement, his tawny eyes alight. It was evident that he was in no mood to discuss important issues with her. Familiar with his moods and whims, the empress withdrew diplomatically; she knew when to let go. With the crowd's roars rising every minute, it was not possible to capture the emperor's attention.

But the empress did not give up easily. That evening, as the couple walked in the garden, inspecting the rose shrubs, she broached the subject once more.

'There is an important matter that needs your attention,' she began.

'Begum, why is it that you want to discuss dull and uninteresting matters just when I begin to enjoy my walk?' Jahangir looked at her petulantly.

'Jahanpanah, state matters need to be discussed at some time or the other. You have such a busy schedule that I barely find a moment to put forth my suggestions.' It was Nur Jahan's turn to complain.

It worked. The emperor, guilt-stricken, turned to her and smiled—'I was jesting, begum. Unburden your mind and tell me what is bothering you.'

She decided on a direct approach. 'I want Shahryar to be sent for the Qandahar campaign.'

'But he is inexperienced. He is too young and the Qandahar campaign would require a tough and experienced commander.'

'Send Mahabat Khan with him. Give him a chance at least.' Nur Jahan knew the Qandahar campaign was an important one and if Shahryar were victorious, his path to the throne would be clear.

'Mahabat Khan cannot be spared for the Qandahar battle. I have decided to send him to capture Shah Jahan. No one else can bring that fool back to my feet. But I can depute Mir Kamran and Prince Vijay Pratap of Amber to assist Shahryar. They are valiant and experienced commanders and will steer Nashudani on the right path. That is if he heeds them.'

The decision was conveyed to Shahryar and the preparations for the Qandahar campaign began in earnest. Troops were amassed and Nashudani strutted off to battle, bloated with self-importance.

Meanwhile, a desperate and exhausted Shah Jahan was kept on the run by the combined Mughal forces led by Mahabat Khan and his brother Prince Parvez. Jahangir had discounted the possibility of Parvez being his heir. Prince Parvez was addicted to wine and opium and had never displayed any interest in taking part in campaigns. Happy with his luxuries and addiction, he had remained unnoticed by the emperor as well as Nur Jahan. When Parvez realised that the emperor was upset with Shah Jahan and was ready to reconsider the matter of succession, he knew that the time had arrived for him to act. He kept up the heat on Shah Jahan, determined to eliminate him from the line of succession.

The emperor had devised a three-pronged attack on Shah Jahan. While Parvez led one contingent which followed the rebel to Mandu, Dawar Baksh, Khusrau's son, marched with another contingent towards Ahmadnagar. The emperor himself proceeded to Ajmer to be closer to the operations. It was a difficult battle; hot weather, humidity and heavy rainfall hampered the operations. Many of Shah Jahan's soldiers deserted him, reducing his already depleted forces to a bare minimum.

Escaping from the royal army, Shah Jahan made his way to Ahmadnagar where he sought the assistance of Malik Amber. The Abyssinian, however, saw his opportunity to make a good impression on the emperor and refused to help the prince. Shah Jahan was forced to flee to Bengal.

Fighting valiantly, he captured the fort of Rohtas. By now, his wife and children were tired of having to move around. Arjumand, ailing and pregnant, needed comfort, so he installed his family at Rohtas and made his way back to Deccan once again. He appealed to the Ahmadnagar ruler for compassion and promised great rewards when he inherited the empire.

A year passed and the fugitive realised the futility of fighting the mighty forces of the emperor. Beaten by hunger, sickness and poverty, his forces had turned against him. A few of his faithful nobles continued to support him, but several had returned to Agra to surrender to the emperor's forces. Shah Jahan himself was seized with illness. Arjumand had just gone through a stillbirth and her health required the attention of skilled physicians, which he could ill afford while on the run.

'Why don't you appeal to the emperor for clemency?' asked Arjumand. 'It aches me to see the children suffering in this manner. Is there no way out of this mess?'

Shah Jahan let flow a flood of invective against Nur Jahan. 'That woman is the worst kind of serpent—dangerous and slimy. She will ruin my father and the kingdom with her plotting. If she puts Nashudani on the throne, it will be disastrous. I have to stop her.'

'But, My Lord, your rebellion may just put the trump card in her hands. She will use it to poison the emperor's mind against you.'

Frustrated, Shah Jahan realised the wisdom of his wife's words, but his ego would not allow him to beg for Jahangir's forgiveness. He travelled through the deserts of Rajputana seeking shelter from his Rajput clan, but they were frightened of facing the emperor's wrath and refused to help him. Shah Jahan's mother, Jagat Gosain, had forbidden her clan from assisting her son.

'My mother will always side with her husband. It is an unwritten Rajput convention that women must stick with their husband against their own sons,' Shah Jahan explained to his wife, sadly. 'Even Queen Jodha Bai, the emperor's mother, had sided with Shahenshah Akbar when Jahangir had rebelled. She had disowned her own son and supported her husband. I can expect nothing different from my mother, who is a proud Rajput queen.'

Shah Jahan then turned to his friend, Rana Karan Singh, the valiant prince of Mewar, and reminded him of their friendship. Years back, it was Shah Jahan who had vanquished the Rana and brought him to Ajmer with honour. It was on his word that Jahangir had received the ruler of Mewar with much respect and honour. Since then, the two had maintained a cordial friendship that extended much beyond the required protocol of a court. The Rana readily extended a warm welcome to the prince and his family and promised to stand loyal to him.

At Mewar, Shah Jahan and his beloved wife finally found peace and happiness. The Rajputs swore to defend the prince with their lives. The Rana constructed a beautiful marble palace in the placid waters of the Pichola Lake for the comfort of his revered guests. When the emperor learnt about the impudence of the Rana, he was livid. Jahangir despatched Mahabat Khan to Mewar to capture his rebellious son. There were only two options before the Rana—either hand over Shah Jahan or fight against the Mughal forces.

When Shah Jahan realised that Jahangir would go to any length to capture him, he decided to surrender before Mahabat Khan. He could not allow the Mughal forces to destroy the beautiful kingdom of Mewar where he had spent a full year in happiness and peace. Although the Mewar soldiers were valiant, they were no match for the emperor's powerful army. Swallowing his pride, Shah Jahan finally wrote a letter to his father, expressing his repentance and begging pardon for all his faults. It was pointless to continue his rebellion when defeat was inevitable.

Jahangir's reply was that, if Shah Jahan would send his sons Dara Shikoh and Aurangzeb to court, and surrender the captured forts of Rohtas and Asir, he would be forgiven.

'Damn the woman. I can see her hand behind this letter,' Shah Jahan fumed on reading his father's letter. His heart broke at the thought of sending his sons as hostage to Agra, and Arjumand wept endlessly, trying to stop him from acquiescing, but they both knew that it was the only way out. As a gesture of repentance he also sent offerings of jewels, arms, horses and elephants, valued at ten lakhs of rupees. The forts were handed over to Mughal commanders. Thus ended Shah Jahan's rebellion after three years of bloodshed.

Meanwhile, news arrived that the imperial army had been defeated at Qandahar. Shahryar returned defeated, much of his ego deflated after the failure of the campaign.

'It is due to Shah Jahan's rebellion that the campaign did not succeed,' Nur Jahan stated, adding fuel to fire. To some extent, she was not wrong: the army and resources had been split between the Qandahar campaign and the rebellion. Jahangir, chagrined that his attempt at regaining Qandahar had come to a naught, once again, could not bring himself to forgive Shah Jahan.

An uncomfortable peace returned to the empire. Parvez had proved himself and the emperor wondered if he should be the one to succeed to the throne. Would he be able to prove himself an able and just administrator? Jahangir consulted his empress about the matter. She dismissed the idea immediately. There was no worthier heir than Shahryar, she said. The emperor, however, did not agree with her. For the first time, it occurred to him that she was promoting her own cause rather than that of the empire.

Nur Jahan had other things to worry about. Mahabat Khan—one of the emperor's most trusted friends, and a skilled general—who she had been trying to suppress, had grown in stature after having subdued Shah Jahan. The trouble between the general and the empress had begun when the former had rebuked the emperor for taking orders from his wife. Mahabat Khan was opposed to the caucus that the empress had created around herself. He was most vociferous when her brothers had been appointed to important positions and given powers, while other able ministers had been sidelined. He had voiced his opinion to the emperor and assured him of all assistance if he would take up the reins of the empire in his own hands.

'There are able ministers and capable soldiers still left to serve the empire. Under such circumstances, the mighty Mughal emperor has no need to resort to the advice of a woman,' declared Mahabat Khan, disgusted with the way Nur Jahan controlled matters of the empire.

Ashamed on hearing the rebuke, the emperor had acted in some measure on his friend's advice for some time, but he soon fell captive to his wife's charms and influence once again. The empress, on finding out what Mahabat Khan had done, decided that the general would need to be stripped of his power and influence.

For several years, she denied him a promotion and pressurised the emperor into sending him for the worst campaigns, keeping him away from the court. He was driven from the Deccan to the frontiers of Afghanistan, across harsh and unfriendly terrains, wherever the most strenuous service was needed. But now, having quelled Shah Jahan's rebellion, Mahabat Khan had not only grown in stature, he had also become close to Prince Parvez. That a legitimate heir had the backing of the emperor's trusted friend was particularly dangerous in Nur Jahan's eyes.

Despite Laadli's warnings, she appointed Mahabat Khan as the governor of Bengal so as to keep him away from Agra. Then she, along with her supporters, convinced Jahangir that Mahabat Khan was plotting against him. Mahabat Khan had remained stationed at his castle in Ranthambore with Prince Parvez despite being asked to go to Bengal. Finally, Jahangir issued a farman ordering the general to either proceed to Bengal or to come to the court at once. Deciding to challenge the absurd accusations against him, the general marched with 4000 seasoned Rajputs to the court at Agra. In the meantime,

Nur Jahan had trumped up several malicious charges against Mahabat Khan, alleging that he had misappropriated large sums of money. Another ridiculous charges was that Mahabat Khan had, without royal permission, affianced his daughter to the son of Khwaja Umar Nakshbandi. The emperor was offended by this breach of protocol. He sent for the young man and threw him into the prison. Orders were given to seize whatever dowry Mahabat Khan had given to the youth and place it in the imperial treasury.

Mahabat Khan was not the man to put up with these affronts. He could discern the empress's hand behind the allegations and realised that she would even resort to his execution to get rid of him. Determined to teach the emperor a lesson, the general decided on a plan.

The royal entourage—having just returned from Kashmir, and about to set out for Kabul—had set up camp near the river Jhelum. While Jahangir rested in his tent, Asaf Khan left him with a couple of attendants, and ordered the royal escorts and soldiers to cross the bridge in order to set up camp on the other side of the river. The royal harem, including Nur Jahan, had already crossed to the other side.

Mahabat Khan had been waiting for an opportunity like this. He had never imagined that Asaf Khan would be foolish enough to leave the emperor virtually unprotected. With 5000 Rajputs, Mahabat Khan proceeded to the head of the bridge. He ordered his soldiers to burn the bridge and proceeded to the royal quarters where Jahangir was resting. The servants who were in attendance rushed to inform Jahangir of the general's daring action. Enraged, the emperor emerged from his tent and took his seat in the royal palanquin. But as soon as he sat down, armed Rajput soldiers closed in and obstructed his path. There was no one with Jahangir but his faithful valet and a few attendants. Realising the futility of resistance, he went back to his tent. The emperor of the Mughal Empire was under house arrest.

When the emperor did not join their camp, Nur Jahan first assumed he had gone hunting. However, she soon found out that he was being confined to his apartment by Mahabat Khan. Furious at her brother's blunder, she summoned the chief nobles including Asaf Khan and reproached them— 'How could you allow such gross negligence to take place? You have imperilled the Emperor's life! You must go immediately and free him from Mahabat Khan's clutches.'

The sun had set and the nobles, tired after the long journey, demurred. Reluctant to take on the valiant Mahabat Khan, but unable to say so, they advised that nothing could be done that evening. They assured the empress that they would embark on a rescue mission the next morning after sunrise and they would defeat the rebel.

The next morning, impatient with the nobles' dithering, the empress herself took charge of the situation. 'I can't think of a more humiliating situation when my brother, who I trusted with the security of the emperor, is not ready to rescue him. If you can't fight Mahabat Khan, I shall do it myself.'

Asaf Khan tried to reason with his sister: 'Your Majesty, most of our soldiers have proceeded to Atak and only a small band remains with us. It is not prudent to take on the enemy with an inadequate number of soldiers. We will have to plan a workable strategy, and this will take time.'

'You are a coward. I shall prove to you that the emperor can be released with a direct attack on the enemy camp.'

Gathering her soldiers, she harangued them for their lack of courage. 'Has the Mughal Empire turned so unfortunate that there are no brave soldiers left to defend the emperor's honour? Shame on you, who call yourselves soldiers, brag about the prowess of your ancestors and wear the uniforms of the imperial army!'

Prince Jai Singh was the first one to respond: his proud Rajput warriors were stung by her remarks and he promised that they would not rest till they had released the emperor from captivity. Leading the band of his valiant soldiers, the young prince charged towards the river, his sword flashing in the rising sun. Unmindful of the danger, Nur Jahan—seated on her elephant along with Laadli's daughter and her nurse—also joined them. Her hair flying loose and her veil thrown back, she shouted at the soldiers to follow her to the other side of the river. Inspired by her command, the soldiers urged their horses into the stream. Soon soldiers, horses, camels and carriages, were in the midst of the river, jostling each other, and pressing to the opposite shore. Brandishing their swords and scimitars, they rushed to fight the soldiers of Mahabat Khan who waited on the other side of the ford. An amused Mahabat Khan, seated on his charge, watched the disorderly army advancing with the empress.

As soon as Nur Jahan's soldiers approached the bank in a disorderly melee, the general's soldiers pushed forward to fight them. Soon the river was a gory mess of red, its waters covered by floating corpses. Nur Jahan tried to bring some semblance of order to her troops but they were in total disarray. Arzani began howling loudly with fright. The empress fired a salvo of arrows at the enemy with great valour. She was a good markswoman and the arrows found their target without effort. All of a sudden the nurse received an arrow in her arm and wailed loudly. With both Arzani and the nurse crying loudly, the empress found herself disconcerted. She pulled out the arrow from the nurse's arm, staining her own garments with blood.

Mahabat Khan's soldiers rushed after Nur Jahan's elephant, determined to capture the empress. Her mahout had been slain and she herself began to drive the elephant and urge it into the deep water, to escape Mahabat's soldiers. When the empress' army saw her elephant turning back, they were confused. Spotting her bloodied garments, the soldiers assumed that she had been wounded and they began retreating.

Wounded and angry, the empress reached the shore without her soldiers and proceeded towards the royal quarters. Mahabat Khan stopped his soldiers from restraining the empress as she made her way to the emperor's tent. The victorious general now confined both the emperor and Nur Jahan within the royal camp, although he treated them with respect. Laadli and the other women soon joined the empress in the camp and were also treated with honour.

Asaf Khan, who was the cause of the debacle, fled with his son and soldiers to the fort of Atak and barred the lofty gates of the fortress. Not willing to let him escape, Mahabat Khan's soldiers attacked and captured the fort.

With this bold coup, Mahabat Khan had imprisoned all the important persons in the empire and was the virtual ruler. But the wily Nur Jahan had not given up. Although she appeared to be spending much of her time with her granddaughter, she was working furiously with Laadli to find a way out of the imbroglio. Together they formulated a plan. Through a spy, the empress delivered a letter to her faithful eunuch, Hoshiyar, instructing him to amass an army of trustworthy soldiers and wait for her at Lahore. The efficient eunuch was able to cobble up an impressive band of 2000 soldiers of the finest kind with the lure of a fantastic salary. On her part, Nur Jahan began fanning communal passions between the two factions—Muslims and Rajputs—in Mahabat Khan's camp. She worked one against the other, arousing fierce hatred. Besides, she knew that there were many in Mahabat Khan's army who still nurtured loyalty to the emperor and were waiting for the right time to change sides.

One morning, the emperor announced his decision to hold a review of the cavalry. He gave orders that all the soldiers should stand in formation in two lines stretching from the royal quarters to as far as the riverbank. He then directed one of his attendants to inform Mahabat Khan that the emperor was holding a review of the empress' Muslim troops that day. It would be better, therefore, for the general to keep away his Rajput warriors, to avoid communal conflict between the two sets of soldiers.

The two lines of the soldiers extended up to the river in an orderly formation. The emperor, followed by Nur Jahan, inspected the troops and the royal couple proceeded towards the river. As Jahangir reached the far end of the parade, he gave a pre-determined signal to the soldiers. Immediately, the soldiers closed the rear to block out the enemy soldiers. Using the opportunity, the royal couple escaped on a boat that had already been hidden at the bank of the river by loyal soldiers.

Jahangir and Nur Jahan passed over the river to the fort of Rohtas, where the army amassed by Hoshiyar was waiting to receive them. It took several hours for the general to realise that the royal couple had escaped. The emperor had been captive for a hundred days; and Mahabat Khan, the great general of the mighty Mughal army, had once again been defeated by Nur Jahan. It was not likely that he would ever forget or forgive her for the trounce.

23

There was to be no respite for Nur Jahan, however. Shah Jahan, in a rebellious mood again, had proceeded to Thatta to test the waters before he took on the emperor's forces once again.

'If I can't muster enough support at Thatta, I will travel to Persia to seek the assistance of Shah Abbas. He hates the emperor and will definitely help me,' Shah Jahan confided to Arjumand when she insisted on accompanying him. 'It is going to be a rough journey and you are not in good health. You must stay with the children at Burhanpur while I cobble up the necessary reinforcements.'

'I can't allow you to travel in this condition,' wailed Arjumand clutching his arm. Shah Jahan had been ailing for a while: the harsh life they had been leading for the past few years had taken its toll on him. 'Let us go back to Burhanpur together. We can stay there till you recoup.'

'You don't understand Arjumand, things are too precariously placed right now. The emperor is suffering from ill health and Nur Jahan has complete control over the empire.

If anything happens to the emperor now, she will place Shahryar on the throne.'

Despite all his wife's misgivings, Shah Jahan set out for Thatta. But he did not get too far—the weather and his own illness changed his course. Overcome with fever and persistent weakness, he could barely ride on a horse or an elephant and was obliged to travel in a palanquin. His progress was slow and painful. Realising the wisdom in Arjumand's advice, he determined to return to the Deccan. And then everything changed.

Shah Jahan received the news that his elder brother, Prince Parvez, had died. He also learnt that Shahryar had been seized by a strange illness. The once handsome prince had lost his luxuriant crop of hair; even the neatly trimmed beard and eyelashes had fallen out in bunches. His skin had turned white, and prominent red patches had appeared in some places. The royal physicians were unable to diagnose the disease. The prince had taken to spending most of his time locked up in the dark, drinking wine and swallowing opium pellets, away from the curious gaze of people.

Nothing could have heartened Shah Jahan more than this news. With Parvez out of the way, and Shahryar suffering from a peculiar malady, there was no one to stand in his path to the throne. Surely the emperor would embrace him with pleasure and forgive his sins.

In the meantime, Mahabat Khan had been ordered by the emperor to release Asaf Khan and to march against Shah Jahan. The general, cut up with the empress who had been behind his downfall, chose to join forces with Shah Jahan. The prince was overjoyed to have the capable general on his side and greeted him with great enthusiasm. 'Victory shall be ours,' he declared. 'I shall not rest till the empress is defeated and rendered powerless.'

Alarmed at this dangerous collaboration between the powerful general and the mutinous prince, Nur Jahan began plotting ways to suppress them. The emperor was very ill by now, and incapable of giving any advice or support. Broken-hearted by one son's death and another's disfigurement, Jahangir had lost the will to live. He could barely breathe; his asthma had reached an incurable stage. Painful coughing bouts kept him awake through the night. No amount of medicine or opium could alleviate his suffering.

'Nur, the Almighty beckons me. Soon, I will have to answer him for all the sins I have committed.'

'Jahanpanah, you must not speak such words. You will live a hundred years, this is just a passing malady caused by inclement weather,' Nur Jahan assured him, her heart pounding with trepidation.

'Perhaps you are right. I need to get away from the foul climate of this city. I yearn for the beautiful valley of Kashmir.'

The royal physicians echoed his sentiments. The emperor needed to recoup his strength in the healthy climes of Kashmir, they opined. Although he was in frail health, the emperor was delighted to leave for his favourite hill station. He was unable to ride on horseback and was carried in a palanquin. His sufferings were great. Sleepless and breathless with chest complaints and lung congestion, Jahangir lost all appetite for food. Nur Jahan was surprised when he even refused opium, which had been his companion for forty long years.

Even Laadli felt sorry for him. The most powerful man in the Mughal Empire was suffering like a common man. She could only imagine the pain of a father, losing two of his sons in the prime of their youth. And out of the two who lived, one was suffering from an incurable disease and the other were baying for his blood. Even his trusted friend Mahabat Khan had deserted him and joined the seditious prince. The wheels of destiny were spinning in an adverse direction, and there seemed to be nothing that could stop them.

Nur Jahan was worried. *Is this the beginning of the end?* she wondered. If the emperor died now, Shah Jahan was too powerful to be halted in his march to the throne. He had the support of Asaf Khan, General Mahabat Khan and many other nobles, while she could count on only a few. Nobles were switching sides every day: opportunism and distrust thrived in uncertain times.

On their way to Kashmir, Jahangir turned to the empress and said, 'Nur, if I die now, promise me that you will put Shah Jahan on the throne. He may be rebellious and disobedient but he is the only one who can rule this empire. Shahryar is incompetent and foolish. I know that you don't like Shah Jahan, but I assure you that he will make an excellent ruler.'

He pointed to his precious sword, Alamgir. Its golden hilt studded with emeralds, it lay in a golden scabbard encrusted with rubies, pearls and diamonds. The Alamgir had been crafted out of a meteor that had chanced, one night, to fall near the royal camp set up for hunt. The emperor considered it a lucky sword.

'I want you to give this sword to Shah Jahan when I die.'

'Hush, don't speak of such inauspicious things. You will live a long time yet,' whispered Nur Jahan, her eyes brimming with unshed tears. She looked haggard. The recent tension had taken a heavy toll on her.

Despite the emperor's pleas, Nur Jahan's mind was made up. It did not matter if Shahryar was inept, she could rule through him. All she required was a puppet on the throne. A fool, who asked no questions and allowed her to reign, suited her more than an intelligent man. She was confident that she and Laadli, together, could rule efficiently.

Once at Kashmir, the emperor seemed to recover. His spirits revived at the sight of the tall cypress trees, well laid out gardens, lofty snow-clad mountains and the myriad cornucopia of colourful flowers. The frothy canals, placid lakes and the saffron fields dotted with apple and cherry blossoms brought out a healthy glow on him once more. With his beloved empress by his side, Jahangir felt at ease. Nur Jahan kept up a regular correspondence with the capital. The empire was in tumult, with speculations about the emperor's health and the matter of succession hanging in the balance. The factions of nobles were quarrelling openly, with no thought to administration. Everything seemed to be in a state of flux, requiring just a trigger to explode.

'Let us return to Lahore,' the emperor announced one day. 'I am in much better health. I have neglected the affairs of the empire too long. I am aware that you have been doing a wonderful job, but I need to get back to the helm. Things are not well with the country.'

Relieved, Nur Jahan gave orders for the royal entourage to leave as soon as possible. Winter was setting in and the flowers were in full bloom when the entourage began its journey to Lahore. The fruit trees were laden and the forests were ringing with the chirping of birds. Jahangir had decided that he would name his successor at Lahore and surrender the obligation of the running of the empire on his worthy son, relieving himself of the burden forever.

Enroute, they encamped at a village near Bhimbhar and the emperor was seized with a desire to hunt. Despite severe opposition from the empress, royal physicians and other nobles, Jahangir was adamant. It was a perfect day for a hunt and he felt confident about his health. Besides, he was just fifty-eight, not old enough to live the life of an invalid, he declared.

'One last time, Nur. I may not be fortunate enough to come this way for many years. Let me indulge myself. It has been such a long time since I hunted. My ill health has kept me away from all my favourite activities. Please don't stop me.'

As Jahangir rode off on his white stallion accompanied by a few of his nobles, Nur Jahan watched the receding figures till the thunder of hoofs dissolved into silence once more. Her heart was heavy with foreboding.

'Laadli, did you feel a tremor just now, as though there was an earthquake?'

'No, I didn't.'

'I feel unease in my chest as though something untoward is likely to occur.'

'Nothing unpleasant is likely to happen. You have been under tremendous pressure for the past few months. You should have accompanied the emperor for the hunt instead of letting your imagination run wild,' Laadli's reply was practical, as usual.

Jahangir was ecstatic, adrenaline pumping through his blood stream. Startled wild rabbits skipped away in fear as the hunters rushed up a forested incline. All of a sudden the emperor's attendant lost control over his horse and plunged into a chasm, his terrified scream renting the peace of the atmosphere. A gaping gorge showed itself just as the emperor's steed stepped on the edge with a terrified whinny. Jahangir struggled with the reins and brought the horse to a halt. The shock of escaping death so narrowly shook the emperor and he felt faint.

The hunters returned to the camp in dejection. Jahangir had taken ill once more. The horror of seeing himself poised on the precipice of death's hands and his own narrow escape had shaken him tremendously. 'I saw death staring at me, begum,' he whispered to Nur Jahan.

Through the night, the empress nursed her delirious husband. The emperor rambled, calling out for Khusrau and Khurram alternately. Nur Jahan kept vigil by his side, wiping his forehead with napkins soaked with rose essence. He clutched at her hand, grasping it in desperation. 'I don't want to die, Nur. I have so much to live for,' he mumbled in his feverish state.

The dying emperor called for a glass of wine, but when it was placed to his lips, he was unable to swallow. It fell in frothy streaks from the side of his mouth, staining his qaba. Laadli took over the vigil from her exhausted mother. She held the emperor's hand as she read the Quran loudly. Jahangir seemed to relax as he heard her recitation; his thrashing head stilled on the cushion for a while. She placed a cool hand on his brow and stroked it lovingly as though he was her father. For the first time she felt tenderness for the suffering man. He was not the emperor she hated, just a tormented soul.

Towards the end of the night he grew worse and called out for Nur Jahan. In an instant the empress was by his side, cradling his head lovingly on her lap. A constant flow of tears stained her cheeks. By midnight, Jahangir could not hear her nor sense her presence although she called out his name repeatedly. He was in a coma and she knew that the end was near. Badshah Nuruddin Muhammad Salim Jahangir died in her arms in the early hours of the following day, in the twenty-second year of his reign.

24

Even before the emperor's body had become cold, the tussle for the crown began. Nur Jahan sent several messages to Asaf Khan but he refused to come. Instead, he sent his swiftest runner to Shah Jahan with the news that Jahangir had died. He also sent his signet ring as a guarantee of loyalty.

At Lahore, Shahryar declared himself the emperor of the Mughal Empire and seized the treasury. Within a week, he distributed seventy lakh rupees among soldiers and nobility in order to gain their support. He managed to cobble up an army of fifteen thousand soldiers.

When Nur Jahan arrived with Laadli at Lahore Fort, she immediately announced her support for the new emperor and ordered week-long celebrations in the city.

Meanwhile, Asaf Khan declared Khusrau's son, Dawar Baksh, as the next emperor. The wily Asaf Khan knew that if Dawar Baksh were crowned as emperor, he would proceed to Lahore to challenge Shahryar. This would enable Shah Jahan to reach Agra without any obstacles. True to his expectations, Dawar Baksh marched towards Lahore to confront Nashudani. In the meanwhile, Shah Jahan rushed to Agra from the Deccan with remarkable swiftness and declared himself emperor.

Hindustan now had three self-declared emperors: Shah Jahan at Agra, Dawar Baksh at Kashmir and Shahryar at Lahore. The parched earth waited impatiently for the bloodshed that was inevitable.

At Lahore, neither Shahryar nor Nur Jahan heeded Laadli's advice for a cautious approach. 'I don't think that our troubles are over. Shah Jahan is definitely going to attack Lahore. He has already declared himself the emperor at Agra and will not rest till he has the control of the entire country.'

'You fret too much,' refuted her mother. 'We will fight back if he dares to attack Lahore.'

Shahryar laughed at Laadli's predictions. 'You are now the empress, Laadli Begum. Leave the thinking to me and enjoy yourself.'

Power had gone to his head. Money flowed like water through his hands and he doled out jagirs and ranks with reckless generosity. No longer concerned about his disfigured looks, Shahryar indulged in drinking and gambling bouts followed by orgies of food and sex. Shahryar invoked revulsion in Laadli with his irresponsible acts. 'Let Shahryar indulge in his fancies, allow Shah Jahan to rule the country,' Laadli advised her mother. 'I do not know what you are planning but my heart is full of fear. Let us forget the throne and the crown. If we appeal to Shah Jahan, he will let us live in peace.'

'You have always lacked ambition. Don't you understand that Shah Jahan will never allow Shahryar to live? Your husband is a threat that has to be eliminated before he steps on the throne. Do you want to be widowed?'

'Does it matter?' bitterness dripped from Laadli's voice. 'I am worried about you and Arzani. We could escape to Persia and seek the protection of Shah Abbas.'

'Let me handle this, Laadli. You are being emotional and one can't be objective when one is emotional. The problem with you is that you think with your heart instead of your brain.'

Soon, they received the news that Dawar Baksh's royal troops were marching towards Lahore and were just ten kilometres away from the fort. The mercenaries raised by Shahryar were sent to counter the attack. The two forces encountered each other outside the city, where it quickly became obvious that the mercenaries were no match for the imperial forces. Shahryar's army broke rank and fled. Only a handful of soldiers remained in the fort to defend it while Dawar Baksh set up camp at the base of the citadel, waiting for an opportune moment to enter the city.

In the meanwhile, the imperial army under Asaf Khan was marching towards Lahore with explicit instructions from Shah Jahan. Both Dawar Baksh and Nashudani were to be blinded and imprisoned.

Although Nur Jahan maintained a calm exterior, she was agitated when she heard the news. Fears of personal safety began to worry her. She knew that Shah Jahan was a dangerous enemy and she would be his first target when the time for retribution arrived. He was not likely to forget his humiliation and the hardship his family had had to endure because of her. Nor would he condone her role in the separation from his beloved sons, Dara and Aurangzeb. Fearful of her fate if Shah Jahan was successful in capturing Lahore, she commanded Nashudani to go to battle.

Shahryar, however, sent his soldiers under the command of Hoshang, a general, and spent his time with nautch girls. Laadli was outraged at his nonchalant stance. 'You should be fighting the enemy troops instead of hiding behind the skirts of the servant girls,' she said, appalled at his conduct.

'Don't worry, begum, there is no need for me to soil my hands when there are others who will bring the crafty Asaf Khan in chains before me.'

Laadli knew that her husband was a coward; she had no doubt that he would abandon her at the first hint of danger. Clutching her daughter to her bosom, she prayed for good sense to prevail. Neither her mother nor Shahryar seemed to realise the wisdom of accepting the inevitable while there was time. Most of the nobles were unreliable and treacherous. Laadli knew that they would throw themselves at Shah Jahan's feet the moment he arrived. If only her mother would heed her pleas and escape, they could still make it to Persia.

Later that day, the fort received news that Hoshang had been killed and that Shahryar's soldiers had either abandoned their post and fled into the jungles or surrendered to Asaf Khan's forces. The sound of victorious cries and drums reached Laadli as the conquerors entered the city. 'There is still time. We can leave undetected if we use the secret passage under the fort's dungeon,' Laadli pleaded with her mother.

'It is too late now. They are already at the gates of the palace,' sighed Nur Jahan. The fight had gone out of the woman. There was resignation on her face.

Shahryar, trembling and sick, crouched in a corner. Laadli looked at her husband with disgust. In the distance, they heard the triumphant cries of the imperial army as they approached the fort. A victorious Asaf Khan entered the harem and warned Nur Jahan—'Hand over Nashudani to us and you will not be harmed.'

His soldiers searched the apartments for the self-declared emperor. In desperation, Shahryar had garbed himself in a woman's costume and joined the women in the zenana. His veil hid his hideous face from the soldiers. But the tide had begun to flow in the reverse direction; one of the harem eunuchs, wanting to curry favour with the victors, betrayed Nashudani. A trembling Shahryar was hauled up before Asaf Khan. Dressed as he was, the soldiers jeered and made fun of him. Laadli tried to shut her ears to the sounds as her husband, screaming and begging, was dragged away from the harem. She had never felt more humiliated in her life.

They never saw Shahryar again, but the imperial guards conveyed the news that he had been blinded on Shah Jahan's orders. Nur Jahan and Laadli were forcibly confined in the harem and a strict watch enforced over them. Asaf Khan did not trust his sister. She still had the resources to resort to mischief and he wanted to take no chances with her. There were some who still nurtured loyalty to the erstwhile empress, however, and they conveyed news of the events to her. They brought bad tidings—Shahryar had been executed and Dawar Baksh had vanished without a trace. Speculations abounded that he had escaped to Persia and sought the protection of the Shah, a decision that Laadli applauded. *If only mother had listened to me*, she thought with a sigh as she waited for Shah Jahan to pronounce judgement on their fate.

25

Shah Jahan was crowned at Agra and Arjumand Begum—now empress of the vast Mughal Empire—was given the title Mumtaz Mahal. Nur Jahan received the news stoically. She now realised the futility of resisting Shah Jahan. It was wiser to declare truce and appeal to his magnanimity. Her very survival depended on his charity. Whether it was a pension or permission to reside at the capital, everything depended on the new emperor.

'Beggars can't be choosers,' she sighed loudly as she sealed the letter she had written to her niece. 'I will have to appeal to Shah Jahan through Arjumand. I hope she will act as our advocate in Agra. The emperor will never deny her anything. Remember how people always appealed to Jahangir through me?'

In her letter, Nur Jahan had composed flattering verses for the emperor. She congratulated her niece on being crowned the empress and expressed her anguish at being imprisoned within the walls of the fort. She requested Mumtaz Mahal to intercede on her behalf and obtain the emperor's permission for her to travel to Agra. 'I want to atone for the wrongs that I have committed and pay my respects to the emperor. I shall throw myself at his feet for mercy and request his clemency.'

Shah Jahan was strolling in the royal gardens debating over the merits of conferring a new jagir on Asaf Khan, who was now the Grand Vizier. He had been a loyal commander and had served him well by furthering his claim to the throne; moreover, Asaf Khan was his father-in-law. His steps halted for a moment as he saw Mumtaz Mahal approaching him. As usual, his heart skipped a beat at her sight and a tender smile lit up his solemn face. She looked dazzling in her jade green costume. He delighted in her simplicity.

'Your Majesty, I have come with a request to you,' she said, smiling.

'Your wish is my command, my queen,' Shah Jahan responded flippantly.

'I am serious, Your Highness. My aunt, Nur Jahan, has written a pathetic letter about her imprisonment at Lahore fort. She appeals to your merciful disposition to release her from the humiliation. Those hapless women can hardly cause any discomfort to you or be a threat to your peace. Let them go. I do not want you to begin your rule with my aunt's curse.'

'You have always been too kind. Have you forgotten the sufferings heaped on us by the woman you call your aunt? It is because of her that we were deprived of a comfortable and normal life. She created a rift between my father and me. It was her machinations that separated our two sons from us for such a long time. She is the one who is to blame for all the ills that haunted us for so many years. Even if you have forgotten it all, I can neither forget nor forgive her.'

'An emperor must be kind and just. Let it not be said that the emperor did not find it in his heart to forgive an old and repentant woman. She has realised the futility of resisting your power and now she wants to atone her sins by paying her respects to you.'

'So the wily woman is trying to appeal through you,' Shah Jahan was suspicious.

'Yes, Your Majesty, she has sent a letter regretting the past and expressed her wish to visit the court and pay her respects, if you permit her to do so.'

'So, that is the reason my beloved Arjumand is advocating her cause. Well, to make you happy, I shall allow that evil woman to visit you. Let me warn you, her stay will have to be short. I do not trust her at all.'

Mumtaz Mahal, relieved at having obtained her husband's approval, sent a reply to her aunt conveying the royal approval for her visit to the court at Agra.

It was only after weeks of exhausting travel that the women reached the palace at Agra. Nur Jahan, ecstatic to be back at the familiar palace, looked around with wonder at the changes made by Shah Jahan. Laadli, cautious and curious, clutched Arzani close to her as their palanquin made its way to the harem. Vivid memories flooded her mind, some happy and some tragic. She remembered the first day she had entered the portals of the palace after the gruesome murder of her father. The fear, excitement, trepidation of the experience of setting foot for the first time in the harem came back to her along with vivid images of the bejewelled concubines. Laadli would never forget her first encounter with the emperor. Nor would she forget her first meeting with Prince Khurram and their fragile friendship.

She was going to meet him once again. He was no longer the Khurram she adored. He was emperor Shah Jahan—ruthless, brutal and all-powerful. He had ordered the killing of her husband, just as his father had ordered her father's death. Would Arzani hate Shah Jahan on learning that he had had her father killed, much as she had hated Jahangir when she learnt that he had ordered her father's murder? Laadli wondered.

As they passed into the beautiful royal garden, Laadli recollected her first meeting with Imraan and her eyes misted at the memory. Was he still alive, hiding in some obscure village, or had he been executed on her mother's orders? She would never know.

Five-year-old Arzani reminded Laadli of herself, decades ago. She had the same confused and excited look at the prospect of staying in Agra.

Shah Jahan did not accord Nur Jahan any of the respect that the dowager queens of the Mughal Empire were normally granted. She was summoned to the Diwan-é-aam before the entire assembly of courtiers and nobles. Heavily veiled, she walked with dignity to the head of the crowd and performed a respectful kornish before the emperor. With great regret in her voice, she declared—'Shahenshah-é-Alam, I come to you with reverence. May Allah give you a thousand years of fruitful reign! I have no desire but to lead a life of piety and peace, wallowing in the memories of my husband, Emperor Jahangir. Your beloved father deserves a grand mausoleum and I am here to request your permission to build a memorial for him.'

Each word spoken by her was directed towards earning the sympathy of the courtiers. Shah Jahan was familiar with her wily ways. From behind the marble fretwork screen Mumtaz

Mahal listened to the cleverly worded appeal of her aunt with admiration. The shrew is invincible! she thought. Laadli, seated with her cousin, was also filled with appreciation for her mother. With just a few sentences she had managed to convey her acceptance of Shah Jahan's rule, gained sympathy as a hapless widow, and also managed to force the emperor's hand for a grant of money for the construction of Jahangir's memorial. Was it any wonder that she had ruled the Mughal Empire for so many years?

Shah Jahan was seething with hatred for the woman, but he camouflaged his feelings and replied with kindness—'Begum Meherunnisa, we appreciate your feelings for the deceased emperor and agree that he deserves a grand monument in his memory. You will be given an adequate pension and a grant of monies to build the memorial.'

A hush fell on the court when Shah Jahan addressed her as Meherunnisa instead of the title, Nur Jahan. With just one word he had made apparent to all her fall from grace. Nur Jahan's face took on an ashen hue. In a single moment he had reduced her to a common woman, divested of all royal trappings. While the crowd cheered his magnanimity with regard to the memorial and her pension, Nur Jahan thanked Shah Jahan, bowed thrice in kornish, and walked back to the harem.

Once there, she allowed her indignation to show. 'He has the gall to insult me in public,' she raged.

'Hush mother! Let no one hear you. We are in no position to rebuke the emperor,' Laadli patted her mother's hand consolingly.

That evening, Shah Jahan visited their apartment—one of the smaller ones in the harem—and spoke to Nur Jahan in private.

'You will never again step inside Agra. I am exiling you to Lahore, forever. You shall be granted a pension of sixteen lakh rupees per annum for your maintenance. As for the mausoleum, you may start the construction of the same in the Dilkhusha gardens. At the smallest hint of any trouble from you, I shall be forced to take the severest of actions. It is because of your relationship with my wife that you have been granted amnesty—but that relationship is not strong enough to withstand treachery.'

He strode away before Nur Jahan could reply. Laadli, who was waiting by the door, hastened to perform her kornish. The emperor smiled and remarked—'You look well, Laadli. I hope that your wisdom will guide your mother's steps and restrain her from imprudence. I may not be merciful the next time.'

'She is a harmless woman, Your Majesty. I guarantee you her loyalty,' Laadli replied quietly.

'You are welcome to approach us whenever you need help.'

Shah Jahan had not forsaken her, Laadli thought, bowing as he walked out of the room.

Despite the undercurrents of hostility, Mumtaz Mahal invited them for a banquet at her palace. Laadli was happy to see that the empress remained the affable Arjumand who had shared many evenings of whispered conversation with her. Nur Jahan wisely refrained from discussing politics and spoke only about the family. Laadli was captivated by the eldest princess, Jahanara, who was reported to be the favourite child of the emperor. All of fourteen, she was as beautiful as her mother. Busy with raising children, Mumtaz Mahal hardly found time to counsel the emperor. In any case, she was not interested in politics, so it fell on the young princess to manage the affairs of the harem and take an interest in politics. Laadli found her to be a very mature and level-headed girl with many talents—arts and music were just some of them. With much in common, there was an instant rapport between the two of them.

After a week's stay at Agra, the two women began their return journey, braving the biting northern winds that numbed their bodies. The mist lifted reluctantly from the streets of Agra as the warm rays of a dilute sun pierced the sky. The smoke rising from a mass of chulahs heralded the advent of another day. Life was stirring in the wayside tea stall where a bunch of shivering bodies in tattered blankets waited for the first cup of warming ambrosia before yet another day of labour. From the east parapet of the walled city, the sun rose. The capital of the mighty Mughuls was poised for another day as Nur Jahan's caravan left for Lahore.

Their progress was slow as Arzani fell ill and a persistent bout of cough overtook her tender body. Nur Jahan, depressed and silent, was lost in thought as they travelled through the familiar streets of Agra.

'You must not take Shah Jahan's harsh words to heart. He is merely retaliating for all the hardship he had to go through before he seized the throne.'

'He has stripped me of the last vestige of dignity. He humiliated me. How can I ever forgive him for that?'

'You must forget it. We are going to Lahore to begin a new life. Everyone respects you there. We will start afresh—you, me and Arzani.'

'Isn't it funny? From Meherunnisa, I was elevated to Nur Jahan, the empress of the Mughal Empire, and now I am

Meherunnisa once again,' Nur Jahan said. And then ruefully, 'The journey from a common woman to an empress took much longer.'

Lahore, beloved Lahore, thought Laadli, her eyes brimming with tears of relief, as she sighted the tall minarets and lofty pillars of the city. 'May Allah grant us peace,' she said, as they entered the portals and made their way towards the mansion that they had been given to reside in. It was modest but spacious; it was a far cry from the royal palaces that they had occupied for years, yet it was home to Laadli. She loved the huge garden, which was lined with fruit trees. It was the right place for her daughter to grow up.

The women led a quiet life. Meherunnisa remained engaged in reading poetry and designing clothes, occasionally venturing out to the dargah. She grew increasingly devout, spending hours in her tiny prayer room.

A whole year passed; the long winter was over and the women heralded the advent of spring with great enthusiasm. Lahore wore a festive look: Shah Jahan was arriving to the city of Lahore for the first time since ascending the throne. There was excitement in the air as people went about decorating their houses, markets and city streets with garlands of flowers. 'The drums are beating at the Naubat Khana of the fort, announcing the arrival of the emperor,' announced Zaib, a servant girl, breathless with excitement.

Shah Jahan was received by the governor, Wazir Khan, and gifted with jewels, gold and silver utensils, carpets, hundreds of horses and camels, valued at lakhs of rupees. The emperor visited the temporary mausoleum of his father and distributed alms to the poor. Then he entered the Lahore fort and inspected the palaces. An expression of displeasure clouded his handsome features. Even as a youth, Shah Jahan had not been impressed by the mosques and palaces constructed by Akbar and Jahangir. The only mausoleum that had invoked some satisfaction for him aesthetically, was the one constructed by Nur Jahan for her parents. As he stood before the Khawabgah-e-Jahangir, which had been used by his father as his sleeping quarters, its red sandstone columns standing stark against the skyline, he squinted thoughtfully.

The quadrangle held many structures made by Jahangir. All sombre and austere, their harsh lines were somewhat softened by the fountains and the water channels. The strong, square, red stone buildings were so typical of his grandfather's style, followed faithfully by Jahangir without much alteration. He preferred something ethereal, soft and delicate.

Summoning Wazir Khan, he ordered—'Have these structures replaced by elegant halls and palaces. I want the most skilled artisans to be employed without consideration of the costs. The palaces should be made of marble instead of these harsh red stones. Use cusped arches and pillars with tapering shafts for beauty.' Shah Jahan wanted the work finished by the time he returned from his sojourn at Kashmir. He then ordered the reconstruction of the ghusalkhana and khwabgah. The reconstruction of the Shah Burj, the royal tower built by Jahangir, was entrusted to Asaf Khan who had won the emperor's admiration with the design of his opulent palace at Lahore, which had taken ten years to complete.

Meherunnisa was predictably indignant when she heard of the reconstruction efforts. 'Replacing red stone with marble cannot wipe out history.'

Although her niece Mumtaz Mahal was residing at Lahore and so was her brother—now an important man—neither of them took the trouble of visiting her. She had not been invited for the grand feasts held in their palaces.

'Fate is a zealous accountant. It keeps faithful account of every sin and charity. The wheels of fortune will turn one day,' Laadli often found her mother muttering viciously. The very name of Shah Jahan seemed to throw her into a nasty mood.

26

Four years passed in a blinking of the eye. Arzani was eight years old. Laadli was determined that the child should lead as normal a life as possible. Meherunnisa busied herself with the construction of her husband's mausoleum, which was coming up slowly. Money was a constraint. The grandiose plans drawn up by Meherunnisa needed unlimited resources. Her fervent appeals to the emperor for financial assistance had yielded no results. From time to time Shah Jahan grudgingly parted with a meagre amount for the structure.

'The great Badshah sleeps in such humble quarters,' Meherunnisa remarked, drawing the outlines of her dream structure. 'If I had the resources, I would make him a mausoleum that would haunt the memory of all who saw it just once. I created a memorable one for my father because I had the money and the power to do so. And now, I have to beg for each coin.'

Laadli looked at her mother's drawing and sighed—it was grandiose and would cost quite a lot of money. 'That design involves an extensive use of marble, Ammijaan. It is likely to cost several lakhs of rupees. Perhaps we could modify the building material and reduce the cost.'

Her statement incensed Meherunnisa. 'If he can ¬end lakhs of rupees on reconstructing each palace buil: by his father and grandfather, surely he can contribute some money for his father's mausoleum?'

'Why don't we design clothes for the harem women just as we did at Agra before you became an empress? That will keep us busy and bring in some money as well,' Laadli suggested.

'As usual, my wise daughter is right. Practical and balanced, you always find a solution. Why not? Neither am I an empress nor are you a princess now.'

'Don't be so bitter, Ammi, it is not good for you. We may not be royalty but we can be happy. I am happy, so is Arzani, and I want you to be happy too. Times change and so does fortune. Accepting the Almighty's decision makes life much easier, so why not accept it with grace. You were always the wise one, running a gigantic empire, counselling the women and creating so many beautiful things. You can still make use of your talents.'

As Laadli had expected, the demand for clothes designed by Meherunnisa poured in as soon as word spread that she was ready to create the beautiful dresses that had once been a rage in the harems of Agra. They worked hard, with Arzani pitching in occasionally. Together, the three of them crafted exquisite ensembles, recreating the magic that had made Meherunnisa's designs popular at Agra.

News of Shah Jahan's campaign at Burhanpur reached them, along with tidings that Mumtaz Mahal, heavy with another pregnancy, was suffering from ill health. 'His destiny seems to be inexorably entwined with that city,' commented

Meherunnisa. 'What I do not understand, is why my niece accompanies him everywhere. Her constant state of pregnancy never ceases to amaze me either!'

It was June. Unbearable whirlwinds of violent sand storms whipped the city. Meherunnisa and Laadli were resting in the cool comfort of their apartment when a maid brought in the news that the entire city of Lahore was in mourning. Mumtaz Mahal had died while giving birth to their fourteenth child. The baby, Gauharara, had survived.

From travellers arriving from Agra, Laadli heard that the emperor, devastated by his wife's death, had become a recluse, refusing to attend to his imperial responsibilities. After Mumtaz Mahal's death, Shah Jahan locked himself in his rooms and refused to eat for eight days. When he emerged from the room, his lustrous black beard had turned completely white. It was left to the young Jahanara to take control of the situation. Laadli's heart went out to the girl who had been burdened with such enormous responsibility at a tender age. Her letter of condolence conveyed the profound grief she felt at the death of Mumtaz Mahal, a cousin she had always loved. It didn't surprise her when Jahanara responded with alacrity and despatched an invitation for Laadli to visit her at Agra.

'Your presence here at this juncture will help in reducing the vacuum we are experiencing. It will give me emotional strength,' the invitation read.

'I wish I could travel to Agra to comfort the family,' Laadli expressed. Meherunnisa was embroidering a bridal dress for the governor's daughter and Arzani was helping her select the sequins and pearls to be used in embellishing the dress.

'I will advise you against the journey. Jahanara has invited you, but Shah Jahan may not welcome us.'

With a heavy heart, Laadli decided not to leave Lahore. The journey would be long, and, her mother was right, she did not know how the emperor would react to seeing them.

The year rolled by slowly as the cold hands of winter gradually erased the heat of summer. Jahangir's mausoleum was almost complete. Shah Jahan was now quick to respond to Meherunnisa's pleas for finances to complete the structure. The loss of his wife had made Shah Jahan understand his stepmother's need to build a memorial for someone she had loved. He was already planning a grand memorial for Mumtaz Mahal; one that would stand eternally as evidence of his everlasting love for her.

The city of Lahore dressed up again to receive the emperor after almost three years. It was rumoured that the eldest prince, Dara Shikoh, was to be married in the city, to his childhood love, Nadira.

Laadli was heartened by the news—she would try to meet Jahanara. She sent a note through the groom to the Shah Begum, as the princess was now known, and was delighted when Jahanara responded warmly, inviting her to the harem. There was excitement as the three women dressed up for the visit. Meherunnisa fussed over her appearance. 'I look so old. Will Jahanara recognise me?' She had greyed astonishingly in the past one year.

'You look very beautiful, Badi Ammi,' assured the twelve-year-old Arzani.

'No one can look more beautiful than you, Arzani,' her grandmother said indulgently. There was no doubt that the girl was a beauty. She had inherited Shahryar's delicate looks and Laadli's lovely complexion and stature. Laadli glanced at her daughter and wondered how time had flown. It was seven years since Jahangir had died and they had come to stay at Lahore. *Soon it will be time to get Arzani married,* she thought sadly. The thought wrenched her heart. *It will be difficult to live without her.*

The women climbed into the palanquin and made their way to the palace. The emperor had decided to spend the winter at Lahore. There would be many more meetings and visits to the royal harem. Meherunnisa was excited. It had been a long time since she had entered the portals of the Lahore fort. As she emerged from the palanquin at the steps leading to the harem, she sighed and looked around wistfully. The old structures had gone; the new palace was like a dream— all white and beautiful.

'There was a time when everyone ran to do my bidding. Today, I enter the harem unheralded.'

She was mistaken. No sooner did she utter the words, than there was a flurry of figures and a rustle of silk and Jahanara was at their side. 'Welcome to the harem, grand aunt! I have been waiting impatiently for your arrival.' She hugged Laadli and kissed Arzani lovingly.

'Allah, what a beauty your daughter has turned out to be.'

She led them to her lavish apartments. The walls of the apartment were ablaze with floral motifs embedded with precious stones. Even the floors, fashioned out of flawless marble, were embedded with jewels. Carved niches broke the uniformity of the walls, their hollows lit up by coloured candles.

Arzani ran around the apartments, amazement writ large on her face. She had never witnessed such opulence. Outside, a large tank shaded by a massive banyan tree, with a fountain and lotuses, caught her fancy. It was a world of wonder; a dream abode.

'It is all so beautiful Apa,' she exclaimed breathlessly.

'Would you like to stay with me for a few weeks? The emperor is staying at Lahore for a couple of weeks before going back to Agra. Dara is to be married and there will be great rejoicing in the palace.'

'Yes, yes, I would love to stay here with you.'

Laadli was reluctant to leave Arzani at the palace. She had kept her daughter away from the glitter of palaces for so many years.

'Please, Ammi, let me stay with Apa for some time,' begged Arzani, sensing her mother's reluctance. 'I promise, I will be good.' Her eyes were dazzled by the magnificence of the quarters. 'I want to attend Prince Dara's wedding. He is a cousin, after all.'

Before Laadli could say anything, Meherunnisa interjected. 'Of course you can stay with your Apa for a few weeks. I am sure your mother will not refuse.'

Laadli suspected that her mother was hopeful that Arzani's beauty would attract the attention of the princes. Her heart heavy with foreboding, Laadli departed after the feast and entertainment that Jahanara had arranged for them. Arzani's days in the harem remained her main topic of conversation for weeks after she had returned. 'I wish we could stay at the palace forever,' she sighed.

It was the memory of her sense of wonderment when she had seen the palace for the first time that restrained Laadli from overreacting. Instead, she smiled at her daughter and said, 'Well, since we are not princesses, it is not for us to stay in palaces.'

Four years passed and the three women continued creating magic with material, their nimble fingers flying over the yards of beautiful silk, soft satins and crisply starched muslin. They could have got by without doing any work, because the pension granted by the emperor was generous, but they needed to keep themselves occupied. Life was dreary, devoid of novelty, its rhythm unbroken. Arzani was almost eighteen, brimming with youthful optimism. She was the only ray of sunshine in the lives of the older women.

'It is time we found a good husband for her,' Laadli sighed, her fingers creating floral patterns on a scarlet brocade. She was embroidering a bridal dress. Worries about Arzani's marriage haunted her whenever she worked on bridal orders.

The emperor had completed ten years of his rule. There was peace in the country and the imperial coffers were overflowing; the voices of dissent had been silenced. Shah Jahan indulged in fancies that were beyond the imagination of people. Lahore was abuzz with the news that the emperor had acquired seven thrones for each day of the week, one covered with rubies, the other with emeralds, yet another with sapphires and one with pearls, diamonds studded another and the sixth one was made of jasper and jade. It was the seventh throne that was most talked about. Shah Jahan's Peacock Throne was a fabulous creation, a magnificent piece of art for which the emperor had commissioned a famous French jeweller, who took seven full years and several lakhs of rupees to complete the marvel.

Shah Jahan had also begun the construction of a grand mausoleum in memory of his beloved Mumtaz Mahal. Hundreds of artisans and craftsmen had been commissioned to give shape to his dream. Masons, craftsmen, sculptors, and calligraphers were summoned from Persia and Europe to work on the masterpiece. The marvel in white marble, was taking shape on the banks of Yamuna river at a colossal cost. Precious jewels from the treasury were used to fill the exquisite engravings that were etched on the marble.

'He is squandering the wealth accumulated painstakingly by his forefathers. One day he will suffer for this indiscriminate expenditure and I shall be the first to celebrate his penury,' Meherunnisa said.

Her dream is never going to come true, thought Laadli. Shah Jahan will gain immortality through the beautiful structures he leaves behind. These will be his gifts to the world.

Gleefully Meherunnisa absorbed all gossip that emerged from the harem. She gloated on the misfortunes of the emperor and grieved on his achievements. One beautiful September morning, the royal family returned to Lahore. This time, happy with a successful campaign, Shah Jahan announced festivities at the palace. As expected, Jahanara invited Meherunnisa and Laadli to the harem for the feast. Since the festivities were to continue for an entire week, with poetry competitions, sports, contests and nautch performances, Jahanara suggested that they stay with her in the harem till the end of the month. Meherunnisa and Arzani greeted this proposal with great enthusiasm but Laadli was sceptical. 'We can travel from our mansion to the fort without much discomfort. You need not fuss about us,' she demurred.

'Jahanara is right in suggesting that we stay at the imperial harem. With my aching joints, I cannot keep shuttling to and from the palace,' Meherunnisa insisted.

The emperor's indulgences were many. He loved good food, lavish clothes and surrounded himself with beautiful women. Stories of the emperor's lustful adventures and licentious behaviour travelled through the country. Some even spoke of an incestuous relationship between him and Jahanara. 'As long as the empress was alive, she could keep Shah Jahan in control,' they whispered. 'After her death he has gone berserk.'

'When will you marry, Apa?' Arzani asked Jahanara, unaware of the unwritten Mughal decree laid down by Akbar— no Mughal princess was permitted to marry. In order to prevent the possibility of the Mughal throne passing to an outsider, the Badshah had enforced a lifetime of spinsterhood for all princesses.

'I am not likely to marry, but why don't we arrange your matrimony with a nice man from the court?' suggested Jahanara.

'Yes, Jahanara, why don't you find a good husband for Arzani? I am besieged with worries about her marriage,' Laadli said. She knew that Jahanara loved match-making.

'In fact, I have someone in mind for Arzani. If you wish, I could begin negotiations with his family. But first, we must seek the emperor's permission for the match.'

'Yes, yes, why not? Who is the fortunate person?'

'I have in mind the son of the Punjab governor's brother, Afzal Khan. He is a handsome and brave man. In fact, the emperor has granted him a rich jagir. Arzani will be happy with him, I am sure of that. Besides, Afzal is the kind of man who will rise to great status.'

Laadli understood the advantage of marrying Arzani to a man who had found favour with the emperor. 'I will be indebted to you if you could finalise this alliance,' she begged earnestly.

Jahanara hugged her aunt and promised to arrange the match. 'Don't worry, Arzani will be married to Afzal as soon as possible.'

Meherunnisa was not amused at the thought of her darling Arzani going away. She sighed and complained constantly till her words began grating on Laadli's nerves.

'Ammijaan, we can't keep Arzani with us forever. She has to marry. Most girls of her age are cradling their babies. Don't worry, she will be happy. Jahannara will not let us down. She is truly fond of Arzani and will do her best to find her the right person.'

The emperor granted his permission and blessed the union between the two young people. In a magnanimous gesture, he granted a promotion to Afzal Khan saying—'This is a marriage arranged by my favourite daughter so it should be the most opulent of all weddings held at Lahore.'

Despite all her misgivings, Meherunnisa finally accepted the match and began working on her granddaughter's bridal dress. Her stiff fingers worked painstakingly on the silk yarn, her weak eyes peering over the patterns, watering with the effort. Laadli's efforts at dissuading her had no effect as the woman stubbornly defied all discomforts to create the most beautiful dress ever worn by a bride.

There was little time for the hectic preparations that had to be made before the wedding, since Afzal Khan had insisted on an early marriage. Jahanara volunteered to take on the task of the nuptial arrangements. Together, they selected the jewellery and other gifts, decided on the food, and made arrangements with the decorators.

Laadli's heart was heavy as Arzani walked towards the wedding dais. The bride's hair was parted in the centre and tied at the back in a graceful knot bound by a lace of gold. On her forehead rested a beautifully fashioned star-shaped diamond pendent. She looked heartbreakingly beautiful.

Laadli could barely hold her tears as the bride sat in the palanquin to journey to her new residence. She hugged her daughter, blessing her repeatedly. Meherunnisa stood by, wiping away the tears that poured down her wrinkled cheeks. A beautiful chapter of her life had ended.

27

The house turned as quiet as a tomb after Arzani's departure. Laadli, with her ability to adapt to situations, took to working harder to keep herself occupied, but Meherunnisa seemed to have retreated into a shell into which she allowed no one. Tremendously lonely, she valiantly groped with her inner turmoil. She had taken to wearing only white and had shed all jewellery ever since Jahangir had died, but now she embarked on a spiritual journey with a frightening intensity. Laadli watched with concern, her mother's obsession with the mystical world. The daily visits to the mazaar of Hazrat Main Mir were interspersed with prayers and fervid readings from the Quran. Meherunnisa, up and about by five in the morning, began her day by placing garlands of white rose buds and jasmine, which she threaded with her own hands, on Jahangir's tomb.

One morning, Laadli found her mother's bedroom in a state of utter confusion. Boxes lay open around the room, their contents strewn all over. Bent over them, the frail body of her mother groped through piles of garments.

'What are you looking for?' Laadli asked.

'Where are my jewellery caskets?' Meherunnisa said, looking up from the heap of clothes before her.

'They must be here somewhere. Let me help you look for them.' Laadli said, joining her mother in the search.

Laadli wondered why her mother had suddenly thought of her jewellery. The last time they had been aired was when Arzani was married. In a generous gesture, Meherunnisa had gifted away a sizeable amount of her precious jewellery to her beloved granddaughter. The enormous rosewood treasure chest overflowing with brilliant diamond-studded necklaces, sapphire rings, emerald ear studs and ruby chokers was finally discovered inside another box.

'Ah, here it is,' Meherunnisa clutched a necklace of priceless pearls possessively. She carried the jewellery box to another corner of the room and laid out its contents.

'This was a gift from the emperor on my lunar birthday,' she sighed, lovingly patting a beautiful necklace studded with gems. 'And this was given to me on our first wedding anniversary.'

Meherunnisa laid out each piece of jewellery on the carpet, describing when she had got it. Why the sudden interest in ornaments, wondered her daughter.

As if sensing her curiosity, Meherunnisa turned and smiled—'I am planning to sell some of these to pay for the marriage of destitute girls. The rest will go towards the expenses for the marble façade which I am planning to construct at Hazrat Mian Mir's mazaar.' These were the two causes closest to Meherunnisa's heart. While she was empress, she had set aside an impressive amount from her personal funds to provide for the marriage of orphaned girls. When they settled down at Lahore, she had continued to arrange the marriages of such girls and provided for their dowry. She was also devoted to the holy man, Hazrat Mian Mir. The saint was a direct descendent of the Prophet and much revered by most of the Mughal emperors.

Jahangir, who had heard of the mystic's powers, once invited the saint to his court. They had a lengthy discussion on various subjects after which, greatly influenced, the emperor expressed a desire to renounce the world and become his disciple. The saint, in his gentle manner, advised him to continue his worldly duties. 'Emperors have been created for the protection of God's people. In doing so, you are discharging an important duty entrusted to you by the Creator. Do not entertain the thought of renunciation.'

Pleased to hear this from the Hazrat, Jahangir stated—'Tell me, oh Shaikh, if you want anything.'

'Will you promise to give it to me?' asked the Pir.

'Most certainly, I will give whatever you ask,' responded the emperor.

The holy man had then replied, 'I only request that Your Majesty will not invite me to his palace again'.

After that day, Jahangir never called for the Pir again, but made it a point to visit the saint whenever he was in Lahore. Nur Jahan, who had been present during the interaction, became a zealous follower as well. When Hazrat Mian Mir was alive, she often consulted him on the difficulties she faced and took his advice seriously. After his death, she began praying at his mazaar, regularly. It was one of her desires to construct an impressive façade and a prayer hall at the saint's tomb.

During one of his visits to Lahore, young Prince Dara Shikoh, the eldest son of Shah Jahan, who was also an ardent devotee of the saint, met Meherunnisa at the mazaar. The prince was a charming man of great learning. The two of them found a common ground and struck an instant rapport. Dara expressed great sorrow at the way Shah Jahan had treated her, delighting Meherunnisa's heart greatly. She invited him to her mansion for dinner, which the prince accepted with alacrity. There was a flurry of excitement in the mansion as it was the first time that a member of the Mughal family had visited them.

After dinner, they sat down in the open baradari to chat about old times. Dara Shikoh updated them on all the happenings at the court and regaled them with stories of his family. Under a canopy of bright stars they conversed about diverse topics, finally launching into a long and animated discussion on theology and spirituality. The women were greatly impressed by the prince's knowledge. He spent many hours telling them about his interactions with religious teachers of various sects. Dara told them that he was planning to construct a massive pavilion, where a thousand people could sit and pray, at the Hazrat's mazaar. 'It was one of the most interesting evenings I have spent in a long time, Meherunnisa told Laadli afterwards. 'He is brilliant, not at all like his father.'

During the day, Meherunnisa involved herself in various activities, but come evening and she would sink into a state of depression. Nights were a torture; unable to sleep, she walked about restlessly through the long corridors of the mansion, till at last she would fall into an exhausted slumber towards the early hours of the morn. She dreaded the sleepless nights when the ghosts from her past assailed her pitilessly. A long string of misdeeds surfaced to chastise her on the lonesome nights.

Guilt and remorse haunted her mind. There were too many ghouls to inter. There was a haunted look in her eyes and dark circles had formed around them.

Alarmed at her mother's condition, Laadli consulted Hakim Al-Badr who had been their physician for a long time. In times of crisis, Laadli had approached him for advice without hesitation. He was like a father figure to her.

'Dear child,' he said, 'your mother has suffered intensely. It is not her body that suffers but her soul that knows no rest. In her heart, she carries humiliation and pain that refuses to heal.' The physician assured Laadli: 'It happens to many of us when we are old. We begin to feel insecure and lonely. There is nothing to be alarmed about. Just try to keep her amused.'

Laadli came back clutching the tranquillisers he had prescribed.

Seated in the garden, Laadli brought up amusing incidents from a shared past. 'Do you remember the time when the emperor had gifted you a beautiful tortoise and you named it Anwari because your maid with the same name was as slow as the tortoise?'

The memory brought a happy smile on the lined face. 'Oh, yes, I remember. Anwari was furious when the women teased her about it.'

'I loved Anwari,' said Laadli, a faraway look in her eyes. 'She sang beautifully. On humid nights when I couldn't fall asleep, I would ask her to sing for me. Her lullabies soothed me to sleep. Firdaus was so jealous of Anwari that she tried singing me to sleep one night.'

'That would have been disastrous!' Meherunnisa said, smiling.

'Oh yes, remember how bad Firdaus' voice was? I had to go sleepless for two consecutive nights after that!'

Both of them laughed at the recollection.

The end came sooner than expected. One morning, Meherunnisa didn't get out of bed. Laadli smelt death as she entered her mother's room. The room was as silent as a sepulchre. Her mind clouded with fear, Laadli bent over her mother.

Meherunnisa's laboured breathing was erratic; her frail body trembled with each breath. The December chill of Lahore froze her bones into icicles of rigidity. The looming shadow of death reached out its ominous fingers to snatch the wasted body of the woman into its fold.

'I am so cold, Laadli, cover me up,' she wailed, unmindful of the three camel hair blankets resting on her. Laadli walked over to the boldly burning brazier and poked at the embers to spark off more heat. 'Don't go away, come near me,' her mother's feeble voice followed her.

'I am here Ammi, don't fret. Just rest. Talking will exhaust you.'

Laadli chafed the cold feet to warm them up. They were stone cold. A teardrop fell on the callused feet as she remembered their past beauty. Slave girls had massaged these royal feet with special emollients made of beeswax, fresh cream, saffron and honey. The henna adorned feet had never known a callus.

'No! Don't stop me from talking. I have to unburden my soul before I leave this earth, else I will not find peace.'

'Hush!' Laadli stroked the dry skin lovingly. It was burning up with fever. 'Later, may be.'

'No, no, I don't have much time. Tell me, do you hate me, Laadli?' the voice pleaded.

'Of course not. Why should I? You are my mother.'

'Because I wronged you. Because I ruined your life. I thrust you upon the princes, unmindful of the way you felt. I know how you winced each time I commanded you to entice Khusrau. I can recall the frightened look on your face. I kept pushing you because I wanted you to be an empress.' The voice faltered.

Laadli moaned softly. The glorious Nur Jahan, feted, dreaded and revered, lay helpless on a cold bed. The fearless empress was cowering in the face of death. This woman had once walked with pride; a single expression of irritation on her face had sent nobles into panic. It now lay shivering under a mound of coarse blankets. Laadli cried at the injustice of it all.

'Hush! Don't talk.'

'Let me finish.' The frail body shook with hollow cough. Laadli held a glass of water to her lips. Meherunnisa pushed it away.

'I loved the emperor. I really did. People said vicious things—they said I loved the crown more than the man. That's not true.'

Laadli turned away. She had thought the same herself many times.

'Please listen, Laadli. I cannot meet my maker unless I have confessed everything,' she said, moving restlessly on the bed, her mind restive with a raging fever.

'I understand,' whispered Laadli, soothing her mother's brow as she dabbed her forehead with a scented cloth.

'That...that young artist...the one you loved...' the voice tapered off.

'Imraan,' whispered Laadli, her voice choking with emotions. It had been such a long time since she had uttered that name aloud.

'Yes, Imraan. I could never have allowed you to wed a commoner Laadli,' Meherunnisa said agitatedly. 'I...did you know that I had him killed?'

'Yes, I did.' She felt sick.

'You knew! All these years...you knew that I was responsible for your lover's murder!'

'In my heart, I had always known my romance was doomed. Benazir warned me repeatedly, but I couldn't help it. I loved Imraan, and foolishly I wanted to believe that we could get away with it. But I knew that you would not allow him to live. Love happened to me despite everything and I am happy it did. Those few months were the happiest of my life. I have never known more joy than those moments we spent together. My only regret is that he lost his life because of me,' Laadli's eyes misted.

'My poor child. I am sorry.' A trembling hand reached out for Laadli.

'Everyone has the right to happiness. You, of all the people in the world, should know what it is to love. You found your happiness with the emperor...Tell me Ammi, did you ever love my father?'

'I do not want to answer your question,' her mother whispered petulantly.

'You must—I have the right to know the truth.'

'The truth is that I was married to him under pressure from Shahenshah Akbar.' There was bitterness in the voice.

'So, it is true that Prince Salim was in love with you before you were married off to Abba.' There was sadness in

Laadli's voice. 'Was that why you married your husband's murderer?'

'Badshah Jahangir did not murder your Abba,' said the empress, but Laadli suspected that she did not quite believe her own statement.

'Anyway, what option did we have? How else would I have brought you up? There are compromises one has to make in life. I made some too.'

'You were a good seamstress and a designer. We could have made a good living,' cried Laadli. 'You wanted to be the empress and that is the truth. All your life you wanted to be queen; that was your dream, wasn't it? And it was more important to you than me.'

In her heart, Laadli knew this was no time to talk of these things, but she couldn't stop herself. Words tumbled out of her mouth, unrestrained. The hot lava of her cached emotions poured into the room.

'That's not true, Laadli, my child. I always loved you more than anyone or anything else. I only wanted the best for you.'

'Or for yourself.'

The room was still, save for the crackling of the fire in the brazier. Two pairs of feverish eyes accosted each other. 'You must hate me,' whispered Meherunnisa.

Hot tears rolled down Laadli's eyes. All the sorrow she had locked in her heart after Imraan's death broke loose. She wanted to hate her mother, but she couldn't. The frail woman lying helplessly before her was to be pitied, not hated.

She shook her head. 'Is it possible for anyone to hate her mother? How can I hate someone who has carried me in her womb for nine months? Nothing you did can alter the fact that you are my mother. Besides, I can't forget the days at

Burdwan when I mattered more to you than anything else.
The memory of those beautiful years of my childhood have
carried me through the long nights of my grief.'

Tears of remorse rolled down the parched skin on the
gaunt face. Outside, the wind howled mercilessly, thrashing
the windows with ferocity.

'Forgive me, my child. I could never be a good mother
to you. I hope you can find it in your heart to forgive me
before I die,' the voice implored.

'Don't talk of death. You will live a long time yet. Don't
you want to see Arzani's children?'

'Arzani's children! I am a greedy woman to want to hold
her baby in my arms, but my maker beckons.'

A soft sigh escaped from the emaciated body. Moments
later the head rolled to a side. Delivered from her guilt, the
empress passed away. With a sob, Laadli hugged the wasted
body.

The remains of the empress were interred in Dil Khusha
gardens, where rested the remains of her beloved husband.
'Bury me near the emperor,' Meherunnisa had instructed
Laadli. In her last days, she had marked the spot for herself.
'I must lie under the shadow of my master. With him watching
over me, I shall not be afraid.'

She had even written the verse that she wanted inscribed
on her grave:

'Bur muzaarey maan ghureebaan ney chiraaghey ney guley. Ney
purey purwaanaa soazud, ney suddaayey bulbuley'
'On the grave of this traveller be so good as to light no lamps
nor strew any roses. This will ensure that the wings of moths

do not get singed and that nightingales will not sigh and weep and lament'

For Laadli, it was as though she could finally breathe. Her last link with royalty had been laid to rest. She was just another middle-aged woman—no more, no less. Ironically, she looked forward to living the rest of her life, alone. No fetters, no regalia nor expectations—the beginning of a long and lonely life.

Epilogue

No one knows what happened to Laadli Begum after Nur Jahan's death. No epic was written about her, nor was she the heroine of any saga. Unwritten, unfeted and unrecognised, the reluctant princess had spent her time on earth embroiled in the intrigues of an ambitious mother. If she bore grudges against the empress, she camouflaged them well in the deep vaults of her heart. Her loyalty and dedication towards her mother was unflinching, to the end.

History is heartless. It records facts as historians perceive them. It has no room for emotions and the intangible. Old monarchs slip into oblivion as new ones emerge. The magic wand of power passes from frail hands to the strong ones and historians are human too. The once feared and feted Nur Jahan simply dissolved into the mist as soon as the spotlight shifted to Shah Jahan and Mumtaz Mahal. History merely states that Nur Jahan lived a quiet life after the demise of Jahangir, at Lahore. She was later buried at Shahdara, where rested the remains of her indolent husband. It describes the unpretentiousness of her tomb as contrasted to the grand mausoleum of her husband.

Nur Jahan survived her husband by eighteen years, and these were spent in quietude, far away from the Mughal court. She had a generous pension to live a comfortable life. Shah Jahan was anything but miserly while granting her monies. But her creativity as a designer continued to delight the denizens of Lahore.

For herself, she desired just twenty-five yards of earth for a simple burial, nothing more. It is said that Nur Jahan, in a communiqué to Shah Jahan, had expressed her desire to be buried under the shadow of the tomb of Jahangir. She had also marked the twenty-five square yards where her body could be buried. Her humility towards the end of her life came from the spiritual disposition she had acquired in the company of her sedate daughter.

Nur Jahan's final resting place was once a beautiful mausoleum filled with cypress trees, and blooms of tulips, roses, and jasmine. Fountains cooled the place with sprays of water and water channels quartered the gardens. There are accounts of an octagonal tower on each corner as well as a pavilion. The interior had arched and columned galleries through which sunlight filtered in gently on the tombs. The structure has since been stripped of its stone cladding, and the garden was irreparably damaged when the British cut a railway line late in the nineteenth century between the tombs of Nur Jahan and her brother, Asaf Khan. Today, her tomb is a sorry sight; hardly the place for the celebrated beauty who wielded so much power and was the de facto ruler of the mighty Mughal empire. It stands forlorn, desolate and uncared for, stripped of its original decorative work and pomp.

What happened to Laadli after Nur Jahan's death? No one really knows. She had never figured in the list of the rich and

the famous; the mousy daughter of a mighty empress has no place in history. Laadli died unsung; her sacrifices unrecognised.

It is a quirk of fate that she was laid to rest beside her mother. The two women had shared an uneasy relationship for most of their lives. An empress, who was insensitive to her daughter's feelings, shares her final resting place with a daughter who was too timid to protest against the wrongs heaped on her. Laadli's austere tomb lies within the premises of Jahangir's mausoleum, a man she hated till the very end. Does the desolate spirit of the reluctant princess baulk at the company she is forced to share, or is it at peace lying near the two people who played such crucial roles in her life?

Throughout their lives, Nur Jahan and Laadli remained diametrically opposed to each other in thoughts and deeds; in death they remain close to each other, cocooned in their respective graves under the same roof, sharing the same rays of sunlight that filter into the vault.

Glossary

abbajaan	:	father
ahadis	:	royal elite guards
aigrette	:	large ornate pin used to decorate the turban
alekum salaam	:	acknowledgment of greetings
ammijaan	:	mother
asharfis	:	coins used during Mughal period
apa	:	elder sister
attar	:	perfume
badi ammi	:	grandmother
badshah	:	emperor
baradari	:	pavilion
bawarchi	:	chef
begum	:	a title used by ladies of class; also meaning wife in some cases.
cabaya	:	robe
caftan	:	long, flowing robe-like garment
champa	:	frangipani
chadar	:	deep-throated marble chutes inlaid with coloured marble

charbagh	:	a type of Mughal garden
chaugan	:	polo
chaupar	:	a form of chess
choli	:	short, usually backless blouse worn over the ghagra
chulahs	:	oven made of clay
churidar	:	tight trousers
durries	:	rugs
dams	:	currency used during early Mughal era
dargah	:	place of worship, usually the tomb of a venerated saint.
dastarkhan	:	carpeted arrangement made for dining on the ground.
divan	:	a low bed
diwan	:	superintendent of the household
diwan-é-aam	:	hall of public audience
diwan-é-khas	:	hall of private audience
fargal	:	jacket
farman	:	royal decree
firanghee	:	foreigner
ganjifa	:	playing cards
ghagra	:	long, voluminous skirt
ghusalkhana	:	bathroom
hakim	:	physician
hammamgah	:	royal bath chamber
houri	:	angel
huzoor	:	sir
jagirdar	:	landlord
jaali	:	delicate fretwork done on marble or sandstone, usually a network of geometric design. Surface

		ornamentation, known as arabesque, included the use of plants or geometric motifs represented in a fancifully combined pattern peculiar to Islamic art. Generally constructed in the palaces to afford privacy.
jagir	:	estate
jahanpanah	:	protector of the world
jannat	:	paradise
jharokha	:	balcony
kafila	:	caravan
kameez	:	long, knee-length shirt worn over tight trousers.
kasam	:	promise
khilat	:	robe of honour; the typical Mughal khilat was a sumptuous set of clothes. The 'core symbol was a cloak which was the outermost, most visible garment of courtly life' (Gordon 1996, 225), but the khilat could include a turban, long coat, gown, jacket, shawl, sash, trousers, shirt, and scarf (Sarkar 1961, 144; Sen 1998, 33). The investiture conferred titles, responsibilities, and rewards, but it also entailed obedience. Protocol demanded that one immediately don the khilat.
kornish	:	courtesy shown by bowing thrice
khwabgah	:	royal bed chamber
lehenga	:	ankle-length pleated skirt

leheriya	:	a type of pattern
mansabdar	:	office holder; mansabdars were divided into 33 classes, each member of each class being supposed to furnish a certain number of cavalry to the imperial army. The three highest grades, 'commanders' of from 7000 to 10,000 were ordinarily reserved for the princes. The other mansabs ranged from ten to 5,000.
mansab	:	estate
mans	:	unit of weight
minakari	:	enamel work on gold
mallika	:	queen
mojris	:	embroidered slippers
mushaira	:	poetry contest
mazaar	:	tomb
nazarband	:	under house arrest, in custody
nazrana	:	gift
nazm	:	couplet
paan	:	betel leaf
nikah	:	marriage according to Muslim laws
nissar	:	special kinds of coins
odhni	:	veil
Panchatantra	:	Indian fables
pir/paighambars	:	holy men and saints
qaba	:	robe like garment
qamargah	:	a form of hunt devised by the Mughul emperors wherein the beaters and soldiers round up the wild beasts within a circle of a few kilometres, by beating drums and closing in gradually.

ustaad	:	teacher
razai	:	quilt
reham	:	mercy
riyaya	:	subjects
shabda bhedi	:	shooting an animal by the sound it makes while drinking water
shahenshah	:	king of kings
shah begum	:	chief queen
shama	:	candle
salaam alekum	:	greetings
shatranj	:	chess
sheesh mahal	:	palace of mirrors
shehzada	:	prince
shehzadi	:	princess
sherwani	:	long, pleated shirt
shikar	:	hunt
shikaras	:	small boats
surkh	:	a unit of measure
zardosi	:	a kind of embroidery
zari	:	golden thread
zenana	:	harem